"I'm talking about us."

There isn't an us," Portia retorted.

"So you keep insisting," Cooper replied. "But I need you to understand something. All that nonsense about men not finding you attractive is just nonsense. You're gorgeous."

Portia smiled. "Thank you. But—"

"I'm not done."

"Oh. Okay."

"But I need you to understand something else. I'm not a nice guy. I'm not selfless. I'm not softhearted."

She was confused by this train of thought. "Oookay."

Well, if she'd been confused before, he was about to make things worse.

He closed the distance between them and pulled her to him. He didn't give her a chance to protest verbally, but pressed his lips to hers. There was a moment of shock. But she didn't resist.

Not even for a second.

* * *

A Bride for the Black Sheep Brother

A BRIDE FOR THE BLACK SHEEP BROTHER

BY
EMILY McKAY

MILLS & BOON

Published in Great Britain 2014
by Mills & Boon, an imprint of Harlequin (UK) Limited,
Eton House, 18-24 Paradise Road, Richmond, Surrey, TW9 1SR

© 2014 Emily McKaskle

ISBN: 978-0-263-91470-2

51-0614

Harlequin (UK) Limited's policy is to use papers that are natural, renewable and recyclable products and made from wood grown in sustainable forests. The logging and manufacturing processes conform to the legal environmental regulations of the country of origin.

Printed and bound in Spain
by Blackprint CPI, Barcelona

Emily McKay has been reading and loving romance novels since she was eleven years old. She lives in Texas with her geeky husband, her two kids and too many pets. Her debut novel, *Baby, Be Mine,* was a RITA® Award finalist for Best First Book and Best Short Contemporary. She was also a 2009 *RT Book Reviews* Career Achievement Award nominee for Series Romance. To learn more, visit her website, www.emilymckay.com.

For my darling daughter, who loves books and reading and stories, despite being bad at "decoding" and being a crappy speller. It's okay, honey. I am, too.

Prologue

Portia Callahan lived her life by one simple rule: when all else failed, make a list.

Today's list was simple, if perhaps a tad more important than most.

- Nails
- Hair
- Makeup
- Dress
- Shoes
- Wedding

Usually, checking items off her list helped her chill out. It soothed her rattled nerves better than a hefty margarita. Not today. Today, she'd checked off the top five items and her insides were still roiling with anxiety. Frankly, she would have ordered the margarita, but a) she was pretty sure smuggling one into the First Houston Baptist Church would put a kibosh on the whole wedding, and b) her hands were shaking so much she was sure she would spill it. If she spilled bright green margarita down the front of the thirty-thousand-dollar gown twenty minutes before the ceremony, her mother's head would actually explode.

A little extreme, maybe, but this was the woman who had taken a nitroglycerin pill this morning when Portia had nearly messed up her manicure.

And that smeared tip on her pinky was nothing compared to her sudden urge to bolt from the church and run down the streets of Houston ripping this white monstrosity off her body. Maybe if her body was moving, her thoughts would stop racing.

Why was her dress so tight? Why was lace so itchy? Why were hairpins so pokey? Had her makeup always felt this sticky?

More to the point, if she felt this panicky now, if she hated the dress and the hairpins and the makeup so much today, when just yesterday they'd all been fine, was it a sign that what she actually hated was the idea of getting married?

Her stomach flipped at the idea. If she didn't do something to calm her nerves, she was going to puke.

But what could she do? Her mother paced along the back of the church's dressing room, critically eyeing every detail of Portia's appearance. Shelby, Portia's maid of honor, stood behind her, doing up the last of the hundred-and-twenty-seven buttons that went up the back of her dress. Portia hated those buttons. Each seemed to cinch her in a little more tightly.

Her body-shaping torture wear constricted her ribs so much she could feel them poking into her lungs. She could barely breathe. And she couldn't help thinking maybe that was the point. Maybe the dress had been designed to squeeze her heart right out of her body.

Just when she thought she couldn't take it anymore, there was a knock on the door.

"Come in," her mother barked.

The door cracked open, and Portia heard the voice of her future mother-in-law, Caro Cain. "Celeste, I don't want to alarm you, but there seems to be a problem with the photographer."

Portia's mother shot her daughter a quick glare. As if this was somehow her mistake, even though she'd personally had nothing to do with the photographer. "Don't move an inch." She looked her up and down. "You look perfect. Just don't mess it up."

And with that, Celeste flounced out of the dressing room to go skewer the hapless person who had created this problem. Portia, meanwhile, sent up a silent prayer of thanks to whatever deity had arranged the snafu.

As soon as her mother left the room, she turned around and grabbed Shelby's hands. "Can you just—?" *Stop trying to strangle me with those buttons!* Portia blew out a breath. Then she smiled serenely. "Could you maybe give me a moment alone?"

Shelby, who had roomed with Portia for all four years at Vassar and knew her better than anyone, frowned and asked, "Are you sure this is a good idea?"

"I'll be fine. I just want a moment to meditate."

"No, I meant—" Shelby gave her hand a squeeze. "Yeah. I'll go keep an eye on your mother. I'll make sure she'd occupied for the next—" She glanced at her watch. "The wedding is in twenty minutes. I can buy you maybe ten minutes alone. That's all."

"Thanks!"

A moment later, Portia was finally, blessedly alone for

the first time in more than nine days. It was almost as good as a margarita. But she felt like every nerve in her body was rubbing against some other nerve and that any second, they might spark and then she'd just—poof—go up in flames.

Her mother had thought the botched manicure was bad. That had nothing on spontaneous combustion.

Alone in the dressing room, she turned slowly in a circle, scanning the room for the distraction she was looking for. Not that there was much room for spinning. Now that she was standing, the acres of white silk that made up the skirt of her dress took up a lot of floor space. She could hardly move in the damn thing. *Huh.* Was that why her mother had insisted on such a monstrously big dress? Had she suspected that Portia might be besieged by last-minute panic and bolt? Had she wanted to guarantee that if Portia did, she'd be easy to take down?

Portia stifled a hysterical giggle at the image of her mother tackling her on the steps of the church.

Not that Portia actually wanted to bolt.

Because she didn't.

This was just nerves. Normal nerves.

Dalton was her match in every way. They were financial and social equals. Which meant that for the first time in life she didn't have to worry about his motives for being with her. She respected him. They got along. And best of all, he was so stable. So steady. And she needed that balance in her life.

They were equals, but opposites. And didn't everyone always say opposites attract?

And she loved him.

Okay, so she was eighty-nine percent sure she loved him. But she was 100 percent sure he loved her. At least, he loved all the parts of her that she showed him. He loved the well-dressed, poised debutante. He loved the best version of her. The person she was trying to be.

And, yes, there was this goofy, rebellious, silly version of Portia, but she was working hard on burying it. Burying it deep. She never went to sing karaoke anymore. She hadn't been skydiving in months. She'd had her Marvin the Martian tattoo removed and the scar was barely visible. Soon, she would be 100 percent the socially acceptable debutante. Soon, she'd be the person Dalton loved.

It wasn't Dalton she wanted to run away from. It was herself.

And the dress. But this was all nerves. She only needed to do something to relieve her tension. Even if it was only for a few minutes. And she knew just what would do the trick.

Coping with the unexpected was one of the things Cooper Larson did best. Zipping down the slopes on his snowboard, he had to be prepared for anything. Everybody knew that snow was mercurial. One second, conditions could appear perfect. The next, it could all go to hell. Cooper's ability to think on his feet and adapt in a spilt second was one of the qualities that had earned him a spot on the Olympic team.

However, both of those skills abandoned him completely when he walked into the bride's dressing room and saw his future sister-in-law standing on her head, her nearly bare legs sticking straight up in the air.

The sight was so unexpected—not to mention confusing—that it took him a while to even figure out what he was seeing. At first all he saw were the legs. It took him a good thirty seconds alone to work his way from the delicate feet down the miles of legs clad only in sheer cream silk, to delicate pale blue garters and eight or so inches of luscious female thigh. And beyond that a pair of bright pink skimpy panties with white dots all over them. Then—just when he thought his head might explode—he realized that the heavy pile of white fluff the legs were sticking out of was an upturned wedding dress.

Shaking his head, he looked again at the legs. Possibly the most fabulous legs he'd ever seen. And they were attached to his future sister-in-law.

Crap.

That was really inconvenient.

What was she doing standing on her head? When she was supposed to be getting married in less than twenty minutes?

And then, he heard her.

"Ba da da da da da!"

Was she singing "Jesse's Girl"?

If that hadn't been Portia's voice, he would have thought he'd wandered into the wrong church. What the hell was going on?

"Portia?" he asked.

The mound of white fluff gave a little squeal. And the legs wobbled precariously. She was going down.

He leaped across the room and grabbed her. Maybe a bit too strongly, because her legs fell against his chest and she kicked him in the face.

"Damn!"

"Ack!"

He stumbled back, dragging her with him.

"Put me down!" she squealed.

But putting her down gently wasn't an easy feat. He took another step back, but then she kicked him again.

"Put me down!" she screamed again.

"I'm trying!"

"Cooper?"

"Yeah. Who else?" Finally, he wrapped an arm around her waist and managed to flip her over. He got a face full of fluffy white lace for his trouble, and her elbow slammed into his chin. He let her go and stepped back, holding his hands out in front of him to ward off her attack. "Are you okay?"

When she looked up, he realized she had a pair of earbuds in her ears and noticed the iPod shoved into the bodice of her dress. She yanked the earbuds out, and he could hear the music playing faintly.

She pushed down her skirt, glaring at him. "Of course, I'm okay. Or rather, I was! Why wouldn't I be okay?"

"You were upside down."

"I was doing a headstand!"

"In your wedding dress?"

She opened her mouth to fire back some quip, but then hesitated, snapped her mouth closed and frowned. "Good point." She grabbed the skirt of her dress and shook it out.

The dress didn't look too bad. Her hair, on the other hand, was a mess. What had obviously once been some kind of fancy twist of curls on the back of her head had started to slide off to the side. One lock of pale golden hair tumbled into her face. Her cheeks were flushed, her lips moist and pink.

He'd known Portia for about two years and in all that time he'd never seen her looking so disheveled. So human. So sexy.

Yeah. And the fact that the image of her bright pink panties and her bare thighs was still seared into his brain had nothing to do with that. And what precisely had been on those panties of hers? From a few feet away, he'd thought they were misshapen white dots, but up close they'd looked like cats. Was that possible? Was there any chance at all that uptight, straitlaced, cold-as-dry-ice Portia Callahan would get married wearing panties with cat heads on them?

"What the hell were you doing?" he asked.

"I was meditating."

"And singing along to eighties pop?"

"I was… I can't…" She blew out a breath that made her hair flutter in front of her face. "It helps me think." And then, she must have realized her hair was mussed, because she grabbed a stray lock of hair and stared at it. "Oh, no! Oh, no, oh, no, oh, no, oh, no!"

She jumped up and ran to the mirror. Still clutching the lock of hair, she turned this way and that, staring at herself in the mirror, muttering "oh, no!" over and over.

He didn't have a lot of experience with panicking women. Zero experience, really. And, to be honest, his mind was still reeling that this was Portia who was panicking. Up until five minutes ago, he would have described her as slightly less emotional than the Tin Man. He would not have pegged her for the type to panic. Or wear pink kitty panties. Damn it, he had to stop thinking about her underwear. And her thighs.

And unless he wanted to be the one to explain to Caro Cain why the wedding was off, he suspected he needed to do some serious damage control.

So he made sure the door was locked and went to stand behind Portia.

He looked at her in the mirror. She was so busy freaking out she didn't notice him until he put his hands on her shoulders. Then she looked up, tears brimming in her dark blue eyes. How had he never before noticed how dark her eyes were? Almost purple, they were so blue.

He dug around in his pocket, but found nothing to give her to wipe her eyes, so he pulled the silk pocket square from his suit pocket and handed it to her.

"Here." She just stared at him, frowning. Crap, he was no good at this. "It's gonna be okay."

"It is?" she asked hopefully.

"Sure."

She stared up at him, a tremulous smile on her lips. "You think so?"

"Yeah." He felt a little catch in his chest. God, he hoped he wasn't lying. "It's just hair, right?" And, that must have been the wrong thing to say, because her lip started wobbling. "I mean, you can totally fix that!" He reached out and gave the lumpy twist a poke. "Just stick in a few more of those pin things, and it'll be fine."

She threw up her hands. "I don't have any more pins!"

"Then how'd you get it up in the first place?"

"I had it done at a salon."

"Oh." He didn't point out that if that was the case, she probably shouldn't have done a headstand. It took a lot of restraint. Surely he got points for that, right? "Well, I bet the ones that came out are still on the ground over there. Let me look." After a minute of crawling around on the floor, he stood up, triumphant. "Five."

She was still sitting in front of the mirror, but she was looking calmer. And she'd done something with her hair so that it looked…more balanced. "Okay. Hand them over."

He did, and then watched as she jabbed them in. When she was done, she met his gaze in the mirror.

"And it's really going to be okay, right?"

"Sure."

"I don't mean the hair."

"Yeah. I got that." He swallowed. Who the hell was he to give relationship advice to anyone? Especially since he couldn't stop thinking about Portia's legs and how adorable she looked in that damn headstand and how she'd always been beautiful but he'd never known how pretty she was until now. "Yeah. It's going to be okay. Dalton is a good guy. And you're perfect for each other."

Except he was lying. Until now, he'd always thought Portia was the perfect girl for Dalton. But this girl? This girl who did headstands in her wedding dress and freaked out and wore pink kitty panties? This girl had more going on inside than he'd ever guessed. This Portia was vibrant and intriguing, and startlingly appealing in this moment of vulnerability. And maybe Dalton wasn't the right guy for her after all.

One

Twelve years later

Portia Callahan wanted to die of humiliation.

Only one thing kept her from actually doing it. If she died during the Children's Hope Foundation annual gala, the charity's silent auction would bomb. Everyone would be so busy gossiping about how Celeste Callahan had finally berated her daughter to death that no one would raise their paddles to bid.

So instead of dying, Portia stood in the service hallway outside of the Kimball Hotel ballroom and let her mother rant at her.

"Honestly, Portia! What were you thinking?" Celeste's crisp pronunciation grated against Portia's already frayed nerves.

She breathed out a sigh and let go of all the logical, sensible answers she could give. *I was thinking of the chil-*

dren. I was trying to do the right thing. Instead she said what she knew her mother needed to hear. "I guess I wasn't thinking."

Which was also true. Three months ago, when she'd visited the inner-city Houston high school on behalf of Children's Hope Foundation, she hadn't been thinking about how her visit might "look" to the Houston society types. She'd been thinking about connecting with the students, encouraging them to dream of a life beyond minimum wage work. She'd been thinking of them and what they needed. There hadn't even been anyone from the Foundation there that day. It had never occurred to her that the teacher snapping photos might send them in to the Foundation or that a few of them might end up in the photomontage that played in the background at tonight's annual gala. And it had certainly never occurred to her that members of Houston high society might be offended by pictures of her playing a pickup game of basketball with former gang members.

"No, Portia. You clearly weren't thinking. That photo…" Celeste sighed.

God, Portia hated that sound. It was how-could-you-do-this-to-me and what-did-I-do-to-deserve-you all rolled into one exhalation of disappointment.

"It's not that bad," Portia tried to explain. She kept her voice low, painfully aware that they weren't really alone. Sure, her mother had dragged her off into one of the hotel's service hallways, but the gala's waitstaff were filtering past with trays of drinks and appetizers. A couple of them had even slowed down, straining to catch what they could of the argument.

"It would be bad enough if it was just the photo," Celeste said. "But with Laney's pregnancy, everyone is watching you, waiting to see how you'll—"

"Laney's pregnancy?" Portia interrupted. Nausea

bloomed in her stomach, turning those butternut squash appetizers into bricks. "Laney is pregnant?"

Laney was Portia's ex-husband's current wife.

Not that Portia had anything against Laney. Or Dalton for that matter.

She was thrilled, just thrilled, that they'd found love and were blissfully happy. She really was. Or she really tried to be. But it would be easier if her own life didn't feel so stagnant.

And now Laney was pregnant? Portia and Dalton had struggled with infertility for years. But apparently all Dalton needed was a vivacious new wife.

Portia pressed a palm to her belly, willing the appetizers to stay put.

"Laney is pregnant," she repeated stupidly.

"Yes, of course she is. They haven't announced it yet, but everyone has noticed the bump. Honestly, Portia, how do you miss these things? All of Houston has noticed, but you're blissfully unaware of it?"

"I just didn't—"

"Well, you need to. You simply have to be more concerned when gossip is brewing around you. And for God's sake, try not to provide all of Houston with photographic evidence of your midlife crisis."

"It's not a midlife crisis!"

Celeste's gaze snapped from self-pity to anger. "It's a photo of you and five gang members, one of whom is staring down your dress and another of whom has his hand entirely too close to your person."

"He was blocking. He wasn't even touching me!" Was that really how the photo looked to other people? "Mother, it's just a picture. There are fifty pictures in the slide show that illustrate the amazing work the foundation does. One of them happens to have me in it. It's not that big a—"

"It is a big deal," Celeste snapped. "The fact that you think it isn't only shows how naive you are. A woman in your position—"

"My position? What is that supposed to mean?"

"A woman's position in society changes when she goes through a divorce. You've seen this in your own life and in Caro's. Thank God you've fared better than she has. So far."

"Right," Portia said grimly. "Caro."

After her divorce from Dalton, Portia had stayed friends with her former mother-in-law. Caro Cain wasn't the warmest person, but she was still easier to deal with than Portia's own mother. And right now, Caro needed every friend she had. Her divorce from Hollister Cain had left her a social pariah.

"Do you know how many people are out there snickering about that photo?" Celeste demanded.

"Nobody but you cares about that photo!"

Celeste took a step closer. "This is how the world works. Stop being naive."

"It's not naive to want to help children."

"Fine, if you want to help children, I can have Dede set something up."

"I don't need Daddy's press secretary to set up a photo op for me."

"Fine. If you don't want my help, do this on your own. Go make puppets with a kid with cancer, but for God's sake, stay out of the ghetto, because—"

But Celeste never got a chance to finish her thought, because just then, one of the waitresses walked by with a tray of champagne and somehow tripped, spilling a flute of the amber liquid down the sleeve of Celeste's dress.

The older woman reared back, gasping in shock.

The waitress stumbled again and barely stepped out of

the way before Celeste whirled on her. "Why you clumsy, little—"

"Mother, it's okay." Portia grabbed her mother's arm, more out of instinct than out of fear that her mother might hit the girl.

Celeste jerked her arm free, her mouth twisting into a snarl. "I'll have your job for this!"

"Let me handle this, Mother." Portia looked nervously around the hall. It was empty now except for this one waitress. "Go on to the bathroom and clean up what you can. Champagne doesn't stain. It'll be okay."

Celeste just glared at the waitress, who glared back, her jaw jutting out.

Portia guided her mother a step away toward the doorway that led into the ballroom. "I'll handle it. I'll talk to the girl's supervisor."

"That clumsy bitch shouldn't be anywhere near a function like this." Then Celeste flounced off to clean herself up.

Portia turned back to the waitress, half surprised to still see her there. The young woman looked to be in her early twenties. Her hair was dyed a dark maroon, cut short on one side and long on the other. She wore too much eye makeup and had a stud in her nose. And she was glaring belligerently at Portia.

"My name's Ginger, by the way. If you're going to go tattle to my boss."

Portia held up her hand palm out in a gesture of peace. "Look, I'm not going to have you fired, but maybe you could just stay out of Celeste's way for the rest of the night."

Ginger blinked in surprise. "You're not?"

"No. It was an accident."

"Accident. Right." Her tone was completely innocent, but there was a slight smirk to her lips as she stepped toward the door into the ballroom. Her smirk made her look so familiar. "Thanks."

"Wait a second—" But the door swung open and two more waiters came into the hall and pushed past them. Portia reached for Ginger's arm and stepped off to the side, where they weren't in anyone's way. "Did you do that on purpose?"

"Tip the glass down your mother's back? Why would I do that?" Ginger smirked again and Portia felt another blast of recognition. Like she should know this girl.

"I don't know," Portia admitted. She looked pointedly at the tray of champagne flutes. "But it seems like it'd be awfully hard to tip just one glass without them all spilling."

"You gonna have me fired or not?"

Portia sighed. "Why would you do that?"

"What? Spill a drink on someone who's verbally abusing her daughter in public? I can't imagine why." Ginger turned as if she was going to stalk off, but stopped and turned back before she reached the door. "Look, it's none of my business, but you shouldn't put up with that. Family should treat each other better."

"Yes. They should." Portia had no illusions about her mother. She wasn't sure why she felt as if she had to justify her mother's words—certainly not to a stranger—but she found herself doing it anyway. "I know my mother can be a bitch. I'm not going to pretend she has my best interests at heart. But when it comes to this kind of thing, she's almost always right. And I'm usually wrong. If she thinks people will misinterpret those photos of me, then I'd bet money they already have."

"That's messed up." Ginger just shook her head. "That doesn't bother you?"

"It does, but it's the world I live in."

"I don't care if that's the world you live in. Family should be on your side. No matter what." Ginger's expression darkened. "The world you live in sucks."

The fierceness in Ginger's gaze took Portia aback for a moment. Portia looked at the girl closely. Again she was struck by how familiar she seemed.

"Have we met before?" she asked impulsively.

Ginger took a step back, the startled movement jostling the champagne flutes on her tray. "No. Where would we have met?"

Before Portia could press her for more information, the waitress spun away and disappeared through the door.

Now Portia was sure they'd met before. It was something in the girl's smile. And something through the eyes.

The eyes.

Portia's breath caught in her chest as the realization hit her.

This young woman. This waitress whom Portia had met by chance had eyes the exact same color as Dalton Cain's. Now that she'd placed the eyes, Ginger's other features seemed to slip right into place. That fierce intensity was pure Griffin Cain. That sarcastic smirk looked just like Cooper's. Ginger was a near perfect amalgamation of the three brothers. Yes, in a more delicate and feminine form, but still, she could be their sister.

Which Portia might be able to dismiss, except for one crucial fact. Dalton, Griffin and Cooper actually had a half sister. They all knew she existed, but no one knew who or where she was. As impossible and unlikely as it seemed, had Portia just found the missing Cain heiress?

Portia looked for Ginger the rest of the night. She constantly scanned the crowd for the waitress's maroon hair and nose stud, but she seemed to have disappeared completely.

By the time Portia had made it back to her small home

at the end of the night, she was determined to track down the waitress. It wasn't that she was obsessed with finding the girl, but it gave her something to think about other than the gossip about her that had been simmering in the background.

Why was it acceptable for people to talk about her merely because her ex-husband was going to be a father? Or because someone had snapped a photo of her playing basketball with some disadvantaged teens? Other people could do truly bad things and no one seemed to care.

The same brutal dynamic was at work with Caro Cain. Hollister Cain, Portia's ex-father-in-law, had had countless affairs. Somehow Caro had held her head up through it all. When Caro divorced him, people gossiped about *her*.

Of course, Hollister and Caro had paid the price for his many affairs. Just last year, when Hollister's health had been so bad, he had received a letter from one of his past conquests. The woman had heard he was on his deathbed and had taunted him with the existence of a daughter he'd never known about.

Whoever had written the letter had known what a manipulative bastard Hollister was. She had known it would drive him crazy to learn he had a daughter he'd never met and couldn't control. When he'd received the letter, Hollister had called his three sons to his bedside—Dalton and Griffin, his legitimate sons, and Cooper, his illegitimate son. He'd demanded that they find the daughter and bring her back into the family fold. Whichever son found her first would be Hollister's sole heir. If she wasn't found before Hollister died, he'd will his entire fortune to the state.

The quest he'd set his sons on had torn the family apart. It had destroyed his own marriage. And now, a year later, the missing heiress still hadn't been found. And Hollister's health had improved. The last time she'd seen him, he'd seemed as bitter and angry as ever, but he was no longer haunted by death. He was just as determined that someone find his daughter.

Maybe it was ridiculous for Portia to think that she might have just found the woman tonight.

As far as she knew, Dalton and Griffin had figured out that their sister was from somewhere in Texas, but that hardly narrowed it down. There were almost thirty million people in Texas.

But of all the people Portia had ever met, only five of them had Cain-blue eyes. Hollister and his sons and now Ginger. This woman with Cooper's smirk and Dalton's determination. She looked just like a Cain.

Not that it was any of her business.

So what if a waitress at a hotel in Houston looked like she could be Dalton's sister?

It didn't have anything to do with Portia.

Except that when Portia thought about Ginger—about the waitress's petulant defiance, about the fierce way she talked about how families should treat each other, Portia felt oddly protective of her. If she was the missing heiress, someone would find her. Someday—maybe someday soon—one of the brothers would stumble on a piece of evidence and they would track her down. Everything about her life would change in a moment. And she was completely unprepared for it.

Ginger was about to be thrust into a world of cutthroat gossips where her every action and motive would be questioned, analyzed and criticized. Where mothers berated their daughters in public and where divorcées were ostracized when they didn't get a lavish divorce settlement.

It was a world of wealth and power, but it was also a crummy world.

But maybe there was something she could do to make this world a little less crummy.

Two

When she was young, Portia had had a reputation among her family for being impulsive, reckless, rash—qualities she had worked hard to banish from her personality in the past fifteen years. And she'd succeeded. No one who knew her now—well, almost no one—would call her reckless.

Now she was not the kind of girl who got a tattoo over summer break—even one of a completely inoffensive, beloved cultural icon like Marvin the Martian. She was not the sort to do headstands in fancy clothes. Those parts of her were gone. It was that simple.

So, a week after the Children's Hope Foundation gala, when she packed her bags and hopped on a plane, it was part of a planned vacation. After all, it was perfectly reasonable for her to take a few weeks of vacation after the months of grueling work on the event. And the Callahans had a condo in Tahoe that she often visited. It wasn't as if she was fleeing from Houston because she couldn't stand the gossip—which hadn't actually been that bad. This was a vacation. A well-thought-out event.

And if she tweaked her travel plans just a smidge so that they included a four-hour layover in Denver, that was totally normal. She'd never liked long flights. Or airports.

And it was also normal—and not at all impulsive—for her to stop by and visit the one person she knew in Denver. Her former brother-in-law, Cooper Larson. Cooper—once the snowboarding darling in the world of extreme sports—was now a successful businessman. He was the CEO and owner of Flight+Risk, which just happened to be head-quartered in Denver. He was also possibly the one person who could help her untangle the identity of the Cain heiress.

This was a slight detour in her life. That was all. Visiting Cooper wasn't impulsive or reckless. It was smart. Of the three Cain brothers, he was the least invested in finding Hollister's missing daughter. He had the least at stake. And he was the most likely to know where the young woman was coming from. Visiting Cooper was only logical.

The litany of logical, sensible reasons echoed through her mind as she paid the taxi driver who'd taken her from the airport to Flight+Risk's office in downtown Denver not far from the Sixteenth Street Mall. The building was an older one that had been refurbished. It was sleek and modern inside, while maintaining the sort of informality that suited Cooper's snowboard accessory business. It was exactly what she'd expected of his office. It suited the black sheep of the Cain family.

The only thing that threw her for a loop was Cooper's assistant. She'd expected some young blond snow bunny type. Someone with more style than sense. Someone she could easily talk her way past.

Instead, the woman—Mrs. Lorenzo, according to the

nameplate on her desk—was nearing fifty, with a humor-less smile and cold, assessing eyes.

"And what did you say your name was again?"

"Portia Callahan."

"Hmm…" Mrs. Lorenzo looked her up and down, as if Portia might be lying. Then the older woman turned back to the computer, clicked her mouse several times and started typing.

Mrs. Lorenzo must have sensed Portia's doubts, because she raised an eyebrow and made a disapproving *mmm* sound.

"I'm his sister-in-law," Portia threw out hopefully.

Mrs. Lorenzo smirked. "Mr. Larson has one sister-in-law—Laney Cain. She's a lovely young woman. And you are not her."

Portia swallowed, suddenly irritated by this woman's superior attitude. She so didn't need one more person telling her how lovely Laney was. "I'm his former sister-in-law."

"I see." Mrs. Lorenzo's mouth turned down as if Portia had just admitted to being pond scum. "Mr. Larson is in a business meeting out of the office this morning. Would you like to reschedule?"

Portia glanced down at her watch. If she'd done the math right, she had about two hours before she needed to head back to the airport. "No. I'll wait."

"Excellent," Mrs. Lorenzo said grimly. "I'll let him know when he gets in."

With a sigh, Portia picked a chair in the reception area and settled down to wait. She pulled a magazine out of her travel tote and flipped it open, but didn't actually read any of it. Instead, she stared blankly at the brightly colored pictures, her mind racing from the lies she'd been telling herself.

Here was the flaw in her logic: if today's visit to Denver

really was logical and not impulsive, she would not have ambushed Cooper at work, hoping to talk her way past his secretary. She would have called ahead and made an appointment. Or better yet, called him and asked to meet for lunch. Or even better yet, just called and talked through this on the phone.

He was her former brother-in-law. Calling him to chat was perfectly reasonable. She'd talked to him on the phone plenty of times during her marriage to Dalton. And even since the divorce, she'd called a couple of times a year to hit him up for donations to the Children's Hope Foundation.

But instead of just calling, she'd changed her travel plans and come to see him in person. Why?

She looked around the office, felt panic starting to choke her and fought the urge to bolt. What was she doing here? Why had she gone to these drastic lengths? And for a girl she barely knew? Based on nothing more than a pair of blue eyes and a gut feeling?

It was ridiculous. Absurd. Completely irrational.

And that was why she'd come here herself.

Because it was irrational and ridiculous. And she knew if she hadn't jumped in feetfirst, she would have backed out. If she had called and tried to explain this over the phone, she would have panicked and changed her story. She never would have had the guts to actually talk about the missing heiress. She had come here to do it in person because now she was committed. Now, she couldn't back out. She could only wait.

In business, as in snowboarding, talent and preparation only got you so far. After that, it was all a matter of luck. Which sucked, because Cooper Larson had never been a particularly lucky man. Ambitious, yes. Talented, smart and ruthless, yes. Lucky, not so much.

But he was okay with that. Luck was for a privileged few. It wasn't something you could control or work for. And personally, he would much rather owe his success to something he'd done.

Still, when it came to important business meetings, like the Flight+Risk board meeting he had scheduled for the afternoon, he never left anything to chance. The meeting would be held at a hotel conference room, not far from Flight+Risk's headquarters. He'd spent the morning at the hotel, putting the finishing touches on the proposal he'd be bringing before the board. Which left him just enough time to stop back by the office and check in before grabbing lunch and heading to the board meeting.

Except Portia was waiting to see him when he got there.

For a moment, he just stopped cold in the doorway staring at her. "Portia?" he asked stupidly. "What are you doing here?"

She stood up, looking strangely nervous. "I had a layover in Denver. And I thought maybe we could talk."

She'd been reading a magazine when he walked in and now she rolled it tightly in her hands, clenching it as if maybe she wanted to swat the nose of some naughty dog.

He studied her, taking in the white of her clenched knuckles. The faint lines of strain around her eyes. He hadn't seen her often since her divorce from Dalton—hell, he hadn't seen her often during their marriage—but he knew her well enough to recognize the signs of stress and nerves.

Even though it would mess with his schedule for the day, he nodded toward his office. "Sure. Come on in." He glanced toward his secretary with a nod. "Hold my calls."

Mrs. Lorenzo narrowed her gaze infinitesimally in disapproval. "Sir, shall I send you a reminder, oh, say thirty minutes before your meeting?"

Good ol' Mrs. Lorenzo could always be counted on to impose a rigid schedule. He grinned. "Make it twenty minutes."

If he skipped lunch that would leave plenty of time to walk back over to the hotel.

He led Portia into the office and gestured toward one of the chairs, admiring the subtle sway of her hips as she preceded him. Portia was built exactly the way he liked—tall and lean. Today she wore her pale blond hair back in a sleek ponytail. She was dressed in skin-tight jeans and a white shirt under a tan sweater. Everything about her looked cool and confident. Everything except those white knuckles.

Though he gestured her toward a chair, he didn't sit behind his desk. Instead, he propped his hips on the desktop and stretched his legs out in front of him. Frankly, he hated the trapped feeling that came with sitting behind a desk for too long. It reminded him of school. And with the board meeting this afternoon, he was going to spend enough time sitting still.

"What's up?" he asked as soon as Portia sat down.

She bobbed back to her feet before answering. "I think I've found the heiress."

"Who?" he asked.

"The missing Cain heiress. The one Dalton and Griffin have been searching for so frantically. Your sister. I've found her."

"What?" He frowned. Her answer was so unexpected, so completely out of left field, his brain spun. No, not even left field. Out of no field. "I didn't even know you were looking for her."

"I wasn't!" Portia started pacing, her words pouring out of her. "I was at a fund-raiser. The big Children's Hope Foundation gala. And I just met this girl. She's about the right age, mid-twenties. Her hair's red, but I'm pretty sure it was dyed. But she has the Cain eyes."

He rolled his own eyes at that, but he was surprised by the way those words drove the tension right out of his body. "The Cain eyes? That's what you're basing this on? The fact that she has blue eyes?"

Portia paused on the far side of his office, right in front of the wall of books he'd never read that the decorator had picked out. He got the feeling that Portia wasn't studying the book spines, but rather summoning her courage before turning back to look at him. She jutted out her jaw as she frowned. "It's a real thing. Don't act like it isn't."

"I'm not acting. Ten percent of the population have blue eyes. They can't all be related to the Cains. Not even Hollister slept around that much."

She blew out a frustrated breath. "Listen, there are some things women are better at than men. Facial recognition— including eye color—is one of them." He waggled his hand in a that's iffy gesture. "Trust me on this. Cain-blue eyes are very unique. I spent ten years staring into Dalton's eyes. I know that color. And I've never seen anyone else with those eyes except for Hollister and his sons. This girl—this girl I saw at the fund-raiser—she's your sister. That has to mean something to you."

Cooper shifted and studied Portia.

She was such a mystery. Half the time, she came off as this coolly serene princess. No, more than half. Eighty percent, maybe ninety percent of the time. But he'd seen another side of her. He knew she had more going on than the ice princess thing most people saw. He couldn't forget when he'd walked in on her doing a headstand on her wedding day. Every time he saw her he thought of those long legs and the pink kitty cat underwear. A guy never forgot a thing like that. He never forgot the sharp punch of desire. Even when the woman had spent a decade married to his brother.

But Portia wasn't married to Dalton anymore. She was here in his office. A thousand miles from her home. Talking to him about something she easily could have told Dalton.

What was up with that?

He ran his thumb along his jaw. "Okay. So let's say this is the girl. Let's say she's really the heiress. Why come to me? Why not just call up Dalton?" And then it hit him—of course she wouldn't call Dalton. He was her ex-husband. Yeah, their divorce seemed civil enough. From the outside. But who knew what it had been like from her side of things? Just because she'd kept in contact with Caro and Hollister that didn't mean she wanted Dalton to win the challenge so that he could inherit all of Cain Enterprises. "Never mind. Sorry I said that. That was stupid. Of course you're not just going to hand him the money. But why not talk to Griffin about this?"

She pulled a sheepish face. "I'm not exactly Griffin's favorite person. I don't know if he'd even believe me. But in reality I couldn't go to him for the same reason I couldn't go to Dalton."

"The same reason? Jesus, how many of us have you married?"

She narrowed her gaze, looking confused for a second before shaking her head. "Very funny. Yeah, sure, I'm not Dalton's biggest fan right now, but that's not what I meant."

"What did you mean?"

"I couldn't talk to Dalton because he wants it too badly," she said simply, like he was the idiot for not seeing it right off.

"You can't tell him you think you've found the girl because he wants to find her?" he asked slowly, drawing the words out while he tried to wrap his brain around what she meant.

"Yes! Think about it—if the girl isn't found before something happens to Hollister, then Cain Enterprises is going to be in serious trouble. If Hollister's shares of the company go to the state, they'll probably be auctioned off, most likely to Cain's competitors. The company will be in ruins. Even though Dalton doesn't work for Cain Enterprises anymore, he doesn't want that to happen. He's worked his ass off for Cain all his life. A new job doesn't change that. He still loves the company. He's always going to pick what's best for Cain Enterprises. He's not going to think twice about his sister."

"So you're telling me you haven't gone to Dalton with this information because you're worried about the heiress?"

"Exactly. Someone needs to think about what's best for this poor girl."

Cooper raised an eyebrow. "This poor girl? If you're right, this poor girl is worth hundreds of millions of dollars. Probably more money than she's ever dreamed of. No one would call this girl *poor*."

Portia seemed to hesitate, then smiled faintly. "Perhaps *poor* isn't quite the word I meant, but I'm sure you'll agree, if Dalton and Griffin do find her, she's going to have a rough time of it."

"What's that supposed to mean?"

"Just that the Cains live in a world of wealth and power that most people can't even imagine. You and I both know that if you're unprepared for that world, it will gobble you and devour you whole. This girl, she didn't grow up with money."

"How exactly do you know she's poor?" he asked with a bit of a sneer. "Are you guessing based merely on the way she was dressed or is this something she told you while you were gazing into her Cain-blue eyes?"

"Very funny. But trust me, I know. She's a waitress, with dyed red hair and one of those little studs in her nose."

"You think rich kids don't rebel? Because I've got to tell you, I've made a lot of money in an industry that's all about rich kids rebelling."

"Exactly. When rich kids rebel, they go snowboarding in Utah. Kids working jobs as waitresses at a hotel? Those kids don't have time to rebel."

Well, she had a point there. And he might even be willing to help her; her heart was in the right place, even if it wasn't really her business anymore. After all, he'd always liked Portia—hell, he'd always more than liked Portia. That was part of the problem, though, wasn't it? It wasn't appropriate to more-than-like your sister-in-law. Not that she was his sister-in-law anymore. Was there some sort of statute of limitations on that?

But he was getting off track. Regardless of how he felt about Portia, it was hard to be too enthusiastic about helping out when her entire reason for asking for his help was because he didn't fit into her world.

"I can't tell Dalton where to find her," Portia said. "He wouldn't think twice about thrusting her into this completely unprepared. And I'm not saying that because I think he's jerk. He just wouldn't even think. He always put business first. He wouldn't hesitate."

"And you think I would?"

"Hesitate?" She shrugged. "I think you know better than anyone where this girl is coming from. She has a middle-class background at best. She won't know what she's getting into. She'll be vulnerable and unprepared—"

"Yeah. I get it." Cooper cut Portia off with a sharp wave of his hand. Jesus, was this how people had seen him when he'd first gone to live with the Cains? "It's probably not as bad as you think. I'm sure she'll at least be potty trained."

"That's not what I meant." Portia glared at him, but she looked more exasperated than angry. "I'm trying to protect her."

"Fine. So mentor her or whatever. Take her under your wing. This doesn't have anything to do with me."

"If I'm right and she really is Hollister's daughter, then she's your sister. It has everything to do with you." She tilted her head just a little and eyed him. "Besides, you can't tell me that you aren't at least a little bit interested in winning. In doing what neither Dalton nor Griffin has been able to do. It's a lot of money."

An ugly thread of disgust wound through his stomach. He got so damn sick of these games people played. If asking didn't get what you want, why not manipulate and pit people against one another? That's exactly what Hollister had been doing for years.

Cooper pushed himself to feet. "I don't give a damn about Hollister's money. I never have. If I had, then I'd been one of Cain Enterprises' lackeys right now instead owning my own company."

"Fine. You don't want the money? Give the money away. Give the money to me."

"You don't need the money any more than I do."

"Please, Cooper—"

"Why?" he demanded. "Why on earth do you care so much about this girl?"

She bumped up her chin again. "Because family is supposed to take care of each other, that's why."

"You're not part of the family anymore."

She went instantly still, and for a second, he would have sworn she'd even stopped breathing. Damn it. It was as if his words had skewered her.

Then resolve settled in her gaze. "You're right. I'm not part of this family anymore. But I was for ten years and I know how hard the Cains can be. I had to fight tooth and nail to get Caro to accept me and treat me with respect. I never won over Hollister, and I'm embarrassed to say I stopped trying long after I should have. He is a hard man. Brutal. And even though I love Caro like she's my own mother, I would be very surprised if she welcomes this girl with open arms. And why should she after the way Hollister treated her in the divorce?" She blew out a breath then, and he could tell she had to work to make it sound even. To make it sound like she wasn't already emotionally invested. "This girl is your family. Don't you want to help her?"

Did he want to help this girl? This stranger who might be his sister? Hell, he didn't know.

Cain family politics didn't interest him. At all.

He didn't give a damn about what happened to the company or to Hollister. None of this was his problem. And frankly, he didn't buy half of what Portia was telling him.

He leveled his gaze at her. "Okay, enough with the warm-fuzzy garbage. What aren't you telling me?"

She pulled back and blinked rapidly. "I don't know what you're talking about."

"Come on, you came here in person to beg me to do this and you expect me to believe your only motive is family loyalty to a girl you spent five minutes with?"

He half expected her to have some visible reaction, but Portia was a cool one, and even though he knew he'd hit on something, she didn't so much as flinch. But he could see the calculations going on behind her eyes, so he didn't trust her words when she calmly said, "Fine. You want a motive? How does this one work? I know you don't want the money, so I'm hoping you'll give it to me."

For a second, all he could do was stare at her. There

was a hard glint in her eyes, a stubborn tilt to her chin, that almost—almost—made her statement believable. But not quite.

"All right," he said, wanting to see where she was going with this.

Her chin bumped up a little. "I…um…the divorce left me destitute. I need the money."

"You're destitute?"

"Totally broke."

"Nice try. I don't believe you're broke. Not for a minute."

She frowned, scrunching her mouth to the side adorably. "Really."

"No. When you and Dalton got married, Hollister told me you had a trust from your paternal grandparents that was worth over fifteen million. I know Dalton didn't touch it. So unless you expect me to believe that you've blown through fifteen million in two years…"

She sighed. "I could be really bad with money?"

"No." He didn't believe that, either. He cocked his head to the side. "But I do believe you want the money. Why?"

She frowned again, and he sensed that she was trying to decide exactly what to tell him. Finally, she said, "Have you talked to Caro lately?"

"Caro?" he asked, surprised by the sudden change in topic. "No. Why?"

"Because things haven't gone well for her since the divorce. Personally. Socially. Financially. And I just thought… if you really don't want the money, then we could give some of it to her."

"She needs money?" But then he waved aside his own question. "Of course she needs money. Hollister's such a bastard, he probably butchered her in the divorce. Jesus. Do Dalton and Griffin know?"

"I don't think anyone knows. She and I haven't always

been close, but we are now. I see it, but she doesn't even admit it to me. Besides, she's not exactly their favorite person right now."

"Yeah. I guess not," he agreed. The mysterious letter about Hollister's missing daughter had turned their lives upside down. Neither Dalton nor Griffin had been particularly thrilled to find out that the letter hadn't been penned by some anonymous former lover of Hollister's, but by his angry and bitter wife. "So Hollister eviscerated her in court and she's too proud to tell her sons that she needs financial help. But you think she'll take money from me?"

"I know she's probably not your favorite person, either—"

"I have no problem with Caro," he said quickly. "I never have."

"Oh," Portia said softly. "I just assumed."

It was a fair assumption. Caro was easy to characterize as his wicked stepmother. But that didn't mean they were enemies or that he wanted her out on the street.

"Caro and I get along fine," he said. "But I don't think she'd take money from me."

"She might if it was Hollister's money. He screwed her over. I think she'd enjoy screwing him back." Portia's face settled into resolve. "I could convince her."

Which brought him back to square one: he didn't have time for this.

"Look, it's not about whether or not I want to help her. I don't have the time. It's not my problem."

"But Caro—"

"Look, I can find a way to help Caro without finding this missing heiress." And he would find a way to help her. Just not now. He glanced down at his watch. "And I've got a meeting I'm going to be late for. I'm sorry, Portia."

He took one last look at Portia. She was perfect and pristine and untouchable. God, sometimes she was so pretty, it almost hurt to look at her. And other times, her beauty seemed almost too fragile. Like she might shatter. He was never sure if the part that would shatter was the real woman or only the outer shell that she showed the world.

In the decade she'd been married to his brother, he'd stayed far away from her because it had been the right thing to do. Now that she was single, he had other reasons for staying away. They weren't from the same world. He'd learned as a kid what it meant to be an outsider in that world. What it meant to be Hollister Cain's bastard son. Seeing the things other people had. Reaching for them. Having your hand slapped away.

Yeah. He knew what it meant to want things you couldn't have.

And yeah, he knew that this mystery sister—whoever she ended up being—was going to have a hell of a time adjusting. But he also knew that nothing he did was going to make it any easier on her. She'd either be strong enough or she wouldn't. She'd have to find her own way. Just like he had.

"She has your smile," Portia said. "If that matters at all."

His step faltered only a little. "If she has you on her side, she'll be just fine."

With that, he left the office, putting the conversation and everything it had stirred up behind him. His future rested on the outcome of the board meeting he was going to. He didn't need this Cain family drama. He didn't need a sister. And he sure as hell didn't need Portia here tempting him.

Three

Three hours later, Cooper sat at the head of the conference table and watched his dreams spiral down the drain.

The board voted no.

By a wide margin. It wasn't even close.

Nine of the twelve board members had voted against his plan to get Flight+Risk into the hotel business. Millions could be made in an upscale resort catering specifically to snowboarders. His gut had told him this was a solid venture. But apparently the board thought his gut was "fiscally irresponsible at this juncture."

Now, as the board members started to filter out of the hotel conference room—the votes cast, the meeting officially adjourned—they could hardly meet his gaze. Which was fine, since he feared he might lunge across the table and slam his fist into Robertson's face. The bastard had been on the board since the company's inception. The man—a staid, lifelong businessman in his sixties—had a background in the retail industry that had proved invaluable, but he had little to no imagination. If you couldn't sell it at Macy's, he wasn't interested. He'd been an opponent of Cooper's resort plan from the beginning, but Cooper had really thought he'd won over enough of the other board members. Clearly, he'd been wrong.

With the exception of a couple stragglers, the room cleared within two minutes. An obvious sign that the board wasn't any more comfortable with the outcome than he was. They may have voted against him, but no one wanted to face him down. As for the part of him that wanted to beat the crap out of someone as a result? Well, that was a part that he'd worked hard to bury beneath the facade of a successful businessman.

So he'd waited quietly for the board to leave. He just sat there at the head of the table, staring blankly at the stack of pages in front of him while the rats fled the sinking ship. When he looked up, only two other people remained— Drew Davis, the only fellow snowboarder on the board, and Matt Ballard, the Chief Technology Officer of FJM, a green energy company out of the Bay Area, and a good friend of Cooper's.

After a moment of silence, Drew said, "Man, you're so screwed."

"I'm not screwed." But Cooper said it grimly and with no real conviction.

"No, you're totally f—"

"No. I'll convince them."

There was too much at stake in this fight. This was *his* company. Flight+Risk made the best, toughest gear for winter sports. The best snowboards, the best jackets, the best thermals. All of it. He knew it was the best for two reasons: first off, because he'd designed most of it himself and demanded absolute perfection. Second, because every top snowboarder in the world wanted to use his gear. Yes, it was that good. He made sure of it himself, because inferior gear put people's lives at risk. And profits as well, though that had always been a secondary consideration for him. Still, his perfectionism, ambition and determination had made him a legend on the half-pipe and in the business world.

So why the hell didn't his board trust that he was right about this?

"How exactly are you going to convince them?" Matt asked, rocking back in his chair. Matt had pulled his laptop out the second the meeting was over and was typing now. He was one of those unique guys who could manage to do multiple things at once. Probably because he was freakin' brilliant. He'd been Flight+Risk's first private investor. In fact, he'd approached Cooper as a fan and offered him start-up money before the company had been more than a business plan and prototype board. They'd become good friends over the years.

Somehow it didn't make Cooper feel any better that the only two members of the board who voted yes with him were his two best friends. It smacked of pity votes.

He looked first at Drew and then at Matt. "You can't honestly tell me you agree with Robertson that investing in another manufacturing facility is a better use of our money?"

"Not better," Drew said. "Less risky."

"My plan isn't risky," Cooper said stubbornly.

"You want to invest forty million dollars in this," Drew said. "Flight+Risk will be overextended. Of course the board is going to balk."

"The company has stellar credit and it will only be for the next eighteen months. The location I've picked is perfect. There's already a resort there—"

"A dated, crummy hotel," Matt interjected.

"And, yes, it needs renovations, but the preliminary inspector said the building was sound." The hotel he'd found, Beck's Lodge, was aging and currently unprofitable, but he knew he could turn it into something amazing. "The snow out there is perfect. As soon as the resort opens, the returns on this investment will be huge. You know I'm right."

"Yeah," Drew said. "I think you're right. But the board cares more about what the stock market thinks."

"Being overextended isn't the problem," Matt said without looking up.

Drew and Cooper both turned to look at Matt.

"What?" Drew asked.

"Then what is the problem?" Cooper asked.

"It's a problem of perception." Matt looked up as if surprised to be the center of the attention. "Come on. Cooper has a reputation for taking crazy risks. That incident with the model after the Olympics when you were reprimanded is a perfect example. And everyone knows Flight+Risk nearly failed in the first two years and would have if you hadn't been pumping your own money into the company to keep it afloat."

"You're saying the board didn't vote against the idea. They voted against me."

"The media loves that stuff," Matt said, shrugging. "It makes for great reading. But the kinds of risks you take scare the hell out of investors."

"Those kinds of risks pay off."

"Barely."

"No. Every one of the risks I've taken in business has paid off huge."

"Yes. They did pay off huge. After you almost failed miserably. You've had a lot of success, but your winning streak is going to end someday. No one wants to catch the flak from that."

"So you're saying everyone just thinks it's my time to fail."

"Yeah."

"But this isn't risky. By the time I'm done with this resort, the best snowboarders in the world will be there. If I were a golfer building one of those golf communities, everyone would be clamoring to invest."

"Maybe." Matt shrugged and looked back down at his laptop. "But golf is different. Those guys know rich. You're just a snowboarder."

Just a snowboarder?

That pissed him off. Yeah, he knew Matt didn't mean it personally, but it was hard not to take it that way.

Because even if Matt didn't buy that argument, plenty of other people did. Never mind that Cooper had been running Flight+Risk for three times as long as he'd been a professional snowboarder. He had more money now than any one man could spend in a lifetime and had earned his money himself, unlike so many other rich bastards. And he'd never once made a business decision that hadn't paid off. Never mind any of that.

In the end, the board was scared he didn't have the business chops to know a great investment from a pipe dream. They'd pegged him as too much of a risk taker just because he'd left college to snowboard professionally. They thought he didn't know the upscale market just because he'd had to work for every one of his successes. Because he'd worked hard to keep his relationship to the Cains on the down low. He'd never wanted people handing him things because of who his father was. He'd never wanted the Cain name to buy him anything. So sure, his lineage was out there for whoever dug around in his past—and reporters loved that nonsense—but he didn't advertise it. He'd never taken the Cain name, even though he'd lived with Hollister and Caro after his mother had died. He never talked about his father or his family connections.

He would have laughed at the irony if it hadn't pissed him off so damn much.

Would he have to put up with this kind of thing if he'd been in the habit of reminding the board who his father was? If he'd trotted out his father's name, the board probably would have rolled right over.

Instead, he did things his own way and his ideas were labeled too risky.

It wasn't fair.

Which was fine. His life had never been fair. He was the king of making not-fair work for him.

He looked up suddenly to realize that his two friends were exchanging worried glances. As if he'd been quiet too long and they were concerned he was plotting Robertson's demise. Well, he was, but not in the way they were worried about.

So he smiled broadly and stood. "It's all good."

Drew stood also. "Are you okay?"

"Yeah. It's just time for Plan B."

Matt raised his eyebrows. "Really? 'Cause I heard you say once that backup plans were for losers without the determination to get it right the first time."

Yeah. That sounded like him. He shrugged. "Okay, we'll call this Plan 2.0."

Matt snapped his laptop closed and stood. "So what's Plan 2.0?"

"I'm going to convince the board that this isn't risky. I'm going to convince them that I do know this market."

"They've already voted you down. Flight+Risk can't move forward unless it comes to a vote again," Matt pointed out.

"I got too eager and pushed the vote too soon. But by

the time I'm done with them, they'll be desperate to get Flight+Risk involved."

"How exactly are you going to do that?" Drew asked.

"I'm going to hire an expert."

In the end, Portia missed her flight to Tahoe and had to reschedule for the next day. The airline had pulled her suitcase off the flight and had held it in Denver, thank goodness, and she'd been able to find a car service to deliver her bag to her hotel. It was all far less inconvenient than it might have been. No matter how Portia tried to tell herself that she'd only lost one day and that she hadn't gone that far out of her way, she couldn't help feeling that the entire trip had been a huge waste of time.

For tonight, she'd checked into a hotel in Denver, not far from Flight+Risk's corporate offices. In the morning she would see about getting another flight to Tahoe. But now, she had room service coming with a salted caramel brownie and carafe of red wine.

Yes, tomorrow she would start her vacation. She'd still get her two weeks of solitude at her parents' summer cabin by the lake. She'd read the dozen or so books already loaded onto her Nook. She'd watch movies. Do some yoga. It would all be very relaxing.

Except she wasn't relaxed. Her mind was still whirling with thoughts of the waitress from the Kimball Hotel, the woman she knew was Hollister's daughter.

Part of her agreed with Cooper. She should just let it go. It wasn't any of her business.

Honestly, she hadn't given the Cain heiress much thought in the year since Hollister had issued the challenge. However, now that she'd met the woman, she couldn't stop worrying about her. She knew better than anyone what a brutal man Hollister was. He was no one's ideal father-in-law. He'd criticized her endlessly. He'd only gotten worse once her fertility problems became public knowledge.

Dalton hadn't put up with that, of course. He'd called his father on it every time he'd witnessed it. But Dalton hadn't been around much. Caro had stepped up to her defense, as well. That was how she and Caro had gotten so close. At first, Hollister's behavior had hurt. She hadn't realized he treated everyone badly. He wasn't picking on her. He was just a jerk.

Would Ginger know that?

She'd seemed tough. Would she be able to defend herself against the likes of Hollister? Would she understand that any sign of weakness would stir up the piranhas? Would she have any defenses against the people who would pretend to be her friend and then turn on her in a second?

Yes, Cooper was right. It wasn't Portia's business. But that didn't stop her from worrying about the girl. She'd been counting on Cooper to take over finding the heiress for her. The hope that some of his reward money would be funneled to Caro was just the salted caramel topping on the brownie. Now that he'd refused, she was left in the hot seat again. She had no other ideas about how to help Caro or the heiress. Unless she went to Dalton.

Still, she couldn't shake the feeling that being found was going to change this woman's life forever, and not necessarily in a good way. But what could she do? Not telling anyone that she'd found the heiress wasn't an option. Damn Cooper for not agreeing to help her. Really, she'd thought better of him.

A moment later there was a knock on the door. Men may never do precisely what she expected them to do, but thank goodness for chocolate. It was there when she needed it.

But when she opened the door, it wasn't room service with her brownie. It was Cooper.

He leaned casually against the wall right outside her hotel room, one ankle crossed over the other. He was wearing the same suit he'd had on earlier in the day, but the tie was gone and the jacket looked rumpled. Like he'd taken it off several times over the past few hours.

He looked up when she opened the door. "Hey, I need a favor."

"You're not a brownie," she muttered under her breath.

He blinked, looking surprised. Then his mouth curled in a wry smile. "Not the last time I checked."

"I ordered a brownie from room service." God, that sounded pathetic. A woman eating a brownie alone in a hotel room? It practically screamed *loser*. "It has a salted caramel topping."

Nope. That didn't sound any less pathetic.

Thank God, she hadn't mentioned the carafe of red wine.

He had texted her over two hours earlier saying he wanted to stop by to talk, so she'd sent him her room number, but when he never showed up, she'd assumed he'd decided against it.

Cooper ignored her babbling and asked, "Can I come in?"

Tempted though she was to demand he go find her brownie as a gesture of goodwill, she stepped aside and let him enter.

He walked into the room and shut the door behind him. Her hotel was one that catered to businesspeople, so her room was a minisuite, with a small living area and kitchen. Before the knock, she'd been about to settle onto the sofa and watch a movie she'd bought on pay-per-view. A sappy romantic drama she'd already seen. The title of the movie was splashed across the screen in pause mode. She clicked the TV off, feeling strangely ashamed of her choice. Next time she was picking an action movie. Or one of those comedies with all the frat-boy humor.

She glanced back over to see Cooper studying her. "What?" she asked self-consciously.

"Nothing." His full lips curved into a smile. "I don't think I've ever seen you looking…" His words trailed off like he didn't have the faintest idea how to describe her appearance.

She glanced down. Her yoga pants and hoodie were about the least glamorous things she owned. "I'm not going to apologize for not being better dressed. It's late. You came to me. You're the one who texted and said you want to talk."

"I'm not criticizing. It's adorable."

There was a gleam of amusement in his gaze. Amusement and something else, as well. Something that made her belly flutter around a bit.

God, he was good-looking. Attractive in a way that completely disarmed her. There was no polish to him. He had no smooth edges. He was rugged and rough-hewn, like the harsh landscapes he snowboarded. But there was an innate humor to him also. A lightness—the way the sun could still shine on a bitterly cold day on the slopes.

Not many men she knew managed to pull that off—his unique combination of tough and disarming. But he did. He wielded his charisma like a surgeon's knife, and if she wasn't careful, he'd lure her in and slice away at her defenses.

She rolled her eyes. "Stop trying to charm me. Just tell me what you want so I can eat my brownie in peace."

"You don't have your brownie yet," he pointed out.

"Exactly. Which gives you from now until whenever the brownie arrives to convince me not to kick you out."

"Then I better talk fast."

And he did. Fast and passionately. She clocked him.

For two straight minutes he talked about his plan to buy and renovate some resort in Southern Utah. He waxed poetic about the perfect powder and the lack of true luxury hotels in the area. He talked about the untapped market. Thirty seconds in, she sank to the sofa and tucked her legs up under her, exhausted just watching him pace the tiny length of the room. He was still talking when there was a knock on the door.

She stood and gestured toward the door. "My brow—"

He stopped right in front of her and grabbed her arm. "Wait. I'm not done."

"But my—"

"You said I had until the brownie arrived." He grinned. "It's not in the room, yet. Give me thirty more seconds."

Cooper on a full tear was an impressive thing. "Look, I'm sorry your board didn't agree. I think it sounds like a great idea. But I don't see what this has to do with me."

"Maybe the board is right. Maybe I don't know that high-end luxury market well enough. I'm just a kid from Denver who happens to be good on a snowboard. But you do know that market. I want you to visit the hotel. See if you agree that it can be turned into a playground for the rich."

"I don't know anything about the hotel business."

"I don't, either. I'm not asking you to run the hotel. I just want your opinion. You grew up with money and—"

"Cooper, *you* grew up with money," she protested.

"No. I grew up with money during the summers. For two miserable years I lived with the Cains in high school. That's not the same and you know it. I never fit in. You said yourself that I was the perfect person to find the Cain heiress because I know what it's like to be an outsider. But you were born to this life. And you have the best taste of anyone I've ever met. And—"

There was another knock on the door and he held out his hand as if to stall for more time.

"Do you really think keeping me from my brownie is going to help your argument?"

A few minutes later, after the waiter had come and gone, she turned back to find Cooper watching her with a mischievous gleam in his eyes. Maybe getting that brownie hadn't been a good idea. Clearly, it had bought him just enough time to concoct some scheme.

"If you help me convince the board to buy Beck's Lodge, then I'll help you find my sister. I'll clear a whole week from my calendar to help her get settled. No, a whole month." He raised his eyebrows. "What do you think?"

"I help you, you'll help me?"

"Exactly."

Her heart rate ticked up a notch. Wasn't that what she wanted? His help with the heiress?

But helping him would mean staying here—or wherever this lodge of his was—at least for a few more days. Maybe more. It would mean spending a lot of time in Cooper's company. For some reason that thought made her deeply uncomfortable. He was an undeniably attractive man. She'd have to be dead not to notice that. Not that she thought of him that way, but it did make this entire situation more confusing.

She gazed longingly at the room service tray and her brownie. Right about now, she could certainly use the comfort only a bakery item could provide. Just a few minutes alone with her brownie. Was that really too much to ask?

"So are you in?" Cooper asked.

"Is there any chance you're going to let me off the hook here?"

"Very little."

So, apparently, yes. It was too much to ask.

"What do you think?" he asked.

"I think you're crazy. That's what I think. You took too many blows to the head on the half-pipe."

"But you'll do it?"

"I didn't say that." His smile brightened as if she'd just given in. "And no. I won't."

His smile deepened. "Yeah. You're going to do it."

"I just said I wasn't going to."

"Yeah. I noticed that. But you'll change your mind."

"I won't," she said, not because she really believed it but because...well, no one liked feeling that transparent.

"You will. You'll do it because you're desperate. You traveled all the way here to talk to me into this. That's how much you want this."

"I'm not desperate!" she protested.

He ignored her. "That's the problem with wanting things too badly. It puts you at a disadvantage when it comes to negotiating." His grin widened, making her breath catch in her chest. "Next time you want something from me, you should play it a little cooler. Maybe call before you rush all the way here."

Damn him for seeing through her so completely. Damn him for calling out her weaknesses. And damn him for making her like him despite those two things.

She crossed her arms over her chest and blew out a breath. "I'll try to remember that in the future."

Four

Twenty minutes later, Portia was washing down the last bite of her brownie with a healthy sip of red wine. She'd shared the brownie with him. He'd eaten his half in three bites; she had carefully divided hers into tiny cubes and eaten it with her fork. Cooper loved the way she turned eating a brownie into an art.

"What do you think?" he asked.

She paused, fork in her mouth, and then studied him through narrowed eyes as she slowly pulled the fork out. "What you really need to do is bring the board out to this hotel. Show them its potential firsthand."

"The place is a wreck right now," he admitted. "I don't think they'll get past that."

"So you make it look like it isn't a wreck. You feed them good food and drinks. You distract them."

"You want me to throw a party to convince them?"

"I'm thinking more a snowboarding exhibition, proceeded by a party."

"So you'll do it?"

"I'm still mulling."

"You can't mull any faster?"

"Not all of us think as fast as you do. Besides—" she glanced at her wrist where a watch would be if she was wearing one "—it's after eight on Monday night. There's a whole twelve hours before you could do anything even if I agree. And you're the one who told me not to appear too desperate."

She leaned forward and carefully set the fork across her plate before putting the silver dome back over it and nudging the room service tray across the coffee table. There was grace in her every movement. She was a woman made for room service and luxury hotels. Elegance practically seeped from her pores. Beside her he felt like a buffoon.

Watching her eat a brownie—a simple brownie for God's sake—reminded him of the thousand and one ways she outclassed him. He was used to feeling outclassed. That's how he'd spent every summer of his youth. He just wasn't used to wanting the kind of woman who made him feel that way.

"I don't think I'm the right woman for you," Portia said, her tone almost distracted.

"What?" He sat up a little straighter.

She frowned, confused for a second, then blushed. "I meant I don't think I'm the right woman for this job. You should hire a professional party planner. Or possibly an independent consultant. Maybe both."

"That's why I'm hiring you. You can do the job of both. I know how flexible you are."

Her gaze sharpened. "What's that supposed to mean?"

He tried to look innocent. "Nothing."

"Cooper—"

"Just that any woman who can do a headstand in a wedding dress and then walk down the aisle ten minutes later can pull off anything."

"I can't believe you brought that up!" she sputtered, burying her face in her palm. "I was hoping you'd forgotten that."

"Trust me, that's not the kind of thing a guy forgets. Your legs straight up in the air—"

"Just stop now!"

"Not to mention that cute little pair of underwear with the kitties on them."

She broke off, her mouth open. "What? My…my cute little…what?"

Her cheeks turned bright pink. As bright as her panties had been.

She looked delightfully flustered. Which was not the end goal, now was it?

If she knew how hot she looked, how much he wanted her, she'd boot him out of her hotel room and refuse to so much as look at him again.

Why had it seemed like a good idea to bring up her panties? Right, because he was going tease her. Playfully.

"Those pink panties of yours. With the little white cat heads on them?"

"My Hello Kitty underwear? You saw my underwear that day?"

"Hey, you were the one doing a headstand." He shrugged. "What did you call them again?"

"Stop teasing me."

He leaned a bit closer and caught a faint whiff of her scent, a combination of something light and pepperminty mingled with warm chocolate brownie. "I happen to think you could do with a lot more teasing."

She glared at him, but there was no real annoyance in her expression. "What's that supposed to mean?"

"People tend to take you entirely too seriously."

"That's not true at all. I'm a socialite. I spend my life doing volunteer work, shopping and lunching. No one takes me seriously."

"You're the daughter of a senator and part of one of the most influential families in the state. I suspect everyone takes you seriously." Something sad and shuttered flickered through her eyes, and he added, "Whether you want them to or not."

But she seemed to shake it off and said with mock severity, "Well, you should take this very seriously—don't tease me about my Hello Kitty underwear. She's a beloved cultural icon."

He held up his hands in mock surrender. "I promise. From here on out, Hello Kitty is off-limits. Now, do you agree to help me?"

"And if I do this, you'll really help me track down the heiress? And you'll stay in contact with her? Make sure she gets settled into her new life?"

"Yes, I will."

She eyed him again. "I can't make any promises. I can't promise that I can convince the board of anything. All I can do is try."

"I understand that."

"And I certainly can't promise that this hotel of yours will be a success."

"You don't have to promise me that." He grinned. "I know it will be."

She leaned forward then and set her wineglass on the coffee table. "Has it occurred to you that you could just do this yourself?"

"Do what?"

"Get financing on your own. Buy Beck's Lodge. Start

a whole new company that's independent of Flight+Risk. You could do that."

"I don't want to do that. I started Flight+Risk. It's my company. The board should trust me. They should trust my judgment."

"So basically, you're just being stubborn?"

"No, I'm—" Then he paused, tilted his head a little to the side as if considering the matter and ultimately smiled. "Yeah. Maybe."

"So this is worth it for you? Spending all this time and energy just to prove to your board that your idea is valid?"

"Yes, damn it." Somehow he managed to smile while conveying the depth of his conviction.

He was so sure of himself. So completely confident that she couldn't help but be drawn in by it. Still, did he know why he was really doing this? Did he get it?

She'd done the research on his board over the years—it wasn't just nosiness on her part. With all the fund-raising she did, she considered it part of her job to know as much as possible about everyone and who their connections where. The curse of being a politician's daughter, she supposed. Of course, at some point, mere research had been eclipsed by her natural fascination with complex human relationships.

Robertson had been a member of the board since Flight+Risk went public. He had the perfect background for the position and Cooper had chosen the man himself. Despite that, they had a history of clashing over the direction of the company. Cooper was a natural risk taker and he just couldn't resist rebelling against authority, even when that authority was his own board.

Still, it didn't take a degree in psychology to figure out the real reason he was desperate to get their approval for his pet project. Several members, Robertson in particular, were men of Hollister's generation. In fact, Robertson might as well have been Hollister; the only difference was that he'd made his name in retail instead of oil. Yes, this was a matter of pride for Cooper, but it was also deeply personal. He didn't just want the board's approval. He wanted his father's.

But Hollister was an ass and that bridge had burned down long ago, ignited from both ends. Cooper could never earn his father's approval. Hell, he could never even ask for it. But he could damn well get the board's support if he tried hard enough.

And, she supposed, she might as well help him get it. "If you really want the board to buy into the idea, you don't sell it to them directly. You find outside investors."

"Flight+Risk doesn't need more investors. We've got the money and the line of credit. I just need the board's approval."

"I know. That's what I'm saying. If you want to get their approval, the way to do that is to convince them that you don't need them. That you have other people interested in investing. Not in Flight+Risk, but you personally."

"So I sell them on the idea by not selling them on the idea?"

"Exactly."

"Okay. How do I do that?"

"Well, we talked about inviting the board up to the resort and show them how much potential it has, right?"

"Yeah. Once they see the powder—"

"No, they don't need to see the powder. If your board is like every other board of directors I've ever met, they don't snowboard. Maybe a couple of them ski. They're in their sixties. They've got power and money, but they're not athletes."

He smiled wryly. "You realize you're making sweeping generalizations about people you've never met, right?"

"Am I wrong?"

"No."

"Okay, so just accept that they don't care about the powder. None of the investors will. All they'll care about is whether the snowboarders—the potential clients—care about the powder. So you invite every snowboarder you know out for an exhibition. You plan a fabulous weekend to woo the investors."

"And I invite the board members."

She cocked her head to the side, considering. "No, not right away. Remember what you said before? About not seeming desperate? That's what we're going for here. We want them to think that you can make a go of this without Flight+Risk. You don't pander to them. You invite other people. Rich, important people. People involved in real-estate investment. That type." She thought for a moment and added, "Preferably people who know a few of the board members. What you want is for the word to spread to them via some other source. You want to make this seem like such a sweet deal that the board comes to you. And in order for that to happen, you have to make them think you don't need them at all."

He nearly laughed. "Well, that's easy. Not needing people is one of the things I do best."

She gave a bark of laughter. "See, you're a Cain after all." Then she tilted her head to the side and asked, "Has it occurred to you that the easiest way to get the money isn't to convince the board at all? It isn't even to find investors."

"It isn't?"

"No. The easiest way to get the money for this project would be for you to just find Ginger and win this damn challenge your father set up." He opened his mouth to protest, but she held up a hand. "I know you don't really want the money, but I also know that Griffin and Dalton have both told your father that if either of them win, they're still splitting it three ways. Or rather four ways, since Ginger will get her share, too. Even if you only take a quarter of the money, you'd still have enough to buy this hotel or a hundred hotels."

"You don't get it. I don't want a penny of that man's money. Ever."

"So what are you going to do once we track down Ginger? When the DNA test confirms she's Hollister's daughter—"

"If the test confirms it."

Portia shook her head. "No. It will confirm it. I'm sure. She looks just like a Cain. When you see her, you'll know what I mean." She said it with so much conviction, even he was starting to believe this woman Portia had stumbled across might be the heiress. "So what are you going to do with the money?"

He shrugged. "Give it to Caro, like you suggested."

"Even if she's thrilled about screwing over Hollister, I doubt she'll take all the money. There's bound to be some left over. Easily enough for this."

"I'll convince her," he said grimly.

"You claim you don't want it, but are you really going to walk away from hundreds of millions of dollars?"

"Dalton and Griffin can keep the money. So can this girl, if she wants it."

"This girl who's your sister."

He narrowed his gaze.

"I'm just saying. Because I've never heard you actually call her your sister."

"Your point?"

"I just want to make sure you remember that. She's your sister. And she needs you. That should matter to you."

Then she leaned forward slightly and for a second she

was close enough he got hit with the scent of her, sweet and fresh. Suddenly he was aware all over again how scantily dressed she was. And that they were alone. And that the last thing he wanted to be doing was talking about his stupid family crap.

"I know you don't get along with the other Cains," she said. "But you might decide Ginger is different. You might actually like her."

He didn't quite know what to say to that. He wasn't in the market for a sister. He didn't particularly want the family he already had. Still, part of him knew that Portia was right. He might actually like this girl. And she would undoubtedly have a hard time of it. In all honesty, the best thing for Ginger would probably be to live out her life without ever knowing who her father was. But there was no way that would happen. Eventually Dalton or Griffin would hunt her down.

Whether he wanted the money or not, maybe finding her first would be the best for everyone. Just so long as it didn't take too much of his time or energy.

This Beck's Lodge deal was his top priority. Flight+Risk was his top priority pretty much always. He didn't need any distractions—not the kind a sister would provide and not the kind Portia would provide, either.

But Portia wasn't interested in him. Not really. Yes, she probably felt that spark of attraction that he felt, but he wasn't even sure if she'd admitted that to herself yet. And she wasn't the kind of girl who would ever act on that attraction.

There were rich women who played with professional athletes like it was a hobby. Something they did in their spare time. Portia wasn't that kind of woman. Headstand or not, she was better than a quick and mindless affair. And if he slipped up and made a pass at her, she would bolt. And as of right now, she was too important to him to scare off. He needed her. If he was going to pull this off, he needed her. Badly.

A fact he'd have to remind himself of constantly when they worked together. Which was probably why he shouldn't be lounging around in her hotel room late at night.

He stood. "I'll pick you up first thing in the morning and take you out to Beck's Lodge."

She frowned, using her phone to check the time. "How long will the trip take? I'd rescheduled my flight to Tahoe for tomorrow afternoon."

"Just give me all day tomorrow." That would give him all of tomorrow to convince her to stay much longer.

Five

Portia had her doubts the next day. To begin with, until Cooper pulled up at the private airstrip, she hadn't considered how they were going to get to the resort. Cooper had chartered a flight to take them to Salt Lake City. From there, it had been an hour drive through the foothills and mountains before they turned off on a private road that wound through snow so bright it made her eyes ache.

Traffic thinned and then disappeared entirely. They appeared to be driving through a land completely uninhabited. But then they turned a corner and the lodge rose up out of the surrounding forest.

"Oh, you have got to be kidding me," Portia muttered as she gaped at the lodge.

He grinned at her. "Yeah. It's a beast of a building, isn't it?"

Cooper stopped the car in the circular drive in front of the building. "Come on, let's go take a look," he said as he climbed from the car.

She clambered out of the car after him and headed for the front of the house, practically bounding up the path, she was so excited.

"Don't we need to wait for a Realtor or someone?" she asked once she reached the steps.

"Nah. I talked to the sales agent and the owners this morning and let them know I was coming up. I'm the only one even looking at the property, so they're giving me a lot of latitude. If you want to meet with them later, they'll come on out, but for now we're alone."

Portia stared up at the building squatting on the road ahead, mouth agape. Building? House? Lodge? Monstrosity? It defied description.

Nestled up against the mountain, built of massive wooden beams and rounded river rocks—some the size of VW bugs—it wasn't so much a lodge as it was a monument. It was three stories of sprawling ego and hubris.

"You didn't tell me it was Bear Creek Lodge," she murmured breathlessly.

Cooper pointed to the cheesy sign planted near the driveway. It was made out of fake wood, with carved letters painted bright yellow, like a sign you'd find in a national park sixty years ago. The sign read: "Beck's Lodge, family owned and operated since 1948."

"Not Bear Creek Lodge. Beck's Lodge," Cooper said.

"Do you know the history of this house?"

"I know this is the best powder on the mountain. I know there's no other location that's anywhere near this perfect. Those are the things I care about."

"But you don't know anything about the house?"

"No." He looked at her, clearly baffled. "Do you?"

"Um. Yeah." She turned her hands up in an exasperated gesture. "You want to buy this place and turn it into an upscale resort and you don't even know the history?"

"What history?" He pointed to the sign. "It's family owned and operated since 1948. What else is there to know?"

"What else is there to know?" She laughed, a gurgling bubble of hysteria. There was so much to know. Among some circles, this house was famous. Either the Realtor listing it hadn't done her research or—more likely—no one thought a snowboarder like Cooper would care about the building's unique history. "There's an American author named Jack Wallace. Wallace became famous writing adventure stories set in the American West and during the Yukon Gold Rush around the turn of the century. The turn of the last century, not this one."

"I know who Jack Wallace is," Cooper said drily.

"Well, then you know how he was larger than life. You probably read his novel *Lost at Bear Creek* in school, right? He was one of the first writers to be a worldwide celebrity. He was a millionaire, which, trust me, meant a lot more in those days than it does now. He bought all this land. Thousands of acres. And in 1910 started building this huge house."

"This house?"

"No. Not this house. Wait for it." She shot him a look, surprised that he seemed to be genuinely interested. She was a history buff. And an old building buff. Not many people had the patience to listen to her rattle on about either, but Cooper seemed glued to the story, and she couldn't help reveling at having a captive audience. "They finished the house in 1923 and it burned down, two weeks before he and his wife moved in. This was before the age of insurance. But Wallace refused to give up. He had them start from scratch. The result was Bear Creek Lodge. The remains of the old house are still standing in the national park, which he donated. But by the time he finished construction, his liver was failing and he lived in it for less than a month before he died. His children inherited the house, but couldn't afford to live here because of the taxes. They couldn't agree about what to do with it and eventually it was auctioned off for back taxes. Which I guess is when the Becks bought it."

As she spoke, she took in every line of the house. This crazy, beautiful building, with its blunt Arts and Crafts style angles and its sharp edges. The house seemed to rise up out of the mountain like some sort of ancient shrine. It was beautiful. Despite its state of disrepair. Despite its age. Despite the attempts the Becks had made to brighten it up, with yellow paint and cheap plastic flowers stuck in the ground in front. It was pure folly.

And in some ways, it reminded her of Cooper himself. It was strong and stubborn and deeply rooted in the outdoors. It was larger than life. The stuff of dreams. Deeply appealing without being soft or pliant. This was a house that wouldn't budge, and she sensed Cooper was the same.

He may think he loved this location because of "the perfect powder," but she knew it was more than that. On some level, he connected to the house, too.

"How do you know all this?" Cooper asked from beside her.

"History of American Architecture class. I was an architecture major for three semesters."

"Why'd you quit?"

She sent him a smile and started walking up the front steps of the lodge. "Because no one builds houses like this anymore."

Listening to Portia wax poetic about the building, Cooper couldn't help wondering what he was missing.

Her enthusiasm was adorable, really, and completely at odds with how he thought of her. Sometimes he felt as if there were two Portias, maybe more for that matter. There was the cool and sophisticated socialite who'd been married to Dalton. Beneath that, there was this bubbly, charming Portia, who seemed like so much fun. She was like a Russian stacking doll. Each layer was different from the one inside. Were there any more layers he hadn't uncovered yet? "You know it's really ugly, right?"

She glared at him. "No. It's really beautiful. You're just blinded by the snow."

Was she pretending to be offended or had he actually insulted her? "The inside is dated and hopelessly dark. It's grimy."

"Are you trying to talk me out of helping you?"

"I just want to make sure you understand. I'm turning this into a resort. Not a national monument to Bear Lodge."

"Bear Creek Lodge," she corrected him absently, her eyes still moving restlessly over the exterior of the building.

Suddenly he was glad that he'd asked the Becks to give him time alone to show her the house. He didn't want anyone there while they discussed it.

"No, no. I know." She stepped through the doorway into the lodge and it seemed to take her breath away. "Oh, my."

The door opened right into the great room. There was a reception area with a front desk made of Formica. It was a massive, sprawling room whose ceiling was two stories up. At one end of the room, a river rock fireplace crawled up the wall. At the other, a staircase spilled out from a second-floor hallway. There were a dozen guest rooms up there.

The place was a wreck on every level. But it was big and that counted for a lot when it came to hotels. Still, how would it look through her eyes? Through the eyes of those rich investors she wanted to lure here? They would see the cheesy Formica and the bright yellow paint. Not the perfect snow and endless potential.

"Eventually we'll have to gut the interior and—"

Portia whirled on him and socked him in arm. "If you touch so much as an inch of this interior without my permission I will hunt you down and hurt you."

He rubbed his arm and faked a wince. "Ouch."

"Except that desk. After you buy this place, you can take that out the same day if you want."

"*If* Flight+Risk buys it. If we can get the board to see our side of this."

"I am no longer worried about that." The gleam in her eyes was almost maniacal. "When we're done here, the board is going to be salivating. And you know why?"

"I'm guessing it's not because of the perfect powder," he said wryly.

"No. Not the perfect powder. You've got that angle covered already. And don't get me wrong, it's a good tack to take. But I'm going to play the irreplaceable slice of history angle. That's something that no stuffy businessman can resist. I'd bet you half of these businessmen grew up reading Jack Wallace books."

"You may be overestimating the intelligence of these men."

Her lips curved in a smile. "Maybe. But at any rate, Jack Wallace's books defined what it meant to be an outdoorsman in America. His stories influenced everything from the settlement of Alaska to the development of the national park system. We just have to remind them that snowboarding is part of that tradition."

"You know that actual snowboarders don't care about any of that, right?"

"You worry about what snowboarders want. I'll worry about the pretentious old men with money and what they want." She ran her toe over the dark green floral pattern in the carpet. "Have you looked under the carpet?"

"No."

"It's probably hardwood. They didn't have wall-to-wall like this when Bear Creek was built. I'd guess this was added sometime in the eighties."

Her voice had taken on a dreamy quality. As if the house entranced her.

"At some point, if we do convince the board to pony up the money, there will have to be massive renovations. You know that, right?"

She swatted away his question. "How many bedrooms upstairs?"

"The Becks have rooms on the third floor in what used to be the servants' quarters. Then there are nine bedrooms on the second floor. But only three bathrooms. There are twenty-four cabins, but they're—"

"I don't care." Her voice sounded dreamy, but her eyes sparkled with delight. "This place is perfect."

"It's a wreck."

"No. It's beautiful."

"It's dark and dingy."

"Which we can fix with the right tricks." She whirled around to look at him. "You've already talked to the owners about renting this place for a weekend for the event, right?"

"Yeah. I did that first thing this morning. They're on board."

"And they're willing to let us make superficial changes?"

"They've said that anything we're willing to pay for, they'll let us do."

She eyed him, making him think she was sizing him up. "You're going to pay for this out of your pocket?"

"If I have to."

"Think I can talk you into pulling up the carpet and having the floors redone?"

Right now, when she was looking at him with the gleam

in her eyes, that pure fiery determination, she could probably talk him into anything she wanted. Her unabashed enthusiasm charmed him. It had been years since he'd seen her this excited about something. He loved the way her lips tilted upward as she spoke. How her eyes sparkled. "This is how you always end up talking me into donating to all your crazy causes."

She propped her hands on her hips, looking indignant. "My causes aren't crazy!"

He chuckled, tucking a loose strand of hair behind her ear. "Relax. I'm just teasing." Then he frowned with mock seriousness. "Your causes are very important. Your ability to coax money out of me—that's crazy."

She frowned. "I don't coax that much money out of you."

Oh, she had no idea. He wasn't a particularly generous man. I wasn't like he went around looking for ways to get rid of his money. But every damn time she called, he couldn't resist. Talking about some charitable cause was the only time she dropped her guard. So, yeah, he literally paid money to see her smile. Sucker.

Suddenly, he realized he was still standing close to her. His fingers were still playing with a silken strand of her hair. He dropped his hand and stepped back.

"Yeah. We can cover getting the floors redone."

Her smile widened into a full-fledged grin. She turned around, taking in the entire room. "If we get rid of the carpet, the curtains and most of this god-awful furniture, this place will be amazing. In four weeks, you won't recognize this place."

"In four weeks?"

She turned to look at him. "You didn't honestly think I could pull this off in less time than that, did you?"

He blew out a breath, doing the math in his head. In four weeks, it would be late March. The snow should still be good. They'd be cutting it close. But it would probably take that long alone to get the exhibition lined up. "Okay. Four weeks. I expect miracles."

"Even in four weeks, I can't pull off a miracle. It'll be mostly staging. And we'll have to get the Becks' approval."

"The couple that ran the lodge when it was still open are too old. Their children are desperate to sell this place. I don't think we're going to have to worry about getting their approval for the things you mentioned."

"Of course they're desperate. Bear Creek Lodge has a reputation for being tainted by misery and failure. It's quite the albatross to be saddled with." She wandered into the center of the room and stared up at the ceiling, slowly spinning around before glancing over at him. "And we have the place to ourselves?"

Her voice was pitched low with excitement. Intellectually, he understood the question. She was asking if there were other quests around. But his body heard a whole different question. Were they alone? Would they be interrupted?

He told his body to shut the hell up and leave him alone.

"The lodge hasn't been opened all season. The Becks' children have had it on the market this whole time."

"Perfect. I want to explore."

And before he could stop her, she dashed off up the stairs to take inventory.

Six

Five hours later, they were having dinner at a restaurant in Provo. Portia had three different notebooks open in front of her—thank goodness she'd had spares tucked in her bag. Each notepad had a different to-do list on it. A piece of cherry pie sat off to her left with a cup of herbal tea beside it. She was still picking at her fries and the ice cream on her pie was starting to melt, but she didn't care.

Cooper sat across the booth from her and fiddled with his iPad. He'd already eaten his hamburger and pie and his plates had been cleaned. He must have the metabolism of a racehorse, because he seemed to inhale food voraciously. How on earth did he eat that much and maintain those washboard abs? Not that she knew his abs were tautly muscled. It was just really easy to imagine that they were. Not that she spent tons of time imagining his abs. Or remembering the way he'd played with her hair as he was teasing her.

No doubt about it, Cooper could lay on the charm like

nobody's business. No wonder he had such a reputation as a ladies' man. Apparently, he couldn't turn off the charm. All the more reason for her to ignore that completely.

She flipped from one page to the next and gaped at the growing list. "Okay, you're inviting all the snowboarders, so I don't need to have anything to do with that."

"Exactly," he said. "I'm going to put Jane to work on it first thing in the morning."

"You can have Jane finalize travel plans, but you should call the talent yourself. Just like you're going to call the investors."

"I am?"

"Absolutely."

"Is that necessary?"

"Yes." She smiled reassuringly. "You're a man who throws himself off mountains for a living. Don't let a few investors scare you. Besides, I'm only going to have you call the ones you either know or have some connection to. If it's someone I know, I'll contact them myself before the invitations go out."

"Someone you know?"

"Sure. And I know a lot of people in real estate. Isn't that why you asked me to help?" She chuckled at the dazed look on his face. She flipped her notebook back a couple of pages and pushed it across the table, turning it around to face him. "Look, it's not that bad. You only have to call the ones with the red stars beside their names. It's all people you've met. You phone them, just like it's a social call, and casually mention the exhibition. Don't mention investing at all. Just be friendly."

He studied the page for a moment and then looked up at her with a teasing smile. "Am I supposed to be able to read this?"

She felt a little flutter in her belly. It would be so easy

to get lured in by his charm. So easy, and so dangerous. She forced her gaze away from his face back to the notebook. "Yeah. I guess my notes are illegible, huh?" The table was just a little too wide to comfortably reach across it, so she wiggled out of her side of the booth and slid in next to Cooper. She looked down at the page in front of him. It was a bit of a complicated mess of web brainstorming she'd done. She traced her fingertip along the writing as she spoke. "Here we are on this side of the page. You. Me. You said Matt Ballard and Drew Davis voted in your favor so I included them on this side. By the way, you've already talked to them right? They're available?"

"Yeah. They're in."

"Good, because I can't wait to meet Drew Davis."

Cooper's mouth turned down at the corners. "Ah. Another Drew Davis fan."

"Oh, my gosh, yes!" She could feel herself getting a little bouncy, which she did when she got worked up. "I loved his interview with Anderson Cooper after his visit to the White House. He's so smart."

"Are we talking about the same Drew Davis?"

"Drew Davis the environmental activist?"

"Drew Davis the snowboarder."

"Yeah. I guess he did get his start snowboarding."

"Get his start..." Cooper sputtered, then exhaled slowly. "Drew Davis is the most important snowboarder of his generation. He practically started the sport in America. He..."

"Hey, calm down." She gave him a surprised look. He sounded offended. She bumped her shoulder against his playfully. "I just meant that I know him more for his work with Save Our Snow. I just think it's really cool that he's trying to inform winter sports enthusiasts about environmental issues. It's a good cause. That's all I meant."

Cooper was still frowning as he said, "You know

Flight+Risk had the first board on the market made from ninety-five percent postconsumer recycled material."

She frowned because Cooper still sounded grumpy. Jealous almost. Which was ridiculous, of course. Unless she'd wounded his ego, first by discussing Drew Davis and then by gushing too much about him.

"Oh, I'm sorry," she cooed in baby tones. "Did I offend you?" She put her hand on his arm and rubbed it. She meant the gesture to be silly and teasing, all mock solicitude. But the second she touched him, she was strangely aware of his strength. Was he just super tense or were all his muscles this…steely? Because even through the fabric of his shirt, it was like touching finely hewn wood. And his arm was so big. Massive compared to hers. Her fingers barely wrapped around it. She'd always thought of herself as a sturdy woman. She was taller than average, nearly five-nine, and fairly athletic. But she felt darn near petite compared to him.

And then, suddenly, she was aware that she was still touching him. That her hand was still rubbing slowly back and forth along his arm. And somehow they both seemed to have stopped breathing completely.

Which was probably for the best, because even without breathing, she could smell the faint hint of his soap. Something woodsy and fresh that smelled so good she wanted to just bury her nose against his neck. Which might be the only thing more awkward than sitting here rubbing his arm endlessly.

Or maybe she would just pass out from being so lightheaded. Yes. That would definitely be the best. Then she could excuse her strange behavior as some sort of aneurysm. She waited for several heartbeats. Just in case she conveniently lost consciousness.

"Portia—" Cooper began, his voice sounding unexpectedly husky.

She didn't give him a chance to finish, but plunged back into her explanation of her notes, talking at breakneck speed to circumvent any possibility of him interrupting. "And then on this side we have each of the nine board members who voted against you. These bubbles around their names are other things they're involved in. Business ventures, companies, well-known charitable organizations. Anything one of us might have a connection to."

She had to pause there to take another breath, because—OMG—she might really pass out now.

"Portia—"

Again she didn't let him get in more than a single word. "So for example, here's Robertson up at the top. You said he was your biggest opponent. He has ties to March's department stores, right? And Bermuda Bob's and Mercury Shoes, because he's on their boards. And Hodges Foundation, because he donates heavily to them. The idea is we need to find anyone we know that also knows Robertson. We're not going to invite Robertson himself. That would be too obvious. Instead, we invite other people. People who will spread the word back to Robertson that you're doing this on your own and that it's going to be a huge success. So we need to look at all the things he's involved in and—"

"How did you find all this out?" Cooper asked.

She breathed out a sigh of relief. Thank goodness he wasn't going to question her excessive arm stroking. Finally, a question she could answer. "Google. And a few phone calls. But mostly Google."

"That's a little alarming."

"Says the man with thirty-four thousand search results."

"You did a Google search on me?"

"Well, duh. By the way, you had quite the adventurous

youth. That scandal with the Swedish model and the photographs of your Olympic medal…wow."

He scowled. "That was not nearly as big a deal as it seemed."

"You were reprimanded by the Olympic Committee," she teased. "Sounds like a big deal to me."

"Apparently, they take their medals very seriously."

"Apparently." She had vaguely remembered the incident when it happened, but that had been right around the time of her first miscarriage, so she hadn't been following the news much. But reading a decade's worth of gossip about him had been…enlightening. An endless array of models had paraded through his life. Each more perfect and beautiful than the last.

The Cooper she knew—the easygoing charmer—was vastly different from the ladies' man the media wrote about. It was a nice reminder for her. This guy she was hanging out with wasn't the real Cooper. Maybe that guy with the Swedish model wasn't the real Cooper, either. She didn't know. Either way, she couldn't let herself become lulled by this false sense of intimacy. She couldn't let herself get drawn in by easy charm and his well-hewn arms. She wasn't the kind of woman he went for. He went for Swedish models who cavorted in fountains, naked but for the Olympic medals around their necks. And with wholesome American models who looked fantastic in Flight+Risk jackets.

Not that it mattered to her. Her interest in his love life… Well, she was just trying to be helpful, that was all.

"By the way," she began, trying to be circumspect. "And don't take this the wrong way, but…"

"What?" he prodded.

"Well, the thing is—" She poked at her pie again with her fork.

"Yes?"

Dang it. She was being such an idiot. She set down her fork and twisted so she was looking directly at Cooper. Of course, looking directly at Cooper was like staring into the sun. Mere mortals couldn't do it for long without risking being blinded. "You realize this is working against you here, right? I mean, the bit with the Olympic medal and all the models and the partying—"

"I don't date that many models. And I don't party." His tone was dark and grim. Again at odds with the guy she knew. Or thought she knew. "I never partied much. It was all just the way media portrays me. They love a bad boy."

"Exactly." Though he'd been holding some of those models pretty close in those photos for it to be only image. Not that she cared. "It's an okay for a snowboarder. It's even okay for the CEO of Flight+Risk. But for this venture, you need something more upscale."

He eyed her shrewdly and then said slowly, "Yes. That's what you're here for."

"No, I mean..." Couldn't the man take a hint? "I know. I'm here to make the event look good. And I can handle that. The staging, the food, the guest list. I can do that. But none of it will make any difference if you show up that weekend with a Swedish model on your arm."

She cringed at the sneer in her voice. But maybe it was impossible for a normal, human-sized woman to say the words *Swedish model* without sneering.

"Let me see if I've got this right. You don't think I can keep my zipper up for even one weekend? You think I'd actually risk blowing this deal by dragging some bimbo along?"

"You're not known for your long attention span when it comes to women." She reached for his arm again, this time to placate him, not to tease him. "To be honest, it's not just this weekend. You want to pull this off, you need to be—"

She couldn't even say the next bit without cringing again. "On your best behavior." She sounded like her mother. "All month long. Total media blackout, okay? From now until after the vote. No models. No cavorting. Nothing."

"Not just the weekend, huh?" His expression turned so grim, she knew at once he was mocking her. "I don't know if I can do it. No cavorting at all? No models? What about model trains? Would that be acceptable? Like Swedish model methadone."

"Ha-ha. You can laugh all you want, but I had to say it. There's no point in doing this if you're going to blow it at the last minute."

"Exactly how much of a player do you think I am?"

His eyes searched her face and something in his expression made her breath catch in her chest. He was so handsome. Not classically handsome, not like Dalton was. Cooper's nose had an odd bump where he'd broken it, maybe more than once. He had a tiny scar just below his right eye, and another longer one on his cheek. His face looked lived in. Rugged. Like he'd carved out his identity on the slopes that had given him those scars.

He'd lived a lifetime in that face. There was adventure and resilience and determination written on it. And suddenly her fingers twitched to trace each beautiful scar.

God, she was staring. Leaning into him and making calf eyes at him, staring. She had to snap out of it! This was not okay!

She bolted back to her side of the booth. Desperate to put some distance between them. She pulled her notebook back toward her.

"Okay. I'll try," he said.

"I'm not joking about this." She pressed him because his tone still sounded too glib for her taste. And—yes—because she was still so off-balance she didn't know what else to say. "I need you to take this seriously. Your fans may think this behavior is cute, but the board members see it as a sign of your immaturity."

"Look," he said seriously, "I can keep my damn zipper up. All that stuff with the model and the Olympic medal, that was just—"

"All part of your bad-boy image. I get it."

"No. You don't." He exhaled sharply and ran a hand through his hair. "I used to do that kind of thing deliberately. It was my way of thumbing my nose at Hollister and all the other rich jerks who thought I was worthless because I was poor. It was stupid and immature. In my defense, I was twenty-two. But I haven't dated a model since I was twenty-five. I don't do that crap anymore."

For a long moment, she could only stare at him, mutely. Because the facade of the charming playboy had slipped briefly, revealing the man he was underneath. His intensity. His drive. And his courage.

Because she knew—better than most—about all those rich jerks who could make a person feel worthless. How society could ostracize someone for being just a little bit different. Wasn't that what she'd been avoiding her whole life? Hadn't she learned that from a young age? You kept your head down and blended in with the herd and maybe you survived. If you stood out too much, the lions took you down.

"I'm sorry," she said abruptly. "I didn't mean to sound like I was judging you."

"Look, this is what you're here to do." He gave another one of those harsh sighs. "I created this mess. If I have a shady reputation as an irresponsible playboy, then it's my own damn fault. I just need you to understand that that's not who I am. Not now. Yeah, when I was younger, I acted like an ass. I'd won this huge honor and I didn't respect the medal like I should have."

"You don't have to explain."

But he ignored her. "I'd slept with the model—hell, I barely knew her. And she 'borrowed' the medal for a while. I wasn't even there when she took the pictures. I didn't know she'd done it until the pictures were all over the internet and the Olympic Committee was calling me on the carpet."

"It's really none of my business."

"I'm not telling you all this to dodge responsibility. I just wanted you to know."

"Okay." She thought about Cooper as he'd been when she'd first met him all those years ago. He'd been so charming, but even then she'd seen that crazy quality. That feckless arrogance that had gotten him into so much trouble.

It didn't take a genius to understand why he'd wanted to thumb his nose at everyone trying to control him. She couldn't blame him. If she was honest with herself, she admired his courage. Sometimes she wished she'd rebelled more when she was twenty-two.

"Don't feel like you have to justify what happened. It's a miracle you don't have more daddy issues."

He grinned, but she could see the glint of sadness behind his eyes. The regret sugarcoated in charm. Part of her wanted to probe deeper, but it wasn't her business, so when he changed the subject a moment later, she didn't protest.

"So there's one thing this abstinence plan of yours doesn't take into consideration."

"What's that?"

"If we're going to pull this off, we're going to be together a lot."

Suddenly, her heart rate picked up and she was aware all over again of the intimacy of sitting across the table from him. Of the way he seemed to take up so much space. Of the implication heavy in his voice. They were going to be together. A lot. Did that mean that he was as aware of her as she was of him?

"And?" she prodded. Her heart was pounding as she waited for his next words. Heat spiraled through her body, a secret, intimate heat.

"If we're together all the time and if you help me host the event, people are going to assume we're together. People will talk about you."

"Excuse me?" She squinted at him. That's what he was worried about?

"Your reputation is pristine," he said dispassionately. "I don't want you to damage that by associating with me. So if you're worried—"

"Wait, you're worried about my reputation?"

"Sure. A nice girl like you might not want to be seen with a guy like me."

"Yeah. I get it." Geesh. Wasn't that just her luck? Here she was thinking he was irresistible and he thought she was nice. Nice.

Cozy sweaters were *nice*. Shortbread cookies were *nice*. Tea was *nice*.

Nice had been the bane of her existence since she was about twelve when other girls got boobs and high heels and she—since she was so nice—got mosquito bites and ballet flats. Which had gotten her a position organizing the school dance instead of a date to the dance.

All these years later and she was still haunted by *nice*. Only somewhere along the way, the connotation had shifted around a bit to mean cool and unapproachable. Which, as far as her love life was concerned, was just as deadly.

She pulled her notebook back across the table and slammed it closed. "I'm not worried."

"Well, I am," he began. "People will—"

"People will not think that." She couldn't quite bring herself to admit aloud that she knew he couldn't possibly want her. "No one in their right mind is going to believe we're together."

"Why?" He narrowed his gaze as tension shifted into his shoulders. "Because you're too good for me?"

She huffed out a breath. She wanted it to convey indifference, but instead it just sounded pathetic. "Not because I'm too good for you. Because I'm too nice. Too boring to hold the attention of a guy like you."

He leaned back in the booth and gave her an assessing look. "A guy like me?"

"Well, yeah. Cooper, you're world renowned as a connoisseur of women."

He cringed. "I'm not world renowned...."

"Thirty-four thousand hits. That's pretty renowned. No one is seriously going to believe you'd actually be interested in me."

"You don't think I could be interested in you?"

She shrugged, suddenly immensely uncomfortable. He must think she was the most insecure woman ever. How needy could she be?

"Portia, you're beautiful and smart and rich."

Her back stiffened. "I'm not fishing for compliments. I'm being realistic."

"So am I. I'm not complimenting you to stroke your ego. I'm being honest."

"Okay, then be honest about this, too. Close your eyes for a second."

"What?"

"Just do it." She waited until he had. Then she ordered. "Think back to the first time we met. What did you think of me?"

"Portia, this—"

"No. No editing. Just honesty, right? What did you think of me?"

He opened his eyes. "This is stupid. I'm not going to play this game with you."

"Humor me. It was Christmas Eve. Caro had planned a big family dinner. You'd flown in from Colorado. Is this ringing any bells?"

He clenched his jaw, and she wondered if he wasn't even going to answer. Then finally he said, "I don't remember."

"You don't remember the dinner?" she prodded.

"I don't remember meeting you that night."

She nodded, drawing the action out to buy herself time to let the sting fade before she responded. "That's about what I thought."

"How did you know?"

"I didn't. Not for sure. But when we met again the next summer, you didn't seem to remember me. That's the way it is with nice girls. We fade into the background. We're uninteresting."

"So what you're saying—" he took a slow sip of coffee as if he was carefully considering his next words "—is that I couldn't possibly be attracted to you because you don't make a good first impression."

Seven

Cooper leaned back in his seat, stretched out an arm along the back of the booth and considered Portia over the rim of his coffee mug. Was it possible that Portia—one of the most beautiful women he'd ever met—had a self-esteem issue? How was that even conceivable? She was gorgeous. More to the point, she was smart, funny and quirky. Not to mention passionate. He'd heard her talking about Beck's Lodge. No woman who got that excited about hardwood floors could be a cold fish.

He just shook his head. "Nope. It's not possible."

"What?" She looked a little offended.

"I'm not buying it. I don't believe—not for a minute— that there's a red-blooded guy between here and the equator that wouldn't—" Then he broke off because he couldn't think of a polite term for *hit that*. "Just trust me."

She shrugged. "You're wrong. I've seen it too many times to count. There's something about me that men find unappealing. They don't hit on me." She cocked her head to the side, considering. "Maybe it's my name."

"Your name?"

"Yeah. Portia. It's an intrinsically rich, boring name, don't you think? I've always wondered why my parents didn't name me Polly or Paige. Or Peggy."

He nearly snorted in derision. "You could never be a Peggy. Trust me. Peyton, maybe, but not Peggy."

"But see, Peggy is a woman a man would buy a drink for in a bar. She's fun."

"Peggy is a generation older than you. If she's fun, it's because men my age expect her to bake them cookies, not because they want to date her."

She slouched a little in her seat, clearly unable to counter his argument. "It would still be better than Portia."

"There's nothing wrong with Portia."

"But—"

"So your name intimidates some guys. Any guy that's turned off by a woman's name is a jerk anyway. Besides, there are several things you're not considering here."

She frowned. "Like what?"

"For starters, you keep talking about first impressions."

"So?"

"So, I know you. I've known you for over a decade. We're long past the point of first impressions. I've seen you doing a headstand in a wedding dress. I've watched you face down Hollister and Caro over things you thought were important. I've danced with you at fund-raisers. For that matter, I've seen you waxing poetic about musty old buildings."

She arched an eyebrow. "What's your point?"

"Just that I know you better than you think I do. And I know you're not the rich bitch you think your name im-

plies. In short, you don't fool me. I know exactly the kind
of person you are."

She looked briefly disconcerted, but then she smiled
coolly. "You forget. It's not you I'm trying to fool anyway.
It's your board and potential investors. And what they think
about me personally is hardly the point. What matters is
what they think about Bear Creek Lodge and more importantly, about your judgment."

"No, the original question was whether or not you were
okay with people thinking we're seeing each other." She
opened her mouth like she was about to talk, but he waved
her protests aside. "No, for a second, just forget about whatever crazy ideas you have about how different we are and
about your name or your pedigree. Just for a second, pretend my instincts as a guy are correct and that every man
who sees us together is going to assume I'd be an idiot not
to do everything in my power to get you into my bed."

Her mouth bowed into a perfect O of surprise. Then,
slowly, she nodded. "Okay."

"So you're going to be okay with people assuming that?"

She thought about it for a minute and then shrugged. "I
suppose so. People have certainly said worse things about
me before."

He was about to ask what she meant by that when the
waitress returned, tapping the bill against her palm. "You
have everything you need here?" she asked, smacking her
gum. "'Cause I'm about to go off shift."

He looked across the table at Portia, who could now
barely meet his gaze. He smiled slowly. "Yeah. We have
everything we need."

He handed a couple of bills to the waitress and didn't
bother to wait for change.

It wasn't until they were back at the hotel—after an endless car ride listening to her run through a to-do list long

enough to stretch back to his apartment in Denver—before he asked, "What do you think? Do we have what we need?"

She pulled the hotel room key out of her bag and then looked down at her notes again. "Sure." She tucked a strand of hair behind her ear. "I, um…yeah. I think I can get started." She looked delightfully flustered. "I can have a finalized guest list for you by tomorrow and I'll need a place to stay here. Probably in Provo. And I'm not good driving in the snow, so maybe we can arrange a driver. But other than that—"

He cut her off by gently nudging a finger under her chin and urging her to look up at him instead of at her notes. "Yeah. Place to stay. Driver. Whatever you need, you've got. But that's not what I meant."

"Oh." She slowly closed her notebook without looking down at it. "Then what were you talking about?"

"I'm talking about us."

"There isn't an us."

"So you keep insisting. But I need you to understand something. All that stuff about men not finding you attractive is just nonsense. You're gorgeous. And if Dalton didn't make you feel irresistible every day you were with him, then that's his problem. Not yours."

Her mouth twisted into a wry smile. "Thank you. But—"

"I'm not done."

"Oh. Okay."

"I need you to understand something else. I'm not a nice guy. I'm not selfless. I'm not softhearted. I'm not overly generous. When I donate to charity, I do it for the tax break. When I help people, it's generally because I think they'll be able to help me at some point down the road."

She was frowning now, clearly confused by this train of thought. "Ooookay."

Well, if she'd been confused before, he was about to make things worse. So much worse.

He closed the distance between them and pulled her to him. He didn't give her a chance to protest verbally, but pressed his lips to hers. There was a moment of shock. He felt it in the stillness of her whole body. The way her breath caught and her muscles tensed. But she didn't resist. Not even for a second. She held very still while her body got used to the idea.

Then, slowly, her arms crept around his neck and her lips parted.

As for him? His body had been gearing up for this moment for about the past decade. So the second he felt her relax, he deepened the kiss. He moved his lips over hers, slowly coaxing her mouth open. He slipped his tongue into her mouth, learning the feel of her lips and the unique taste of her. She was sweet and tart, like the cherry pie she'd been eating. But her flavor was more complex than that. There was an underlying smokiness. A hint of darkness. His senses had barely registered all of that when she molded her body against his.

Her purse dropped to the ground beside their feet and he instinctively backed her up against the door until she was arching into him. Seeking him with the same desperation he felt.

Damn, but she felt good. Right. Like she'd always belonged there. Her curves were sexy and strong without being outrageous. Her body was sleek and muscular, but feminine in all the right places. There was so much hidden passion here. So many hidden depths. And he couldn't wait to delve deeper into all that complexity. But they were still standing in the hallway outside her hotel room. Which was entirely too close to her bed. And while he had no problem taking her to bed immediately, he also knew that she was not ready for that.

So he pried himself away from her tempting body and took a step back. He ran a hand through his hair, because—frankly—it gave him something else to do with his hands beside touching Portia.

She just stared up at him, her eyes wide and shocked, her lips pressed together like she was trying to seal in the last of their kiss. "What was that for?"

"That was so you'd know."

"Know what?"

"How much I want you."

"You want? Me?"

"I do. And unless you tell me right now that you're not the least bit attracted to me—unless you ask me to leave you alone—then I'm going to pursue you until you want me just as much. I know you're not there yet. I know you're nowhere near ready. But I'm a patient man and I can wait. But I wanted you to know, right now, what's coming. Because sometime in the next couple of weeks, you're going to convince yourself that I'm flirting with you because I'm just a friendly guy. And that every time I touch your elbow or put my hand at your waist or can't resist touching your hair that it's because I'm just stroking your ego. That I must pity you and I'm just trying to make you feel better."

Her eyes had gone even wider by this point and he couldn't resist stepping closer again. He didn't kiss her this time—but he wanted to. Instead, he ran his thumb just under her lip until she opened her mouth again.

"Just remember, I'm not a nice guy. If I'm pursuing you, it's because I want to take you to bed. It's because I've wanted you ever since I saw you doing that headstand. First impressions be damned. Your relationship with Dalton be damned. I wanted you. And I'm tired of waiting."

* * *

Portia stood in her hotel room just inside the door for several long minutes as she processed Cooper's words.

It didn't bode well for her that she hadn't even been able to enter her room under her own willpower.

No, after making the rather startling proclamation that he wanted her—*Cooper Larson wanted her?*—he nabbed the hotel key card from her hand, popped open her door and gently guided her into her room before handing the key back to her and closing the door behind her. Then a second later, he'd said loudly, "Lock the deadbolt."

Only then did she hear him go into his own hotel room, which was right next door to hers. A moment later, she heard the shower crank on and she stood there imagining him undressing and stepping into it. Naked.

Holy crap.

Not only was Cooper Larson naked in the room next door. He was taking a shower. And if the searing kiss he'd just given her was any indication, quite possibly a very cold shower.

Why was it that she'd never given a second thought to him showering before, but now the idea made her head spin?

Well, no mystery there.

Before, he hadn't dropped that bomb on her. Before, he hadn't told her that he'd wanted her for years. What on earth was she supposed to do with that information?

How was she supposed to work with him during the next month knowing that? How was she supposed to concentrate when all she could think about was the way he'd kissed her?

How was she supposed to—?

Portia suddenly realized that she'd started pacing. A familiar buzz skittered along her nerves. Energy all but bounced through her. When was the last time she'd been this wound up?

She hated this. And damn Cooper for making her feel this way.

And here he was, just blissfully taking a shower, like nothing had happened between them. Like nothing had changed at all.

Well, that was bull.

She grabbed her key card off the dresser where she'd carelessly tossed it and stormed out of her room. It took a solid three minutes of knocking on Cooper's door before the shower cranked off and another minute before he opened the door.

He stood there, dripping water, towel wrapped around his waist. For an instant, a smile flickered across his face, like he thought there was a chance she'd come over here to take him up on his bargain. But then he had the good sense to read her expression.

"What. The hell. Was that?"

For a second, he seemed taken aback, but then he grinned. "Just fair warning."

"How the hell am I supposed to work with you now? How the hell am I supposed to do my job when I'm distracted thinking about the fact that you want to take me to bed?"

Concern flickered across his face. "Is this a sexual harassment thing? Because I never meant—"

She waved her hand dismissively. "I know that. And you're not my boss. I didn't mean my job in that sense. I just meant—" She looked around and noticed that she was in his room. Damn it, she was pacing again. What was wrong with her? She forced herself to be still. What had she meant? "What exactly did you hope to achieve by telling me that? Did you think that once we had the sexual tension out on the table, I'd just come over and rip your clothes off?" She glanced at the skimpy towel. At his naked chest, which was so beautiful her fingers ached to touch him.

"Of course I didn't think that," he protested.

"Because that would be really stupid of me." The words sort of sputtered out of her. Apparently, she could no longer form a coherent thought. She took a step closer to him. And then another. "I just mean, I'm not the type of girl to do this sort thing. And it would be really stupid to do it now."

"It would be extremely stupid," he agreed. But his perfect, irresistible lips had begun to curve into a smile and his voice had dropped to a husky purr.

Sure, she hadn't had sex in a long time. And it had been even longer since she'd felt attractive. Since she'd felt wanted.

But that was exactly how Cooper made her feel. Desirable. Irresistible.

And before she even knew what she was doing, she'd taken yet another step closer and plastered her body against his.

Eight

Portia moved before he had a chance to, rising on her toes and pressing her chest against his. He barely noticed her room key dropping to the ground. Her hands burrowed into his hair, angling his head so their lips could meet.

Everything about this surprised him. From the way she took full command of the embrace to the instant heat of her kiss.

After an hour of watching her nibble at a slice of pie, he expected a hesitant peck. After all her talk of being a nice girl, of being the boring one, he expected timidity. He expected another kiss like the one in the hall. He thought he'd have to be the aggressor, that he'd have to gently tease a response out of her. Instead, she was greedy. Enchanting.

Her hands clung to him even as her tongue traced the crease of his lips. She didn't have to ask twice. He opened his mouth to her, nearly shuddering with desire when her tongue, eager and fast, darted into his mouth. She was almost clumsy. There was no artifice to her. No planning or thought. No seduction. Just pure, searing desire. Whatever else he thought about her, he knew this: she was here because she wanted this. Because she wanted him.

The thought that Portia wanted him—that this amazing, smart, unbelievably beautiful woman picked him, got him hard faster than he would have thought possible given that he'd just stepped out of glacially cold shower.

Yeah, sure. He'd taken plenty of beautiful women to bed, but this was different. *She* was different. Because this was Portia. The woman he'd wanted for a third of his life. The woman he'd never dreamed he could have. She was his fantasy. She was the dream that woke him up in the middle of the night, hot and hard and aching. And she was reaching for the towel at his waist with eager hands. If he didn't slow this the hell down, he was going to come the second she touched him.

There was no way he was going to let that happen. This was his dream. There was no way he was going to let her control it.

He grabbed her wrist, stopping her just shy of pulling his towel off.

She paused for a second, pulling back from the kiss. Her eyes were wide with confusion and doubt. Just looking at her made him go rock hard, but at the same time, that question in her gaze slayed him. Still, after everything he'd said to her, she doubted that he really wanted her. After all this, after the very physical evidence of his desire that she had to have noticed, she still doubted.

He opened his mouth to reassure her. There were a thousand things he wanted to say. And every one of them scared the hell out of him. So instead of speaking, he grabbed her other wrist and whirled her around so her back was up against the wall. He pinned her wrists to the wall on either side her of head and crushed her mouth beneath his. She tasted like red wine and cherries. He couldn't get enough of her. He had the heart-stopping, terrifying thought that he'd never get enough of her.

He shoved the thought aside and pressed his body to hers. She was tall for a woman and fit against him perfectly. There was no finagling, no floundering to position their bodies together. There was just her against him. His mouth on her neck. Her hands plowing through his hair and his erection nuzzling the V between her legs. Like they'd been made for one another. Pure perfection.

Her leg crept up to the outside of his thigh, and she bumped against him, groaning as he nipped at her honeyed skin. His hand slipped under her sweater, up over the silken lace of her bra to cup her breast and pluck at her nipple. Her head tipped back, and she let loose a groan that rocked him to his very core.

She arched onto her toes, straining against him. When he cupped her ass and lifted her, she wrapped her legs around his hips, grinding herself against him. Her hands moved greedily over his shoulders and back. He sucked in a breath as he felt her heels kicking his towel aside. That was it. She had on entirely too many clothes. If he was going to be naked, then damn it, so would she.

He might not have intended to push her, but turnabout was fair play. He stepped away from the wall, squeezing her delectable ass as he carried her across the hotel room to the bed. It took only a few seconds to yank the bedspread off. Then he lowered her to the bare sheets. But he didn't follow her down. As much as he wanted to bury himself inside of her, he didn't want to rush this. He'd wanted her for years. He could wait a few more minutes to make sure this was as mind-blowing for her as it was for him.

He undressed her slowly, lavishing attention on every

inch of silken skin. First, he stripped off her cream sweater and pulled off her jeans. The sight of her nearly naked sent desire rocketing through him. Her perfect breasts were encased in a hot-pink bra that matched her panties.

Because she dressed so conservatively, he never dreamed she'd be wearing something so damn sexy underneath. It wasn't hot-pink kitty panties, but it would do.

Somehow the combination of hot-pink silk and her naked flesh cast in the half-light was almost too much. She was too perfect to look at; she had to be felt to be believed. She had to be tasted.

He shimmied her panties down her hips and kissed his way to the sensitive flesh he'd just revealed. He parted her flesh to reveal the delicate bud of her sex. He lapped at her folds, intoxicated. Desperate. Until she was as needy as he was. Until she bucked against his mouth. Then he slipped a finger inside her. And then another. He suckled her bud as she rode hard against his fingers, groaning. Panting. And finally screaming. Screaming his name as she fell to pieces around him.

The sound of his name on her lips as she came was almost too much to bear. He almost came, too. Without her even touching him. Somehow, he managed to hold back, until he'd found a condom and plunged into her. Thankfully, she was still on the brink. The spasming muscles of her sex were enough to send him over the edge. He came almost immediately. Her voice echoing in his ears, her name on his lips.

Cooper woke up early, content with the knowledge that whatever else happened, this bargain he'd made with Portia was the smartest thing he'd ever done.

He had no doubt her plan was going to work. She was going to convince the board that he could get financial backing all on his own, which would win them over more quickly than any of his arguments had. She was going to help him achieve the goal that had dominated the past year of his life. And he'd slept with her.

Now as far as he was concerned, any day he woke up with a beautiful woman in his bed was bound to be a good day, but with Portia, it was different. Because she was Portia. The one woman he'd always wanted and could never have. Now he'd had her. And if he had his way, he'd have her again. As often as possible over the next month.

Which would be plenty of time to get her out of his system. Portia would never fall for a guy like him. She'd made that clear enough with all her jabs about Swedish models. They had no future together. Which was fine. He didn't want a future with her. Or any woman for that matter. No woman he'd ever known had held his attention for longer than a couple of months. Tops. So there was nothing to worry about with Portia. There was no reason they shouldn't continue sleeping together as well as working together. And he had no doubt that she would agree. No one would turn down sex that explosive. That right.

All he had to do was think of the way she'd come against him and he got hard all over again.

Her body was warm and soft against his, her buttocks nuzzling his growing erection. He could wake her up slowly, kissing the back of her neck. She'd make that little sound in the back of her throat, halfway between a yummy noise and a groan.

Except they'd made love twice more in the night and now she was deeply asleep, her breathing deep and even.

So instead of waking her, he propelled himself from the bed and got dressed, heading downstairs for an early morning jog. He'd burn off some of this extra energy and grab breakfast before she even woke up. He'd ply her with coffee and fresh croissants and then make love to her again. He didn't need to wake her up now. They had all the time in the world.

Nine

From the moment Portia woke up in Cooper's bed, it took her less than thirty seconds to get from *Damn, that was amazing!* to *Holy crap, I slept with Cooper!* to *What the hell is wrong with me?*

Cooper was her brother-in-law!

Okay. Not really. Not anymore.

But he had been once and surely that put him off-limits forever. Surely there was some sort of societal rule about not sleeping with former brother-in-laws. Jeez, even Shakespeare had covered it. *Hamlet* made it pretty damn clear. It was like number three on his lists of big don'ts, right after not strangling your wife—*Othello*—and not murdering your houseguests—*Macbeth*. Marrying, flirting with or sleeping with your former brother-in-law was bad news.

Or did that only count if he was an evil bastard who had poisoned your husband and tried to kill your son?

Ugh. This was *so* not helpful.

When had her life gotten so confused?

For that matter, where was Cooper now?

She sat bolt upright in bed and looked around the hotel. He was gone.

Then, she cocked her head to the side and listened carefully, just in case he was in the shower. But nope, there wasn't a peep from that direction. No running water. No off-key signing. No soft, moving-around-the-bathroom noises. He wasn't here.

Was that a good thing or a bad thing?

She looked around the room, sucking in panicky gulps of air. It was good, right? This would give her time to think. To plan. To get her act together.

She scrambled from the bed and yanked on the clothes she grabbed off the floor until she was decent enough to duck out into the hall. The rest she merely tucked under her arm. She found her room key on the floor a few feet from the door. The swath of hallway from his door to hers may have been the shortest walk of shame ever, but she was keenly aware of every step and she didn't stop shaking until she was standing in the shower, hot water washing over her skin. Washing away Cooper's touch.

She stilled for a second then stepped out of the stream of water, shaken all over again. Was that really what she wanted? To wash away his touch?

Shakespearean life lessons aside, it wasn't as though what she'd done was actually wrong. It was just complicated.

And wonderful. Because no man had ever made her feel the things Cooper had made her feel.

She finished rinsing off and dried herself quickly before putting on the first item of clothing she pulled out of her bag—a simple gray dress. She didn't bother to look for the tights or cardigan to go with it. Instead, she tugged her comb through the long strands of her hair, her mind automatically going back to Cooper and the amazing things he'd done to her body.

Which wasn't to say that sex with Dalton hadn't been good. It had been. But with Dalton, she'd had trouble really letting go. She'd always been so aware of everyone's expectations. Even when she was in bed with him, she'd been conscious of the fact that they were supposed to be the perfect couple. She'd never felt free to just be herself. A problem she simply hadn't had with Cooper. Somehow, for the hours she'd been in his arms, she'd let herself forget that he was her former brother-in-law, that there were countless reasons they couldn't have a relationship and that she was supposed to be the nice girl. The boring girl. The girl who never had crazy, reckless sex with a man who was off-limits.

The question was, which of these two people did she want to be?

Before she could ponder that any further, there was a tap on the door.

She felt unprepared to face Cooper, but she couldn't hide in her room forever. But when she opened the door, she didn't have a chance to voice any of the things she wasn't even sure she wanted to say. Cooper immediately took her into his arms and kissed her. His mouth moved over hers with the same surety and passion he'd displayed the night before. Heat poured through her veins, searing away her doubts. After a long moment, he pulled away from her, tucking a strand of damp hair behind her ear.

"I brought croissants."

"What?" she asked stupidly.

"Croissants. Pastries." He raised a hand to show off a white paper bag and gave it a little shake. "Breakfast?"

She looked from him to the bag and back again, all her doubts rushing back to her. "I can't do this," she blurted out.

"You don't do breakfast?"

"No. I mean, yes. Of course I eat breakfast. I mean, this—" She gestured to the two of them. "I've never done this before. The one-night stand thing." Suddenly she couldn't even look at him anymore. Her panic mingled with her embarrassment and the cocktail made her feel almost light-headed. "I've never had a one-night stand in my life. I only had a few serious boyfriends before Dalton and next to nothing since then. I never in my life did anything like this and I'm just—"

Before she could get anything else out, she felt his hands on her shoulders. He gently turned her to face him. "You're thinking about this way too much."

"I am?"

"Yes. Why make this complicated? We're attracted to each other. We get along. There's no reason why we can't just do this for the next few weeks, enjoying each other in and out of bed."

A knot of tension loosened in her chest. "Right," she said softly. "Just enjoy it."

"Yeah." His lips twisted into a half smile. "This isn't rocket science. You said yourself I'm not known for my long attention span when it comes to relationships. Neither of us wants something long-term. Neither of us is expecting forever here, so let's just have fun."

That gave her pause. "Neither of us is expecting forever?" she repeated.

But he must have taken her words as a statement rather than a question. "Exactly. I'm just not a forever kind of guy."

"And you don't think I'm a forever person, either?"

"Come on, you bought into the fantasy once. You know

better than most that happily ever afters aren't real. That forever never lasts."

For a moment she was shocked into silence. How was she supposed to respond to that? What could she say? She couldn't argue with him. She couldn't deny the truth to his words. Her own marriage—the one that was supposed to be so perfect—hadn't been forever. Far from it.

Of course there was only one response she could give— the one he so obviously expected. She forced a smile. "Of course you're right. The idea of love, of forever. That's just—" The word *silliness* had been on the tip of her tongue, but she couldn't force it out. She couldn't make herself say aloud something so antithetical to her ideals. Instead, she waved her hand dismissively. "I mean, if I couldn't make it with Dalton, then I'm not going to make it with anyone, right?"

Even as she said the words, they curdled in her stomach. She didn't want to believe that. Maybe it didn't make any sense at all, maybe she had no evidence in her life to prove that love could last, but that didn't mean she didn't want to believe.

She looked up to see Cooper watching her, his expression pensive. There was something a little...well, almost hurt in his gaze.

Ugh. She'd been an idiot. What kind of fool brought up her ex with the guy she'd just slept with?

She smiled again, and this time it felt a smidge more natural. "See? This is what I mean. I have no idea what I'm doing here. Bringing up my ex? Isn't that a total rookie mistake? Shouldn't I know better? Isn't that completely against the rules?"

His expression softened. "There aren't actually any rules."

"There aren't?" she asked, frowning. Sure she had dated

a little since Dalton, but not much. And she hadn't been with another man. For all she knew, there were all kinds of rules she didn't know about. "Are you sure? Because I'm totally new at this."

"Yeah. I'm sure. Look, I enjoy your company. We have fun together. The sex is great. It would be great if we could just enjoy this. But if that's too weird for you, I understand. No pressure."

She thought about it. Let the idea of this no-pressure, just-temporary, just-fun relationship roll around in her mind. She had never had a relationship like that in her life. There had always been pressure of one kind or another. The pressure to be with the right guy. The pressure to twist herself into the perfect wife.

But in all these years, had any of those things made her happy? Ever?

It made her a little bit sad to think about giving up her dream of having forever with someone. But in a way, hadn't she already done that? When she'd started looking into adopting a child—all on her own, without a husband—hadn't she known that was going to drastically reduce her chances of finding Mr. Right? Sure, there were still men who fell in love with single moms, but she had to be shrinking her dating pool. Besides, if she was diving headfirst into the mothering thing, she was going to be too busy to date for a very long time.

So maybe for now, an easy, no-pressure affair was just what she needed. Maybe she really had been going about this wrong all these years. Maybe Cooper had the right idea after all. The idea was terrifying and exhilarating all at the same time.

"What about Bear Creek Lodge?" she asked.

"What about it? Unless you think you can't work with me now that we're sleeping together, I don't see that anything about the project has changed. There's no reason this needs to be complicated."

Laughter bubbled up in her chest. "You're my boss and my former brother-in-law. It doesn't get any more complicated than that."

"You say the word and I'll back off," he said, his expression suddenly serious. "If it's too weird, we don't even have to work together on the Beck's Lodge project."

She tilted her head and thought about it for a moment, but it didn't take long for her to realize that she didn't want him to back off. Never in her entire life had she felt this desirable. She loved the way he made her feel. She didn't want to stop feeling that way. She didn't want to stop sleeping with him. But despite what she'd said about not being a forever kind of person, she still needed boundaries.

"If we're going to do this—" she began, but then broke off when his face split into a grin. "I said *if.* If we're going to do this, then we need to have a few rules."

He shrugged, sauntering across the room to wrap his arms around her from behind. "I thought we agreed there were no rules."

He trailed a delicious path of kisses along the curve of her neck, making her mind spin. His hand slipped up to her breast. He cupped her flesh, giving her nipple a tweak. That simple gesture, so compelling, so masterful, reminded her of how completely at his mercy she'd been the previous night.

"Oh, there needs to be at least a few guidelines." Her mind was whirling as excitement suddenly buzzed along her veins. "For starters, I need my own room."

"Sure."

The line of kisses on her neck got wetter, firmer, nipping playfully at her tender skin.

"Even if you're here only on the weekends, I still need my own space."

"Only on the weekends?" He stilled, lifting his head.

She turned to look at him. "Well, sure. You have to go back to Denver, right?"

"Back to Denver?" He was looking at her with a puzzled frown.

"Of course. You can't stay here. Not when you have Flight+Risk to run. If you're going to keep your board happy, you have to continue to do your job. You can't drop everything to babysit me."

"No. Of course not. Wouldn't dream of it."

He didn't sound the least bit concerned.

Of course that might have been because he was intent on nudging the hem of her skirt up so he could cup her bottom. A moment later, the dress was gone entirely, along with whatever other rules she'd intended to list. She was sure she'd had more in mind. Things designed to create personal and emotional space between them. But as his hands pushed her panties down her legs and his fingers found the very core of her, she couldn't think of a single one.

Ten

When Cooper returned to Denver on Monday morning, he found staying away from Portia was harder than it should have been. But after all, she'd been right. He did have a business to run. Normally, he worked long hours. The work demanded it. He demanded it of himself. If he didn't expect himself to give Flight+Risk everything he had, then he wouldn't ask employees to do the same. Despite that, as one week bled into the next, he found himself increasingly distracted by Portia.

They spoke on the phone almost every night. The nights they didn't talk, they video chatted. Every telephone conversation was ostensibly about the project, but that didn't mitigate the intimacy of lying in bed at night, listening to her talk about her day. He automatically found himself describing the ups and downs of running Flight+Risk. Maybe it came from her years of marriage to Dalton, or maybe from the psychology degree she swore she never used, but she had a keen understanding of what it took to run a company and manage so many personalities. All of which made her very easy to talk to.

Worse still were the hours the hours they spent video chatting. She insisted he needed to see things like sample fabrics and invitations and that the easiest way to do that was through Skype. Who was he to complain when it gave him the chance to see her relaxed with a glass of wine in one hand, her hair twisted up in an easy knot on the top of her head, dressed in adorable pajamas dotted with snowmen. He never would have thought snowmen could be sexy, but on Portia, they were more tempting than the hottest lingerie.

He delighted in taking them off her over and over again the following weekend when he visited her in Provo. Yes, he was there to check on her progress, but in reality, they spent much of their time in bed. The weekend after that, he didn't even bother going up to Bear Creek Lodge more than once. Instead, they stayed in Provo. There seemed to be an unspoken agreement between them that they would only be together as long as the project lasted. Suddenly, a month didn't seem like nearly enough time.

It was early Sunday morning, before they'd even finished their coffee, he looked up to see her savoring a bite of her croissant. Her eyes drifted closed as she licked the flaky pastry off her fingertips.

She looked delightfully sensual, and it was all he could do not to take her back to bed right then. Instead he skimmed his hand up her bare leg and teased. "Didn't I tell you they had the best food in town?"

She shifted into his touch. "You were right. I will never doubt you again for as long as I live."

The husky promise in her words sent a thrill through

him. It was the first time she'd so much as hinted at anything beyond this month.

She must have realized her meaning as soon as he did, because she stilled instantly, then pulled back. "I mean, for as long as we're together. Which won't be more than a few more weeks."

He studied her, taking in the panic written clearly on her face. "Right," he said grimly.

She scooted off the bed and slipped into the robe she'd dropped on a nearby chair. He scrubbed a hand down his face, trying to wipe off what he feared was a kicked-puppy expression. Man, could she make it any clearer that she was in this for the short-term?

"I didn't mean anything by that." She turned back around, frowning. "You know that, right?"

"Yeah. It's pretty clear."

She laughed nervously. "Good, because I know this can't last. I know that. It's like, the weirdest relationship ever, right?"

"What?"

"You and I. I feel like we're horribly mismatched."

He felt like he'd been sucker punched by her words. Part of him knew he should let it go. Change the topic. Distract her with sex. Anything. But instead, he asked the really stupid question. "Why do you say that? Is it because of Dalton? Are you still in love with him?"

"Dalton?" she asked, sounding vaguely surprised.

"You were with him a long time." Why was he asking this? He didn't really want to know, did he? Just like he didn't really want to know why she insisted on having her own hotel room when he came into town or why she was always pushing him to go back to Denver on Mondays. Clearly, she took this no-pressure fling thing very seriously. Did he really need her to spell it out for him? "And

I know you asked for the divorce, but…hell, I don't know. Just because you couldn't stand to be married to the guy anymore doesn't mean you don't still miss him."

"Dalton?" she asked, her expression shifting from panicked to something more serious. "No. I don't miss him. And I don't love him anymore, either." She was silent for a long moment while she considered. "But I do miss the part of me that married him."

Cooper raised an eyebrow, and she laughed nervously, ducking her head as she tucked a strand of hair behind her ear. At least she didn't look like she was going to run from the room anymore.

"I mean, I miss the innocence and hope that I had when I married him. I miss the girl who thought she had love all figured out. I miss her. I miss being her."

She sounded so sad when she said it. So mournful. And listening to her talk, Cooper actually missed that girl, too. That young Portia, who'd been so full of hope. Jesus, had he ever been that young? Had he ever felt like that? Like he might have love all figured out? No. Not that he remembered.

If it had been any other person, he would have sneered at her sentimentality. But it was Portia. So instead he just wanted to comfort her. To protect her.

"You could get married again," he suggested.

Why the hell had he said that? What if she thought he wanted to marry her? Because, damn, what kind of idiot brought up marriage to a woman he was sleeping with if he didn't want to marry her?

But thankfully, Portia didn't go there. She shook her head. "I think I'm past that stage of my life. I think I'm just done hoping for a happily ever after." She raised a hand to ward off any objections he might have voiced—if he'd been the type to believe in happily ever after. "I don't mean to sound bitter. I'm not. It's just that I tried dating after Dalton. No one was worth the effort. No one wanted the things I do and I'm past twisting my expectations to fit someone else's reality."

"What do you mean no one else wants the things you do?"

"Do you know why Dalton and I got divorced?"

"Because he was a heartless bastard who spent too much time working and never appreciated what an amazing woman you are?"

Her mouth twisted into a half smile and she chuckled a little. As if she didn't really believe the compliment but appreciated it anyway. Then her smile faded. It was like the time-lapse photography version of the way she'd dimmed over the years she'd been with Dalton.

"Actually, that wasn't it at all. I never minded how dedicated he was to Cain Enterprises. I knew what I was getting into when I married him. I knew I'd always come second. It wasn't that. I could have put up with that indefinitely."

"You shouldn't have had to," Cooper said gently.

She ignored him. "But I wanted kids."

"And he didn't?"

"No, he was fine with the idea of kids. We tried for years, in fact. It just didn't work out."

Her head was tipped down as she said it, making her expression impossible to read, but he heard the sorrow in her voice. The unspoken pain. He remembered now—one Christmas when Caro had whispered something about a miscarriage. The implication that it hadn't been the first. And he couldn't help thinking about the toll that had taken on Portia.

"I'm sorry." Sorry didn't begin to cover it. Not even close, but there was so little he could say. She shrugged, something in the movement making him think that it wasn't his sympathy she wanted, but something else entirely. "And that's why you got the divorce?"

"Yes, it is. I wanted to keep trying. He didn't."

"He should have—"

"Don't get me wrong. I don't blame Dalton. Infertility takes its toll on a relationship. It's easy to become obsessed with it. I was so desperate for kids, sometimes I think he was right to put a stop to it. I wanted more and more fertility treatments. Then when those didn't work, I wanted to adopt. He insisted we slow down, take a break. I asked for a divorce."

Her voice was oddly quiet—almost emotionless—as she recounted the end of her marriage. Still, he heard the guilt in her words. She blamed herself, not Dalton, for how things had ended. But Cooper knew the truth—Dalton was a heartless bastard who'd ignored his wife's needs. Maybe that wasn't the whole story, but that was how Cooper saw it.

"He should have been a better husband."

She smiled again. Another one of those smiles that was a little sad and a little wry and broke his heart a little. "That's not the point of the story."

"Okay, then what is?"

"You asked why I didn't think I'd marry again. This is why. While I'm the first person to admit I got too obsessed with it last time around, becoming a mother is still very important to me. After Dalton, I thought I would meet someone else. Someone who wanted kids like I did. That hasn't happened and I'm weirdly okay with that. I don't need a husband to be a mom."

"You're going forward with the fertility treatments," he summed up.

"No. That was what made me so crazy last time. This time, I'm going to adopt."

He sat back in his chair slowly. "I see."

Her gaze darted to his, suddenly sharp. "You do?" she asked suspiciously.

"Yeah." Because this was Portia and she didn't do anything halfheartedly. She held herself coolly distant from something until she'd decided to commit, then she threw herself into it 100 percent. "I'm thinking you're not the type to adopt some rosy-cheeked baby, are you?"

"Of course, I thought about that first. I've been working with an adoption attorney for over a year now. So far no luck."

"Why not? You'll be a great mom."

"Private adoptions are tricky. There's a lot of putting out feelers and then waiting to see if you get any takers. And there are a lot of couples out there trying to adopt. I guess when a woman is looking for the perfect parents to raise her baby, she automatically thinks of two parents. Not just one." She gave a little shrug. But then her eyes took on the glow of excitement. "Which is why I'm thinking about going through the foster care system. Adopting an older kid. There are so many who need homes and—" Then she broke off nervously, as if she'd just spilled a secret she hadn't meant to share. "I haven't told this to anyone yet. I don't know why I'm telling you now."

He leaned back and studied her, marveling all over again that she was just as beautiful at thirty-two as she'd been at twenty-one. And that the more he got to know her, the more attractive he found her. The deeper layers of Portia's personality revealed intelligence and passion, selflessness and sensitivity. Which frankly kind of sucked.

"You were telling me why we made the strangest couple ever." He couldn't help the note of grim finality in his voice.

She didn't seem to hear it though. "But I guess it doesn't matter if this isn't anything more than just two friends who happen to enjoy each other's company in bed."

"Right," he said, suddenly feeling unexpectedly deflated. "Because we were never going to be anything more than a brief fling."

"Exactly," she said, sounding more cheerful than she had earlier. "If I was looking for anything more than that, you would be my last choice."

"Your last choice? Ouch."

"Don't pretend to be wounded. You don't want to be a father. And even if you wanted something longer than this, you and I in a real relationship would be very messy."

"It's already messy. We jumped right past the part where it would have been anything else."

Her lips twisted into a smile. "True, but I've already had my heart broken by one Cain brother. I don't think I'm up for round two."

And that was one argument he couldn't possibly defend himself against, because in the end, she would always be Dalton's ex-wife. Neither of them could outrun that. And she was right. They could never have more than just this month, because he couldn't give her the things she really wanted.

He took another sip of her coffee and then asked, "Is that the real reason you're doing this?"

She turned and looked back at him. "Pardon?"

"Your adoption plans? Are they the real reason you're so desperate to find the missing heiress?"

She frowned. "I don't understand—"

"You're so worried about how she's going adapt to having wealth and social position thrust upon her. You're so desperate to make sure she can handle it. It's not really about her at all, is it? It's about this kid you want to adopt."

"I—" The furrow between Portia's brows deepened as she blinked in confusion. "I hadn't thought about it." Slowly, her shoulders sagged. "I don't know. Maybe it is.

I'm trying to be smart about this adoption thing. Trying to plan ahead and think through all the hidden pitfalls. But in the end, I'm planning on taking some kid out of her world and bringing her into mine. She'll have all kinds of resources that she doesn't have now, but she'll still be living in a world that's harsh and cutthroat."

He couldn't help but smile at that. "If you're adopting some kid out of foster care, there's a decent chance she's coming from a world that's harsh and cutthroat."

"Good point. But at least that world is familiar. She knows the rules. She knows what to expect."

"You're forgetting one thing. She's going to have you in her corner. With you at her back, she'll be fine."

She reached across the table and gave his hand a friendly but dismissive squeeze. "I'm glad we're friends."

Friends? Was she kidding? They'd just had some of the best sex of his entire life and now she was relegating him to the friend zone?

But he was the one who'd worked to sell her on the idea of a no-pressure, just-sex relationship. It was just that he'd never had that with someone he was friends with. Sex with a friend was so much more than he'd ever bargained for. And he couldn't help thinking that whatever time they had left wasn't going to be nearly enough.

With two weeks to go before the exhibition, he actually thought about taking time off from Flight+Risk—not to manage the project, but to be with Portia. He certainly had plenty of vacation days. And, hell, what was the point of being the CEO if he couldn't occasionally take time off to do what he wanted?

The second the thought crossed his mind, he panicked. He'd never once taken a vacation just to take time off. Sure, he went on plenty of snowboarding trips—that was just part of the job, in addition to being the thing he loved best. But there'd never been any woman in the world he'd wanted to ditch work to hang out with. The fact that he felt that way about Portia was enough to send him back to Denver fast.

Not that that put her out of his mind. But he took to emailing her instead of calling. He got the endless stream of texts. Although he tried to keep his answers short, he found himself texting her back, responding not only to her questions about work, but sending her personal messages, as well. Before he knew it, he was text flirting with her, for God's sake.

By the time Thursday rolled around, the first thing he did in the morning was reach for his phone to see if Portia had texted him when she woke up. Like him she was an early riser. Sure enough, there was a text from her.

Made you a reservation at the hotel for Friday and Saturday night. OK?

In fact, it should have been okay. After all, he'd told her he was coming out for the weekend, but the way his heart rate picked up at the idea made him nervous. Before he could analyze his response, another text came through.

Also made appointment for tasting at the bakery on Saturday morning. Ate a croissant on your behalf.

A second later she sent him a photo of a croissant with a large bite taken out of it.

He chuckled at the picture, but there was something else underneath. A pang of longing maybe. He had a day full of meetings and idea pitches—the stuff that was the lifeblood of his company—and all he wanted to do was hop on a plane to Utah so he could feed her bites of croissant.

Annoyed with himself, he typed a quick reply.

Will be off-line most of today. Might not make it out to Provo this weekend after all. Then he added, Keep the hotel res just in case I need a place to crash.

Then he tucked his phone into his pocket, determined to not even glance at it again.

He made it precisely eleven hours and forty-two minutes before reading the texts she'd sent him throughout the day. There were a couple early in the day, then a flurry later in the afternoon. Then nothing.

By the time he texted her back that night, he hadn't heard from her in hours. When she didn't respond right away, he knew he should let it go. Instead, he found himself dialing her number.

She answered quickly, but her voice was subdued. "Hi." She gave a nervous-sounding chuckle. "Sorry I flooded you with texts today about the flooring."

"Don't apologize," he said, too harshly really. But why the hell was she apologizing? He was the jerk who'd been dodging her texts. "I was just in meetings all day."

"Sure. No, it's okay. I got it sorted out. The Becks are still being super accommodating. I shouldn't have even bothered you."

"Don't worry about it. I trust you."

"That's just it," she said abruptly. "I know you do. You've got total faith in me. And the Becks, too. Every time I suggest something, they jump right on it."

"They really want to sell," he mentioned.

"They're depending on me to get the hotel in shape for you. You're depending on me to win over investors. Are you sure you should be trusting me with this?"

"Hey, calm down. You're sounding all panicky."

She went instantly silent.

"Why don't you take a deep breath and tell me what's really going on here."

"I don't know!" she admitted. "Suddenly this just all feels very important. You're spending a huge amount of money. You may never see returns on this investment. And basically we're trying to hoodwink your board. This whole endeavor could be doomed. What if we fail? What if I fail?"

"You're not going to."

She gave a little snort. "Yeah, your confidence in me is really great, but you know this isn't *Peter Pan,* right? If you clap long and hard and swear you believe in fairies, that still doesn't mean I'm going to be able to pull this off."

"I don't think I have a response to that," he said.

"Why? Because secretly you know I'm right?"

"First off, snowboarders are prohibited from understanding any and all references to *Peter Pan*. Or any other Disney movie for that matter."

She gave a bark of laughter. "You are not."

"Of course we are. It's in the code."

"The code?" she asked suspiciously. "There's no code."

"Oh, yeah, there's totally a code. We also can't stop and smell flowers or order drinks with pink umbrellas."

From her laugh, Cooper could tell she was beginning to feel less panicked. It was a genuine chuckle, not the crazed bark of laughter that had escaped her a moment ago.

"It sounds like a pretty tough code. What if the bartender gets your drink wrong and puts an umbrella in your Scotch?"

"Well, if that happens you have to just beat the crap out of him."

"So this snowboarder's code is all about being tough and manly, huh? Is that why you're not nervous about this? Frankly, you should be even more panicked than I am. Is it just that all those years of throwing yourself off mountain-tops has deadened your ability to perceive risks?"

He laughed then. "I guess it might seem that way, huh?"

"Yes, it does."

"You know the thing about snowboarding, though? People talk all the time about how dangerous it is. And I'm not going to lie. It is dangerous. But when you're a professional, when you do this for a living, you don't take unnecessary risks. Planning, knowledge, preparation…those are all things that mitigate the risks. Now you can't plan for everything, but you prepare for the things you can and you don't let your fear get in the way. So sure, we all get nervous. We just do it anyway."

"You don't seem nervous," she said begrudgingly.

"Well, that is part of the code. You do what you need to do so you don't let the nerves show. The nerves, they help you focus. They help you commit to the run. You just hang on. But you never let them get in your way." He paused for a second to let his words sink in. "This project at Beck's Lodge, it's the same thing. Sure, I'm nervous. But I'm also ready. I've done the research. I've hired you—and believe me, despite any doubts you're having right now, you are the best at what you do. I'm sure there are plenty of things that will happen in the next month that I can't prepare for, but that's just life."

Again, there was silence on the other end of the line. "You're not saying anything," he prodded gently. "Do you need to go do a headstand?"

"Shut up," she said with a soft chuckle.

"So we're good here?"

"Yeah. I still don't understand how you can be so relaxed about everything."

"Because I've got you working on my team. That's how."

* * *

After her bout of hysteria, she expected him to get off the phone quickly. There was no way he'd want to stay around for more of her crazy cakes, especially not after he'd been distant for so much of the day.

Honestly, she didn't quite know what to make of him sometimes. He was confident to the point of being cocky. He was smart as hell and ambitious. Despite all that, she couldn't shake the feeling that he was also lonely.

She knew better than most how hard it could be to find true friends when your net worth put the county budget to shame. It wasn't easy making friends under those circumstances. Which was why you had to be loyal to the ones you did make. All the more reason for her to step up and protect Caro. And to take care of the heiress.

But what about Cooper? Who was going to take care of him?

They stayed on the phone a few more minutes after that. Quietly talking. Though she'd gotten used to the phone calls from Cooper from her bed, she was still keenly aware of how close she felt, talking to him. Somehow, their nightly chats seemed more intimate than the hours they actually spent in bed. But eventually, they did hang up. She lay there in bed for several minutes after that, just thinking about Cooper.

She'd never had anyone talk her out of a panic attack before. For that matter, she wasn't sure there was anyone other than her therapist who even knew she had panic attacks. And Cooper also knew she was trying to adopt, something only her lawyer and social worker knew. Moreover, he hadn't dismissed the idea.

It felt odd that he knew these secret private things about her that no one else knew.

And it still made her unthinkably sad that he seemed

to not have anyone he was close to. Maybe she had it all wrong. Maybe he really was that emotionally self-sufficient. Maybe that was part of the snowboarder's code. But the more she thought about it, the more she wondered if he didn't need his sister just as much as she might need him.

Later, Portia did what she should have done two weeks ago. She dug through her contact list for the name of a private investigator that her father's secretary sometimes used. Portia had only met the man once. When her mother had learned that she and Dalton were getting a divorce, she'd tried to strong-arm Portia into hiring the guy to dig up dirt on Dalton. Turned out the P.I. was too ethical to go behind Portia's back. She liked the idea of an ethical P.I. Especially one she trusted with sensitive information and whose email address she had handy.

Eleven

It about killed Cooper to stay away from Provo the week before the exhibition. It killed him to be in Denver when his dream was taking place at Beck's Lodge. At least that's what he repeatedly told himself was causing the pain.

His biggest challenge as CEO of Flight+Risk had been learning to delegate. His temptation had always been to do everything himself. Sure, it was hard to keep his ass in Denver where he needed to be. The four times he hopped in the car and made it halfway to the airport before turning around and driving back home were proof of that. But it had nothing to do with Portia and everything to do with the fact that he was a very hands-on CEO.

He limited their contact to emails and to the occasional telephone conversation. Still, most of the phone calls—like the one he was on now—happened late at night, after they'd both had dinner and their schedules were clear.

If he wanted to push his luck, he could say something

licentious. He pictured her blushing. She had the kind of pale skin that blushed beautifully and often. And when she blushed, it tinted not just her cheeks, but her neck and chest too. The thought of all her delicate skin flushed pink with titillation was almost more than he could bear.

"Well, okay then," she said in the cheerful tone she always used as she was transitioning from work talk to anything more personal. "I think that's about it."

"Okay, I'll—"

"No, wait. That's not it. I just remembered. I got an email from Drew Davis yesterday and then he called today to confirm. He said a couple of his friends are going to come up tomorrow to build the slope for the exhibition. They'll be—"

"Wait a second." Cooper sat up in bed. "Did he say a couple of his friends or *The* Friends?"

"I don't know. Why?"

"Because The Friends are a very specific group of guys. They're five of the best snowboarders in the world. They all came up through the competitive ranks about the same time and that's how they got their nickname."

"And Drew is one of them?"

"No, he and I are both about ten years older. Which is why it never occurred to me…"

"Wait, didn't you invite the snowboarders?"

"Most of them, sure. But Drew said he'd invite some guys he knew and I let him handle it." And he'd been too distracted by Portia to follow up and ask whom Drew had invited. It was the first time in his life he'd let work slide to be with a woman. "Damn it, I guess it's too late to do anything about it now."

"You sound stressed out about this. You said these guys are good, right?"

"They're some of the best," he admitted grudgingly.

"If they're coming to help build the slope or whatever and they're going to board in the competition, that seems like a good thing to me. Won't that just impress everyone?"

"Yeah. Sure."

"Then what's the problem?"

The problem was all of The Friends—one or two in particular—were total players.

"There's no problem," Cooper finally said aloud, but only because he couldn't think of anything else to say without sounding like a jealous ass. "Just, you know, watch yourself, okay?"

"Watch myself? What's that supposed to mean?"

"Just be careful. Some of these guys have reputations as womanizers."

"You have a reputation as a womanizer," she pointed out.

"Which I've told you is largely exaggerated."

"Then I'm sure theirs is, too."

Yeah. Well, he was not at all sure about that. In fact, he'd bet money that Stevey Travor was going to show up, take one look at Portia and dial the charm up to eleven. Not that she'd fall for it. At least, not right away. Not while she was still with Cooper.

But they'd both agreed that their relationship would end after the exhibition. And he'd worked damn hard to convince her that no-pressure, commitment-free sex was the way to go. Had he inadvertently primed her for the likes of Stevey Travor?

"Just don't listen to anything they say, okay? And don't spend too much time alone with any of them."

She chuckled dismissively. "I think I can handle it. Besides, it's not like I'm going to be with them. I have things to do. The floor guys will be there tomorrow putting down the final layer of wax. Drew promised me that he was going to oversee everything and that I didn't even have to leave the lodge."

"Drew said that?" Ah, great. This just kept getting better and better. "Drew is coming with them?"

"Yeah. Didn't I say that?"

"No, I must have missed it." However, he didn't miss the implied intimacy of her words. Just how friendly had she gotten with Drew over the course of the past month, when he'd been stuck here twiddling his thumbs in Denver?

"Are you worried they won't do a decent job?"

"No," he muttered tightly. "They're the best. I'm sure they'll do a great job. I'm thrilled they're all chipping in."

He ended the call a few minutes later—before he could make any more of a fool of himself—assuring her he was thrilled with her progress.

And he was. Of course he was. Just like he was thrilled that The Friends had gotten involved. They were some of the hottest snowboarders around. He knew all of them personally and two of them had endorsement deals with Flight+Risk. Their involvement would draw a lot of media attention, as would Drew's. He was glad he had business associates who agreed with his visions enough that they were willing to jump in and help.

He just wished that Portia hadn't sounded so damn starstruck the times she'd talked about Drew Davis. He also wished that freakin' Stevey Travor wasn't coming. Because the guy was notorious. And even though she would never admit it, she was vulnerable to that kind of charm.

Stevey was a scoundrel looking for nothing more than a willing woman. Cooper knew damn well that was exactly the kind of guy who could talk his way into her bed. She'd fallen for it with him, hadn't she?

As beautiful as she was, she'd somehow never learned the power of her own beauty—probably because Dalton was such a class A idiot. Her innocence—combined with her romanticized view of relationships—made her particularly vulnerable to the charms of a guy like Stevey. Or Drew for that matter.

And now that he thought about it, hadn't Drew just finalized his third divorce?

Damn.

There was no way he was leaving her alone up there on his mountain with those two.

Portia hadn't really believed Cooper had anything to be suspicious about when it came to The Friends. First off, she was so busy that she doubted she'd even see them, at least not until they were finished with whatever snow-related job they were doing—which she didn't really understand, despite Drew's attempts to describe it. She had been working twelve-hour days getting the hotel ready for the exhibition and the party the night before. In what little spare time she had, she'd been furthering the search for Ginger. Despite Cooper's doubts, she was still convinced that Ginger was the missing heiress. The information the P.I. had turned up only confirmed her conviction. And Cooper's protests had only strengthened her resolve.

She'd been in contact with Dalton and Laney about the matter and had even called Griffin. They had been intrigued enough by her theory that they had shared the information they'd discovered about Hollister's indiscretion all those years ago. But as eager as Portia was to delve into that mystery, she was still determined to pull off an exhibition worthy of Cooper's ambition, even if she was starting to have doubts about the project.

Of course that was before a pair of passenger vans pulled up in front of the lodge just before lunch. She'd been overseeing the work on the floors, which needed to be waxed a second time and buffed at least twice before anyone walked on them, when she heard the noise. She hurried out the front door only to stop short on the deep wraparound porch.

Each of the vans pulled a trailer with four snowmobiles. The doors swung open and out poured a dozen guys. Or maybe it was fewer—they were all so big. And rowdy. It was hard to tell how many there were exactly.

Drew was the only one she recognized, because she'd seen footage of him when he'd talked at the UN about climate change. Plus, he'd competed in the Olympics on the American team with Cooper, so she'd actually seen him board. Like Cooper, he was all lean muscle, though if she had to guess, she'd say he was an inch or so shorter than Cooper. He wore his hair long and scruffy. Though he was handsome, he lacked the intensity that made Cooper so irresistible.

When Drew spotted her, he bounded up the stairs and gave her a big bear hug like they were old friends, even though they'd only spoken on the phone a handful of times.

"Portia! Great to finally meet you!"

"Um, yeah," she squeaked, even though he'd squeezed all the air out of her lungs. "Nice to meet you—" he gave her another bone-crunching squeeze as effective as a trip to the chiropractor "—too."

As he released her, he laughed like she'd said something funny. "Come on. I'll introduce you to The Friends. They can't wait to meet you."

She surveyed the group of guys at the bottom of the stairs. Some of them were already unloading the snowmobiles, others were unpacking massive bags from inside the vans. While they worked, they jostled and pushed one another like a litter of rambunctious puppies.

Drew called them each over to meet her, as if she could possibly remember their names, when they all looked so much alike—young and handsome, with ruddy, wind-roughened cheeks. Most of them immediately went back to work. A couple hung nearby and seemed to be waiting to talk to Drew about something.

When he introduced Wiley, the cameraman, and Jude, the director, she looked back and forth from the men to Drew.

"Cameraman and director?" she asked. "Aren't they snowboarders, too?"

"Only amateurs," one of the younger guys who hadn't gone back to work interjected. His name was something with an *S*. Scotty maybe? No, Stevey.

"So they're here to…"

"Film the project," Drew said simply. "They've been wanting some footage of what it takes to build a jump. So they'll film us for the next two days. And then they'll film the exhibition, too."

"You know Drew here is going to be movie star, right?" Stevey had edged closer to her and bumped his shoulder against hers playfully.

Drew looked embarrassed. "Hardly a movie star. They're making a documentary about Save Our Snow."

"That's fantastic!" she said. "You know I've been following the work you've done with—"

"You're going to come up and watch us work, right?" Stevey interrupted her.

She nearly smiled when she looked at him. If the other guys were like puppies, Stevey was like an Australian shepherd. He'd started tugging at her heel the second her attention strayed from him.

"I really can't," she said truthfully. "I've got too much to do."

"You have to come! If you've never seen a jump being

formed before, now's your chance. You're gonna love it. I promise."

He might as well have started waving and shouting, "Look at me! Look at me!"

She glanced at Drew for support. "I really—"

"If you're busy, you don't have to stay the whole time. I'll bring you back down the mountain myself."

She looked up at the lodge and then at the vans. It was true that until the floor guys finished inside, there wasn't a whole lot she could do here. "How exactly do we get up there?"

"We'll take the snowmobiles up. Scout out a location and then get started."

"The snowmobiles?" she asked doubtfully.

This was a hiccup she hadn't considered. It had never occurred to her that they would need snowmobiles to get up the mountain for the exhibition. There were over thirty confirmed guests and technically, the event was open to the public. That had gotten them some good press coverage in the local papers.

Frowning, she looked from the snowmobiles to the guys.

"You're coming, right?" Stevey asked again.

"Oh, sure." She nodded mindlessly. It would give her a chance to talk to Drew about this transportation problem. She certainly hadn't come this far to give up now. After all, she hadn't let the debacle with Cooper slow her down. Why would a little thing like snow stop her?

Twelve

Cooper left for the lodge first thing in the morning. He wasn't about to leave Portia alone with those guys any longer than necessary. Despite that, the earliest flight he could get to Salt Lake City wasn't until ten. By the time he took the helicopter from the airport down to the lodge, it was well after lunch. He was annoyed, but not particularly surprised, when he talked to the flooring crew and discovered Portia was not there, but rather off with Drew Davis and The Friends. Of course she hadn't taken his concerns seriously. He hadn't been exactly laying it all out on the line because he hadn't wanted to sound like an ass or an idiot.

But by the time he talked to Drew and figured out where they were, and then borrowed a snowmobile from the Becks and made it up the mountain, he was done worrying about how he looked.

When he pulled up, the guys were almost done building the jump.

Something in his heart clenched when he saw Portia. She was dressed in her bright pink ski gear, looking like she'd planned on staying out for several hours. She looked ridiculously adorable among all the rugged guys. Pale blond hair in braids on either side of her neck peeked out from beneath her snow cap. Her cheeks were rosy, her eyes hidden behind oversized sunglasses. She looked like Heidi by way of a *Vogue* photo shoot.

She waved when she saw him, but her smile froze. "I thought you weren't coming up for a few more days," she said as he shook hands with Drew.

Drew was the only one near her. Cooper recognized the director and cameraman from a previous meeting, but they were both focused on filming the other guys.

"I had an unexpected opening in my calendar." Drew was standing closer to Portia than Cooper liked, so he stood on her other side, casually dropping his hand onto her shoulder. "So I decided to come on over and keep an eye on things."

Drew grinned as if he saw right through Cooper. "Hey, things are fine, man. You have nothing to worry about."

Cooper nodded toward the jump. "Sure, you and The Friends are experts at this, but sometimes you need a more delicate touch."

"You don't think I have a delicate touch?" Drew asked.

"I just think I have a little more invested in this than you do."

Drew threw back his head and laughed. "Good point, man. Good point. But don't worry, I'm watching out for your interests here."

Portia was looking back and forth between the two of them, her brow furrowed in confusion. Apparently, she'd missed the entire subtext of the conversation. Which frankly relieved him. He didn't need her to know how tied up into knots he was over her.

Portia practically beamed at him. "Do you see what they're doing?" She pointed off toward the jump, rising up and down on her toes. Either she was very cold or very excited. And it was adorable. "They've been building the slope all morning. They actually moved the snow from over there—" she pointed off to her left "—to over here. In big blocks like bricks. And then they packed in the rest of the snow to make it swoopy like that."

"Swoopy?" he asked.

"Yeah. Swoopy." She made a motion with her hand that could only be described as...well, swoopy.

"It's a jump, not a slope. And that's the kicker, not the 'swoopy part.'" He shot Drew a glare. "Have you been letting her call it a *slope* and a *swoopy part* all morning?"

Drew just flashed her a charming smile and threw an arm around her shoulder. "It's adorable."

"Oh." For a second, she looked embarrassed, but then she waved it away. "Anyway, it's amazing to watch. I had no idea they were going to do this."

Cooper shrugged. "This is how it's done."

"I think I expected more machinery to be involved or something."

"Nah, real snowboarders don't want anything messing with their powder."

"It's a lot of work," she said. "All these guys must really like you for them to come all the way here to do this for you."

He looked at the jump. They were already smoothing out the snow on the kicker, dragging the backs of snow shovels down the curve. The kicker was nice and tall, so they'd have a ton of air when they jumped. They would put on an amazing show.

"Nah," he said. "They would come do this anywhere, anytime, if it meant they'd get to ride it later. That's the thing about these guys. It's always all about the snow."

She tilted her head to the side, looking at him as if she wanted to say something else. Or maybe she wanted to protest. Before she could, Stevey Travor stopped goofing around on the snow and sauntered their way, a cocky grin on his face.

Portia changed the subject and because she seemed to be talking about something related to the exhibition, Cooper tried to focus on that instead of the need to charge head-first into Stevey and beat the crap out of him.

"I was worried about transportation," Portia was saying. "It hadn't even occurred to me to think about where the exhibition was going to be and how to get the money types up here to see it."

"Hmm," he said noncommittally.

"I know!" she said. "I can't believe I didn't think about that. I've just been so busy working on the party Saturday night and arranging accommodations for everyone, I just didn't think about it. And—"

"And I told her that as long as we made sure we could get a snowplow up here, we could build the jump close to the road," Drew chimed in.

"Did you know they could do that?" she asked Cooper. "Just move the snow around and make a jump anywhere they want? How crazy is that?"

He arched an eyebrow. "You do remember that I'm a snowboarder, too, right?"

"Well, yeah, but—"

Just then Stevey reached them. "Hey, old man." He clapped Cooper on the shoulder and winked at Portia. Cooper wanted to break the guy's hand. "You can't blame her for being impressed. I mean, everything we do is golden, right, babe?"

Cooper felt a wave of irrational anger wash over him. He didn't just want to break Stevey's hand; he wanted to rip it off. He wanted to tear the guy limb from limb so that he never boarded again. And just for good measure, break the guy's nose in a couple of places to knock that pretty-boy sheen off his face.

And that was it right there—the moment Cooper knew he was in deep trouble. Hell, he'd nearly lost his cool and beat the crap out of an innocent—well, sort of innocent—guy who was basically his friend, even if he was a bit of a jerk. And it was all over a woman he was supposed to be done with by the time the weekend was over. Done.

Except he apparently wasn't done at all.

"Okay," he said, taking Portia by the shoulders and steering her over to his snowmobile. "I think it's time I get you back to the lodge. The flooring guys said they needed your input on something."

"Is it about the wax? Because I wasn't sure about that shade of brown and—"

"Yeah. Absolutely. Total wax nightmare."

She dug in her heels a few steps later. "Wait. Don't you want to watch them finish? It's really pretty impressive."

"Yeah, man," Stevey said with a cocky grin. "If you want to stay, I can take her back."

"No. It's fine. I know what you're capable of. It's nothing I haven't seen before."

"I don't understand," Portia said as she stared at the empty entrance hall of Bear Creek Lodge. The floor guys were nowhere to be seen. Their van wasn't even out in front. They'd left yellow caution tape strung across the door with a note saying no one could walk on the floors for at least twelve hours. More to the point, the wax job was clearly finished and looked amazing. She turned to Cooper. "What's going on?"

He took a step forward like he was going to walk right through the tape. She pushed a hand into his chest. "Oh, no, you don't, mister."

When she broke off suddenly, he raised his eyebrows in question.

Damn. Why had she touched him? His muscles were firm beneath her hand, despite the layers of clothes separating them. She couldn't think when he was near. She had to force a casual note into her voice. "Didn't you read the sign? No walking on the floor."

"So, what, we're just supposed to stand out here in the cold?"

She pointed down the porch. "No, we can go in through the back door to the kitchen if we need to, but let's not touch much there, either. The cleaning crew worked for four days to get it inspection-ready and the inspector is coming tomorrow."

Once she'd let them in the back door, she turned to him, frowning. "So what's the deal? You acted like there was some big emergency. What's wrong?"

"I just don't want you hanging out with Drew and Stevey and The Friends, that's all."

"Oh." She blew out a breath, unsure what she was supposed to do with this information. "So you don't want me around your friends."

"It's no big deal. It would just be best for everyone if you spent as little time with them as possible."

"I see." His words stung more than she wished they did, and she turned away from him so that he couldn't see the hurt in her eyes. They weren't together. Maybe they had seemed like a couple for the past few weeks, but they weren't. She'd momentarily forgotten the boundaries of their no-pressure fling. There was no need for her to be around his friends.

Maybe she was being too sensitive. Maybe this shouldn't hurt her, but it did.

She stared sightlessly at the kitchen. It wasn't much by the standards of a modern industrial kitchen, but it was one of her favorite rooms in the lodge. If you looked beyond the aging stainless-steel appliances, you could see the bones of the grand kitchen it had been when Wallace had first built Bear Creek Lodge. Thankfully, the Becks had only done the bare minimum of updates, leaving the solid maple cabinetry and massive butcher-block table in place. But like much of Bear Creek Lodge, you had to look beyond the surface to see the real beauty. Some people were no good at that. "Well, I guess that makes sense. Okay."

"Thank you," Cooper said gruffly.

But still it stung. And maybe she should have let it go. After all her years of marriage to Dalton, she was good at letting things go. But wasn't that the kind of thinking that had gotten her into trouble with her marriage in the first place? When she'd filed for divorce, hadn't she sworn that she was done just letting things slide? That she was going to fight for herself more often?

So why wasn't she standing up for herself now? Because she genuinely liked Cooper and she didn't want him to think she was a bitch?

She was so bad about that. In general, the more she liked someone, the more important they were to her, the less likely she was to show that person the real her. She was always so afraid of screwing up or doing the wrong thing or being an embarrassment. So she hid all her silliness, her propensity for panic attacks, her sensitivity. She buried it deep. But—as Cooper had pointed out—this wasn't long-term.

Besides, Cooper had seen beneath the polished facade long ago. He knew she had the heart of a flibbertigibbet. He knew she was overly sensitive and flighty and a little bit wack-a-doodle.

So there was no reason not to tell him exactly how she felt.

Even though Portia had said it was fine, when she turned back around to face him a moment later, he could see in her expression that it wasn't. Not at all. Her brow had furrowed and her eyes had darkened to match her tumultuous expression. Her lush, gorgeous lips twisted into a grimace.

"But you know, it's really not okay."

Uh-oh.

"It isn't?" he asked.

"No. It isn't. I was getting along fine with them. And, frankly, I'm a little annoyed that you even feel like you have to barge in and say anything."

"Oh, so I'm supposed to just stand there and say nothing while you hang out with Stevey freaking Travor?"

"Look, I get it. We're not really together and you don't want them thinking we are. Fine. You want me to stay away from your friends, and I'll do it. But it's kind of rotten, you know? Because they were genuinely nice to me and now I have to act like the bitch and be all cool and distant. I'll do it, but just so you know, I think you're a jerk for expecting me to."

She seemed to run out of steam then, because she just stood there, glaring at him. Her delicate skin had flushed a deep pink and her chest was rising and falling rapidly—as if she'd just run a mile. Or torn him a new one.

"You done?" he asked softly.

Her gaze narrowed, like she was thinking it over, trying to decide if she had anything else she wanted to throw at him. But then she nodded.

"First off—" he started walking toward her, slowly, because he was half-afraid she was so amped up she'd bolt if he moved too fast "—I'm not asking you to be a bitch. I don't care if you like them and want to be their friend. I don't even care if you want to start a frickin' book club with them."

Her frown deepened. "Then why were you so adamant about me not hanging out with them?"

Her complete and total confusion charmed him. She truly didn't see it. At all.

By now he'd closed the distance between them. She had backed herself into the corner of the kitchen. She still looked skittish, like she might want to run, but he reached out a hand and cupped her cheek.

"I don't want you hanging out with them because I'm trying to protect you."

"You're protecting me from them?"

"Stevey Travor is a womanizer. He'd talk your pants off you in a second if he had a chance."

She looked completely baffled, then she laughed. "You're worried I might sleep with Stevey Travor? That's absurd."

Her amusement did not improve his mood. "I've seen Stevey in action. He's quite charming."

"He's like a big puppy dog. And he's a decade younger than me. He's a child."

"Great," he groused. "I'm glad this amuses you."

She shook her head, a smile playing across her lips. "And I'm pretty sure it would never occur to him to seduce me. It's just silly."

"It's not silly. And it's driving me crazy."

"It's driving you crazy?" she asked, her voice sounding breathless.

"Yes." He stood a few inches away from her, taking in everything about her. He'd been away from her for over two weeks. It felt like a lifetime. Why was that? How was it that this woman—whom he'd known for years and had always been able to force out of his mind in the past—was suddenly someone he could hardly function without? He studied her, taking in everything from her adorable Heidi braids to her sun-kissed cheeks. She'd blossomed these past few weeks, but her appeal went far beyond her physical appearance.

"Should I apologize?" she asked sheepishly.

"I can't explain it. It doesn't make any sense, but the thought of you with any of those guys—hell, with any guy—it drives me crazy with jealousy."

Something that looked like sorrow flickered through her gaze. "I'm sorry, Cooper. I'm sorry it makes you uncomfortable. But it doesn't have anything to do with me."

"Are you kidding? It has everything to do with you."

Her face set into stubborn lines and she pushed her way past him. "No. It really doesn't. You said yourself that you don't want to be in a relationship. You have no interest in me outside the bedroom. Isn't that the point of a no-pressure fling? That means you don't get to be jealous. A husband would have the right to be jealous. A boyfriend would. But not you. All you ever wanted was to take me to bed. That's just about my body, so I don't see what that has to do with me at all."

"You think this is just about sex?"

"Do you think it's about anything else?"

"If it was your body I lusted after, I would have found a way to take you to bed years ago. I wouldn't have spent the past decade tormented by the idea that you were in love with and married to my brother. It's not just your body that I want. It's not thoughts of your body that keep me up at night. It's you. With all your quirks and funny little personality ticks. It's your pride and your stubbornness and your compassion. It's your sheer mule-headed determination to do the right thing no matter what. It's your very soul." He laughed then, because if he didn't know better, if he didn't know that love was a fantasy, he'd think that what he'd just described was a man in love.

Thirteen

Standing there, listening to Cooper talk about how much he wanted her, she knew there were a lot of reasons why she shouldn't be falling a little bit more in love with him with every word. But somehow she couldn't stop herself from hearing him. Couldn't stop herself from believing everything he said. In fact, all she could do was reach for him. Give herself what she most wanted. In that moment. Which was to rise up onto her toes and press her mouth to his.

That simple invitation was all that he needed. He met her move for move, tracing the seam of her lips with his tongue until she let him in. He tasted like mint and sweet spring water. He stroked her tongue with his in a way that made her tremble. Cooper kissed the same way he did everything—with confidence that bordered on arrogance, with skill that made her mind spin.

He was fearless in a way that took her breath away. As if he'd never had a single doubt about kissing her. As if he knew this was exactly what she wanted.

And it was.

This time, when he kissed and touched her, he lacked the finesse he'd had the previous times they'd made love. Instead of skill, he was all need. Instead of expertise, he was barely controlled desperation.

His hands moved down her back, pulling her to him until she was molded against him. Only her hands were between them, moving across his shirt, exploring the rock-hard muscles of his chest.

And then his hands skimmed down her side to squeeze her hips before slipping around to cup her bottom. Pleasure spiraled through her, and a low groan was torn from her throat.

"Damn, Portia," he muttered, his words nearly a groan, as well.

He lifted her up and against him, his mouth trailing a hot line of kisses down her neck. Each place his lips touched her skin lit a fire that spread through her body. She arched toward him. Then suddenly, she was off the ground. He'd lifted her clean off her feet onto the counter, and her legs automatically wrapped around his hips, pulling his hard length against her core. A shudder of raw pleasure coursed through her body. Somehow, he seemed to know exactly what she needed. Just how to touch her so that she came undone.

His kiss affected her in a way nothing else ever had. And maybe this was the last time she'd ever get to experience it. It was as though his very touch heated her blood and made her head spin. As though his kisses sucked the air right out of her lungs. She drew in quick, desperate breaths, but he only filled her senses more, the warm woodsy scent of him hitting her in the gut, making her greedy for him. She wanted him naked before her. She tugged at his shirt, pushing her hands under the fabric so that her palms could knead his bare skin.

And still that pressure inside her kept building until she was desperate. For all of him.

A moment later he was whipping her turtleneck up and over her head. The rest of her clothes followed so quickly she barely remembered them coming off. No man had ever seemed so eager to get her naked. And it felt good. Amazing to have him still wanting her like this. Cooper, who was like a rock star, who was so sought after that his assistant had to turn women away, who was handsome and accomplished and an amazing lover. And he wanted her. The experience was so heady, she didn't even protest as her clothing fell away.

For the briefest instant, she wondered if this was really her at all. The entire experience seemed beyond anything she'd ever done. Even anything she'd ever thought about doing.

But none of that seemed to matter, not when he was touching her. His fingertips trailing down her body, into her body, pushed all thoughts aside, burying who she really was so completely that when he slipped her panties down and knelt between her legs, she was beyond thought, let alone protest.

Because this woman, this woman sitting bare-assed naked on the counter while he devoured her, wasn't even her. That's what she told herself even when she shattered into tiny bits.

Cooper had meant to stop. Or at least to slow down. Or maybe just to ask and make sure that this was what she really wanted.

Instead, he'd lost himself in Portia's kiss. In her heated

response to his every touch. To her low moans and greedy mewling sounds. To the cool flutter of fingertips and the hot thundering of her heart. To the soft mounds of her ass and the damp folds of her sex. To her desperation. Her need. Her surprise.

At every step of the way, he told himself he was going to stop. Just one kiss, he'd said. Just one peek at her breasts. Just one nibble on her neck. Just one taste. Until he felt her coming apart against his tongue as tremor after tremor of her orgasm rocked through her body. That's when he stopped lying to himself.

He wasn't going to stop. Not until he'd driven her mad with pleasure at least a few more times tonight. Not until he'd felt the last of her defenses crumble as she'd climaxed while he was buried deep inside of her. Not until he'd erased every other man from her memory and her mind.

He carried her up the stairs to one of the empty bedrooms and then slowly made love to her. All the while forcing from his mind all the reasons they couldn't really be together. Not just the stupid, selfish reasons he'd always given to himself for not being in a real relationship, not that crap about not believing in love or happily ever afters. Those were the excuses he'd always given himself. The things that haunted him now were her reasons. All the reasons she didn't want to be with him. The fact that she'd been hurt too badly. That she wanted to adopt. That she couldn't see him as a father. That she couldn't imagine him in her life long-term.

And as long as he kept touching her, he was able to forget them.

He kissed his way back up her body, leaving a trail of pink where the day's growth of his beard scuffed her tender skin. Maybe he should have felt bad. Instead, he felt a deep surge of satisfaction at the sight. A sort of primitive pride that he didn't remember feeling with anyone else. He'd marked her as his. Not for forever, but for now. She was his.

He pinned her hands over her head and waited until she was looking him in the eye before he plunged into her. He needed her to see him. To acknowledge that he was the one making love to her. That he was the one who brought her pleasure over and over again. Making love to her was almost too much pleasure and in the end, he was the one who looked away. Because as much pleasure as he brought her, just being with her brought him more.

Portia awoke alone in the bedroom in Bear Creek Lodge that she'd been staying in whenever she worked too late to call the driver to take her back into town. After what had happened in the kitchen, Cooper had swept her up into his arms and carried her here to make love to her again. At some point after that, she'd slept, Cooper's body wrapped around hers, his hand clasping her breast possessively. Had she ever slept like that before? So closely entwined with someone else's body so that she felt it every time he moved? Had she ever felt that connected to a man?

She didn't think so.

She rolled over and buried her nose in the Cooper-scented pillow beside her and she was hit with another punch of that great scent. All pine-y and smoky. He smelled good. He always had.

He wasn't here, but that didn't surprise her. He'd probably gone out to see what Drew and The Friends were doing. He wouldn't want them to come looking for her and then to have to answer the inevitable questions any more than she did.

Still, lying there in bed, she had to admit this wasn't just sex. It was something so much more complicated than that. In the past few weeks, she'd grown to know Cooper. To understand how smart and driven he was. To respect him. To care deeply about him. What had started as a no-pressure fling had grown into something deep and complicated and nearly out of control.

But there was no room in her life for anything like that.

Things might have been different if he wanted a real relationship. She could have given herself over to the flame and let it burn her whole. But he didn't want that. He only wanted brief and shallow. He wanted sex without love.

At least that was what he'd said when they started this. She'd thought this afternoon that maybe he'd changed his mind. That maybe he felt more.

And when he'd carried her to the room and made such beautiful love to her, she'd been sure he'd been on the verge of saying so out loud.

Except, he hadn't. They'd had great sex and then he'd walked away.

She'd foolishly thought that she could let herself have this passionate fling, that as long as she knew going into it that it was just sex that she'd be safe. She'd been so wrong.

She was in way over her head. She wanted more. She needed more or nothing at all.

Settling for less than what she wanted seemed dirty and petty. It seemed small. It seemed disrespectful of her marriage.

Yes, her marriage to Dalton was over, but those ten years were still part of her life. It wasn't as if she could get them back or unwind them. She couldn't undo them. She wouldn't if she could. She certainly wouldn't turn her back on that part of herself. She had been so young and hopeful.

Portia respected that person too much to settle for something like this with Cooper.

She wouldn't settle for a cheap affair, but that didn't mean she was giving up, either. Somehow, inexplicably, she'd fallen in love with Cooper over the past three weeks.

She was dressed and heading down the servants' staircase in the back of the house when she heard the roar of snowmobiles outside the lodge. For just an instant, her hand gripped the railing. Was she ready for this? Ready to face the half-dozen rambunctious puppies as if nothing had happened?

Well, she supposed that was the good thing about puppies. Unless she met them on the porch wailing her heart out, they probably wouldn't notice. A few deep breaths later, she exited onto the porch via the kitchen door and followed the sounds of their raucous laughter.

Cooper was with them. In his snow gear, he blended seamlessly with the group as they parked their snowmobiles under a nearby copse of trees and started loading their equipment back into the waiting van. There was a lot of backslapping and boasting about who had done the most work and who had been a dumbass. For the first time, she felt a twinge of doubt about the coming days, not just about her relationship with Cooper, but also about whether or not this party of hers was a good idea at all. And about Cooper's idea for the lodge. He wanted to open an exclusive high-end lodge for snowboarders, but would snowboarders actually want to stay here?

Nothing about this group said exclusive or high-end. These guys didn't look as if they'd know luxury accommodations if they bit them on the nose.

Not for the first time, Portia felt a heartbreaking panic. She had doubts upon doubts. Fears on top of fears. Because

in that moment she understood something about her relationship with Cooper. Yes, he wanted Bear Creek Lodge,
but he wanted it for all the wrong reasons. He wanted pres-
tige, the social acceptability that would come with owning
a high-end resort. It wasn't the lodge he loved. It was the
idea of the lodge. What owning the lodge would bring him.

Was his relationship with her just the same? Were they
together because he wanted her, or because she represented
success and wealth and privilege?

The idea made her sick to her stomach. But before she
could flee back into the house, Stevey noticed her standing
there and he nudged a couple of the other guys so they knew
she was there, too. They settled down a bit. He bounded up
the stairs to the porch.

"We finished! We'll be back tomorrow for test runs
and to shoot some footage for the doc. You'll come watch,
right?"

She glanced back down to see Cooper looking up at her,
his expression unreadable. Then she smiled at Stevey, trying to hide her sorrow and confusion. "I don't know. I'll
just have to see how things look here tomorrow."

"You should come," he insisted.

"I'll try," she agreed, but knew that *try* was the opera-
tive word there. She couldn't make any promises until she
knew how things went with Cooper.

A moment later, Drew and The Friends all piled into the
vans and headed back down the mountain.

Cooper came up onto the porch, propping his shoulder
against one of the rough-hewn posts that held up the roof.
"What were you talking to Stevey about?" he asked.

"He asked if I was going to come watch them practice
tomorrow."

"What did you say?" he asked as he followed her in
through the back door to the kitchen.

"I told him I'd have to wait and see." She sucked in an icy, bracing breath and plunged into the conversation she knew he wouldn't want to have. "I don't think this is a good idea. But Cooper, you and I need to talk."

Fourteen

He gazed at her through narrowed eyes, like he was just waiting to be sucker punched.

"I hired a P.I.," she said without ceremony.

She had wanted this conversation to go very differently. She had wanted to tell him after the exhibition as sort of a celebration. But then she'd met the snowboarders and now she had doubts about the lodge. Suddenly, she knew she had to tell him this now, while there was still a chance he'd listen.

"A P.I.?"

"His name is Jack Harding. I know Hollister said it was 'against the rules.'" She added air quotes in case he couldn't read her low opinion of Hollister's rules from just her tone. "But the way I see it, those rules are for you, Dalton and Griffin. I'm not competing for the money. I'm not technically in the game. So I figure I'm exempt. Which means I can hire anyone I want to find the heiress."

Cooper had crossed his arms over his chest and was watching her with an inscrutable expression.

She crossed to the kitchen counter, grabbed her tote bag and pulled out the few pages of emails from Jack that she'd printed out at the hotel business center. "I had him start looking for Ginger at the hotel where we held the Children's Hope Foundation gala." She flipped through the papers. "They had no idea who Ginger was, which seemed odd at first. But then the catering manager admitted that it wasn't unusual for them to hire temp waitstaff for events like that." She held out one of the papers to Cooper. "Here's the email from the temp agency. They don't have an employee named Ginger, either. Which made me think she must have given me a false name."

She paused, half expecting him to ask why Ginger would have done that. Portia looked at him expectantly, but he said nothing. Instead, he just stared at the page in front of him almost as if he wasn't even seeing it.

Then she continued, trying to recapture her previous interest in the search, but floundering a bit. When she and Jack had discussed all this, it had seemed like such a revelation. It had seemed important. "After all, when I talked with her, she'd just tipped a drink down my mother's back. She probably thought she was in trouble with her boss. So I asked Jack to go to the hotel and ask the other employees, which he did. And here's where it gets weird."

She paused again. This time, Cooper looked up at her, eyebrows raised infinitesimally.

"He talked to twenty-one employees and twelve of them remember a waitress matching her description, but no one remembers hiring her. Or paying her. And of those twelve employees, five of them remember different names. She's a phantom."

Cooper pushed the printouts back across the table toward

her, some of the tension in his expression fading. "I don't see what this has to do with anything. You found nothing."

She pushed the papers back defiantly. "This isn't nothing!"

"You didn't find her."

"No. I didn't find her real identity, but I definitely found her."

He tapped a finger in the center of the top page. "There's nothing here to indicate this is the woman at all."

"I found a woman who is trying very hard to hide her identity from us."

"Why on earth would she do that?"

"I think she knows we're looking for her. I think she knows she's Hollister's daughter." She was sure she was right. So sure about it that her heart was racing, slamming into her ribcage. "Everyone in Houston knows the Cains attend the Children's Hope gala. If she found out she was a Cain and just wanted to scope out the situation, that would be the perfect opportunity. She could walk in disguised as one of the waitstaff and watch the family members and see how they interact, all without revealing her identity to us."

"Your logic there is faulty," he said with a sneer. "You assume she's trying to hide her identity from *us*. When in fact, she may have no idea we exist. All we know for sure is that she's trying to hide her identity."

"What other reason could she have for showing up at the gala and working without getting paid?"

"She could be a pickpocket or a thief."

"Right. Your long-lost sister is a character in a Dickens novel." Why didn't he see it? Why was he so damn determined to make this complicated? "Or we could figure that maybe since the Cains have been searching for her for over a year that maybe somebody did something to tip their hand." She waited, heart still pounding, for some glimmer of interest from him. "Why are you so determined to downplay this? This is a clue about the identity of your sister."

He whirled on her. "No, it's not. You haven't discovered anything about her. This is just more information about a woman we're not even sure exists. What is it you expect me to feel here?"

She threw up her hands. "I don't know. I don't even care. I just want you to feel something."

"Why?" He stalked a step closer to her. "Why should I feel anything about this? Even if you actually found Hollister's daughter, even if she was standing right outside the door, why should I feel anything about her?"

"Because she's your sister."

"No. She's not. I don't have a sister. This woman, whoever she is, is just another one of Hollister's bastards. For all we know, there are dozens of women just like her. Hell, there are probably hundreds. So why the hell are we all so hot to find this one woman?"

"Because she's your sister," Portia repeated, softly this time, because she almost couldn't speak past the lump of emotion clogging her throat.

"I have nothing in common with this woman. Shared genetic code does not make her my family."

"Is that how you feel about Griffin and Dalton, too?"

"Yes."

"Even though you spent summers with them since you were ten."

"Yes."

"Even though you lived with them after your mom died? Even though Caro took you in?"

"The fact that I lived in the same house with them never made me part of the family."

Her frustration burst out. "You know what, you're right. It didn't." Now it was her turn to stalk closer to him. "You know what makes someone part of the family? Spending time with them. If you'd wanted to be part of the Cain family, then you damn well should have made an effort. For years, I invited you to visit. I invited you for Thanksgiving and Christmas. Every time we had any kind of family gathering, I invited you. You almost never showed up. Half the time you didn't even bother to reply, so don't bitch now about not being part of the family."

He tipped his head back and laughed. "That's great. Just great."

She blinked, startled by his mercurial mood shift. "What?"

"You. Giving me a hard time about not coming to family functions."

"Why is that funny?" He was still laughing and it unnerved her. What didn't she know?

"It's not funny so much as ironic." The laughter settled into a grin tinged with bitterness. "You ever think about why I didn't attend all those warm family gatherings?"

"You were busy. You had work and travel." She parroted the excuse he'd always given her. And then, so she wasn't the only one thrown off-balance, she added, "And I assume plenty of Swedish models to keep you occupied."

"Right. The Swedish models. Haven't you ever wondered why all those Swedish models bother you so much?"

He was clearly baiting her, so she bumped her chin up and narrowed her gaze. "As a feminist I don't like to see any woman devalue herself so much that she'll sleep with a guy merely because he has an Olympic medal."

He smirked. "Nice try, but no. The Swedish models bother you for the same reason I never came to Cain holiday functions."

She frowned. "There's no connection—"

"I stayed away all those years because I knew I was attracted to you. I stayed away because I knew you felt it, too."

She wanted to protest, but all her words were encased in shock. And he didn't give her a chance to say anything anyway.

He closed the distance between them in a few quick steps and cupped her jaw in his hands. His touch was gentle, but firm, unrelenting, so that she had no choice but to meet his gaze.

"There's been an attraction between us since that day in the church. I've wanted you. I stayed away because it was easier than being around seeing you married to my brother."

She shook her head. "I would never have—"

"I know that. You're a good person, maybe the best person I know. Decent in a way that Dalton didn't even deserve. And I know you never would have acted on that attraction. But that wouldn't have stopped me from being the jerk who tried to tempt you. So I stayed away."

She just stood there, staring into his amazing blue eyes, watching the emotions flicker in his gaze. A horrible pain spread through her chest, crushing her lungs, breaking her heart.

Because until now, she hadn't been ready to face the real reason they couldn't be together—her relationship with Dalton. Sure, they'd talked about Dalton and about her marriage, but neither of them had gone so far as to admit that this attraction had been simmering for years.

As long as this was just a fling, it didn't matter. It was just between the two of them and neither of them had to face the reality of what a relationship would mean.

"You're right," she said numbly.

"I am."

"I mean, yes, there always has been something between us. Neither of us ever would have acted on it, but it was there. And as long as this was just a mindless fling, I could pretend that none of this—what's happening now—had any connection to my real life. But I don't think I can pretend that anymore."

He just stared at her blankly. "So then we're over," he finally said.

His words made her heart break a little more, even though she had no idea why, because their relationship had always had a sell-by date. They were never going to last forever, so why did it hurt so much to end it?

"Yes."

He strode over to her and grabbed her arms, pulling her toward him just a little, searching her expression. "I'm not okay with this."

"I'm not, either," she admitted. "But what's the alternative? That we start dating? That I take you home to meet my parents? That we tell your brother that we're sleeping together? For what? All because we happen to enjoy each other's company in bed? Look, I know that's not how this works. Women are like accessories to you. The naughty models and Olympic scandal were for the rebellious stage of your life. But now that you want respectability, you're going for the nice rich girl and the high-end hotel. This has been fun, but I never expected it to last forever."

She purposely threw his words back at him. It was petty of her, the way she wanted to hurt him just a little bit because he'd hurt her so much, but she did it anyway.

He dropped her arms and stepped back. "No. I guess neither of us wants that." He shook his head, letting out a bitter little laugh. "But I'm still not okay with it."

"Well, if you don't like that, then you're really not going to like this. I don't think this is a good idea."

"You and I?" he asked grimly. "I think we just covered this territory."

"Not you and I. This. Turning Bear Creek Lodge into a luxury resort."

His gaze narrowed. "You've gotten too attached to it, haven't you? You got caught up in the romanticism of the history and—"

"That's not it." He started to say something else, but she held up her hands to cut him off. "Stop interrupting me and let me get this out. It's not that I don't want you messing up the lodge. It's that I think anything you do to this place is getting in your own way."

"That doesn't even make sense."

"Yes, it does. You're so sure that there's a market for a high-end resort for snowboarders, and I'm sure you're right. But would you actually want to hang out with the snowboarder who would come here? I've met your friends. They would come here because you're here, but they wouldn't come here just for the resort."

"You think Drew and Stevey and those guys are my friends?"

"They came here to help you, didn't they?"

"They came here for the snow."

"No. They came here for you. Because they think you're great. You weren't out there when they were building the jump. You didn't hear the things they said about you. I know you think they were just hitting on me, but you're wrong. It never even crossed their minds, because they all assumed we were together. They all talked you up to me. They may enjoy the powder, but they came here for you. Because you're their friend."

For a second, he just stared at her, like he couldn't quite wrap his brain around her words. Then his gaze dropped and he gave a little nod. "Maybe."

"And if I had to guess, I'd say you genuinely like them,

too. That you admire them more than you do some jerk like Robertson or your father."

His lips twisted into a smile. "That's obvious."

"So then why are you so desperate to prove yourself to Robertson and Hollister? Why do you give a damn what they think? Why not do whatever the hell you want to with this lodge? Why not market it to people whose opinion matters to you?"

When he looked back up at her, his expression was flat. "I'm marketing it to people like you."

She felt a stab of pain near her heart. "Exactly. You're marketing to people like me."

People who he thought cared about luxury and style more than substance.

"Don't you get it?" she asked. "You're marketing this hotel to people you don't really like. People you wouldn't want to spend time with. I think it's a mistake."

He just looked at her. "After all this work we've both put into this, now you're telling me? What's the point?"

"The point is, I'm not going to be around to tell you these things next week or the week after. If I think you're making a mistake, I have to tell you now. Now is all I have."

That had seemed so simple just a few weeks ago. But in this moment, it broke her heart to admit it aloud.

She waited to see if he would acknowledge her words, if he would admit that she was right. But instead, he just shook his head.

"You're wrong. Beck's Lodge is going to be amazing. It's the best thing I can do with Flight+Risk."

She wanted to keep arguing with him, but what else could she say? In the end, it was his decision. Maybe Bear Creek Lodge would be his downfall after all. It had certainly been hers.

Fifteen

Until she saw the resort through Cooper's eyes, she hadn't realized how much she had accomplished. It about killed her, because she still knew that this was a mistake; there was just nothing she could do to convince Cooper of it. Still, if she blocked out how miserable this was going to eventually make him, if she pretended this was just a business move and not deeply personal, then she could appreciate the amazing changes in Bear Creek Lodge.

The only renovations they'd done to the building itself were to demolish the ancient registration desk and pull up the carpet to restore the original hardwood floors.

All the other changes were staging. She'd moved out the aging lobby furniture and replaced it with only a few clusters of chairs. A small stage had been set up in the corner for the band she'd hired. Buffet tables had been set up where the registration desk had once been. The rest was lighting, lighting, lighting. It was amazing how you could manipulate the beauty of a room by highlighting its best features and casting its bad ones in shadow. Portia took comfort knowing that when the guests arrived this evening for the exhibition kickoff, they would have to look very closely to see the toll that the past sixty years had taken on the once-glorious lodge. It was small comfort, but she took it where she could get it.

In fact, things appeared perfect as Portia strolled around the room, surveying everything. The guests would start arriving in the next thirty minutes. The caterers was already putting out appetizers. The band—a popular cover band from Provo—was already set up in the corner.

Cooper walked up to her, stopping to survey the room. He stood close, but pointedly didn't touch her. There was space between them that hadn't been there before. An immeasurable gulf of misunderstandings and cross-purposes.

Part of her yearned for his touch—nothing romantic or sexual—just something comforting. But he didn't reach for her and she didn't budge in his direction, either. She'd dressed in a pair of navy palazzo pants and a flowing top with just a little bit of shimmer to it. Her hair was swept up into a relaxed twist. She hoped that she looked cool and wealthy. Like the perfect hostess for this event, even if she didn't feel like it on the inside.

"Everything looks just right," he said, his tone cold. "I knew you could pull it off."

She turned to look at him. "We haven't pulled it off yet. We still have the rest of the evening to get through and tomorrow. And that's just the beginning, right? After that, we have to see if you've convinced any investors that this is a safe bet. Or if you can sway the board. There are still a lot of ifs in play."

Cooper looked around the room, his gaze taking on a possessive glint. "No. There aren't. This place looks amazing. No one who comes here is going to have any doubts that this is meant to be."

Her stomach soured and she knew he was right. He was so determined—so focused—it was impossible to believe that he wouldn't succeed. Even though this was the last thing he needed.

The party was in full swing a few hours later when Cooper looked up from talking to one of the investor types to see the last man he would have expected walking through the front doors—his brother Dalton. Laney was on his arm. Dalton paused just inside the door to help her out of her coat, which he handed to the attendant. Laney looked lovely in a vibrant yellow dress. Once her coat was off, they both stepped aside to reveal Griffin and his wife, Sydney, right behind them.

Jesus. It was like a Cain family reunion.

Who the hell had invited them?

Before the thought could even settle in his mind, Portia crossed to their side. She gave Laney and Sydney hugs and brief air kisses. And then Dalton gave her a real hug. Somehow the sight of that made Cooper's gut twist with jealousy. Not the superficial jealousy that he'd felt about Drew and Stevey, but something deep and dark. Something rooted in a lifetime of resentment.

By the time he reached them, Portia was shaking Griffin's hand with a friendly smile.

"Dalton. Griffin." Cooper nodded. "I didn't realize you'd been invited."

"I invited them," Portia said smoothly.

"You did?" Cooper turned to look at Portia, who smiled back innocently.

"Yes. Did you know, Cooper, that Sydney's youngest brother has an interest in snowboarding?"

"I did not know that," he said through a tight smile.

"Trust me, it's not something I encourage." Sydney laughed. "But we all wanted to see what you've been up to." To Portia she added, "After all the praise you heaped on this place, we're hoping it was a real showstopper."

"And what do you think?" Portia asked with a smile.

"It's amazing," Laney said. "I can see why you're so enthusiastic."

He shot Portia a look, trying to read her expression. Had she invited Dalton and Laney before or after she'd decided this whole project was a crappy idea? Had she invited them to support him or prove a point?

The band was playing a song from the sixties. The kind of classic anyone would love to get up and dance to, and the crowd was eating it up.

"You should go dance," Portia said. She pulled out her phone, where she somehow had the queue of songs listed. "The next song is a jazz ballad. It'll be perfect. After that, I can fill you in on the fascinating history of the building and tell you all about Cooper's plans."

Right on cue, the band drifted from the dance classic to a sultry jazz standard.

Portia smiled at him as if she hadn't just fed him to the wolves. "Perhaps you'd ask me to dance, Cooper?"

He wanted to tip his head back and howl with frustration. He wanted to storm out, find a board somewhere and get lost in the icy snow. To walk away from her and everything she represented, everything he couldn't have. Because he couldn't have her, no matter how much he wanted her. Instead, he took her arm and led her out onto the dance floor, relishing the feel of her body against his even as his anger threatened to boil over. But he tamped that all down, and grasped her hand in his. He let his fingers rest at the small of her back, just where her blouse hung loose, so that his fingertips grazed her bare skin.

"That was a nice trick," he said. "You invite them here just to prove a point?"

She met his gaze coolly. "Yes, but probably not the point you think."

"Okay, I'll bite. What point are you trying to make? That I don't have what it takes to open this hotel? That in the end, I'll always be outclassed by Dalton and Griffin?"

"See? I knew you were going to misinterpret things." Despite her chiding words, she smiled up at him. There was something sad and heartbreaking about her smile. "I invited them here because you hadn't seen them in years."

"Thanks to Hollister's stupid quest and their weddings, I've seen more of them in the past year than I ever have."

"I hardly think meeting against the backdrop of Hollister's ridiculous challenge counts as fertile ground for a healthy brotherly relationship."

"That's assuming I want that kind of relationship."

She stopped dancing. They were in the middle of the dance floor, and other couples moved around them seamlessly in time to the music. "I think you've spent so much of your life resenting them just because they're Hollister's sons that you no longer know what you want, let alone what you need." She continued to meet his gaze unflinchingly. "You need friends that appreciate you for who you are. You need a family that loves you. The thing is, you already have those things. They're right there. You just refuse to acknowledge them."

"And this seemed like a great idea? To drop this on me right now?"

She tipped her head slightly to the side. "No. Not at all. But when else do I have? You and I are over after this weekend. This is my last chance."

"You think you know exactly what I need? Just like you think you know what I should do with Beck's Lodge?"

"No. I don't care what you do with this place. I love this building, but I only care about what you need. Make it into a hotel or don't. But you know what I think you do need? You need more people in your life who care about you. Either way, I don't want to be your excuse for not having a relationship with your family."

"I don't need a relationship with them."

"Yes. You do. Everybody needs family. And you're the one who told me you've stayed away from yours for years because of me. I'm not okay with that. I don't want to stand between you and your brothers."

He dropped his hands from her body. "So. That's what this is about?"

"Your relationship with the Cains? That's what this has been about for a while now."

"No. That's not what I meant." A few of the other couples had noticed that they weren't dancing, so he stepped closer to her and pulled her back into his arms. This time, he felt only cold anger as he held her. "You just can't resist fixing people, can you?"

She frowned, looking off-balance for the first time tonight. "I don't...I don't know what you mean."

"You think I want to be another one of your charity projects? Like the heiress you're so determined to protect? Like Caro? Like those foster kids you plan to adopt?"

"I don't... That's not what this is."

"Are you sure?" Doubt flickered through her gaze and just like that his anger dissolved into something softer but no less painful. How could he still be angry with her? "You are so damn sensitive. You care so much about other people. You can't help it. But I am not another fixer-upper. I will not be an object of pity for you."

He dropped his hands from her body and this time he walked away. He was done dancing.

She must have been done, as well, because at the end of the night, when the last busload of guests went back down the mountain to the hotel in Provo, she went with them. And she didn't come back the next day.

Sixteen

Cooper had consumed her life for those brief weeks she'd been at Bear Creek Lodge.

The whole time she'd been there, part of her had been convinced they were going to fail. That Bear Creek Lodge would be Cooper's folly. It had never occurred to her that it would be her own.

And yet the exhibition had been a huge success. She had seen that even though she'd left partway through. The lodge had looked amazing. The guests had had a fabulous time. More importantly, the guests who were also investors had been impressed.

She had left Utah with no doubt at all that Cooper would be able to purchase, renovate and open Bear Creek Lodge. Either his own board would support the decision and the resort would open under the Flight+Risk name or other investors would step forward. She wouldn't be surprised if he'd already received numerous offers. Offers she would never know anything about.

She still didn't believe opening the lodge would make him happy, but what could she do? She'd tried her best to give him an opening to repair his relationship with his brothers. She couldn't do any more than that—other than hope.

Before leaving Bear Creek Lodge, she'd cleared out the little room she'd stayed in occasionally—the room she and Cooper had made love in. She'd headed back into Provo for the night and taken the first flight out in the morning. She hadn't even waited for the first flight to Texas, but instead had just headed east. Between long flights and rushed connections, it took her almost eighteen hours to get back to her cozy house near the Galleria. It felt like years had passed since she'd been there.

She didn't even give herself a chance to settle in but immediately called Jack Harding for the latest update on the missing heiress. Then she printed up all the information in the file and delivered it to Caro. Caro might be too proud to tell her sons about the state of her finances. She might be too proud to ask for help from anyone. But it had occurred to Portia that if Caro found the heiress on her own and presented the information to Dalton and Griffin, then they would almost definitely split the money with her. It was the simplest and easiest solution.

And Portia felt like an idiot for not thinking of it sooner. Instead, she'd come up with a solution that had complicated everyone's lives.

After that, like a bear going to ground for winter, she hunkered down, living like a shut-in for a week, talking on the phone only to her mother, who was baffled by her behavior.

Of course her mother—being a supreme gossip hound— had heard all about the exhibition and Portia's part in it.

There were phone calls—lots of them—from her mother. Fretful ones. Anxious ones. Critical ones.

It took a week for Celeste to run out of things to say. Portia knew Celeste could have held out a lot longer if Portia had given her anything to work with. But Portia refused to comment or defend herself, so eventually Celeste ran out of steam and left Portia alone. After that, Celeste had just ordered Portia to get herself together in time for the next gala on the society schedule.

It wasn't until two days later when her doorbell rang that she decided she'd had enough. For once in her life, her mother just needed to bug off.

Except it wasn't her mother at the door. It was Laney.

Portia just stood there in her yoga pants and Scooby Doo T-shirt, gaping at the sight of the woman on her doorstep. Laney's pregnancy was just beginning to show and she had an adorable little bump tenting her vintage dress, a bump that her gorgeous gown from the other night had hidden. Her hair looked thick and glossy. Her cheeks glowed. She did not look like she'd spent the past week watching Nicholas Sparks movies and eating Pizza Rolls. And an entire Sara Lee pound cake.

Unfortunately, Portia was pretty sure that's exactly what she looked like.

Laney seemed not to notice. Instead, she threw her arms around Portia and gave her a rib-crunching hug. The bag Laney was holding swung around and bumped Portia's hip.

"Okay, I know it's weird, me coming over," she said as she pulled back. "But your mom called Dalton and asked him to come talk to you. He said that was a sure sign things were bad and that he really should come. But I thought him coming would be even weirder. Besides, he clearly didn't even know what to say and he wasn't going to bring ice cream. Or any kinds of snacks. At all. Men."

Brushing past Portia, she held up the bag and gave it a jiggle. "I didn't know if you were a sweet snacker or a savory snacker, so I brought some of each." She plopped down on the sofa and started putting things out on the coffee table. "We have chips, guac, salsa, wasabi nuts, chocolate-covered almonds and five different flavors of Ben & Jerry's. What's your poison?"

Portia could only stare in amazement as Laney made herself at home. Laney.

Laney Cain was in her house. Her ex-husband's current wife had to visit. Apparently to make sure Portia was prepped for the zombie apocalypse.

That was bizarre, right?

"What are you doing here?" she asked stupidly.

Laney looked up, her cheeks flushing. "Look, I know it's weird." She looked down at the table and nudged the various jars of things so that they all lined up perfectly. "Everyone is really worried about you. When we saw you in Provo, we thought something was up between you and Cooper. We thought maybe something—" she gave an awkward shrug and tried to smile "—good. Dalton thought it was weird at first, but he got used to the idea. We were hopeful. Except you came back here early and Cooper's completely incommunicado, which just made us think maybe we should be worried. No one wanted to tell Caro because Hollister took a turn for the worse the other day and she's busy with that."

"Everyone's worried about me?"

"Yes! Sydney offered to come by instead of me, but she and Griffin are leaving the country tomorrow morning. But if you need them, they'll postpone the trip." She gave a little shrug. "Look, I know you probably don't like me. I can't blame you. And you don't even have to talk to me. You can just take my food and show me to the door. But if you want a friendly ear and a shoulder to cry on, you've got it. Besides, we're family, so you know whatever you tell me isn't going any further."

What could she say to that?

No, she didn't like Laney. She was the love of Dalton's life. Of course, Portia didn't like her.

Still, she was floored by the idea that Laney considered her family—let alone that she would go to all this effort on her behalf. The fact that Griffin and Sydney were talking about canceling their trip—for her—was baffling. Yes, she still had a good relationship with Caro, but she'd figured she was persona non grata with the rest of the Cains.

She walked over to the table and picked up the five pints of ice cream. "These will melt if we leave them out too long."

She headed off into the kitchen, wanting to steal a moment alone. She shoved the ice cream in the freezer and then stood there for several long heartbeats, her forehead pressed to the front of it. Mostly just feeling sorry for herself.

Then Laney said, from the doorway, "Dalton said you were too smart to let a guy like Cooper break your heart, but me…I know smart has nothing to do with it."

Part of her wanted to yell at Laney. Or have a temper tantrum. Or maybe just throw up her hands and cry.

She whirled around to face Laney. "Look, I appreciate the gesture. Thank you for coming and trying to help or whatever, but it's just too weird, okay? I'm not going to cry on your shoulder. There's not enough Ben & Jerry's in the world for that."

Laney just stared at her, an expression of sympathy on her face. Then she said softly, "You take care of a lot of people. Would it kill you to let someone take care of you for a change?"

Portia tilted her head to the side and just looked at Laney, trying to see past the layers of complication that separated them. She tried to imagine opening up to this woman, spilling her guts, crying her eyes out, eating Phish Food straight out of the container.

But she just couldn't see it.

So instead of bursting into tears and throwing herself into Laney's waiting arms, she answered the question that still hung in the air. "Yes. I think today it would kill me to let you take care of me. I can handle a lot, but I can't handle pity from you."

Laney looked like the protest she wanted to make was clawing its way out of her throat. But finally, she nodded, slowly crying the tears Portia wouldn't let herself shed. "Would it be better if it was one of the other Cains?"

Portia shook her head. There was only one Cain she wanted to see.

"Okay. I'll go," Laney said. But at the door she stopped and added, "You're wrong, though. It's not pity that brought me here. I know what it's like to be alone. To feel like you have no family. Not wanting you to feel like that isn't pity."

Laney left then, without giving Portia a chance to reply. She waited until she heard Laney's car drive off before she let the tears fall.

Cooper didn't know what to do with himself the next week, despite the fact that the rest of the weekend went off without a hitch. If Portia's quick departure could be considered without a hitch. Portia had planned everything so well that things ran smoothly without her. The guests were impressed. The snowboarders had a great time. The media ohhed and ahhed. By the following week, several investors had already approached him about buying in. By the week after that, his board, Robertson included, was clamoring to move forward and commit Flight+Risk to the project.

And none of it mattered.

He felt none of the joy or satisfaction he should have felt at his success.

In fact, he felt nothing at all, until he came home to his loft in Denver one night to find Dalton waiting on his doorstep. Even then, it was only mild surprise.

"Hey," he said with a nod as he opened the door.

Dalton waited until they'd entered the condo, then asked, "Did you sleep with Portia?"

Cooper didn't answer, but Dalton must have seen the truth in his face, because he hauled off and straight up punched him.

Cooper staggered back a step in surprise. "What the hell?"

He didn't have a chance to recover though because Dalton slammed into him again, this time shoulder first into his chest, plowing him back several steps until they both went feet over ass over the arm of the sofa.

"What the hell?" he asked again.

Still Dalton threw another punch. At that point, Cooper was just done. He caught Dalton with a jab to the kidneys. Dalton grunted and tried to dodge the blow. Cooper rolled on top of his brother and landed one more solid punch in Dalton's stomach before scrambling back. "I don't want to hurt you."

Dalton pushed himself up, the rage on his face dimming somewhat. "Yeah, well, I still want to hurt you."

"Why?" Cooper asked.

"Portia," Dalton answered, panting and rubbing his hand across his kidneys. "Because you screwed with Portia."

"Oh." Shock rocked him back on his heels. It took him a few seconds to process what his brother was saying. Then he pushed himself to his feet and stood, holding out his hand to Dalton. As he pulled Dalton up, he asked, "You want to hit me some more?"

"Yeah. I do." He rubbed his hand down his cheek and flexed his jaw. "But I think I'll give it a rest."

Cooper nodded and headed for his refrigerator. He pulled out two Sierra Nevadas, popped them both open and handed one to Dalton. "She's not yours."

Dalton glared at him before taking a long draw from the beer. "You think I don't know that? Of course she's not mine." He muttered something under his breath that sounded like *dumbass*. "But who the hell else does she have to come kick the ass of the guy who broke her heart?"

Cooper froze, the beer not quite to this mouth. That statement gave him pause for several reasons. First off, apparently he'd broken her heart. He'd known he'd hurt her. He'd known he'd pissed her off. He had not known he'd broken her heart. Secondly, apparently she'd shared this news with Dalton. Which surprised the hell out of him. But to Dalton, he merely said, "No one kicked your ass when you broke her heart."

"Someone should have."

Cooper raised his beer slightly in toast. "You wanna have another go? I'll do it right now."

Dalton ignored the jab and said, "Portia is an only child. Her parents are selfish nightmares. She's essentially alone in the world. You wouldn't know it to look at her, but she doesn't make friends easily." He took a drag of beer. "I did a lot of things wrong when I was with her, but I always treated her with respect. And I have a hell of a lot of admiration for her. She deserves better than to be jerked around by someone like you."

"Yeah. I couldn't agree more." The words were out of his mouth before he even knew he was saying them. "She does deserve better. If I thought for a second that she really did love me, then things would be different."

Dalton eyed him for a long moment. "So you're just

going to leave it at that? You're just going to let her go? You're not even going to try to fight for her? Because you never struck me as the kind of guy who would back down from a fight."

"I'm not."

Finally, Dalton shook his head, a smile pulling at his lips. "Then what the hell are you doing here? If you want to be with her, then you should be in Houston, begging her to take you back."

Seventeen

Having Laney come to her house was just what Portia needed to pull herself out of her funk. There were a lot of things Portia could put up with, but being pitied by Laney was not one of them. She was done moping around.

Still, it was hard to get back to her normal routine when she didn't really have a normal routine. Much of her life was defined by the fund-raising schedule for Children's Hope Foundation and the other organizations she worked with, but this was a particularly slow time of year for her. However, she did follow up and make an appointment with a social worker she knew. The process of adopting through the foster system was totally different than the private adoption she'd been pursuing with the adoption lawyer. She was starting over. If she was going to adopt then she had a lot of paperwork to get started on. There were classes to take and applications to fill out. She had enough to keep her so busy she wouldn't have time to think about Cooper. Almost.

She was just returning from her appointment when she noticed an unusual car parked in front of her house. But then she saw it was a sporty model with a rental agency sticker on the back and she only knew one guy who rented a sports car every time he came to Houston. Her foot hesitated on the accelerator as she pulled into the driveway, tempted, if only briefly, to drive right on past and ignore Cooper's presence.

But that would be cowardly, and Cooper wasn't the kind of man who would take being put off forever.

He was sitting on her doorstep, waiting, and he stood when she climbed out of the car.

He was dressed in jeans and a navy Henley that made the blue in his eyes seem deeper and more mysterious. His expression was dark and heated as he looked at her. He held a leather-bound book in his hands. The very sight of him made her heart race and her knees weak. How could she be this close to him and not just throw herself in his arms? Why was he here? What could he possibly want?

Despite her endless questions, she didn't say anything, but just unlocked the door to let him in.

"We had a deal," he said as she shut the door behind them.

It took her a second to realize what he was talking about. "We did. I held up my end of it."

He nodded, holding the book out to her. "You never gave me a chance to hold up my end of the bargain. I'm supposed to help you find the heiress."

She looked at him suspiciously. "What's this?"

"It's my mother's journal."

"And how is this supposed to help me?"

He ducked his head for a second, scrubbing his palm over his hair before meeting her gaze again. "Just look at it, okay?"

She flipped open the book and thumbed through the pages. There were handwritten pages interspersed with newspaper clippings. All articles about Hollister or Cain Enterprises.

"I don't understand," she said.

"When I was a kid, my mother was obsessed with Hollister. She was convinced that their brief fling was true love. That he was going to divorce Caro and marry her. She read and collected everything about him. She got the Houston newspapers for years so that she could clip the articles. This book is all the information she had about him. It's from about the time when he probably had the affair with the heiress's mother. I don't know if there's anything in there or not. Maybe there's some clue about what Hollister was up to. It might help."

Portia stared at the pages in front of her, unable to stop looking. Without taking her eyes from the book, she backed up to the sofa and slowly sat down. The journal was detailed. Exhaustive. As Cooper had said, obsessive.

Cooper had brought it to her because it might have information about Hollister's life, but she couldn't help thinking about the glimpse into Cooper's life it provided. What had it been like to grow up with a mother like this? How had it shaped Cooper's view of the Cains? Of the world?

Almost as if he had read her mind, he said, "I don't want you to think she was crazy."

She glanced up, her heart breaking a little at the protective glint in his gaze. No matter what else he thought about his mother, he had loved her. He still did.

"I don't think that," she said.

"They had met when she was skiing in Europe. She was a model. It was her first international photo shoot. She got pregnant. Her modeling career was over. Her parents hadn't wanted her to go into modeling and refused to take her back in when they found out she was going to have a baby. She didn't have a lot of options."

"But Hollister supported her, right?"

"Yeah. She didn't have any education. She didn't make good choices with the money. She paid for skiing lessons and vacations in Vale, but we lived in crap apartments." He let out a laugh that was sad and bitter and lonely. It was the laugh of countless disappointed hopes. Of crushed paternal affection. "She wanted us to be ready for the good life when Hollister came back and married her."

Portia carefully closed the book and set it on the coffee table before standing. She wanted more than anything to pull him into her arms. To stroke his back. To comfort the child he'd been. To protect that boy from the heartless cruelty Hollister had undoubtedly bestowed.

She knew what a bastard Hollister was. Yes, he'd been charming and handsome and charismatic when he wanted to be. But all that covered a ruthless ambition and a lack of concern for others that bordered on sociopathic.

When she thought of Cooper as a child—hopeful, energetic, eager—coming face-to-face with his own father's apathy…well, when she thought of that, she wanted to drive across town and drive a stake through Hollister's heart, because surely monsters like him could only be killed that way.

However, she didn't pull Cooper into her arms, because she knew if their positions had been reversed, if it had been her revealing that information, she wouldn't have wanted comfort. Wasn't she the one just the other day who'd told Laney to leave because she couldn't stand her pity? Wasn't she the one who—

Ah, screw it.

She threw herself at him, and he caught her. She held

on tight, trying to squeeze a lifetime of love into that one embrace.

For the first time, there was nothing sexual about his embrace. It was just comforting.

After a moment, he whispered, "I didn't come here for your pity."

"This isn't pity," she whispered back against his chest.

"I told you, Portia, I need you to believe I'm a man of my word. I needed to fulfill my end of the bargain."

"I don't care about the heiress anymore!" Her voice rose, and she hugged him more tightly. "I don't know why I ever did, but—"

"I know why you cared about the heiress." He pulled back just far enough to tip her chin up so she met his gaze. "You cared about her because she'll probably have trouble fitting into this world and you've always had trouble fitting into it, too. You cared about her because you care about everyone, even when you don't show it. I'm just hoping that you care more about me than you've been letting on. I didn't come here to fulfill the bargain we made, I came here because I want a second chance."

"A second chance at what?"

"I want a second chance to make you fall in love with me."

This time, she wrenched herself out of his arms with such force, he had no choice but to let her go. "Don't you get it? I'm already in love with you! Why do you think I couldn't stay in Utah?" He didn't answer, so she turned to look at him. A grin split his face. "This isn't funny!"

"I'm not laughing. I'm happy." He took several steps toward her, but she held up her hands palm out to stop him.

"I don't know why you're happy about it, because I'm sure not. You think you want me now, but how long is that going to last? Forget whether or not I'm in love with you,

I'm not coming back to Colorado with you. I'm not turning my life upside down to be with you only to have you get bored in a few weeks and then decide you'd rather have another no-pressure fling with some Swedish model."

He ignored her outstretched hands and closed in on her. But instead of taking her into his arms again, he stopped a half foot away from her. Still, he had backed her against a wall. She had nowhere to go and nothing to do but hear him out.

"I'm not going to change my mind about this. Don't you get it? I'm all-in. Remember when I said you should never let the person you're negotiating with see how desperate you are? Well, I came here because I'm done pretending I'm not desperate," he said softly. "I can't blame you for not trusting me. I fought this tooth and nail. I did everything I could to keep from falling in love with you." He gestured toward the book where it lay on her coffee table. "Can you blame me? Knowing my family history, can you blame me for being afraid to lose myself in love?"

She shook her head. "No, I can't. But love doesn't have to be like that."

He pulled her roughly back into his arms. "But it feels like that. When we're together, I feel crazy and out of control. I feel jealous and obsessive. And it terrifies me. And the only thing I can hope is that maybe it'll all be okay, because maybe, just maybe you love me back. Maybe I can make you understand you're the most important thing in the world to me. I've screwed up before. You probably don't want to believe that I can do this, that I can be there for you. But I can."

"Cooper—"

"Let me finish, Portia." His voice was forceful and loving and so, so right that it reached deep inside of her. It turned her fears on their heads and shook her resolve.

"I realize this isn't orderly and it doesn't fit into your plan. You can't make a list about this. But I see you, I see the real you and I want you more than I've ever wanted anything in my life. I love you more than I've ever loved anyone."

He paused, took a deep breath. "I know this scares you. It scared me, too. I know you've been hurt before. And maybe it would be easier, safer, if we just walked away from this. But I can't do that. Loving you is the biggest risk I've ever taken in my life, and I know—*I know*—that it's going come with the biggest payoff. If you'll just believe me. If you'll just trust me. If I've learned anything in my life, it's that some things are worth any risk.

"For me, that's you, Portia. You can't be predicted. And I want nothing more than to ride this thing for the rest of our lives. I promise you, if you just trust me, if you just let go, I'll hang on to you with everything I have." He reached up, ran his fingers softly down her cheek. "I'm hanging on to you, Portia. Hang on to me. Please."

Her heart stuttered in her chest. She wanted to believe him so badly that it was an open, aching wound inside of her. She loved him, adored him, wanted him more than she'd ever wanted anything in her life. But could she reach out and take him? Could she do what he said and trust him enough to hang on forever—through the good and the bad, the dangerous and the delightful?

His face moved closer to her, his sapphire eyes bright with hope and love and a need so great it shook her world, turned it upside down. At that moment she was on the edge of a precipice, balanced on the side of a cliff looking down into the yawning emptiness her life would be without him. The same yawning emptiness that had echoed inside her from the moment she walked away from him in Utah.

"Portia—" he started, but this time she was the one who interrupted him.

Lifting one shaky hand to his face, she covered his mouth with her fingers. "I'm scared, Cooper."

"I know, baby. But—"

"Let me finish." She smiled at him. "I've never been a risk taker. I've always played it safe, always done what others expected me to do. But this time, this time I'm going to do what I want. What I need.

"I need you, Cooper. I've always needed you—I just didn't know it. But I do now. And if you want, I'm yours. For now. For tomorrow. Forever."

His face lit up like the sun and he grabbed on to her, pulled her into his arms. And she went, without protest, without struggle, with her heart and her arms open wide. And it felt so good.

If she'd known letting go would be this easy, she would have done it a long, long time ago.

She lifted her face for his kiss and as his lips touched hers, she realized that no, she wouldn't have. Because everything she'd done, everything she'd been through, had been leading her here, to this moment. To Cooper. To the life they would have together. Messy and imperfect though it would be, it was a life she would hang on to with everything she had. Because she was his and he was hers. Forever.

When he lifted his head, he said, "Would you really move to Colorado for me?"

She considered the issue for a moment. "I'm sure not going to ask a snowboarder to move to Houston where it's hot and muggy and never, ever snows. Why? What were you thinking?"

"Actually, I was hoping we might split our time three ways. I need to be in Denver at least half of the time—I can't move Flight+Risk, but I can work remotely a lot. But I wouldn't mind giving Houston a try some of the time. After all, you're the one who keeps telling me I need to be closer to Dalton and Griffin."

She arched up on her toes and kissed him. "Thank you for trying. I would hate it if you let me get in the way of being close to them."

"Yeah. I got that."

"But what's the third place?"

"Bear Creek Lodge. You were right. I got plenty of investors who are interested in funding the resort. Now I just have to decide how to parlay that into something we both can live with. You're right about that, too. I don't want the place overrun by a bunch of trust fund brats."

"You do realize I'm a trust fund brat, right?"

He ignored her jab. "I need you to help me find a happy medium. Someplace you and I can both be comfortable. The way I see it, you and I are both misfits. We need someplace we can both fit in. And maybe someday, if we adopt a bunch of misfit kids, they'll fit in, too. Do you think we can do that?"

He was searching her face, as if he still couldn't believe she loved him. She rose up on her toes and kissed him again. "Yeah. I'm pretty sure I can do that."

After a long minute, he asked, "Is it going to be weird for you?"

"What?"

"Being with me. Since I have the Cain eyes. You're the one who said you'd spent ten years gazing into these eyes." He looked a little sheepish. "I mean, that's got to be weird for you, right? Having me look at you with these same eyes."

She pushed up onto her toes and pressed a long slow kiss to his lips. Then she cupped his cheek and answered him.

"You look at me like I'm the most precious woman in the world. Like you know all of my crazy flaws and love me for them. You look at me with eyes of love. Dalton never looked at me like that."

With those words, he crushed her against him and ground his mouth to hers. A long time later, she pulled away from him and asked, "What would you have done if I'd said it did bother me?"

"I would have bought a lot of sunglasses."

* * * * *

If this new Megan tried to play on his sympathy, it wasn't going to work.

So help him, whatever it took, he was going to nail her to the wall.

She'd been looking straight ahead, but now she turned toward him with a frown. "Is something wrong, Cal? Another crisis back home?"

He managed a wry laugh. "Not that I know of. I could say I was just passing through and decided to stop by…" He saw the flash of skepticism in her caramel-colored eyes. "But you wouldn't believe me, would you?"

"No." A smile tugged a corner of her luscious mouth. The sort of mouth made for kissing. When was the last time she'd been kissed? he caught himself wondering.

But never mind that. He was here for just one reason.

Although, if getting to the truth involved kissing her, he wouldn't complain.

A SINFUL
SEDUCTION

BY
ELIZABETH LANE

Published in Great Britain 2014
by Mills & Boon, an imprint of Harlequin (UK) Limited,
Eton House, 18-24 Paradise Road, Richmond, Surrey, TW9 1SR

© 2014 Elizabeth Lane

ISBN: 978-0-263-91470-2

51-0614

Harlequin (UK) Limited's policy is to use papers that are natural, renewable and recyclable products and made from wood grown in sustainable forests. The logging and manufacturing processes conform to the legal environmental regulations of the country of origin.

Printed and bound in Spain
by Blackprint CPI, Barcelona

Elizabeth Lane has lived and traveled in many parts of the world, including Europe, Latin America and the Far East, but her heart remains in the American West, where she was born and raised. Her idea of heaven is hiking a mountain trail on a clear autumn day. She also enjoys music, animals and dancing. You can learn more about Elizabeth by visiting her website, www.elizabethlaneauthor.com.

For Pat, my wonderful sister
who loves Africa

One

San Francisco, California, February 11

The headline on Page 2 slammed Cal Jeffords in the face.

**Two Years Later
Exec's Widow, Foundation Cash
Are Both Still Missing**

Swearing like a longshoreman, Cal crumpled the morning paper in his fist. The last thing he needed was a reminder that today was the second anniversary of his best friend and business partner's suicide. And he didn't need that grainy file photo to help him remember Nick and his wife, Megan, with her movie-star beauty, her designer clothes, her multimillion-dollar showplace of a home and her appalling lack of human decency that let her steal from a charity and then leave her husband to carry the blame.

With a grunt of frustration, he crammed the newspaper into the waste basket.

He had no doubt that the whole ugly mess was Megan's fault. But the questions that still haunted him two years later were *how* and *why?* Had Megan coerced Nick into complying? Had the demands of their lavish lifestyle driven Nick Rafferty to embezzle millions from J-COR's charity foundation? Or had Megan embezzled the money herself and forced her husband to take the blame? She'd had plenty of opportunities to siphon off the cash her fund-raisers brought in. He'd even found evidence that she had.

But Cal would never know for sure. The day after the scandal went public, he'd found Nick slumped over his desk, his hand still clutching the pistol that had ended his life. After the private funeral, Megan had vanished. The stolen money, meant to ease the suffering of third-world refugees, was never recovered.

It didn't take a genius to make the connection.

Too restless to sit, Cal unfolded his athletic frame and prowled to the window that spanned the outer wall. His office, on the twenty-eighth floor of the J-COR building, commanded a sweeping view of the Bay and the bridge that spanned the choppy, gray water. Beyond the Golden Gate, the stormy Pacific stretched as far as the eye could see.

Megan was out there somewhere. Cal could feel it, like a sickness in his bones. He could picture her in some far-away land, living like a maharani on the millions stolen from his foundation.

It wasn't so much the missing cash itself that troubled him—although the loss had cut into the foundation's resources. It was the sheer crassness of taking money earmarked for food, clean water and medical treatment in places rife with human misery. That Megan hadn't seen fit to make amends at any point after her husband's death made the crime even more despicable.

She could have returned the money, no questions asked. Even if she was innocent, as she'd claimed to be, she could have stayed around to help him locate it. Instead, she'd simply run, further cementing Cal's certainty of her guilt. She wouldn't have run if she didn't have something to hide. And the woman was damned good at hiding her trail. Not one of the investigators he'd hired had been able to track her down.

But Cal wasn't a man to give up. Someday he would find her. And when he did, one way or another, Megan Rafferty would pay.

"Mr. Jeffords."

Cal turned at the sound of his name. His receptionist stood in the office doorway. "Harlan Crandall's outside, asking to see you. Do you have time for him now, or should I schedule an appointment?"

"Send him in." Crandall was the latest in the string of private investigators Cal had hired to search for Megan. A short, balding man with an unassuming manner, he'd shown no more promise than the others. But now he'd come by unannounced, asking for an audience. Maybe he had something to report.

Cal seated himself as Crandall entered, wearing a rumpled brown suit and clutching a battered canvas briefcase.

"Sit down, Mr. Crandall." Cal motioned to the chair on the far side of the desk. "Do you have any news for me?"

"That depends." Crandall plopped the briefcase onto the desk, opened the flap and drew out a manila folder. "You hired me to look for Mrs. Rafferty. Do you happen to know her maiden name?"

"Of course, and so should you. It's Cardston. Megan Cardston."

Crandall nodded, adjusting his wire-rimmed glasses on his nose. "In that case, I may have something to tell you. My sources have tracked down a Megan Cardston who appears to fit the physical description of the woman you're looking for. She's working as a volunteer nurse for your foundation."

Cal's reflexes jerked. "That's impossible," he growled. "It's got to be a coincidence—just another woman with the same name and body type."

"Maybe so. You can decide for yourself after you've looked over this documentation." Crandall thrust the folder across the desk.

Cal opened the folder. It contained several photocopied pages that looked like travel requests and personnel rosters. But what caught his eye was a single, blurry black-and-white photograph.

Staring at the image, he tried to picture Megan as he'd last seen her—long platinum hair sculpted into a twist, diamond earrings, flawless makeup. Even at her husband's funeral, she'd managed to look like a Hollywood screen goddess, except for her pain-shot eyes.

The woman in the photo appeared thinner and slightly older. She was wearing sunglasses and a khaki shirt. Her light brown hair was short and windblown, her face bare of makeup. There was nothing behind her but sky.

Cal studied the firm jawline, the aristocratic nose and ripe, sensual lips. He willed himself to ignore the quiver of certainty that passed through his body. Megan's face was seared into his memory. Even with her eyes hidden, the woman in the picture had the same look. And Megan, he recalled, had worked as a surgical nurse before marrying Nick. But was this image really the woman who'd eluded him for two long years? There was only one way to be sure.

"Where was this picture taken?" he demanded. "Where's this woman now?"

Crandall slid the briefcase off the desk and closed it with a snap and a single word.

"Africa."

Arusha, Tanzania, February 26

Megan gripped the birth-slicked infant and delivered a stinging fingertip blow to its tiny buttocks.

Nothing happened.

She slapped the baby harder, her lips moving in a word-less plea. There was a beat of silence, then, suddenly, a gasping wail, as beautiful as any sound she'd ever heard. Megan's knees slackened in relief. The delivery had been hellish, a breech birth coming after a long night of labor. That mother and baby were both alive could only be counted as a miracle.

Passing the baby to the young aide, she mopped her brow with the sleeve of her smock, then reached over to do the same for the baby's mother. The air was warm and sticky. Light from a single bulb flickered on whitewashed walls. Drawn by the glow, insects beat against the screened windows.

As Megan leaned over her, the woman's eyelids fluttered open. *"Asante sana,"* she whispered in Swahili, the lingua franca of East Africa. *Thank you.*

"Karibu sana." Megan's deft hands wound a cotton string, knotted it tight and severed the cord. With luck, this baby would grow up healthy, spared the swollen belly and scarecrow limbs of the children she'd labored so desperately to save in Darfur, the most brutally ravaged region of Sudan, where a cruel dictator had used his mercenaries to decimate the African tribal population.

Megan had spent the past eleven months working with the J-COR Foundation's medical branch in the Sudanese refugee camps. Two weeks ago, on the brink of physical and emotional collapse, she'd been ordered to a less taxing post for recovery. Compared with the camps, this clinic, on the ramshackle fringe of a pleasant Tanzanian town, was a luxury resort.

But she would go back as soon as she was strong enough. She'd spent too many years feeling purposeless and adrift. Now that she'd found focus in her life, she was determined to finally make the most of her skills and training. She should be where she was needed most. And she was sorely needed in Darfur.

By the time the afterbirth came, the aide had sponged the baby boy clean and swaddled him in cotton flannel. The mother's eager hands reached out to draw him against her breast. Megan took a moment to raise the sheet and check the gauze packing. So far, everything looked all right. She stripped off her smock and her latex gloves. "I'm going to get some rest," she told the aide. "Watch her. Too much blood, you come and wake me."

The young African nurse-in-training nodded. She could be counted on to do her job.

Not until she was soaping her hands at the outside faucet did Megan realize how weary she was. It was as if the last of her strength had trickled down her legs and drained into the hard-packed earth. Straightening, she massaged her lower back with her fingers.

Beyond the clinic's corrugated roof, the moon glimmered like a lost shilling through the purple crown of a flowering jacaranda. Its low angle told her the time was well past midnight, with precious few hours left for sleep. All too soon, first light would trigger a cacophony of bird calls, signaling the start of a new day. At least she'd ended the day well—with a successful delivery and a healthy new life. The sense of accomplishment was strong.

Tired as she was, Megan knew she had no right to complain. This was the life she'd chosen. By now her old life—the clothes and jewelry, the cars, the house, the charity events she'd hosted to raise money for Nick and Cal's foundation—seemed little more than a dream. A dream that had ended with a headline and a gunshot.

She'd tried not to dwell on that nightmare week. But one image was chiseled into her memory—Cal's stricken face, the look of cold contempt in his glacial gray eyes, and the final words he'd spoken to her.

"You're going to answer for this, Megan. I'll hold you accountable and make you pay if it's the last thing I do."

Megan hadn't embezzled a cent, hadn't even known about the missing money till the scandal had surfaced. But Cal would never believe that. He'd trusted Nick to the very last.

Seeing Cal's look and hearing his words, Megan had realized she had no recourse except to run far and fast, to someplace where Cal would never find her.

That, or be trapped with no way to save her own soul.

But all that was in the past, she reminded herself as she flexed her aching shoulders and mounted the porch of the brick bungalow that served as quarters for the volunteers. She was a different person now, with a life that gave her the deepest satisfaction she had ever known.

If only she could put an end to the nightmares....

As the sleek Gulfstream jet skimmed the Horn of Africa, Cal reopened the folder Harlan Crandall had given him. Clever fellow, that Crandall. He alone had thought to look in the last place Megan would logically choose to hide—the volunteer ranks of the very foundation she had robbed.

The photocopied paperwork gave him a summary of her postings—Zimbabwe, Somalia and, for most of the past year, Sudan. Megan had taken the roughest assignments in the program—evidently by her own choice. What was she thinking? And if the woman in the photo was really Nick's glamorous widow, what in hell's name had she done with the money? She'd stolen enough to live in luxury for decades. Luxury even more ostentatious than the lifestyle her husband had given her.

Cal couldn't repress a sigh as he thought of the expensive trappings Nick had lavished on his wife. He'd always wanted her to have nothing but the best. His taste might have been over-the-top, but Cal had always been certain that Nick's intentions were good, just as they had been back when the two had become friends in high school.

They'd graduated from the same college, Cal with an engineering degree and Nick with a marketing major. When Cal had come up with a design for a lightweight modular shelter that could be erected swiftly in the wake of a natural disaster or used at construction and recreation sites, it had made sense for the two friends to go into business together. J-COR had made them both wealthy. But they'd agreed that money wasn't enough. After providing shelters for stricken people around the world, it had been Cal's idea to set up a foundation. He'd handled the logistics end. Nick had managed the finances and fund-raising.

Within a few years the foundation had expanded to include food and medical services. By then Nick was married to Megan, a nurse he'd met at a fund-raiser. Cal had been best man at their wedding. But even then he hadn't quite trusted her. She was too beautiful. Too gracious.

Too private. Beneath that polished surface he'd glimpsed something elusive; something hidden.

Her cool distance was a striking contrast to Nick's natural openness and warmth—particularly given the way Nick clearly doted on her. He had showered his bride with gifts—a multimillion-dollar house, a Ferrari, a diamond-and-emerald necklace and more. Megan had responded by using her new position in society to supposedly "help" the foundation. The charity events they'd hosted for wealthy donors at their home had raised generous amounts for the foundation. But of course, those events had done much more to line Megan's pockets. Three years later, after a routine tax audit, the whole house of cards had come tumbling down. The rest of the story was tabloid fodder.

Cal studied the photograph, which looked as if it had been snapped at a distance and enlarged for his benefit. Megan—if that's who it really was—may not have even known it was being taken. She was gazing to her left, the light glinting on her sunglasses—expensive sunglasses. Cal noticed the side logo for the first time. He remembered her wearing that brand, maybe that very pair. His mouth tightened as the certainty slid into place. Megan hadn't quite abandoned her high-end tastes.

It was a piece of luck that she'd been sent to Arusha. Finding her in Sudan could have involved a grueling search. But Arusha, a bustling tourist and safari center, had its own international airport. The company jet was headed there now, and he knew how to find the clinic. He'd been there before. If he so chose, he could round her up with the help of some hired muscle and have her on the plane within a couple of hours.

And then what? Tempting as the idea was, Cal knew it wasn't practical to kidnap her in a foreign country without a legal warrant. Besides, would it do any good if he could?

Megan was smart. She'd know that despite her signature on the checks that had never made it to the foundation's coffers, he had no solid proof she'd kept the money. If she stuck to her original story, that she'd had no knowledge of the theft and knew nothing about the missing funds, he'd be nowhere.

He didn't have grounds or authority to arrest her; and it wasn't in him to threaten her with physical harm. His only hope of getting at the truth, Cal realized, was to win her trust. He wasn't optimistic enough to think he could make her confess. She was too smart to openly admit to her crimes. But if he got close to her, she might let something slip—drop a tiny clue, innocent on its own, that could lead Crandall to the location of the hidden accounts.

That could take time. But he hadn't come this far to go home without answers. If that meant wining and dining the lady and telling her a few pretty lies, so be it.

The slight dip in the angle of the cabin told him the plane was starting its descent. If the weather was clear, he might get a look at the massive cone of Kilimanjaro. But that was not to be. Clouds were gathering off the right wing, hiding the view of the fabled mountain. Lightning chained across the distant sky. The seasonal rains had begun. If this kept up, which it likely would, they'd be landing in an African downpour.

Fastening his seat belt, Cal settled back to watch the storm approach. The plane shuddered as lightning snaked over its metal skin. Rain spattered the windows, the sound of it recalling another time, a rainy night three years ago in San Francisco.

It had been the night of the company Christmas party, held downtown at the Hilton. At about eleven o'clock Cal had bumped into Megan coming out of the hallway that led to the restrooms. Her face was white, her mouth damp, as if she'd just splashed it with water. Cal had stopped to ask if she was all right.

She'd laughed. "I'm fine, Cal. Just a little bit...pregnant."

"Can I get you anything?" he'd asked, surprised that Nick hadn't told him.

"No, thanks. Since Nick has to stay, I'm going to have him call me a cab. No more late-night parties for this girl."

She'd hurried away, leaving Cal to reflect that in all the time he'd known her, this was the first time he'd seen Megan look truly happy.

Was she happy now? He tried to picture her working in a refugee camp—the heat, the flies, the poverty, the sickness.... What was she doing here? What had she done with the money? The questions tormented him—and only one person could give him the answers.

Megan sank onto a bench outside the clinic, sheltered from the rain by the overhanging roof. The day had been hectic, as usual. The new mother and her baby were gone, carted off by her womenfolk early that morning. Her departure had been followed by a flood of patients with ailments ranging from impetigo to malaria. Megan had even assisted while the resident Tanzanian doctor stitched up and vaccinated a boy who'd been foolish enough to tease a young baboon.

Now it was twilight and the clinic was closed. The doctor and the aide had gone home to their families in town. Megan was alone in the walled compound that included the clinic building, a generator and washhouse, a lavatory and a two-room bungalow with a kitchen for volunteers like her. The utilitarian brick structures were softened by the flowering shrubs and trees that flourished in Arusha's rich volcanic soil. The tulip tree that shaded the clinic had ended its blooming cycle. Rain washed the fallen petals in a crimson cascade off the eave, like tears of blood.

Closing her eyes, Megan inhaled the sweet dampness. She'd yearned for rain in the parched Sudan, where the dusty air was rank with the odors of human misery. Going back wouldn't be easy. But the need was too great for her not to return. The need of the refugees for care and treatment—and her own need to make a difference.

She was about to get up and brave the downpour when she heard the clang of the gate bell—an improvised iron cowbell on a chain. Rising, she hesitated. If someone had an emergency she could hardly turn them away. But she was here alone. Outside that gate there could be thugs intent on breaking into the clinic for drugs, cash or mischief.

The bell jangled again. Megan sprinted through the rain to the bungalow, found the .38 Smith & Wesson she kept under her pillow and thrust it into the pocket of her loose khakis. Grabbing a plastic poncho from its hook by the door, she tossed it over her head as she hurried toward the sheet-iron gate. The key was in the rusty padlock that anchored the chain between the gate's welded handles.

"Jina lako nani?" she demanded in her phrase-book Swahili. She'd asked for the person's name, which was the best she could manage.

There was a beat of silence. Then a gravely, masculine voice rang through the rainy darkness. "Megan? Is that you?"

Megan's knees crumpled like wet sand. She sagged against the gate, her cold hands fumbling with the key. Cal's was the last voice she wanted to hear. But hiding from him would only make her look like a fool.

"Megan?" His voice had taken on a more strident tone, demanding an answer. But her throat was too tight to speak. She should have known that Cal wouldn't give up looking until he found her—even if he had to travel half-way around the world.

The lock fell open, allowing the heavy chain to slide free. Megan stepped back as the gate swung inward and Cal strode into the courtyard. Dressed in a tan Burberry raincoat, he seemed even taller than she remembered, his gray eyes even colder behind the rain that dripped off the brim of his hat.

She knew what he wanted. After two years, Cal was still looking for answers. Now that he'd found her, he would hammer her mercilessly with questions about Nick's death and the whereabouts of the stolen money.

But she had no answers to give him.

How could she persuade Cal Jeffords to see the truth and leave her in peace?

Two

Cal's eyes took in the cheap plastic poncho and the tired face beneath the hood. Something in his chest jerked tight. It was Megan, all right. But not the Megan he remembered.

"Hello, Cal." Her voice was rich and husky. "I see you haven't changed much."

"But you have." He turned and fastened the gate behind him. "Aren't you at least going to invite me out of the rain?"

She glanced toward the bungalow. "I can make you some coffee. But there's not much else. I haven't had time to shop…" Her voice trailed off as she led him through the downpour to the sheltered porch. Rain clattered on the corrugated tin roof above their heads.

"Actually I have a taxi waiting outside," he said. "I was hoping I could take you to dinner at the hotel."

Her eyes widened. She seemed nervous, he thought.

But then, she had plenty to hide. "That's kind of you, but there's no one else here. I need to stay—"

He laid a hand on her shoulder. She quivered like a fawn at his touch but didn't try to pull away. "It's all right," he said. "I spoke with Dr. Musa on the phone. It's fine with him if you leave for a couple of hours. In fact, he said you could use a nice meal. His houseboy's on the way over now, to watch the place while we're gone."

"Well, since it's all arranged..." Her voice trailed off.

"Dr. Musa also mentioned that you're doing a great job here." That part was true, but Cal made a point of saying it to flatter her.

She shrugged, a slight motion. The old Megan would have lapped up the praise like a satisfied cat. This thin-drawn stranger seemed uncomfortable with it. "I've just finished cleaning up in the clinic. I'll need to wash and change." She managed a strained laugh. "These days it doesn't take long."

"Fine. I'll open the gate for the cab."

As Cal slogged back across the compound, he spared a moment to be grateful that he'd thought to bring a pair of waterproof hiking boots before his thoughts returned to his encounter with the woman he'd come to find. Meeting Megan tonight was like meeting her for the first time. He was puzzled and intrigued, but still determined to get to the bottom of the money question. If this new Megan tried to play on his sympathy—and she likely would—it wasn't going to work. So help him, whatever it took, he was going to nail her to the wall.

Minutes after the cab pulled up to the bungalow, Benjamin, Dr. Musa's strapping young servant, arrived. Megan emerged from her room wearing a white blouse, fresh khaki slacks and a black twill jacket. A corner of the folded plastic poncho stuck out of her beat-up brown leather purse—Gucci, he noticed the brand. Some things at least hadn't changed.

Giving Benjamin her pistol, she thanked him with a smile and a few words. Cal lifted a side of his raincoat like a wing to shelter her as they descended the porch steps and climbed into the cab. Her face was damp, her hair finger-combed. She hadn't taken more than ten minutes to freshen up and change, but it had worked. She looked damned classy.

"When did you get in?" she asked him, making small talk.

"Plane landed a couple of hours ago. I registered at the Arusha Hotel, cleaned up and headed for the clinic."

She'd been looking straight ahead, but now she turned toward him with a frown. "Is something wrong, Cal? A crisis back home?"

He managed a wry laugh. "Not that I know of. I could say I was just passing through and decided to stop by..." He saw the flash of skepticism in her caramel-colored eyes. "But you wouldn't believe me, would you?"

"No." A smile tugged a corner of her luscious mouth. The sort of mouth made for kissing. Though he had never warmed to her personally, he'd never denied that she was an attractive and desirable woman. When was the last time she'd been kissed? he caught himself wondering. But never mind that. He was here for just one reason. Although, if getting to the truth involved kissing her, he wouldn't complain.

"I know you better than that, Cal. I left you with a lot of questions. But if you're here to charm the answers out of me, you could've saved yourself a trip. Nothing's changed. I don't know anything about where you could find the money. I'm assuming Nick spent it—which, I suppose, makes me guilty by association. But if you're looking for a big stash under my mattress or in some Dubai bank account, all I can do is wish you luck."

It was like her to be direct, Cal thought. That trait, at least, hadn't changed. "Why don't we table that subject for now. I'm more interested in why you left and what you've been doing for the past two years."

"Of course you are." Something glimmered in her eyes before she glanced away. The cab's windshield wipers swished and thumped in the stillness. Rain streamed down the windows. "For the price of a good steak, I suppose I can come up with a few good stories—entertaining, if nothing else."

"You never disappoint." Cal kept his voice as neutral as his comment. He had yet to pin down this new Megan. The inner steel she'd always possessed gleamed below a surface so fragile that he sensed she might shatter at a touch.

He knew she'd been sent here for rest and recovery. Nothing in the documents he'd seen explained why, but Dr. Musa, the tall, British-trained Chagga who ran the clinic, had expressed his concern about her health and state of mind to Cal over the phone. Cal needed to learn more. But right now, he was still taking in her presence.

He recalled the perfume she used to wear. The fancy French name of it eluded him, but he'd always found it mildly arousing. There was no trace of that scent now. If she smelled like anything at all, it was the medicinal soap used in the clinic. But strangely, her nearness in the cab was having the same effect on him as that perfume used to have back then.

Things were different now. Back in San Francisco she'd been his best friend's wife. Megan had been widowed for two years, and if there was anyone else in her life, there was no mention of it in Crandall's report. As long as the end justified the means, bedding her would be a long-denied pleasure. A little pillow talk could go a long way in loosening secrets.

If nothing else, it would be damned delicious fun.

Megan had spent little time outside the clinic since her arrival, so the remodeled nineteenth-century Arusha Hotel was new to her. Catering to wealthy tourists, it featured a lobby decorated in rich creams and browns with wing-back chairs and dark leather sofas, a bar and a restaurant with an international menu. Through the glass doors at the rear of the lobby, she glimpsed a large outdoor swimming pool, deserted tonight except for the rain that whipped the water to a froth.

Cal's big hand rested beneath her elbow as he ushered her toward the restaurant. Megan was of average height, but she felt small next to him. He was almost six-three, broad-shouldered and athletic, with a hard-charging manner that defied anyone to stand in his way. John Wayne in an Armani suit—that was how she would have described him back in the day. Even tonight, in travel-creased khakis, he looked imposing. John Wayne in the old movie *Hatari* came to mind—maybe because it was also the name of the hotel bar. She'd always found Nick's best friend over-bearing. But there'd been times when she'd wished her husband was more like him.

She wasn't surprised that he'd found her. Once he set his mind, Cal Jeffords could be as fiercely determined as a pit bull. And he'd come too far to leave without getting something to make his trip worthwhile. She'd told him the truth about the money. But he hadn't even pretended to believe her. Her signature on the donation checks she'd endorsed and given to Nick to deposit had convinced him she was guilty. Megan's instincts told her he had a plan to wear her down and make her pay. It would do her no good to fight. Cal was as much a force of nature as the storm raging outside. All she could do was wait for it to pass.

Sitting at their quiet table, she allowed him to order for her—filet mignon with mushrooms, fresh organic vegetables and a vintage Merlot. She could feel his gaze on her as the white-gloved waiter filled their wine goblets and set a basket of fresh hot bread between the lighted candlesticks.

"Eat up," Cal said, raising his glass. "You need to put some meat on those lovely bones."

Megan broke off a corner of the bread and nibbled at the crust. "I know I've lost weight. But it's painful to fill your plate when people around you are starving."

His slate gray eyes narrowed. "Is that what this is all about—this life change of yours? Guilt?"

She shrugged. "When I was married to Nick, I thought I had it all—the big house, the cars, the parties…" She took a sip of the wine. The sweet tingle burned down her throat. "When it all fell apart, and I learned that my lifestyle was literally taking food out of people's mouths, it sickened me. So, yes, you can call it guilt. Call it whatever you want. Does it matter? I don't regret the choice I made."

A muscle twitched in his cheek, betraying a surge of tightly reined anger. "The choice to run away without telling me? Without telling anybody?"

"Yes." She met his eyes with her own level gaze. "Nick left a god-awful mess behind. If I hadn't run, I'd still be back in San Francisco trying to clean it up."

"I know. I had to clean up most of it myself."

"There wasn't much I could do to help. The house was mortgaged to the rafters—something I didn't know until the bank called me after Nick's death. I told them to go ahead and take it. And the cars were in Nick's name, not mine. I'm assuming your company took those, along with the art and the furniture. I boxed up my clothes and shoes

for Goodwill and pawned my jewelry for travel money—
cash only. I knew my credit cards could be traced."

"By me?"

"Yes. But also by the reporters who kept hounding me
and the police who seemed to think I'd have a different
answer the fiftieth time they asked a question than I did
the first."

"If you'd stayed, I could have made things easier for
both of us, Megan."

"How could I take that chance? I knew the questions
from the police, from the press and from you wouldn't
stop. But, so help me, Cal, I didn't have any answers. It
was easier to just vanish. I was half hoping you'd believe
I'd died. In a way, I had."

The waiter had reappeared with their dinners. Megan
half expected Cal to start grilling her about the missing
funds, but he only glanced toward her plate in an unspoken order to eat her meal.

The steak was surprisingly tender, but Megan's anxiety
had robbed her of appetite. She took small bites, glancing across the table like a mouse nibbling the cheese in
a baited trap. Her eyes studied Cal's craggy face, trying
to catch some nuance of expression. Was he about to trip
the spring?

He'd aged subtly in the past two years. The shadows had
darkened around his deep-set eyes, and his sandy hair was
lightly brushed with gray. Nick's betrayal and suicide had
wounded him, too, she realized. Like her, Cal was dealing
with the pain in his own way.

"I was just wondering," he said. "When you joined that
first project in Zimbabwe, was the director aware of who
you were?"

"No. He was a local, and Zimbabwe's a long way from
San Francisco. My passport was still in my maiden name,

so that was the name I used. I showed up, described my nursing training and offered my help at the AIDS clinic. They needed a nurse too badly to ask many questions."

"And the transfers?"

"Once I got on the permanent volunteer roster, I could go pretty much where I wanted. Early on I was nervous about staying in one place too long. I moved around a lot. After a while it didn't seem to matter."

"And in Darfur? What happened there?"

The question shook her. Something too vague to be called a memory twisted inside, silent and cold like the coils of a snake. Megan willed herself not to feel it.

"You were there for eleven months," he persisted. "They sent you here for recovery. Something must have gotten to you."

She shrugged, her unease growing as she stared down at the weave of the bright brown-and-yellow tablecloth. "It's nothing. I just need rest, that's all. I'll be ready to go back in a couple of weeks."

"That's not what Dr. Musa told me. He says you have panic attacks. And you won't talk about what happened."

Megan's anxiety exploded in outrage. "He had no right to tell you that. And you had no right to ask him."

"My foundation's paying his salary. That gives me the right." Cal's leaden gray eyes drilled her like bullets. "Dr. Musa thinks you have post-traumatic stress. Whatever happened out there, Megan, you're not going back until you deal with it. So you might as well tell me now."

He was pushing too hard, backing her against an invisible wall. The dark coils twisted and tightened inside her. Sensing what was about to happen, she willed herself to lay down her fork. It clattered onto her plate. "I don't remember, all right?" Her voice emerged thin and raw. "It doesn't matter. I just need some time to myself and I'll be fine. And now, if you don't mind, I need to get back to… the clinic."

Her voice broke on the last words. As her self-control began to crumble, she rose, flung her linen napkin onto the table, caught up her purse and walked swiftly out of the restaurant. There had to be a ladies' room close by, where she could shut herself in a stall and huddle until her heart stopped thundering. Experience had taught her to recognize the symptoms of a panic attack. But short of doping herself with tranquilizers, she had little control over the rush of irrational terror that flooded her body.

She reached the lobby and glanced around for the restroom sign. The desk clerk was busy. No matter, she could find it by herself. But where was it? She could hear her heart, pounding in her ears.

Where was it?

Caught off guard, Cal stared after her for an instant. Then he shoved out his chair, stood and strode after her. She hadn't made it far. He found her in the lobby, her wide-eyed gaze darting this way and that like a cornered animal's.

Without a word, he caught her shoulders, forcing her to turn inward against his chest. She resisted, but feebly, her body shaking. "Leave me alone," she muttered. "I'm fine."

"You're not fine. Come on." He guided her forcefully through the lobby and out the back door to the patio. Sheltered by the overhanging roof, they stood veiled by a curtain of rain. Her body was rigid in his arms. He could feel her heart pounding against his chest, feel the slight pressure of her breasts. She'd stopped fighting him, but the trembling continued. Her breath came in muted gasps. Her fists balled the fabric of his shirt.

He might not be the most sensitive guy in the world, but even he could tell that the woman was terrified.

What had she been through? Cal had visited the Sudan refugee camps—a hell of human misery if ever there was one. Tens of thousands of people crammed into tents and makeshift shelters, not enough food, not enough water, open sewers and latrines teeming with disease. Organizations like the United Nations and private, nongovernment charities, known as NGOs, did what they could. But the need was overwhelming. And Megan had spent eleven months there.

He wouldn't have been surprised to find her dispirited and worn down—which she clearly was. But there was something more here. Harsh conditions wouldn't have made her this fearful. Something had happened specifically to her. Something so terrifying that the briefest reminder of it was enough to make her quake.

He was here about the money, he reminded himself. She was guilty as hell, and he couldn't let himself be moved by sympathy. But right now Megan's need for comfort appeared all too real. And besides, hadn't he wanted to get close to her—close enough to learn her secrets? Here was his chance to take that first step.

"It's all right, girl," he muttered against her silky hair. "You're safe here. I've got you."

His hand massaged her back beneath the light jacket. She was bone thin, the back of her bra stretched tight across shoulder blades that jutted like wings. He'd come here to get the truth out of her and see that she was punished for any part she might have played in Nick's suicide. But arriving at that truth would take time and patience. Megan was fragile in body and wounded in spirit. Pushing her too hard could shatter what few reserves she had left.

Not that Cal was a saint. Far from it, as his hardening

arousal bore witness. It might have been an indelicate response to the situation, but it was the only way he knew to reply. His relationships were usually short-lived affairs, with plenty of heat that burned out quickly. With all the time he devoted to J-COR and the foundation, he had little to spare for romantic entanglements. Brief, passionate flings were usually his preference—the sort of relationship shallow enough for every conflict to be solved by taking matters to bed. He had little experience comforting genuine distress, and his body shifted into default mode, wanting to solve the problem by replacing her troubled thoughts—and his own niggling guilt for causing her such distress—with ecstasy for them both.

The desire was there, smoldering where her hips rested against his, igniting the urge to sweep her upstairs to his luxury suite and ravish her till she moaned with pleasure. Maybe that was what the woman needed—a few weeks of rest, good food and good loving to restore her health and build her trust.

But that wasn't going to happen tonight. It was comfort and support she needed now, not some big, horny jerk making moves on her.

Giving himself a mental slap, Cal shifted backward, easing the contact between them. She was calm now. Maybe too calm. "Want to talk about it?" he asked.

She exhaled, pushing away from him. "I'll be fine. Sorry you had to see me like that. I feel like a fool."

"No one's blaming you. I've seen those camps. You've been through eleven months of hell."

"But not like the people who have nowhere else to go. Seeing their children die, their women—"

"You can't dwell on that, Megan."

"I can't forget it. That's why I plan to go back as soon as I'm strong enough."

"That's insane. I could stop you, you know."

"You could try. But if you do, I'll find another way."

The defiance in her gaze stunned him. Back in San Francisco, where he'd known her as a charming hostess and a lovely ornament, he would never have believed she could possess such an iron will. But her will looked to be all she had left. She was like a guttering candle, on the verge of burning out.

"You should go back and finish your dinner," she said. "I've got my rain poncho. I can catch a *matatu* back to the clinic."

"One of those rickety little buses? You'd end up walking for blocks, alone in the rain. I'll take you." Cal wouldn't have minded inviting her upstairs for a hot bath and a chaste, restful night in his suite's second bed—as a simple act of kindness. But she was certain to turn him down. And even if she accepted, he didn't trust himself to behave. For all her devious ways, Megan was an alluring woman, made more so by her surprising strength and the unspoken challenge in her manner. The urge to bury himself between those slim, lovely legs might prove too much to resist.

But an idea had taken root in his thoughts—one so audacious that it surprised even him. First thing tomorrow he would make some calls. What he had in mind might be just the thing to restore her health and win her trust.

Minutes later Megan was huddled beside Cal in the cab's backseat. The rain had stopped, but the night was chilly and the black blazer she'd worn to look presentable was too thin for warmth.

"You're shivering." Cal peeled off his Burberry coat and wrapped it around her shoulders, enfolding her in the heat and manly scent of his body. A thread of panic uncurled inside her. She willed it away.

"We've talked about me all evening," she said, making conversation. "What's new with you?"

"Nothing much, except that I'm here. The company's doing fine. So is the foundation. I've hired a team of professionals to do the fund-raising. But they don't have your elegant touch. I miss you and...Nick."

Megan hadn't missed the beat of hesitation before he spoke her late husband's name. "That time seems like a hundred years ago," she said, then tactfully changed the subject. "Any special lady in your life? As I recall, you always had plenty to choose from."

"Having a special lady requires an investment in time. More time than I can spare."

"Remind yourself of that when you're a grumpy, lonely old man," she teased. "You're what? Forty?"

"Thirty-eight. Don't make me out to be more decrepit than I already am."

"Fine. But one of these days you're going to look back and wish you'd had a family."

"You're a fine one to talk," he countered.

"Well, at least I tried." She remembered telling him about the baby. Had Nick let him know she'd miscarried? Or had her statement made him think of her wedding day, when his best man's toast had congratulated the two of them on the new family they were making together?

His answering silence told Megan she'd pushed the conversation onto painful ground. Cal had been as devastated as she was by Nick's death. Devastated and angry—or at least, there had been anger on *her* part, when she'd learned about the embezzlement. Cal had seemed determined to find some way to clear Nick of any blame...which had meant shoving that blame on her, instead. Now, more than two years and half a world away, she was sitting beside him with his coat wrapped around her. It was as if they'd come full circle. She'd done everything in her power to put the past behind her and find peace. But it was no use. Being with Cal had brought it all back.

Three

Cal had offered Benjamin a cab ride back to Dr. Musa's. The distance wasn't far but by the time they arrived, jet lag from the long flight had caught up with him. He was nodding off every few minutes.

"Won't you come in, sir?" the husky youth asked as he climbed out of the cab. "I can make you tea."

"Another time, thank you. And give my best to the doctor. Tell him I'll ring him up tomorrow."

As the cab headed on to the hotel, splashing through the backstreet ruts, Cal reflected on his evening with Megan. Nothing had been as he'd expected. She was so fragile, and yet so powerfully seductive that he'd been caught off guard. It would have been all too easy to forget that the woman had either stolen or driven his best friend to steal millions from the foundation before killing himself, and that the money was still missing. In the days ahead he'd do well to remember that.

A few evenings out weren't going to break down her resistance. He was going to need more time with her—a lot more time, in a setting calculated to put her at ease. A safari would be perfect—days exploring Africa's beautiful wildlands, and the kind of pampered nights that a first-class safari company could provide.

Tomorrow he would put his scheme into action. First, as a courtesy, he would ask Dr. Musa's permission to take Megan out of the clinic for a couple of weeks. If need be, he could fly in another volunteer to take her place. Arranging a photo safari on short notice shouldn't be a problem. Business tended to slow during the rainy season. Most companies would be eager to accommodate a well-paying client.

Not until everything was in place would he let Megan in on his plan. She might argue. She might even dig in her heels and refuse to go along. But in the end she would go with him. If he had to knock her out and kidnap her, so help him, she would go.

Evenings were long and peaceful on safari, with little to do except eat, drink, rest and talk. As for the nights... But he would let nature take its course. If things went as planned, Megan would soon be stripped of any secrets she was hiding.

But first he wanted to cover all his bases. Tomorrow he would compose an email to Harlan Crandall. If the man was sharp enough to locate Megan, he might also be able to ferret out more details about the last months of Nick's life. He might even be able to locate the missing money.

For now—Cal punctuated the thought with a tired yawn—all he wanted was to go back to the hotel, crawl between the sheets and sleep off his jet lag.

On a cot veiled by mosquito netting, Megan writhed in fitful sleep. Her hellish dreams varied from night to night.

But this one from her time in Darfur dominated them all, replaying as if it had been burned into her brain.

Saida had been just fifteen, a beautiful child with liquid brown eyes and the doelike grace of her people, the Fur. Because she spoke fair English, and because her family was dead, Megan had given her a translating job at the camp infirmary, with an out-of-the-way corner for sleeping. Bright with promise, Saida had one failing. She had fallen in love with a boy named Gamal, and love had made her careless. Checking on the patients late one night, Megan had found Saida's pallet empty. Earlier, the starry-eyed girl had mentioned her trysting place with Gamal, a dry well outside the camp. That had to be where she'd gone.

Leaving the camp at night was forbidden. Beyond the boundaries, bands of rogue Janjaweed mercenaries prowled the desert like wild dogs in search of prey. No one was safe out there. Megan had known that she needed to find the two foolish youngsters and bring them back before the unthinkable happened. Arming herself with a loaded pistol, she'd plunged into the darkness.

Now the dream swirled around her like an evil mist. She was sprinting through pools of shadow, the waning moon a razor edge of light above the naked hills. Behind her lay the camp; ahead she could make out the gnarled trunk of a dead acacia, its limbs clutching the sky like the fingers of an arthritic hand. Beyond the tree lay the well, a dry hole marked by a cairn of stones.

Near the cairn she could see the two young lovers. They were locked in a tender embrace, blind and deaf to everything but each other. A turbaned shadow moved behind them. Then another and another. Raising the pistol, Megan cocked it and aimed. Time slowed as her finger tightened on the trigger.

Before she could fire, a huge, sweaty hand clamped over her mouth. Pain shot up her arm as the pistol was wrenched away. She tried to fight, twisting and scratching, but her captor was a wall of muscle. Powerless to move or cry out, she could only watch in horror as a knife sang out of the darkness and buried itself to the hilt in Gamal's back. He dropped without a sound.

Saida's screams shattered the darkness as the Janjaweed moved in. One of them flung her to the ground. Two others pinned her legs as the circle of men closed around her. Megan heard the sound of ripping cloth. Again Saida screamed. Again and again…

Megan's eyes jerked open. She was shaking violently, her skin drenched in sweat beneath her light cotton pajamas. Her heart slammed in the silence of the room.

Easing her feet to the floor, she brushed aside the mosquito netting, leaned over her knees and buried her face in her hands. The dream always ended the same way. She had no memory of how she'd managed to escape. She only knew that Gamal had been found dead outside the camp the next morning, and Saida had vanished without a trace.

She'd soldiered on, hoping time would help her forget. But even here in Arusha the nightmares were getting worse, not better. Maybe Dr. Musa was right. Maybe she did have post-traumatic stress. But so what if she did? As far as she knew, there was no simple cure for the malady. Otherwise, why would so many combat veterans be suffering from it back in the States?

All she could do was go on as if nothing had happened. If she could control her fears, she could still do some good. One day she might even be able to live a normal life.

But normal in every respect? She shook her head. That would be asking too much.

* * *

Wednesday was vaccination day at the clinic. While the aide managed the paperwork, and Dr. Musa took care of the more urgent cases, Megan spent the hours giving immunizations. Most of her patients, babies and children, had departed squalling. She loved the little ones and was grateful for the chance to help them stay well; but by late afternoon she'd developed a pounding headache.

Taking a break as the stream of people thinned, she gulped down a couple of aspirins. She couldn't help wondering where Cal was. He'd promised to come by the clinic, but she hadn't seen him for two days. Had some emergency come up, or was he just avoiding her?

But why should she care? Cal wanted to stir up memories she would be happy to keep buried. Seeing him again would only sharpen the loss that had dulled over time.

Dared she believe he'd given up on her and left? But that wasn't like Cal. He'd come here seeking satisfaction, and he wouldn't walk away without it. Was it just the money? Or was he looking for some closure in the matter of Nick's death? Either way, he was wasting his time. She had no insight to offer him.

But her conflict over the prospect of spending time with him went deeper than that.

The other night when the calming strength of his arms had temporarily eased her panic, she'd been grateful for his comfort—and troubled by how it made her feel. Cal was a compelling man, and he'd touched her in a way that had sent an unmistakable message. There was a time when she would have found him hard to resist. But when he'd held her so close that his arousal had hardened against her belly, it had been all she could do to keep from pushing him away and running off into the rain. Only when he'd stepped back had she felt safe once more.

Over the past months, it was as if something had died in her. The things she'd witnessed had numbed her to the point where she doubted her ability to respond as a woman.

The issue had come to light a few months ago when a volunteer MSF doctor in one of the camps had invited her for a private supper. He'd been attractive enough, and Megan had harbored no illusions about what to expect. Such things were common enough between volunteers, and though she'd never indulged before, she'd actually looked forward to a few hours of forgetting the wretched conditions outside. But when he'd kissed her, she'd felt little more than a vague unease. She'd tried to behave as if everything was all right; but as his caresses grew more intimate, her discomfort had spiraled into panic. In the end she'd twisted away, plunged out of the tent and fled with his words echoing in her ears— *What the hell's the matter with you? Are you frigid?*

By the next night the doctor had found a more agreeable partner. Megan hadn't attempted intimacy again. She'd hoped it had been a fluke, but her reaction to Cal had confirmed her suspicions.

Her problem hadn't gone away, and most likely wouldn't. If Cal had seduction in mind, the man was in for a letdown. For that, and for every other reason she could think of, it would be best if she never saw him again.

But that was not to be. The next morning, as Megan was eating a breakfast of scrambled eggs and coffee, he roared through the gate in an open jeep that bore the logo of one of the big safari companies. A flock of brown parrots exploded from the tulip tree as he pulled up to the bungalow.

Dr. Musa stepped out of the clinic, grinning as if in on some secret joke.

Cal vaulted out of the jeep. "Pack your things, Megan," he ordered. "You're coming with me—now."

"Have you lost your mind, Cal Jeffords?" She faced him on the porch steps, her arms folded across her chest. "What gives you the right to come in here and order me around as if I were six years old?"

His eyes narrowed, glinting like granite over a sharklike smirk. "I'm the head of the J-COR Foundation and you're a volunteer. Right now I'm volunteering you to come with me on safari for ten days. I've already cleared it with Dr. Musa." He glanced toward the doctor, who nodded. "Your replacement's flying in this afternoon, so the clinic won't be shorthanded. Everything's been arranged."

"And I have no say in any of this?"

"Dr. Musa agrees with me that your work here isn't giving you enough rest. You need a real break. That's what I'm offering you."

"Offering? Does that mean I can refuse?"

"Not if you're smart." He stood his ground at the foot of the steps, his slate eyes level with hers.

"What if I say no? Will you haul me off by force?"

"If I have to." He didn't even blink, and she knew with absolute certainty that he wasn't bluffing. Once the man made up his mind, there'd be no moving him.

Not that the idea of a safari seemed so bad. It might even speed her recovery. But how was she going to survive ten days with Cal? Scrambling for a shred of control, she squared her jaw.

"Fine, I'll go with you on one condition. If I'm fit and rested by the end of the safari, I want to be sent back to Darfur."

One dark eyebrow twitched. "Are you sure that's a good idea?"

"Is it a good idea for any of those poor people who have nowhere else to go? It's where I'm most urgently needed.

And without that goal, I can't justify wasting ten days on a…vacation."

He scowled, then slowly nodded. "All right. But while we're on safari, you're on orders to relax and have a good time. That's the best medicine you can give yourself if you want to recover. And as you said yourself, you'll need to be fit and rested to return there."

She took a moment to study him, the jutting chin, the steely gaze. Cal Jeffords wasn't spending precious time and money on a safari just to help her get better. The next ten days would be a contest of wills. She would need to be on her guard the whole time.

"So, do we have a deal?" he demanded.

Megan turned toward the door of the bungalow. Pausing, she glanced back at him—long enough for him to see that she wasn't smiling. "It won't take me long to pack," she said. "The coffee's hot. Have some while you're waiting."

The single-engine Piper Cherokee circled the rim of the Ngorongoro crater, a place designated by *National Geographic* as one of the world's Living Edens. Cal had been here two or three times over the years and knew what to expect. He was more interested in watching Megan, who was seeing it for the first time.

As the pilot banked the plane, she pressed against the window, looking down at the grassy floor of the twelve-mile-wide caldera. "This is amazing," she murmured.

"It's all that's left of an ancient volcano that blew its top." Cal shifted comfortably into the role of guide. "Geologists who've done the math claim it was as big as Kilimanjaro. Can you believe that?"

Megan shook her head. She'd been quiet during the short flight, and Cal hadn't pressed her to talk. There'd be plenty of time for conversation later. He studied her finely chiseled profile against the glass. Even in sun-glasses, with no makeup and wind-tousled hair, she was a beauty. No wonder Nick had been eager to give her any-thing she wanted.

"We could've driven here in less than a day," he said. "But I wanted your first view of the crater to be this one, from the air."

"It's breathtaking." She kept her gaze fixed on the land-scape below. "Why is it so green down there? The rains have barely started."

"The crater has springs that keep it watered year-round. The animals living there don't have to migrate during the dry season."

"Will we see animals today?" Her voice held a childlike anticipation. Once Megan had resigned herself to going, she'd flung herself into the spirit of the safari. Despite his hidden agenda, and his long-nurtured distrust of her, Cal found himself enjoying, even sharing, her enthusiasm.

"That depends," he replied. "Harris Archibald, our guide, will be meeting the plane with our vehicle. Where we go will be mostly up to him. You'll enjoy Harris—at least, I hope you will. He's a relic of the old days, a real character. Be prepared—he's missing an arm and he'll tell you a dozen different stories about how he lost it. I've no idea which version is true."

He'd been lucky to hire Harris for this outing, Cal re-flected. The old man usually guided trophy hunters, and his talent for it had him in high demand. But when Cal had called on him in Arusha, Harris had just had a client can-cel. He'd been glad for the work, even though shepherd-ing a photo safari had meant changing the arrangements he'd already made.

The old rogue swilled liquor, swore like a pirate and had been through four wives; but when it came to scouting game, he had the instincts of a bloodhound. There was no doubt he'd give Cal his money's worth.

"Will we be sleeping in tents tonight?" Megan asked as the plane veered away from the crater toward the open plain.

"You sound like a little girl on her first camping trip." Cal squelched the impulse to reach out and squeeze her shoulder. She seemed in high spirits this afternoon, but he sensed the frailty beneath her cheerful facade. Or was that an act? He'd have to remember to be on his guard against her. This was a woman used to wrapping men around her little finger.

"Wait and see," he said. "I want you to be surprised."

And she would be, he vowed. By the end of the next ten days, Megan would be well rested, well fed, well ravished and trusting enough to tell him anything.

The plane touched down on an airstrip that was little more than a game trail through the long grass. Cal swung to the ground, then reached up for Megan. Using his hand for balance, she climbed onto the low-mounted wing and jumped lightly to earth.

A cool wind, smelling of rain, teased her hair and ruffled the long grass. Far to the west, sooty clouds boiled over the horizon. Lightning flickered in the distant sky. Megan counted the seconds before the faint growl of thunder reached her ears. The rain was still several miles away, but it appeared to be moving fast. Their personal gear had been unloaded and the plane was turning around to take off ahead of the storm. If no one showed up to meet them, she and Cal would be left in the middle of nowhere with no shelter to protect them from the weather or the wildlife.

But there was no way she'd let Cal know how nervous

she was. Glancing over her shoulder, she flashed him a smile. "So our big adventure begins."

He wasn't fooled by her bravado. "Don't worry, Harris will be here," he said. "The old boy hasn't lost a client yet."

As if his words were prophetic, Megan saw a mottled tan shape approaching in the distance. Lumbering closer, it materialized into a mud-spattered heavy-duty Land Rover with open sides and a canvas top. There were two men in the front seat—a tall African driver and a stockier figure in khakis and a pith helmet.

Waving to the pair in the Land Rover, the pilot gunned his engine. The little plane droned down the makeshift runway, cleared the ground and soared into the darkening sky.

Cal hefted the duffel bags and strode toward the vehicle, where he tossed the gear in the back, keeping hold only of the case he had told Megan held the binoculars and cameras. Once the bags were arranged, he opened the door for Megan to climb into the rear seat. The driver gazed politely ahead, but their aging guide turned around to give Megan a look that could have gotten him slapped if he'd been a generation younger.

The man reminded Megan of an aging Ernest Hemingway, with battered features that would have been handsome in his youth. His bristling eyebrows and scruffy gray beard showed lingering traces of russet. His blue eyes held a secretive twinkle that put Megan at ease.

"I'll be damned, Cal." He spoke with a trace of lower-class British accent. "You told me you were bringing a lady friend, but you didn't tell me how classy she was. Now I'll have to be on my best behavior."

Cal settled himself on the backseat. "Megan, my friend Harris Archibald needs no introduction," he said. "Harris, this is Ms. Megan Cardston."

"It's a pleasure to meet you, Mr. Archibald." Megan extended her hand, then noticed, to her embarrassment, the pinned-up right sleeve of his khaki shirt.

He chuckled and accepted her handshake from the left. "You can call me Harris. I don't hold much with formality."

"But I'm holding you to your remark about being on your best behavior, Harris," Cal said.

"Oh, you needn't worry on that account. I've long since learned my lesson about fooling around with the client's womenfolk. See this?" He nodded toward the stump of his arm, which appeared to have been severed just above the elbow. "Jealous husband with a big gun and a bad aim."

Cal rolled his eyes heavenward. Remembering what he'd told her about Harris's stories, Megan suppressed a smile. "And our driver?" she asked. "Are you going to introduce him?"

Harris looked slightly startled, as if most clients tended to ignore the African staff. "Gideon," he said. "Gideon Mkaba. We'll be in good hands with him."

"*Hujambo,* Gideon." Megan extended her hand over the back of the seat.

"*Sijambo.*" The driver smiled and shook her hand.

"So where are we going, Harris?" Cal broke the beat of awkward silence.

The guide grinned. "Thought you'd never ask! Elephant! Whole bloody herd of 'em down by the riverbed. We were scouting 'em when we saw your plane."

As the engine coughed to a rumbling start, lightning cracked across the sky with a deafening boom. The roiling clouds let loose a gush of water that deluged down on the vehicle's canvas top. Wind blew the rain sideways, dousing the passengers.

"Move it, Gideon!" Harris shouted above the storm. "They won't be there forever!"

"But it's raining!" Megan protested, shivering in her wet clothes.

Twisting in the front seat, Harris shot her a devilish grin. "Excuse me, miss, but the elephants don't bloody care!"

Four

By the time they came within sight of the riverbed, Cal had managed to clamber into the back of the jouncing Land Rover and find Megan's duffel among the gear. Pulling out her rain poncho, he reached over the seat, tugged it past her head and worked it down around her shivering body. It was too late to keep her dry, but at least the plastic sheeting would act as a windbreaker and help keep her warm.

As he moved back to the seat, she looked up at him. Her lips moved in silent thanks. A freshet of tenderness welled inside him. Even a strong woman like Megan needed someone to care about her. Something told him she hadn't had anyone like that in a long time.

But he hadn't come on this trip to feel sorry for her. He couldn't let sympathy—or any other emotion—divert him from his purpose.

"There." On a slight rise above the riverbank, Harris motioned for the driver to stop. The growl of the engine dropped to a low idle. Glancing back at Cal and Megan, the guide touched a finger to his lips and pointed.

At first Cal saw nothing. Then, not fifty yards ahead, a huge, gray silhouette emerged through the sheeting rain. Then another and another.

Cal could feel Megan's hand gripping his arm as the herd ambled toward them on silent feet. Did the tension in her come from awe or worry? He wasn't quite sure what to feel, himself. He knew that most animals in the game parks were accustomed to vehicles. But these elephants were close, and the open Land Rover offered little in the way of protection. He could only hope that Harris knew what he was doing.

Somewhere below them, hidden by the high bank, was the rain-swollen river. Over the rush of water, Cal could hear the elephants. They were vocalizing in low-pitched rumbles, their tone relaxed, almost conversational. Gideon slipped the gearshift into Reverse, ready to back away at the first sign of trouble. Surely, by now, the herd was aware of them. But the elephants continued on, undisturbed.

The leader, most likely an older cow, was within a stone's throw of the vehicle's front grille when she turned aside and disappeared through an opening in the riverbank. The others followed her—adult females, half-grown teenagers and tiny newborn calves trailing like gray ghosts through the rain, down the slope toward the river. Megan's grip tightened. Cal could sense the emotion in her, the fear and the wonder. He resisted the impulse to take her hand. They had just shared an unforgettable moment. He didn't want to risk spoiling it.

The last elephant had made it down the bank to the water. The contented sounds of drinking and splashing drifted up from below. Harris nodded to the driver, who backed up the Land Rover, turned it around and headed back the way they'd come.

"You had me worried, there," Cal admitted. "Any one of those elephants could have charged us."

Harris chuckled. "No need to fret. I know that herd, and I knew they'd be thirsty. They always take the same path down to the river. As long as we didn't bother them, I was pretty sure they wouldn't pay us much heed."

Megan hadn't spoken. "Are you all right?" Cal asked her.

Her voice emerged as a nervous laugh. "Unbelievable," she breathed. "And we forgot to take pictures."

Cal could feel her trembling beneath the poncho, whether from cold or excitement, he couldn't be sure. But her green-flecked caramel eyes were glowing beneath the hood. It had been a good moment with Megan, the elephants and the rain, he mused; maybe the best moment he'd known in a long time. But he couldn't forget what he'd come to do.

Megan had expected that being on safari would involve roughing it in a tent. In her cold, wet condition, the luxury lodge on the outer slope of the Ngorongoro Crater came as a welcome surprise. Less welcome was the discovery that Harris had clearly misread her relationship with Cal. He had reserved just one bungalow for the two of them. With one bed.

"Don't worry. I'll take care of this." Cal stood beside her in the open doorway surveying the elegantly rustic quarters, decorated in native rugs, baskets and tapestries. "While you shower and change for dinner, I'll go talk to the manager. They're bound to have an extra room somewhere."

With the door locked behind him, Megan stripped

down and luxuriated in the hot, tiled shower stocked with lavender-scented soap and shampoo. It wouldn't be a good idea to get used to this, she lectured herself. In the camps, a bucket of cold water was often as good as she could get. Much of the time she'd had to make do with sponge baths, reminding herself that even that was better than most refugees had.

If she could move beyond the panic attacks and the nightmares, Cal had promised to send her back to Darfur. Ten days wasn't much time. But if she could relax and focus on getting well, it might make a difference.

She wanted to go back, needed to. Working among the poor and dispossessed had given her the only real sense of worth she had ever known—something she had craved after her world had collapsed under her feet.

In her naïveté, she hadn't learned about Nick's embezzlement of the charity funds until days before he'd shot himself. Between his death and his funeral, she'd done a world of soul-searching. For years, she'd taken it for granted that her husband was rich, and she'd spent accordingly. But how much of the stolen money had gone to support her extravagant lifestyle? Megan had no way of knowing. She had known, though, that while she couldn't return the money, she could at least make some restitution through her own service.

Cal's cold anger at the funeral and his threat to make her pay had startled her. Until then she hadn't realized that he blamed her for the theft and for his friend's suicide. Knowing that he would find some way to go after her legally and that she had no power to fight him had pushed her decision—she'd had no choice except to run far and fast, where Cal would never think to look for her.

Using her political connections and her knowledge of the J-COR Foundation, she'd managed to expedite the paperwork and lose herself in the ranks of volunteers. What surprised her was the fulfillment she'd found in working with the refugees. They had needed her—and in that need she'd found the hope of redemption.

She was proud of the work she'd done in Arusha, but she could do so much more in Darfur. She had to go back; and she couldn't let Cal stop her.

Megan had put on fresh clothes and was fluffing her short damp hair when she heard a knock on the door. She opened it to find Cal standing on the threshold with his duffel bag.

"No luck," he said. "They've got a big tour group coming in tonight, and everything will be full-up. I even asked about borrowing a cot. Nothing."

"Can you room with Harris?"

"Harris has a single bed in the main lodge. He'll probably come in drunk, and even when he's sober he snores like a steam calliope. I let him know about his mistake—the old rascal just grinned and told me to make the best of it."

He glanced around the bungalow, which, except for the bath, was all one L-shaped room. Near the window, a sofa and two armchairs were grouped around a coffee table. "Sorry. I'll be fine sleeping on the couch. I even have some sheets and an extra mosquito net they gave me at the desk."

Grin and bear it. Megan sighed as her gaze measured his looming height against the modest length of the sofa. "I may be a better fit for the couch myself. But I suppose we can work that out. Come on in. You'll want to clean up before dinner."

While Cal showered, Megan opened the camera bag and went over the instruction manual for the small digital camera Cal had bought her in Arusha. In the background, she could hear the splash and gurgle of running water as he sluiced his body—probably a very impressive body, she conceded. But she'd been married to Nick for five years; and working in the camps, she'd seen more than her share of nudity. If Cal were to walk out of the bathroom stark naked, she would do little more than shrug and look the other way.

The small intimacies of sharing a room didn't bother her. It was Cal's constant, looming presence that would take some getting used to.

The shower had stopped running. The door opened a few inches to let out the steam, but it appeared he was getting dressed in the bathroom. A few minutes later he stepped out, freshly shaven and combed, and dressed in clean jeans and a charcoal-gray sweater that matched his eyes. The clothes should have seemed casual, but something about his presence lent a rugged elegance to whatever he wore. She'd always noticed that.

Megan had done some needed shopping in Arusha before their departure, but she'd bought mostly plain khakis and T-shirts, a fleece jacket and a pair of sturdy boots, which she could take back to Darfur. Her one indulgence had been a colorful but practical jade-green scarf, which she'd knotted at her throat tonight. It was as dressed-up as she was going to get.

She surveyed him from head to toe. "You look like a page out of *GQ*."

He grinned. "And you look like Ingrid Bergman in *For Whom the Bell Tolls*. Shall we go to dinner?"

It was still raining, but there was a good-size umbrella in the room. Stepping out onto the terrace, Cal opened it and sheltered Megan while she locked the door. With rain a streaming curtain around them, they followed the brick walkway across the grounds to the dining room.

The lodge stood on an old coffee plantation, its original German owners exiled by the British, who'd taken over the country at the end of World War I. The trees, the gardens and some of the old buildings had been preserved and beautifully restored. A high brick wall around the property kept out prowling animals. Veiled by rain and twilight, memories of a forgotten world lingered in the shadows. It seemed so distant from any world she'd been used to—in America or in Africa—that it almost felt like a dream. She'd have to remind herself not to get lost in it. This wasn't a fairy tale, she was not a princess and Cal was no Prince Charming. He was a man with an agenda, and she would do well to keep that in mind.

Gideon would be sleeping and eating in the staff quarters; but Harris was waiting at their table in the dining room. Already glowing from the whiskey in his glass, he kept them riotously entertained through the five-course gourmet meal. Megan was grateful for his presence, which saved her from making awkward conversation with Cal. She found herself liking the old rogue, despite his proclivities for strong drink and colorful curses. Even when he flirted outrageously with her, she took it in the good humor it was meant to be.

"Join me in the bar for a nightcap?" He gave her a sly wink as their dessert plates were whisked away. "We might even invite that old sourpuss Cal along if he asks nicely."

"Thanks, but I can barely keep my eyes open now," Megan said, rising. "Of course, I can't speak for Cal. But I'll see you tomorrow morning."

The men had risen with her. "I'll excuse myself, too, Harris," Cal said. "It's been a long day, and I know you'll want to get an early start in the morning."

"Where will we be going?" Megan asked.

"Wait and see," Cal teased. "More fun that way."

"Fine, but can you at least tell me where we are now? I've totally lost my bearings."

"Sure. I've got a map of the country in my bag. That'll give you a better idea."

They stepped outside to discover that the rain had stopped. The clouds had swept away to reveal a dazzling expanse of stars. Water dripped from the trees as they walked back down the path to their bungalow.

"How early does Harris expect us tomorrow?" Megan asked.

"Six, maybe. Early morning's the best time to see animals. He may be up half the night drinking, but don't worry, he'll be there first thing. And we'll be there, too, if we know what's good for us."

"You seem to know Harris pretty well. How did you meet him?"

"Partly luck. A few years ago I took one of our big donors to see some projects in Africa. The man was a hunter and wanted a safari while he was here. Harris was available."

"You hunted with them?"

"I just went along for the ride. Took a few pictures. Harris thought I was a wuss. Probably still does, but we managed to become friends. I've sent him other clients over the years, but after seeing those beautiful animals go down under the gun, I've no desire to hunt anything. Life's too short and too precious."

"I like that about you," Megan said, meaning it. "And I never thanked you for commandeering me on this trip. So far it's been wonderful."

She waited, expecting some kind of response, but Cal was silent. He hadn't brought her along on this trip for pleasure, Megan reminded herself. Or if he had, it was only because he thought that he could get her guard down and pry away her secrets.

Two years ago, Cal had been the one to walk into Nick's

office and find him dead at his desk. A shock like that would leave a lasting scar. If Cal had blamed her, even in part, for his best friend's suicide, the blame would still be there, festering like an infected wound beneath the veneer of charm and affability he was showing her now. Even before Nick's suicide, he'd never approved of her. He must hate her now.

Had he come here to punish her? Maybe she should simply ask him. She doubted he'd tell her the truth. Worse, voicing her suspicions might raise his guard. But at least it would let him know he wasn't fooling her.

"I've been thinking about our sleeping arrangement," she said. "If you try to stretch out on that sofa, you'll hang over the ends and keep us both awake with your tossing and turning. But I'm short enough to fit—not to mention the fact that, after living in the camps, I can sleep anywhere. You're taking the bed. End of discussion."

"Fine," he answered after a beat of silence. "I bow to your common sense. But you get one of the pillows and your first choice of blankets."

"Deal." They'd reached the terrace of their bungalow. She fished in her pocket for the key. "How long will we be staying here? Surely you can tell me that much without spoiling any surprises."

"We'll be using this lodge as our base for the next few days, so you can go ahead and unpack for now. After that… you'll see."

"Sorry, but I've grown accustomed to being in charge of my life."

"For the next nine days, your only responsibility will be to relax. Leave the logistics to Harris. That's what I'm paying him for."

"And what are *you* getting out of this?"

The slight intake of his breath told her that her question

had thrown him. In the silence that followed, she turned the key in the lock and opened the door. Before she could step inside, he touched her arm. "It's early yet. Let's sit outside for a while. If you think you'll be cold, I'll get a blanket."

"Thanks." The overhanging roof had kept the rain off the bench under the window, but the night breeze carried a chill. Megan took a seat, huddling for warmth while Cal went inside and turned on a lamp. He hadn't answered her question, but at least he seemed willing to talk.

Moments later he returned with a light woolen blanket. It was long enough to cover them both as he sat next to her. Megan was acutely conscious of his body heat and the rain-fresh aroma of his skin. She'd always found Cal intimidating, like facing down a lion. There was something about him that shriveled her self-confidence. It had gotten much worse after Nick's death, when he'd begun to treat her as an adversary. But she'd have to put her discomfort aside if she wanted him to deal with her as an equal.

The night was still except for the lightly rustling wind and the drip of water off the leaves and buildings. A night bird called from outside the wall, a shimmering sound that, in Megan, touched a chord of sadness.

"You asked me a question," Cal said.

Her heart stumbled. "I did. You don't owe me anything, Cal. You've no reason to like me, or do me any sort of kindness. For all I know, you still blame me for Nick's death. So why should you invest your time and money in this adventure? That's why I'm asking, what's in it for you?"

He stirred beside her. "Peace of mind, maybe. Or at least some answers. I've never gotten past what happened with Nick, or his death. For years he was my closest friend. I thought I knew him. But it appears I didn't know him at all. I want to move on. But for that, I need to understand

Nick and what motivated him to kill himself. I need to see him through your eyes."

Megan swallowed the ache in her throat. As expected, he hadn't asked her about the money directly. But his words had stirred up some painful emotions. She'd asked for this; but even after two years she wasn't ready to talk about her marriage.

"I don't know if I can help you," she said. "When the theft was discovered and Nick took his own life, I was as shocked as you were."

"So have you been able to move on, Megan?"

Had she? Megan struggled with the question. She'd dealt with Nick's death by running away to a part of the world where tragedy was commonplace. But the past was still there, like an unhealed wound, and now Cal wanted to rip that wound open.

"Maybe we can help each other," he said. "It might do us both good to talk."

"Talk about Nick?" She shook her head. "If that's what you want from me, you've come a long way for nothing. It still hurts too much."

Turning away from her, he fixed his gaze on the night sky. Megan studied his craggy profile, the Roman nose, the determined chin, as she waited to see how he'd respond to her refusal of his request. Cal Jeffords wasn't a man to take no for an answer.

"If talking about Nick's too painful, why don't you tell me about yourself?" he persisted. "I don't know much about your background, except that you were a nurse. Where did you grow up, Megan?"

Even talking about her early life was hard. But Cal wasn't about to let up. "I grew up in Arkansas," she said, "in a little hill town you've never heard of."

He looked at her again, one eyebrow quirked. "I'd never have guessed it. You don't sound like a Southerner."

"I was born in Chicago and lived there till I was six. Then my parents died in a car accident—New Year's Eve, drunk driver, no insurance."

"Sorry. Tough break for a kid."

"My grandmother agreed to take me and raise me up 'in righteousness,' as she was fond of saying. Granny was a good woman, and she meant well, but…"

The words trailed off as Megan remembered the spankings with a hickory rod, meant to drive out the devil, the long passages of scripture learned by rote, the endless hours of sitting on a hard bench in revival meetings while the preacher raged hellfire and damnation.

"I get the picture," Cal said. "And I'm guessing some of that so-called righteousness was a hard pill to swallow right after losing your parents. No kid wants to be told that her parents had to die so they could be in a better place without her. It explains, in part, why you left that all behind so completely."

"Don't try to psychoanalyze me, Cal. I've done enough of that on my own."

"Fine. Go on." He shifted beneath the blanket, his knee brushing hers. Megan sensed a shift in his manner, but she willed herself to ignore it.

"We were so poor that we wore clothes from the church's charity bin. But Granny had inherited her little house and the acre of land it sat on. When I was seventeen, she died of a heart attack and left it to me. I sold the property to pay for college and never looked back."

"And so you became an angel of mercy." His tone was razor-edged. But given the extravagant way she'd lived with Nick, Megan could hardly blame him for being cynical.

"Oh, at first I had some idealistic dreams about what I

could do with a nursing degree," she said. "But by graduation I was broke, and the top-paying job I could find was with one of San Francisco's best-known plastic surgeons."

"I take it the good doctor didn't hire ugly nurses."

"That's not fair!" Megan reined the impulse to slap him. Apparently he'd dropped the pretense of just wanting to know her better. Now he was firmly back into judgmental mode—the way he usually was when he spoke to her, back before Nick's death. Their interactions had been limited, but his tone with her had always made his disdain perfectly clear.

"I was good at my work—very good," she insisted. "But yes, we had to project the right image for the clients—hair, makeup, fitted uniforms, the whole package. And I didn't mind. After years of donated clothes—washed out, shapeless and worn down nearly to rags—I enjoyed having nice things that I could buy new, and money to spend on a hairdresser or a manicurist. I learned a lot from the women who came in for procedures—where to shop, how to dress, where to get my hair done. Some of them were even friendly enough to invite me to their charity galas. That was how I met Nick." She paused, sensing she'd stepped onto dangerous ground. "That's it. You know the rest of the story."

"Yes. Cinderella went to the ball, met her handsome prince and they lived happily ever after…or, whatever the hell really happened."

The anger that flashed through Megan was as instantaneous as torched gasoline. She'd tried to be patient and open with the man. But he'd repaid her with sarcasm and contempt. Twisting on the bench, she faced him with blazing eyes.

"It's my turn to ask the questions, Cal Jeffords!" She flung the words at him. "I didn't steal the money! I didn't kill Nick! I've done nothing immoral or illegal! What gives you the right to be my judge and jury? What have I done to make you hate me so much?"

"Hate you? Damn it, Megan, all I want is to understand what happened—and to understand you! Why do you make it so hard?"

"You're the one who's making it hard," she flung back at him. "You didn't come here for a good time. You came because you wanted something. Why can't you just be honest with me for a change? What kind of game are you playing?"

With a muttered curse, he seized her shoulders and jerked her close. For an instant his eyes burned their anguish into her soul. Then his mouth captured hers in a brutal, crushing kiss.

Five

The heat of Cal's kiss jolted through Megan like the burn of a bullet. She felt a rush of sensation—too sharply intense for her to decide if it was even pleasurable or not. Then her pulse went crazy as stark panic set in. Wild with senseless fear, she thrashed against him, fists flying at whatever target they could find.

Shoving her to arm's length, he released her and sank against the back of the bench. His face reflected shock—and a few red marks from where her wild blows had connected—but he spoke calmly. "Megan, it's all right. Nobody's going to hurt you."

Something in his voice reached her. She willed herself to clasp her hands in her lap and breathe. She was safe, she told herself firmly. Cal hadn't meant to harm her. The only danger was in her mind.

As the panic ebbed, she began to tremble. Her shoulders sagged. Her head dropped into her open hands. How could she have let this happen?

"Forgive me, Megan. I should have known better." He made no effort to touch her; but when she found the courage to look up, his stricken eyes met hers. With wrenching effort, she found her voice.

"Please…I'll be fine. Just don't do that again," she whispered.

Releasing a long breath, he stood. "Relax. I'll get you something to drink." Stepping inside, he returned a moment later with one of the water bottles from the room and held it out to her. Megan took long sips, letting the cool water calm her. Her senses took in the fresh smell of rain and the musical drone of crickets in the darkness as her heartbeat calmed enough for her to hear past its thudding in her ears.

"Better?" he asked.

She managed to nod. "Getting there. Not quite the reaction you get from most of the ladies you kiss, is it? But I'm in no mood to offer any sort of apology. You were out of line. What were you thinking?"

"I won't even try to answer that question." His chuckle sounded strained. "Is there anything I can get you?"

"Not really. But some time alone to settle my nerves might help."

"Fine. I'll go keep Harris company in the bar. You won't be going anywhere else, will you?"

"Just to bed." The panic attack had drained her. She barely had the energy to speak. "Take the key. With luck I'll be asleep when you get back."

"Got it." His voice was edged with caution. "Rest, now. We've got a long day ahead of us tomorrow. Let's put tonight behind us and make it a good one." He turned to go, then glanced back at her. "I've learned my lesson, Megan. You have my word. I won't frighten you like that again.

You're right that you don't owe me an apology—I owe you one. I'm truly sorry for upsetting you."

Unable to form a response, she looked away and heard his footsteps fade around the corner of the bungalow. Outwardly she was calm enough. But Cal's kiss had set off a maelstrom of inner turmoil. Wrapping herself in the blanket, she struggled to sort out her thoughts.

Cal was experienced enough to read most women. If he'd had any idea she might fight him, he would never have kissed her. Had he picked up on signals she wasn't even aware of sending? Had she actually *wanted* to be kissed? By him, of all people? He was an attractive man, but she could honestly say she'd never imagined him in an intimate context. He'd always seemed so cold toward her—coldly disdainful at first, and then, at Nick's funeral, coldly vengeful.

She recalled, in vivid detail, the white-hot sensation that had flashed through her body as his lips crushed hers. There had been nothing cold about him in that moment. With the last man she'd kissed—the doctor in the camp— she'd felt nothing. With Cal, what she'd felt was a sensual overload so powerful it had terrified her.

What did it mean? Was she healing or getting worse?

What would happen if she let him kiss her again?

Trembling, she hugged her arms against her ribs. For now there was little chance of that. Cal had promised to leave her alone for the rest of the trip. If she was wise, she would hold him to that promise. The boundaries they'd set tonight were meant to keep her safe. Pushing those boundaries would involve more risk than she had the courage to take.

But there was one thing tonight had taught her. Cal wasn't the problem. She was.

Rising, she walked into the bungalow, locked the door and set herself to making her bed on the sofa.

Cal was in no frame of mind to sit around in the bar. His restless pace carried him along the darkened walkways, through the coffee grove and around the inside perimeter of the wall. With each stride, his thoughts churned.

He hadn't planned on kissing Megan. In fact, he'd warned himself not to. But it had happened—and the brief seconds it lasted had only sharpened his appetite for more. Even after her fear-driven response, his body ached with the desire to sweep her into bed and pleasure her torment away.

But never mind his own needs. There were darker forces at work here, and deeper concerns.

Megan's frenzied reaction had opened his eyes to what he should have realized earlier. She wasn't just exhausted from her time in the camps. And she wasn't just traumatized by the things she'd witnessed.

Something had happened to her.

Lack of cell service rendered Cal's mobile device useless here. But the lodge had a bank of antiquated computers with internet available for guests. Sitting in an empty spot, he logged in to his email and checked a few incoming messages, then opened a new window. Taking his time, he composed a message to the director in charge of volunteer records for the J-COR Foundation, requesting a copy of Megan's performance evaluations and medical history for the past two years. The records were supposed to be confidential; but as the foundation's head, he had the power to override that rule.

Megan would be upset if she knew he was meddling. But he needed to get to the root of her fear. Otherwise, how could he hope to understand her, or get her some help? Whatever their past connection, he could tell she was deeply troubled. How could he be so callous as to turn his back and leave her hurting?

He'd come to Africa with one purpose—to track down Megan and get justice for the loss of the money and Nick's death. But he hadn't counted on the complications. He hadn't counted on Megan's fragility or on his own accursed need to rescue the woman. He hadn't counted on becoming emotionally involved.

Now he was scrambling for answers—answers to questions he wouldn't have thought to ask a week ago. And it wasn't in his nature to walk away. He wouldn't rest, he knew, until he'd learned everything he needed to know about her.

Megan heard Cal come in and lock the door; but she pretended to be asleep. As his footsteps paused beside the sofa, she willed herself to keep perfectly still. She knew that he was no threat to her safety. But he might want to talk—and the last thing she'd wanted was to be grilled about what had happened tonight. Cal wasn't her doctor or her therapist. The mess inside her head was her private concern. She would deal with it in her own time, in her own way.

Before long, he was asleep in bed, snoring lightly. She lay awake in the darkness, comforted by the peaceful, masculine sound. Strange, how safe that sound made her feel.

If only she'd felt that way in his arms.

But Cal was a complication she didn't need right now. She was too damaged for any kind of relationship—especially with a man whose past history with her was one big red flag.

She was beginning to drift. The couch wasn't the most comfortable bed, but she'd slept on far worse; and the long day had worn her out. She'd come here to rest, she reminded herself; to relax and do her best to heal...if only she could.

For a time she slumbered quietly. Then, the specter rose from the darkness of sleep once more. Like bones exposed by blowing sand, it emerged, took shape, took on life and substance to become living memory. Once again she heard Saida's cry as her young lover fell. She saw the shadowy forms close around the helpless girl, heard the rough laughter as they flung her to the ground, heard the helpless cries and the sound of tearing cloth. Beyond the dry well, Megan writhed against the sinewy arms that held her, screaming into the greasy palm that clamped her mouth. She could smell the sweat, taste it...

Something jolted Cal awake. He sat up, eyes staring into the darkness. As his senses cleared, he heard muffled whimpers and the sound of thrashing from the couch.

Flinging the covers aside, he switched on a bedside lamp and stumbled out of bed. As he neared Megan, he saw that she'd become tangled in a web of netting and covers. Eyes closed in sleep, she was fighting to get free.

"Megan." He spoke softly, knowing better than to grab her or shake her. "Megan, wake up. You're dreaming."

Clearly in torment, she continued to struggle. Working with care, he pulled away the netting and the twisted sheet and blanket. It seemed to make a difference, ending her frantic writhing—though her expression remained tense and fearful. She sprawled in her cotton pajamas, calmer now as he bent over her. Daring to touch her, he smoothed the damp curls back from her forehead. "It's all right," he murmured. "You're safe. I'm here."

Her eyelids fluttered open. She stared up at him. "Cal?"

"You were dreaming. Do you know where you are?"

He saw the flicker of uncertainty in her eyes. "You're in the bungalow with me," he said. "Everything's all right."

Her breath came in hiccupping, dry sobs. Cal remembered her panic attack in the hotel, when she'd allowed him to draw her close. It had helped her then. But after she'd fought her way out of their kiss, he knew better than to reach out to her without her permission. "Would you like me to hold you?" he asked.

She hesitated, then nodded. Ever so gently he circled her with his arms, pulling her against his chest. She clung to him like a frightened child, her heart still hammering her ribs.

Megan, Megan, what frightened you so? What can I do to help?

This was no time to voice his questions. Maybe the medical report would tell him something. Until then, he could only do his best to comfort her.

The room was chilly. A glance at the clock confirmed that it was too early to get up. But he didn't want to risk leaving her alone on the couch. There was only one thing to do.

"Let me carry you to the bed," he said. "You'll be safe there, even from me, I promise. All right?"

When she didn't answer he lifted her in his arms. Her hands crept onto his shoulders as he carried her across the floor. Parting the mosquito net, he lowered her to the mattress and pulled the covers over her. She was still quivering when he left her to walk around the bed and switch off the lamp.

Could he really climb between the sheets with this woman and keep the promise he'd made to her? He didn't entirely trust himself awake, let alone half-asleep. But there was a precaution he could take.

Lifting the blankets, he slipped under them, leaving

the top sheet as a discreet layer between his body and Megan's. He couldn't recall ever sharing a woman's bed without planning to make love to her. But there was a first time for everything.

She lay curled slightly away from him, but he could feel her trembling body through the sheet. She couldn't possibly be asleep. "Are you all right?" he asked her.

"I will be."

"Tell me about your dream." Was he pushing her too fast? He wasn't sure she'd answer, but after a slow, unraveling breath, she spoke.

"There was this young girl who used to help me, when I was in Darfur. She was just fifteen, a beautiful child. She left the camp at night to meet a boy. I went after them, but I was too late."

"They were killed?"

"The boy was killed. The girl was…raped. Afterward she was never found."

"Janjaweed?"

"Yes."

"And you saw it happen."

"There was nothing I could do."

"I'm sorry, Megan." Acting on instinct, he laid an arm across her shoulders, on top of the covers. He half expected her to pull away, but the weight seemed to calm her. She was no longer trembling. Encouraged, he tightened his clasp. With a sleepy murmur she snuggled against him, warm through the sheet. "Go to sleep," he murmured. "No more bad dreams. I'm here."

She relaxed with a sigh, the cadence of her breath deepening. Wide-awake now, Cal lay holding her in the darkness. He had nothing but admiration for the volunteers who served in the refugee camps. The work demanded courage, compassion and the strength to look death in the face. Until Harlan Crandall's report, he would never have believed Megan capable of such fortitude. But her time in the camps had taken its toll. He'd seen evidence of that toll tonight.

He was familiar with the Janjaweed, of course—mercenaries paid by the Sudanese government for the express purpose of genocide against the black African population. Known as Devil Riders for the horses and camels they rode, they swept down on innocent civilians, killing, robbing and raping. Now that much of the bloody work was done, groups of Janjaweed had turned to banditry, even going so far as to rob the big white U.N. trucks that carried food and supplies to the camps. The refugees had little worth stealing, but if the marauders happened to catch an unguarded woman...

Cal's arm curled protectively around Megan's slumbering body. He could scarcely imagine the bravery it must have taken for her to go after that young girl and boy in the dark of night. At least she'd made it safely back to the camp. Thank heaven for that. Maybe now that she'd talked about the experience, she could begin the healing process.

She stirred, shifted and settled back into sleep. Now he could see the dark outline of her profile, fine-boned and elegant against the white pillowcase. His memory of the pampered ice queen he'd known in San Francisco was fading. This was Megan, as he thought of her now. And it was getting harder to reconcile her with the cold, high-living trophy wife whose extravagance had driven his best friend to suicide.

Cal had seen the checks himself—the generous donations from the charity events Megan oversaw that had never made it into the foundation's bank account. The graceful signature on the back had been Megan's, but they'd gone to a joint account in a different bank—an account in her name and Nick's. The online statements had gone to their home computer, which was registered to Megan. By the time the theft was discovered, the account had been almost empty.

How could he not believe she'd been involved in the theft, or even responsible for it?

Was there more to the story than what he knew? He wanted to believe that Nick was innocent—or that, at worst, he'd crossed the line solely to please his demanding wife. Nick had seemed so proud of her, so anxious to satisfy her every whim. But the woman beside him now didn't seem the type to manipulate her husband into theft—especially since the money had been earmarked for aid to the very same people she'd spent the past two years nursing.

Had Nick's death triggered a change of heart, making her regret her past actions? Had she changed…or had he been wrong about her all along?

Whatever was going on with Megan now, Cal couldn't let himself forget what had happened back in San Francisco. He'd been betrayed by the friend he would have trusted with his life. If he'd mistrusted Nick, how could he let himself believe that Nick's wife was blameless?

He couldn't afford to trust her until he knew the whole truth, no matter how ugly.

Megan woke alone in the bed. The bungalow was dark, but as her confusion cleared she became aware of water running in the bathroom. Beneath the closed door she could see a sliver of light.

Sitting up, she switched on the bedside lamp. Now she remembered the dream, and the aftermath—Cal's comforting voice, his strong arms lifting her off the couch and carrying her across the room to the bed. Amazingly, she'd slept for the rest of the night without nightmares.

She'd just flung back the covers when he stepped out of the bathroom, shaved, combed and dressed. He gave her an easy grin.

"Good morning, sleepyhead. I was about to wake you."

"What time is it?" she asked with a yawn.

"Five-thirty. Harris wants us on the road by six, so get a move on. There'll be coffee and a light breakfast in the lobby."

"Where are we going?" She dropped her feet to the cold tile floor.

"You'll see. It's a surprise."

"A surprise! Why do you and Harris insist on treating me like a five-year-old?"

His laughter followed her into the bathroom as she closed the door with a decisive click. She remembered what he'd said last night. Yes, it was time to put the drama behind her and start the day fresh.

By the time Gideon pulled the Land Rover up to the front of the lodge, Megan had finished her breakfast. The trees were alive with bird calls, and the amethyst sunrise promised clear weather. She looked forward to a day of adventure. Maybe this trip was exactly what she'd needed.

She stole a glance at Cal, where he stood talking with Harris. Her gaze traced the taper of his back from well-muscled shoulders to taut buttocks. By any measure, the man was prime stud material. But last night had proved she wasn't fit for any kind of physical relationship. Maybe she never would be.

At least he seemed to understand that. Since that disastrous kiss, he'd treated her like a kid sister. Even sharing the bed with him had been a chaste experience—perhaps a first for a man like Cal.

She tore her gaze away from his body. Under different conditions, she might not have minded sharing more than a blanket. But something vital in her was broken, shattered by forces she couldn't even name. If she was going to panic again, as she surely would, the last person she wanted it to happen with was Cal Jeffords.

"Ladies aboard!" Harris gave her a wink as he crushed his cigar with his boot heel and swung into the front passenger seat. "And may I add that you're looking right pert this morning, Miss Megan! Are you ready for your surprise?"

"Bring it on!" She tossed her day pack into the vehicle's bed, behind the backseat. It bounced off a basketball-size chunk of broken concrete lying next to the tailgate. "Is that what you plan to throw at anything that attacks us?" she joked.

"That's my wheel block," Harris said. "Believe me, if you get a puncture out there or need to park on a hill, you don't want to have to go looking for a rock. There could be some nasty surprises in that long grass. I've never had to use it—hope I never will. But it pays to be prepared."

Giving him a grin, she climbed into the backseat and spoke to the driver. "Good morning, Gideon. It's nice to have you with us."

"Thank you, miss." His tone was formal, but his expression told her he was pleased with her greeting.

"Let's go." Cal climbed into the backseat with Megan. The air was cool now, but the rising sun promised to be hot. Megan tightened the chin strap on her canvas hat. She was going to need it.

Cal studied Megan as the Land Rover climbed the winding road to the rim of the Ngorongoro Crater. She had just discovered where they were going today, and she was as excited as a child at the circus. Last night he'd feared for her mental state. But seeing her this morning, radiant and laughing, with her jade-green scarf knotted at her throat, was worth every dollar this safari had cost him. If he were meeting her for the first time today, with no past history between them, he could easily see himself falling for her charm.

This must have been the woman Nick saw when he looked at her. For the first time, Cal understood why Nick had fallen so hard and so fast. And Cal could no longer really say that he blamed him.

The thought shook him. Nick had been the type to fall in love easily, but while Cal had known plenty of women, he hadn't fancied himself in head over heels since high school. He'd been too serious, too driven for such frivolous emotion. He'd always felt that it was an advantage he had over Nick. But it didn't feel like too much of an advantage at the moment.

He put the thought out of his head. Megan was a fascinating package, but not what he'd call a candidate for a stable relationship. And he'd be a fool to let desire color his need for justice.

This morning he'd taken a moment to check his email. The medical report hadn't arrived. It might not arrive for days. Meanwhile he had no choice except to be patient—and Cal was not a patient man.

A flock of doves whooshed out of a flowering tree and soared skyward against the sunrise. "Beautiful…" The word was a whisper on Megan's lips. Cal remembered kissing those lips, crushing them with his. And he remembered what had followed. What had thrown her into panic? Was it him?

The Land Rover had crested the top of the crater and

was starting down the graveled road to the vast caldera below.

"Can you see any animals yet?" Cal asked Megan. "Here, take the binoculars."

Looking out the open side of the vehicle, she scanned the landscape below. "All I can see is grass and brush."

"You'll see a lot more when we get to the bottom," Harris said. "Last time I was here I saw a black rhino. Poor buggers will be extinct if the poachers get many more of them. The horns are worth big money. Arabs buy them for dagger handles. And powdered rhino horn's the rich Chinese version of Viagra. Works on the mind if nothing else, I suppose. Not that I've tried it—or needed to." He shot Cal and Megan a mischievous look.

"Are there poachers here in the crater?" Megan asked.

"They've been known to sneak in at night. Rangers have the go-ahead to shoot them on the spot. I'd do the same if I caught the bastards."

"But you guide hunters, don't you Harris?"

"Not here. This place is a national park. The animals here are meant to be protected. And legal hunting's not like poaching. Hunters pay thousands for a license to take one trophy animal. Part of the money goes to fund game management, including protection for animals like our rhino friend. And the cash that goes into the economy encourages the locals to see wild animals as the resource they are. Poaching's like the dark side. It takes all the good away."

"I see something." Cal pointed to a cluster of black dots. "Down there to the right, four o'clock."

Harris nodded. "Cape buffalo. Tough and mean as they come. We can get closer in the vehicle, but don't let them catch you on foot. I learned that lesson the hard way—see this?" He pointed to his empty, pinned-up sleeve. "Biggest bull you ever saw. Damn near killed me."

Lifting an eyebrow, Cal glanced at Megan. She rewarded him with a wink and a sexy smile that kicked his pulse into overdrive. He cursed silently. A few hot nights between the sheets would suit him fine. But with her panic attacks, her shadowed past and her connection to Nick and the stolen money, Megan was the last woman he should get serious with.

He could see it happening, and it made a delicious picture. Sharing some pillow talk with Megan had been his plan all along. But he hadn't planned on becoming emotionally involved. He was walking a fine line, and Lord help him if he stepped over. He could find himself in serious trouble.

Six

Megan gripped her camera, hesitant to raise it and risk triggering a charge. She'd heard how dangerous the huge black Cape buffalo could be. But these seemed accustomed to vehicles. They barely raised their massive heads as the Land Rover passed at a fifty-yard distance. Egrets—fairy white—stalked among their ebony legs, unafraid as they probed for insects in the grass.

"They seem so peaceful," she whispered to Cal. "And look, there's a little black calf—and another!"

"All the more reason to be careful." Cal's low voice was close to her ear. "They're family animals. Very protective."

"We should be seeing more babies." With the buffalo upwind of them, Harris spoke in his normal tone. "Now that the rains have started, there'll be plenty of grass—plenty of meat for the predators, as well. Good time to raise young ones."

Megan gazed ahead to an open plain where dainty

Thomson's gazelles were grazing. The ebony stripes along their sides glimmered in the morning sunlight.

"Do you have children, Harris?" she asked.

"A boy by my second wife. She took him home to England after the divorce. I hear he's a barrister of some sort, but we don't talk."

"I'm sorry."

"That's life, girl. You play the hand you're dealt and make the best of it."

Wise words, Megan thought. She'd been trying to make the best of her own life. But surprises kept throwing her off track. Surprises like Cal Jeffords showing up and turning her world upside down.

"How about you, Gideon?" she asked the driver. "Do you have a family?"

A smile broadened his long face. "Yes, miss. Three fine boys and two girls. They keep my wife very busy."

"I can tell you're very proud of them."

"Yes, miss. Good children are a blessing from God."

Something had spooked the gazelles. Their heads and tails shot up, and they burst into glorious flight, leaping and bounding like winged creatures. Even the little ones, all legs, were fleet enough to keep up with the herd as they vanished over a rise.

Gideon glanced at Harris, who nodded. "Lion, maybe. Come up easy."

Lion. Megan's heart crept into her throat as the Land Rover slowed to a crawl. She'd been in Africa for two years, but there were few, if any, large wild animals left in the places where she'd worked. Outside of a zoo, she'd never seen a lion.

In the open-sided vehicle, they were fully exposed to any creature that might decide to attack them. She'd glimpsed the high-powered rifle Harris kept mounted next to the passenger door, but he didn't seem concerned about having it ready.

She glanced at Cal. Reading her anxiety, he laid a light hand against her back. She moved closer to him. He might not be much use against a lion, but his size and strength made her feel safer.

The Land Rover inched around a bend in the narrow road, and suddenly there they were—two lionesses, sprawled on the grass a mere stone's throw away. The larger one studied the vehicle and its passengers with calm amber eyes. Her huge mouth opened in a disdainful yawn that showed yellowed fangs as long as Megan's fingers.

"Mother and daughter, I'd say," Harris whispered. "Look, the older one's pregnant. Big sister will likely stick around to help raise the cubs. Go ahead and take a picture. They're posing for you."

Megan's hands shook as she centered the pair in her viewfinder and pressed the shutter. The click was startling in the silence, but the lionesses barely glanced toward the sound. Gideon was about to move on when Harris touched his arm. "Hold it," he whispered. "Here comes papa!"

Megan was aware of a stirring, like wind in the long grass. She forgot to breathe as a majestic male lion strolled into view. Regal and unhurried, he seemed more interested in the females than in the Land Rover and the lowly humans inside. There was no need to prove who was king here.

Megan managed a few more shaky photos before Gideon pulled away, leaving the lions in peace. Harris grinned. "Now there's a life for you! The women raise the cubs and bring down the meat. Nothing for the old man to do but fight and make love."

"Not that he has it that easy." Cal's voice was close to

Megan's ear. "He has to defend his territory and his family from gangs of rival males. The stakes are life and death."

"That's a grim thought," Megan said. "Oh, look! Zebras out there in the open! And what's up there, next to the road? Something black!"

"Warthogs," Harris said. "A family of them, rooting for their breakfast."

"And they've got babies!" Megan rose in the seat, aiming her camera and snapping. "Look at them! So tiny and so cute!"

"Again, it's the male's job to protect them." Cal steadied her with a hand at her waist. "He may not be very big, but those tusks can rip a lion's belly, and the lions know it."

She glanced down at him. "Why aren't you taking pictures?"

He gave her his Hollywood grin. "I've got plenty of pictures from other trips. Right now I'm having more fun watching you."

Cal had spoken the truth. Being with Megan today was like being with a little girl at Disneyland. She was so natural and so excited; every minute with her was a delight.

He remembered the glittering ice queen who'd been married to Nick—perfect hair and makeup, runway clothes, the best of everything. Which one was the real her? Was this exuberance a part of her that she'd stifled all those years? If so, then he could almost understand Megan running away to escape the person she'd become.

What if it hadn't been about the money, after all? Today he could almost believe that. But no—he brought himself up short. Megan was as changeable as the wind. He'd be a fool to start trusting her.

Last night he'd watched her fall apart. Today she was behaving as if nothing had happened. Had the panic attack and the nightmare been some kind of performance, staged to gain his sympathy?

But how could that be? How could any person with a shred of honesty be capable of such deception? He couldn't believe that of Megan. But what *could* he believe about her? He had little choice except to wait for the report he'd ordered and hope it would give him some insight.

They stopped to eat bagged lunches on a safely fenced rise with primitive restrooms, picnic tables and a wide vista of the grassland below.

"I still can't believe one of those lions didn't jump right into our laps." Megan took a sip of her bottled water. "What would you do, Harris, if something like that happened?"

"I'd fire into the air and try to scare the bugger away. There'd be no end of trouble if I shot one of those babies in the park. Best way to keep that from happening is to read their body language. If they're looking uneasy, you keep your distance. Those lions we saw back there were as mellow as big pussycats. Otherwise we'd have given them a wide berth."

"Have you ever had an animal charge your vehicle?"

"Just once. White rhino in Tarangire. Made a bloody dent in the door and crushed my arm. That's how this happened." He glanced toward the pinned sleeve. Megan shot Cal a knowing glance, her eyes dancing, her smile a flash of white in her tanned face. He'd thought she was beautiful when she was married to Nick. Today she was spectacular.

The breeze had freshened. Harris squinted toward the far rim of the crater, where black clouds churned above the horizon, ready to stampede across the empty sky.

"We'd best be heading back," Harris said. "But there's plenty of time. We'll take a different road, off the beaten track as they say. Might see something new."

Megan climbed into the backseat and settled next to Cal. The morning had been incredible, but the hours spent in the hot sun and the jouncing, swaying vehicle had taken their toll. As time passed, her energy had begun to flag.

Back in the camps, she'd spent her days working in the infirmary from first light to bedtime, collapsing on her cot and then getting up at dawn to more of the same. Only now that she had the luxury of rest did Megan realize how exhausted she'd become. Even so, she missed being useful. When she got back to the bungalow, she would find some paper and write letters to people she'd known and worked with in the refugee camps. If she could let them know she meant to come back, that would strengthen her own resolve to get strong again.

After she finished the letters, maybe she'd look for some light reading in the lodge gift shop—a thriller or maybe a romance, anything to engage her mind and block the nightmares before she went to sleep.

The distant growl of thunder pulled her back to the present. Cal was watching her, mild concern in his eyes. "I thought you were about to nod off," he said.

"Would you have let me?"

"Only until we saw something you wouldn't want to miss. If you're sleepy, my shoulder makes a good pillow."

For an instant Megan was tempted. But accepting Cal's offer might be courting fate. Bad enough that Cal had witnessed one of her nightmares. She didn't want Harris or Gideon to see them, too. She shook her head. "I'm fine—and I don't want to miss anything."

The sky was getting darker now as fast-moving rain clouds blocked the sun. The Land Rover had cut off onto a side trail and was crossing an open plain dotted with thornbush. A herd of zebras and dark-hued wildebeest grazed in the distance. There were no other vehicles in sight.

"Along here is where I saw the black rhino," Harris said. "If he's still in the neighborhood, we might get lucky. Keep your eyes open."

He'd no sooner spoken than the sky split open as if someone had slashed a giant, water-filled balloon. Thunder roared across the horizon as sheets of gray rain turned the road to a quagmire of flowing mud.

Gideon muttered what Megan assumed to be a curse. Harris, however, was undeterred. "What's a little rain?" he shouted, grinning. "We can't stay here, so nothing to do but keep going!"

The canvas roof kept off the overhead downpour, but water was still blowing in. Megan, who hadn't thought to bring her rain poncho, was already drenched. There had to be a way to roll down the side covers. But she assumed it would involve stopping and having someone get out—impractical now because they'd just come up on another herd of Cape buffalo.

Something—maybe the lightning and thunder—had disturbed the hulking black beasts. More numerous than the first group, they were milling and snorting like range cattle on the verge of a stampede. Megan remembered Harris's words about reading an animal's body language. The signs that she could read from them made it clear that danger was very real.

The others seemed to agree. Gideon was driving as fast as he dared, trying to get past the herd without agitating them further. As the vehicle swayed along the muddy road, Megan found herself shivering, not only with cold but with fear.

Reaching across the seat, Cal circled her with his arm and drew her close. She huddled against his side. There was little warmth to be had, but she found the hard bulk of his body comforting, like a rock to cling to for safety.

What happened next happened fast. A low, dark shape—a warthog—shot across the road, almost under the front wheels. Instinctively, Gideon slammed the brake. The animal streaked away unharmed, but the Land Rover fishtailed in the thick mud and crunched to a stop with one rear wheel resting in a water-filled hole at the roadside.

Gideon revved the engine and tried to pull out—once, then again, rocking forward and back. It was no use. The mud was so slippery that the heavy-duty tires could find no purchase. They spun in place, shooting geysers of mud and water.

For a tension-filled moment nobody spoke. But Megan guessed what the men were thinking. The rain could go on for hours, making the road even worse. Even if they could radio for help, it was doubtful that anyone could get here before the storm let up. If they were going to free the vehicle, somebody would have to brave the buffalo and push from behind.

Since Gideon knew the vehicle best, it made sense for him to stay at the wheel. With one arm, Harris could neither push nor shift and drive efficiently. That left Cal—the huskiest of the men—to climb out into the mud.

The buffalo had turned as one to watch them. Frozen in place for the moment, they were perhaps fifty yards away—a distance that a charging animal could cover in a heartbeat.

Harris lifted the rifle from its bracket next to the door. "I'll cover you," he said. "If the bastards get any closer, I'll fire over their heads, try to scare them off."

Megan read the knowing glance the two men exchanged. If one of the massive bulls were to actually charge, there'd be little chance of stopping it, even if Harris aimed to kill. A single rifle shot, even a lucky one, wouldn't be enough to drop it on the spot. And a wounded Cape buffalo would be a murderous foe.

"Why not scare them off now?" Megan asked.

"Risky," Harris grunted. "Spooking them could make them more aggressive. Safest thing is to keep them calm, if we can."

"What can I do to help?"

"Pray," he snapped, dismissing her.

Harris shouldered the rifle with his left hand, resting the barrel on the door. Megan had wondered briefly whether he could handle a gun with one arm. Evidently he could.

He glanced back at Cal. "Whatever you do, keep your head down and stay close to the vehicle," he said. "If the buffalo see you in the open, you're in trouble. Ready?"

"Ready." Ducking low, Cal climbed into the back of the Land Rover and bellied over the tailgate. Megan's heart crawled into her throat as she watched him go. More than anything she wanted to stop him. Harris had told her to pray, but her mind had lost the words. There was nothing she could do but watch.

She could see the back of Cal's head and shoulders as he braced himself behind the rear bumper. "Hit it," he growled.

Gideon slammed the vehicle into gear and gunned the engine. The wheels inched forward, spattering mud, then the rear sank back into the hole.

Cal muttered a curse. "Can you back it out?"

"I already tried. No good," Gideon said.

"There's a shovel back here. Can we dig out a track?"

"Better not to try," Harris said. "That much activity could set off the buffalo." He was looking not at Cal but at the herd. As lightning crackled across the sky, they were becoming more agitated, stamping, lowing and tossing their heads. The biggest bull of all, with curling horns as broad and thick as the bumper on a truck, had moved front and center. His nostrils flared as he processed the alien odors of motor exhaust and human sweat.

Cal repositioned himself behind the tailgate. "All right. Again."

Once more the engine roared. Cal's shoulder muscles strained like steel cables as he pushed back and upward. The tires spun and spat showers of mud before he gave up and slumped forward. "We need something to brace that wheel." His voice rasped with fatigue. "A rock, maybe to jam in the hole."

A rock! Megan remembered the chunk of concrete she'd seen in the back of the truck. It might work, but Cal couldn't shove it in place while he was pushing. He would need a second pair of hands. Hers.

The buffalo were massing behind their leader. Rain poured down their sleek black sides and dripped off their horns. Megan forced herself to look away and concentrate on her task as she slipped into the back bed of the vehicle and found the concrete. Harris and Gideon were watching the herd. They hadn't noticed her, but Cal did.

"What in hell's name do you think you're doing?" His eyes blazed in his mud-coated face.

She hefted the gray chunk, which was even heavier than it looked. "Hold this," she hissed, passing it to him.

He took it, but when she started to scramble over the tailgate, his gaze narrowed dangerously. "For God's sake, Megan, stay put!" he growled.

"You need me." She dropped to the ground, staying close to the vehicle. Taking the piece of concrete from him, she knelt and set it rough-side-up against the back of the mired wheel. She tried not to think about the buffalo and how close that big bull might be. Rain soaked her hair and streamed down her body, but she no longer felt the chill.

"Tell Gideon to try it again," she said, hoping Cal had one more push left in him. He was a powerful man, but he was only human and the effort would be excruciating.

He positioned himself against the bumper, feet braced, eyes meeting hers through the gray veil of rain. "Be careful," he muttered. "This thing could roll back and crush your hand."

"I'll be fine."

"If there's a charge, roll under the vehicle. That'll be the safest place. Understand?"

She gave him a nod, willing herself not to look toward the buffalo. "Ready."

"Hit it!"

Gideon gunned the motor to a roar. Grunting with the strain, Cal pushed and lifted. Spitting showers of mud, the mired wheel inched forward, leaving just enough space and time for Megan to shove the lump of concrete into the hole.

But would it be enough? As she tumbled backward, out of the way, Cal eased off long enough to let the tire settle onto the solid surface. Gideon was still racing the engine. Now, finding slight purchase, the wheel began straining forward.

"Now!" Cal began pushing with all his might. Scrambling to her feet, Megan flung herself next to him. Her weight was scant, her strength meager, but coupled with his it might be enough to make a difference.

Inch by inch the Land Rover crept forward. Now it was out of the deep mud, moving forward onto the main trail and gaining speed. Harris was whooping like a cowboy on Saturday night.

Hoisting Megan in his arms, Cal dumped her over the tailgate and clambered after her. She sat up and swung her attention back to the buffalo. The bull had burst into a false charge but stopped short, snorting and tossing its horns in what could almost pass as a victory dance at the sight of their retreat.

Bracing her by the shoulders, Cal looked her up and down as if inspecting her for damage. His hat was gone, and he was coated with mud from his hair to his boots. Megan realized she must look the same. "You're all right?" he asked.

She gave him a grin. "Never better. We did it!"

"You crazy woman! You could've been killed!" He caught her close, holding her fiercely against his chest. She was dimly aware of Harris and Gideon in the front seat, but it was as if the two men were far away and nobody was here but Cal. Adrenaline rushed through her body. She felt wonderfully wild and reckless.

"You brave, beautiful fool!" Laughing, he cradled her close, muddy clothes and all. His arms were warm and safe, his laughter like a joyful drug. Carried away, Megan was surprised to find herself wanting to be kissed—really kissed—by him.

But there was no way Cal was going to kiss her. Not after what had happened the last time. If Megan wanted a kiss from him, there was only one thing she could do.

Fueled by euphoria, she hooked his neck with her arm, pulled him down to her and pressed her parted lips to his.

Seven

Megan sensed the shock of Cal's surprise. Her heart shrank as he stiffened against her. But he was quick to recover. With a little growl of laughter, he took charge. His compelling mouth molded to hers with a teasing flick of tongue—playful and, at the same time, so sensual that she experienced a delicious twinge at the apex of her thighs.

The fear was still there, slumbering in the depths of her awareness. But the thrill of Cal's kiss swept her away like a plunge over a waterfall. For a fleeting moment, she savored the sweetness of something she'd believed lost.

Too soon, he ended the contact. "We have an audience," he muttered in her ear.

Megan glanced forward to find Harris turned in his seat, grinning back at them. "I'll be damned," he said with a wink. "I knew you two would come around. All it took was a thunderstorm, a stuck wheel and a herd of buffalo."

"Eyes front, *mzee,*" Cal said, using the Swahili term for

an old man. He smiled as he spoke, but Megan sensed that any more kissing would have to wait for a private time.

Riding in the bed of the Land Rover was rough and wet. Cal boosted her over the back of the seat and took his place beside her. His arm circled her shoulders, pulling her against his side to protect her from the worst of the storm.

Megan's heart hammered as she weighed the risky step she'd just taken. Had she turned a corner? Was she really getting better, or had the moment's excitement swept her away?

She yearned to be emotionally well again. To go through life unafraid of intimacy, to make love, even to remarry and have children—that was what she'd wanted all along. But over the past months she'd lost hope. The fear that had frozen some vital part of her—a fear so dark and deeply rooted that she didn't fully understand it herself—still lurked like a monster in its cave, waiting to reach out with its cold tentacles and crush her courage.

Back in America she might have sought professional help. But here what little help there was to be had was focused on treating the trauma of refugees—which was as it should be. And going home would only bring her up against the demons Nick's death had left behind.

For the first time she felt a glimmer of hope. She'd fought her attraction to Cal for as long as she'd known him. Now there was no more reason to fight. Something about his solid strength wrapped her in a sense of safety. His kiss had left her with a delicious buzz. But was it enough? Could she risk more, especially when she knew the reason he'd come here? Could she trust him not to manipulate her, or use her vulnerability against her? He'd been so good to her the previous night, but could she truly trust him? And could she trust herself not to get too invested?

Even if she dared go the distance, she knew better than

to think a fling with Cal would last. He wasn't the sort of man to settle on one woman. Even if he was, his dark suspicions and the painful history they shared would drive them apart. But he was an exciting man—a very sexy man. And she had little doubt he'd be willing to cooperate with her present needs.

Was it time she faced her fear?

The Land Rover crawled upward toward the rim of the crater. The going was treacherous, with rain churning the road to mud; but soon the long drive would be over. Chilled to the bone, Cal looked forward to a hot shower, dry clothes, a gourmet dinner at the lodge—and just maybe something more.

Megan nestled against his side, the contact of their bodies providing the only spot of warmth. As his arm tightened around her shoulders, she glanced up and gave him a quiet smile. She'd been amazing today, braving the buffalo to climb out of the vehicle and brace the wheel. How many women—or men—would have shown that kind of courage?

Her kiss, he suspected, had demanded a different kind of courage. After last night's panicked response, her sweet passion had caught him off guard. Whatever she'd meant by it, he wasn't complaining. But now what?

Clearly Megan was up to something. But he knew better than to push her. Be patient, Cal lectured himself. Let her take the lead; then follow to where they both wanted to go.

Hadn't he meant to seduce her all along? If that was what the woman had in mind, she was playing right into his hands. Get her warm and purring, and maybe she'd open up about what had happened in San Francisco.

It was still raining by the time they topped the crater and made it downhill to the lodge. Gideon pulled up in front to let his weary passengers climb out of the vehicle. Harris headed inside, probably for a warming glass of whiskey at the bar. Cal helped Megan out of the backseat. Chilled, muddy and cramped from sitting in the rain, they made their way down the brick path to their bungalow. They paused to leave their muddy boots on the doorstep for the staff. Then Megan used her key to open the door.

Inside, Cal fished a Tanzanian shilling out of his pocket. "I'll flip you for the first shower."

Meeting his eyes, she took the coin out of his hand. "It's a big shower," she said.

Cal was quick to get her meaning, even though her fingers trembled as she laid the coin on the table. This was her call, he reminded himself. All he had to do was follow her lead. He would have Megan right where he wanted her.

Their clothes were dripping mud. It didn't make sense to shed them anyplace but in the spacious, tiled shower, where they could at least rinse out the worst of the dirt. Megan walked into the bathroom, leaving the door open. Turning on the water, she stepped into the shower and began unfastening her mud-soaked blouse. Her quivering fingers fumbled with the buttons.

"Let me give you a hand." After shedding his leather belt, his watch and his wallet, Cal stepped in beside her and took over the buttons. He heard her breath catch as his knuckle brushed her breast. Slow and easy, he reminded himself. Megan was putting herself out to make this work. The last thing he wanted was to frighten her back into her shell.

Her jade-flecked eyes widened as the front of her blouse fell open to reveal a lacy black bra—perhaps a relic of the old days in San Francisco. The sight of that dark lace against creamy skin triggered an ache of raw need. Cal suppressed a groan as his sex rose and hardened. All he wanted right now was to rip off her wet clothes, sweep her into bed and bury himself inside her.

But haste could ruin everything. Megan was clearly willing to try. But he knew she'd been traumatized, and one wrong move could spoil everything. If he wanted her, he would have to hold back, be patient and let her set the pace.

If he could manage to keep himself under control.

Cal's shirt was open to his chest. Willing herself to stay calm, Megan freed the remaining buttons, down to the waistband of his trousers. There was nothing to be afraid of, she told herself. She'd been married to Nick for five years. Being naked with a man and having sex was nothing new. And she *wanted* this. She needed it. So why was her heart pounding like a jackhammer gone berserk?

She could feel his eyes, those perpetually cold gray eyes that had always seemed to look right through her. Eyes she remembered as contemptuous, especially after Nick's death. If she looked up, what would she see in them now?

Maybe she was making a fool of herself. Why would Cal want to make love to a woman he had every reason to dislike?

But then again, why wouldn't he?

The warm, clean shower spray rinsed their hair and sluiced down their bodies, running brown with African mud before it gurgled down the drain. A shiver of anticipation passed through Megan as Cal pushed her wet blouse off her shoulders. It slid down her arms and dropped to the tiles.

"Look at me, Megan." His voice was husky. His thumb caught the curve of her jaw, tilting her face upward. The eyes she'd remembered as cold burned with raw need.

Her hand moved upward to rest against his cheek. His

skin was warm, the stubble rough against her palm. "Kiss me, Cal," she whispered.

Leaning down, he feathered his lips against hers. The contact passed like a glowing thread of heat through her body, warming her to an aching awareness of how much she needed him. She strained upward to deepen the kiss and felt him respond, his arms pulling her close, his lips nibbling, tasting, moving to her cheeks, her throat and back to her mouth. His hand unhooked her bra and pushed at the waistband of her slacks. The fit was loose enough for them to slide off her hips and drop, along with her panties, to the shower floor. She stood naked in his arms—a trifle self-conscious because she was so thin, but Cal didn't seem to notice—or at least not to mind.

Finding a bar of scented soap, he lathered his hands and then reached for her, his palms slicking the warm suds across her shoulder blades and down the long furrow of her spine. Sweet sensations melted her body like hot fudge flowing over ice cream. Her tension eased out in a long sigh. Almost purring, she arched against the exquisite pressure of his hands. Her eyes closed as his fingers worked their delicious way down to trace the deep V of her lower back, splaying to cradle her buttocks. For a moment he held her that way, cupping her hips against his. Through his wet trousers she could feel the hard ridge of his sex pressing her belly.

A memory glimmered, awakening the cold coils that slumbered inside her. Megan willed herself to block the fear. She wanted to let Cal make love to her. She wanted to believe that she could heal. She wanted *him*.

He lowered his mouth to hers, his kiss gentle and lingering. "I want to touch all of you," he whispered, turning her around so that her back was toward him. His big soapy hands slid over her breasts, caressing them, cupping them in his palms, thumbing the nipples until they ached with yearning. A moan quivered in her throat.

"You're so beautiful, Megan. You were made to be loved." One hand lingered on her breast, and the other slid down to skim her navel, splay on her belly and brush the dark triangle of hair where her thighs joined. She wanted the burst of sensation that his touch would awaken when he explored further. But as his fingers moved lower, a chill passed through her body. The coils of fear shifted and tightened, and she sensed that she was losing the battle to hold them at bay.

Maybe things were happening too fast. If she took more time she might still be all right. Shifting away, she turned to face him.

"You need to clean up, too," she said, forcing a smile as she found the soap. "Let me wash your back."

Ignoring his slightly puzzled expression, she turned him away from her, pulled the mud-soaked shirt off his shoulders and tossed it onto the shower floor.

He had a magnificently sculpted back, broad and tanned and powerful. His smooth skin warmed to her touch. Megan luxuriated in the feel of him, letting her soapy hands glide over his muscular shoulders and down the solid, tapering curve of his spine. Little by little, as she stroked his warm, golden skin, she felt her fear ebbing. It was going to happen, she told herself. All she had to do was relax and let nature do the rest.

Reaching his waistband, she hesitated. With a raw laugh, Cal reached down, yanked open the fly and let his pants and briefs drop around his ankles. "Don't stop now," he said. "I'm enjoying this."

Ignoring a prickle of uneasiness, Megan soaped his taut buttocks. His body was perfect, everything tight and in flawless proportion. Any woman should be thrilled to have him in her bed. Her hands caressed curves and contours, moving forward to skim the ridges of his hip bones. She could feel the tension growing in him, sense the urgency in the harsh cadence of his breath. Her own pulse had begun to race—but was it from desire or from that unknown terror that had given her no peace since the night she'd gone after Saida?

He cleared his throat. "I think my back is clean enough. If you want to wash the rest of me, I'm all yours. Otherwise, just say so and I'll shut off the water and grab us some towels. I look forward to drying you off."

Megan glanced down at her soapy hands. Her heart lurched as she imagined Cal's jutting erection, gleaming like wet marble in her hands. She knew what he wanted. Heaven help her, she wanted it, too. But she could feel the cold dread, as sure and silent as death, rising inside her.

She froze.

"What is it, Megan?" He glanced back at her, his eyes narrowing with concern as he shut off the water. "What's the matter?"

She'd begun to shiver. Her arms clutched her ribs. Tears might have helped, but she hadn't shed them since that awful night in Darfur.

"I'm sorry." She choked out the words. "I thought I could do this, Cal. But I just can't. There's something wrong with me—something I can't control." She stared down at the shower drain, wishing she could just dissolve and flow away.

"You're getting cold." Stepping out onto the mat, he reached for one of the two white terry-cloth robes that hung on the back of the door. Gentleness masked his obvious frustration as he laid it over her trembling shoulders. Slipping her arms into the sleeves, she knotted the sash around her waist. Little by little her racing heart began to calm. By the time she forced herself to look at him, he'd donned the other robe.

"I was hoping this wouldn't happen," she said. "I should've known better. I feel like a fool."

"At least I appreciate your honesty," he said. "I wouldn't want to make love to a woman who wasn't enjoying herself."

"Not even if she *wanted* to enjoy herself?" Megan gripped her sash, yanking it tighter around her waist. "Do you think I want to be this way—flying into a panic whenever I'm faced with intimacy? All I want is to be a normal woman again. So I took a chance. It didn't work. Not even with you."

Not even with you. It was too late to bite back the words. The subtle shift in his expression told her what he'd read into them. He wasn't just another man to her. He was a man who meant something—even if she wasn't completely sure what. Their past together had been so troubled, but the things she admired about him—his strength, his determination, the intensity of his feelings—had made her hope that he could carry some of this burden for her, lighten the load enough to let her heal.

"Come sit down." His hand at the small of her back guided her out of the bathroom and across the bedroom floor to the couch. Sitting, he pulled her down next to him and covered them both with a woolen blanket. Tucking her bare feet under her, she nestled into its warmth. Rain drummed on the tile roof and streamed down the windowpanes.

"You were amazing out there today," he said. "I mean it."

"It was an adventure—and somebody had to help."

He slipped an arm around her shoulders, a friendly gesture, meant to be comforting. "You're a brave woman,

Megan—and strong. I'm just discovering how strong. But something's frightened you badly. When did these panic attacks start?"

"Are you trying to analyze me, Dr. Freud?" She attempted a feeble joke.

"I'm just trying to understand you—maybe even help if I can. When did you become aware that something was wrong?"

"I'm not sure." She wasn't about to describe her fiasco with the doctor. That disastrous date wasn't the source of her problem, just a symptom.

"The incident you dreamed about—going after that young girl and boy, seeing them attacked. When was that?"

She shrugged, uneasy with the question. "Five, maybe six months ago. It's hard to keep track of time there. But I remember it was the dry season."

"Where were you when you saw it happen? If you were afraid to help them—"

"No, I was *trying* to help them. I'd brought a pistol. But before I could use it, somebody grabbed me from behind and took it away. I couldn't move, couldn't scream. I could only watch." Megan felt the fear rising. "Don't ask me to talk about this, Cal. I don't want to."

"Fine." His breath eased out in a long exhalation. "Just one more question. How did you get away?"

The cold coils tightened. "I don't know. Maybe the Janjaweed let me go because I was American. Or maybe somebody came from the camp and scared them off. The next thing I remember, I was waking up in the infirmary."

"You really don't know what happened?"

"I was probably knocked out—or fainted—and somebody found me. That's the only explanation that makes sense." Agitated now, she flung the blanket aside and rose from the couch. "No more questions, Cal. Two innocent young lives were destroyed that night. I'll remember it forever, but that doesn't mean I want to talk about it."

Pulse racing, she strode to the wardrobe where she'd hung her meager supply of clothes and went through the motions of rummaging through the hangers. "Isn't it about dinnertime? I'm starved, and I can hardly wear this bathrobe to the dining room. So please excuse me while I get dressed." She grabbed a set of clothes without really looking at them and glanced back at him. "That debacle in the shower never happened. I never want to hear about it again."

Cal glanced across the table to where Megan was conversing animatedly with Harris. Since he'd grilled her about the incident in the camp, she'd barely spoken to him. Clearly his questions had made her uncomfortable. All the more reason to keep pursuing them, but in a more subtle way.

He'd come to Tanzania to track down the stolen money and learn what he could about her role in Nick's suicide. That goal was still high on his list. But what drove him now was Megan—finding the key to understanding this maddeningly complex woman. He couldn't seem to make the pieces line up in his mind.

She had a fortune tucked away, but chose to work in one of the grimmest refugee camps in the world. She was equally at home in designer brands and mud-stained safari gear. She kissed him as if she couldn't get close enough to him, but froze at the feel of his hands on her body. She was brave but frightened. Passionate but withdrawn. Charming and at ease in this moment with Harris but still the same woman who had trembled with pain and fear barely an hour before.

The more he learned about her, the less he understood.

And the more driven he became to figure her out, find the key to unlock her inner demons and set her free.

Earlier he'd looked forward to making love to her. But even as she undressed him, he'd sensed that she was pushing herself too far. By the time she'd finally crumpled, he'd been prepared to back off. Bedding a terror-struck woman wasn't his idea of a good time—for him or for her.

Not even with you.

Her anguished words came back to him—the words that had told him he was more than just another man to her. She'd wanted him, and only him—the awareness of that made him all the more determined to break through her fear. Whatever it took, he would get to the bottom of what she was dealing with—and make love to her as she was meant to be loved.

A stray thought reminded him that he hadn't checked his email tonight. After dinner he would make his excuses and wander down the hall to the front desk. By now he should have a reply to his request for Megan's file. If it wasn't there, his next request would be less cordial.

By the time they'd finished their tiramisu, Cal was getting restless. It came as a relief when Megan accepted Harris's invitation to have a drink at the bar. Promising to join them later, he strode down the corridor to the front office. The computers were busy with people from the tour group using the antiquated machines, but he managed to find an empty spot and log on to his email.

The file was there, as he'd hoped. But it was a long one, and he didn't want to read it in this crowded room, with people jammed around him, awaiting their turn at the machines. Sending the file to the office printer, he picked up the sheaf of pages and went in search of some privacy.

Two doors down the hall from the dining room was a small library, the shelves stocked with books and out-of-date magazines left behind by past guests. It was furnished with two well-worn leather chairs, both empty. Switching on a lamp, Cal took a seat and began to read.

The first few pages were routine—lists of assignments and duties, along with evaluations, all of them praising her work. He was halfway through the file before he found what he was looking for—her medical history, including a doctor's account of the night Megan had described.

As he read, his fingers gripped the page, crumpling the edges of the paper.

Dear God. Megan...Megan...

Eight

With mounting horror, Cal reread the doctor's account—how searchers had found Megan unconscious outside the camp one morning, bruised and smeared with blood, her clothes ripped away. She'd been eased onto a stretcher and carried back to the infirmary, where an examination confirmed that she'd been raped, most likely multiple times.

For four days she'd lain in a stupor with an IV in her arm. The medications she'd been given were listed in the report—antibiotics along with a light sedative and drugs to prevent pregnancy and sexually transmitted diseases.

The doctor had attempted to make arrangements to have her airlifted to a hospital, but there was no plane readily available. On the fifth day, while they were still awaiting transport, Megan had opened her eyes and sat up. She'd insisted that the flight be canceled and that she be allowed to go back to work. She appeared to have made a full recovery except for one thing—when asked about the incident, she had no memory of anything beyond the attack on the young Sudanese girl.

Heartsick, Cal read the concluding paragraph.

After consulting with other medical staff, I made the decision that, given her emotionally fragile state, it would be a dangerous risk to inform Miss Cardston about the rape. It is my recommendation that she seek counseling at the first opportunity at which time she can be told and deal with the issue. Meanwhile, since she appears to be in good physical condition, and since we need her help, I see no reason why she shouldn't resume her work.

So Megan didn't know.

Cal sank back into the chair, feeling as if his blood had drained out his legs and onto the floor. No wonder she was scared at the thought of physical intimacy. No wonder she was having panic attacks. Her conscious mind had blocked the rape. But her body remembered and reacted with terror.

Lord, he'd done all the wrong things—grilling her with questions that made her feel vulnerable and under attack even when he wasn't touching her, pushing her to have sex with him, thinking he could fix her problems with a good old-fashioned roll in the sack. That Megan had been so willing to try, so desperate to feel normal again, made him feel like an even bigger heel.

The papers had slid off his lap and onto the floor. Cal gathered them up and folded them in half. He wasn't ready to go back to the bar and face Megan—especially in the presence of Harris and his teasing innuendos. And he needed to get the documents out of Megan's sight. It might be prudent to shred or burn them. But going back to them at a later time, when he'd had a chance to calm down, might give him more insight into her state of mind.

For now, he would take them back to the bungalow and hide them in his bag. Maybe the walk from the lodge would help clear his mind—as if anything could. He hadn't meant to get involved in Megan's problems. But he'd brought this mess on himself; and now he was in deep, way over his head.

"Another one?" Harris shot Megan a devilish grin as he signaled the waiter. "It's on Cal's bar tab, and he can bloody well afford it."

Megan shook her head. The man was shameless, but she couldn't help liking him. His outrageous manner, she sensed, hid a genuinely kind heart.

"One banana daiquiri's enough for me," she said. "Too much alcohol gives me a headache. Maybe you should think about cutting back yourself. All that whiskey can't be good for you."

He lifted his freshly refilled glass. The cut crystal reflected glints of flame from the candle on their table. "No lectures, m'dear. An old man like me has few enough pleasures in life—a sunrise over the Serengeti…an occasional drink with a pretty lass…and the taste of a good Scotch on your client's dime. Doesn't quite make up for coming home to an empty bed, but it's close enough." He sipped from the glass, taking time to savor the taste. "Speaking of beds, how are you and Cal getting along in that cozy bungalow?"

Megan felt the heat creep up to the roots of her hair, embarrassed not just by the indelicate question but by the memory of how close they'd come to being *very* cozy— before her panic ruined things. "All right. We've made some…accommodations."

"Right sorry about the mix-up," he said. "When Cal told me he was bringing a lady friend along, I just assumed…"

"You assumed wrong. But it was an honest mistake."

"When I saw that kiss today, I was hoping it wasn't a mistake, after all."

Megan faked a chuckle. "We were just celebrating our safe getaway. Nothing's changed."

"I'll just have to take your word for that, won't I?" He gave her a knowing look. What would he do if he knew the truth? Would he offer her fatherly advice or just shake his head in disbelief? "Speaking of Cal, where do you suppose the lad's run off to? I'm beginning to wonder if he's lost his taste for my company."

"He said something about checking his email." Feeling the need for a break, Megan rose. "Why don't I go and look for him? I shouldn't be long."

Harris rose with her, minding his manners. "I'll be right here. If you don't come back, I'll assume you've found another diversion." The teasing light in his eye gave way to something warmer and more genuine. "Whatever's happening between you two, I can tell he cares for you. Whenever you step into view, you're all that he sees."

Don't. Megan bit back the word. Harris was pulling her strings; that was all. The old man enjoyed stirring up intrigue.

"Take your umbrella with you," he said. "You may want to go outside."

With a murmur of thanks, Megan took the umbrella Cal had left with her and walked down the hall to the front desk. Cal wasn't in the computer alcove, but the clerk told her he'd been there and had printed out a file before leaving.

Glancing around the lodge, she failed to find him. Why hadn't he joined her and Harris in the bar? Had he received some unsettling news? Would she find him in the bungalow packing his bag to leave?

Cal was a busy man, she reminded herself. He had

responsibilities and concerns in the outside world. If he needed to fly home, she'd be a fool to take it personally, or to expect any kind of promise to return. But she would always wonder what might have happened between them if he'd stayed. Would they have found some answers to whatever they were seeking—or only more disappointment?

Megan opened the umbrella and stepped outside to find that the rain had stopped. The clouds had moved on, leaving a glorious panoply of stars in a sky as black as a panther's coat. Closing the umbrella, she hurried down the brick path. Cal was an adult, she reminded herself. There was no need to go looking for him. But a sixth sense whispered that something had changed—something that had stopped him from rejoining her and Harris. She needed to find out what it was.

Cal had hidden the volunteer report between the folds of the map, which he'd zipped into the inner pocket of his duffel. Now, seated on the bench under the window, he pondered what to do next.

Sharing what he'd learned with Megan was out of the question. He was sure that her first reaction, if she learned what he'd done, would be fury at him for accessing her private information. But that much he could live with. It was the reaction that would follow, once she discovered the information in the file itself, that had him more worried. How would it affect her to know she'd been raped?

Would the awareness push her over the edge—or might it be cathartic, even helpful? Either way, he couldn't be the one to tell her. He had no right to make that decision—nor did he want to. He agreed with the doctor who'd written the report. Megan would need professional help to deal with the way she'd been hurt. And here in the wilds of Africa, there was little help of that kind to be had.

So what now? Should he try to get her back to the States? He couldn't imagine she'd be willing to go without knowing why. Should he try to help her himself, maybe get her talking? Lord, he wouldn't know where to begin. In his blundering way, he could make things worse.

For now, he could only behave as if nothing had changed. Megan was a proud woman and she was smart. If he showed pity or an excess of concern toward her, she'd pick up on it. And she'd demand to know what was wrong.

Leaning back on the bench, he closed his eyes and let the memories of the day crumble around him. Warring emotions flailed at him from all sides—worry, rage and frustration. He found himself wishing he could find a wall and punch it till his knuckles bled.

Megan hadn't asked him to come and find her, Cal reminded himself. She hadn't asked him to get involved in her life. But he *was* involved, and now he couldn't just walk away.

For the first time he found himself asking whether Megan had suffered enough. Whether she was guilty or innocent in the embezzlement, surely she'd paid the price for anything she might have done. If she returned to the States, there'd be legal entanglements—the civil suit he'd filed against her after she'd disappeared had been the first and not the last—but he could withdraw his own charges and hire a lawyer to help her with the rest.

But what was he thinking? The money was missing and his best friend was dead. How could he let that go without learning more about what had happened? He still needed answers, still had to understand what kind of person Megan truly was. The report was just the tip of the iceberg. There was still so much he wanted to know.

"Cal?" Her low voice startled him out of his reverie. "What are you doing out here? Is everything all right?"

"Fine," he lied. "I must've dozed off."

"Why didn't you come back to the bar? Harris was concerned about you."

"Sorry. The rain had stopped. I felt like some fresh air. I'll apologize to Harris tomorrow." More lies. Megan deserved better. But if he was going to be around her, lies were something he'd have to get used to.

Coming around the bench, she stood gazing down at him. She looked so fresh and pretty with the stars behind her and the night mist glistening on her hair. *Brave, sweet Megan...how could those bastards have hurt you the way they did?*

"You're sure everything's all right?" she asked. "The desk clerk mentioned you'd printed a file."

"Just business. Something that needed my okay." Another lie.

"When you didn't come back, I was afraid I'd find you packing your bags."

"I wouldn't do that without telling you." That much, at least, was true. "Sit down. It's a nice night, and it's too early to go in."

She took a seat on the bench, at a stranger's distance. Cal guessed she was still smarting from their near miss in the shower. He ached to cradle her in his arms, but he pushed the urge away, struggling to rebuild the emotional walls that had always kept him strong and centered, thinking clearly. They'd taken a bad blow tonight, and he felt uncomfortably certain that Megan's warm body in his arms would wreck them completely. He had to stay focused and rational, and not lose sight of why he was here.

"Was Harris upset about being abandoned in the bar?" he asked, making small talk.

"I hope not. He told me that as long as the drinks were on your tab, he'd be fine." She shifted her gaze to the stars. "I get the feeling Harris is a better man than he pretends to be."

"You're right. He'd deny it if you asked, but I know for a fact he's paying to educate Gideon's children. And no one works harder to make sure his clients are safe and taken care of. I'd trust the old man with my life—and have."

She gave him a tentative smile. "Somehow that doesn't surprise me. What's the real story behind his losing that arm?"

"I haven't a clue, and I've heard at least a dozen different versions. Part of his white hunter mystique, I suspect. Harris is one of a dying breed. These days, your safari guide is more likely to be African."

"That's as it should be, I suppose. Still, there's that old Hollywood image—John Wayne, Clark Gable…" A visible shiver passed through her body. She'd worn a light jacket to dinner but now the night air was getting chilly.

"Stay put. I'll get a blanket." Rising, Cal strode inside. Tonight Megan seemed relaxed and willing to talk. He very much wanted her to stay that way.

Seconds later he returned with the blanket. She snuggled into one end, leaving the rest for him.

"Better?" Cal pulled his end of the blanket over his chest.

"Better, thanks. The sky's beautiful tonight, isn't it?"

Cal murmured his agreement, suppressing the urge to circle her shoulders with his arm and pull her close.

"I always wanted Nick to take me with him to Africa when he made trips for the foundation. But when I asked him, he told me I wouldn't like it. Can you imagine that?"

"Imagine your not liking it?" Cal shook his head. "Not after seeing you out there today." Back in California, he might have agreed with Nick that his pampered, high-maintenance wife was ill-suited to the wilderness. He knew better now…and suddenly found himself wondering just how well Nick had bothered to get to know his wife.

Her smile flickered in the darkness. "Oh, today was wonderful. But it's not just the wild country and the animals I love. It's the people—like those poor souls in Darfur. They've suffered unthinkable wrongs, lost their homes and their loved ones, seen their women raped and their young boys marched off to be soldiers. But I see so much courage in the camps, so much selflessness—the way they take care of each other and share what little they have. They're the reason I want to go back to that awful place, Cal. The reason I *need* to go back."

Gazing at her, he shook his head. After what had happened to her, how could she even think of going back to Darfur?

"You're quite a woman, Megan." The understatement was deliberate. To say more might reveal too much.

"It's not me. It's them. They showed me the person I was meant to be—the person I'm still trying to become. I know that might sound maudlin to a man like you, but it's the truth."

"A man like me?" Cal quirked an eyebrow, teasing her a little to lighten the mood. "How am I supposed to take that?"

"Oh, not badly, I hope. But you've always struck me as a very pragmatic man, more focused on charging ahead and getting things done than on sentiment."

"A cold-blooded cynic, in other words."

"I didn't say that." Something flashed in her eyes. She looked away, her gaze tracing the path of a falling star. She used to do that back in California—find some excuse to turn away from him whenever they talked. What had she been hiding? Dissatisfaction with her glittering lifestyle? Unhappiness in her personal life? Or…had she been hid-

ing something more sinister, such as her crimes against
the organization where she now worked?

As he studied her sharply etched profile, a thread of
doubt crept into his mind. Had Megan really changed?
Could he take her words at face value, or was she con-
ning him? What if the money was still out there, waiting
to be drawn on when she felt safe enough—or when she'd
volunteered long enough to salve her guilty conscience?

The report verified everything she'd told him, Cal reminded himself. Her spotless service record was real. The
rape was real. But so was the crime that had come before
all of that. Someone was responsible for taking the money,
and Cal still didn't want to believe it was the friend he
would have entrusted with his life.

He didn't realize how long they'd been silent until she
spoke.

"Looking back, I don't think Nick knew me at all—
maybe because I didn't know myself. I became what I
thought he wanted. Not that it made any difference in
the end."

Cal shot her a startled glance. Her words matched his
own thoughts, but he was surprised to hear her bring it
up. She'd seemed firmly against discussing Nick with him
earlier. "I thought you and Nick had the perfect marriage,"
he prompted, testing waters. "It certainly looked that
way."

She gazed up at the sky. "We put on a good show. But
we both knew better."

"Would you have stayed with him?"

"You mean, if he hadn't shot himself when the money
scandal broke? I've asked myself the same question. I was
raised to believe that marriage vows are sacred. But when
your partner is cheating and doesn't care how much he

hurts you, those vows can seem more like a prison sentence. Maybe if I hadn't lost the baby…" Her voice trailed off.

So Nick had been cheating on her. The discovery tightened a raw knot in the pit of Cal's stomach. He and Nick had been best friends since high school. True blue all the way, or so he'd thought. But if Nick had been faithless to his beautiful wife, what else would he have been capable of?

"What happened with the baby, Megan?" he asked. "Nick never said much, except that you'd lost it."

"That doesn't surprise me. I'd hoped having a baby might make a difference, force him to take our marriage more seriously, but it barely seemed to register with him. As for the miscarriage…" She shrugged. "It was what it was—nothing I could have prevented. At least that's what the doctor said. I've always wanted children. But maybe it isn't in the cards. Especially not now."

Cal studied her profile in the faint light. How could any man have cheated on a woman like Megan? Nick had always been a flirt, quick with compliments and flattery whenever a beautiful woman was involved, even after he was married. Cal had simply chalked it up as part of his friend's personality. He'd never imagined the man would cheat—Nick had given every indication of worshipping his beautiful wife. Had it really all been for show?

There was no denying the aching resignation in Megan's tone. Nick hadn't just indulged in an indiscretion or two—it sounded as if Megan was saying he'd never been faithful at all. Now that Cal thought about it, Nick had always been one to take his commitments lightly. Instead of apologizing for missed meetings or deadlines, he was more likely to brush it off with a shrug and a smile, confident that he could charm his way into forgiveness. The truth of that hurt like hell. But how much more had it hurt Megan?

If things were different between them, Cal thought, he might try to make it up to her—show her how a woman should be treated by a man who claimed to care for her.

But given the past, that wasn't in the cards, either.

Megan wrapped the blanket tighter, taking care to leave enough slack for Cal. The moon had risen above the distant hills. Full and ripe as an August peach from her grandmother's old tree, it flooded the brick terrace with light and etched Cal's craggy face into ridges and shadows. She'd thought she'd managed to put her old life behind her. But being with Cal had brought it all back—and not in a good way.

"Maybe the camps have been an outlet for your mothering instincts," he said.

"Are you trying to analyze me again?" She didn't like being examined, especially by Cal.

"I wouldn't dream of it," he said. "But as long as we're on the subject, wouldn't it be worth getting professional help for those panic attacks and nightmares?"

"Maybe." A prickle of distrust stirred. She faked a chuckle. "If I could find a good witch doctor to rattle the bones."

"You're not going to find help here." He turned on the bench, impaling her with his eyes. "I've glimpsed the pain you're in, Megan. Come home with me and get the therapy you need. I'll do whatever it takes to help you."

Megan lowered her gaze, alarms going off in her head. Of course, she told herself. This was why Cal had come here. He was determined to get her back to the States, where he could go after her legally, maybe even have her arrested. This wasn't the approach she'd expected him to take, but the end result was the same either way.

And she'd actually begun to trust him. What a fool she'd been!

Meeting his eyes again, she shook her head. "Cal, I know you mean well." *A necessary lie.* "But I'm not leaving Africa. If I were to go home, there's a chance I'd never make it back here."

"Not even if I promised to send you?"

"I can't depend on that. Things get in the way. Besides, there's nothing wrong with me that time and hard work won't heal."

"But to go back to the very place where—" He broke off, as if he'd been about to say too much.

"Don't you see? That's exactly what I need to do—go back and deal with what happened. If I can face it, and understand it, it won't have the power to frighten me."

The breath exploded out of him. "Damn it, Megan, if you'd just listen—"

"Stop pushing me, Cal. I'm not a child."

"You're working for my organization. I can order you home for treatment."

"Not if I resign. Believe me, there are plenty of NGOs who'd be happy to have an experienced nurse." She stood, tossing the blanket aside. "I'm too tired to argue any more. If you'll excuse me, I'm going to turn in. Truce, all right?"

"Truce." He rose with a weary sigh. "I'll go and spend some time with Harris. That'll give you a chance to get settled. We'll be off to another early start tomorrow."

"Fine." She opened the door, which was unlocked.

"Megan."

She turned at the sound of her name.

"Take your side of the bed. I promise to be a perfect gentleman."

A gentleman? Is that what he called someone who flew halfway around the world to hound a woman into his idea

of justice? Did he really think she didn't know about the
civil suits waiting to fall on her the minute she reentered
the United States? What kind of gentleman—what kind of
man—was he to do this to her and pretend it was for her
own good? She was angry with herself for even listening
to him, much less beginning to trust him. And that wasn't
even mentioning the way she'd let him kiss her, or the way
she'd started to feel in the shower with him before her fear
had taken over. For a short while, she'd actually thought
that he was the man who could make things better for her.

She stepped into the bungalow and closed the door. If
only she could close the door as easily on her frustrating
feelings toward the man.

Nine

By the time Cal crossed the grounds to the bungalow, the moon had risen above the treetops. A bat flashed past his head, its wings slicing the dark like scimitars. The haunting cry of an owl shimmered through the night.

He'd spent the better part of two hours with Harris, gently urging him to call it a night and go to bed. The old hunter hadn't looked well tonight—not really sick, but sad and fatigued. At sixty-six, his rough life and hard drinking had begun to catch up with him, and it showed. Cal had been worried enough to stay with him and walk him to his private room in the rear of the lodge. It would be a relief to get him away from this place and out on the Serengeti with no hotel bar to keep him up drinking at night.

The bungalow was dark. Hopefully Megan would be asleep. She'd been tired, too—and prickly, he recalled. He should have known better than to bring up the idea of flying her home for therapy. But she'd given him an opening. He'd seized it and come away with his whiskers singed.

He'd learned where she stood on the question of going home. But he also knew something Megan didn't. She needed serious help—and going back to Darfur without that help could send her spiraling into an emotional abyss.

Unlocking the door, he stepped inside. Moonlight fell between the parted curtains, softening the darkness. Relief lifted his mood as he glanced through the mosquito netting and saw the slight form raising the covers. At least she'd trusted him enough to share the bed. Or maybe she'd wanted him close by to protect her from the lurking monsters in her dreams.

Moving closer, he gazed down at her. She lay curled with her lovely rump toward his side of the bed, sleeping as sweetly as a child. Something tightened around Cal's heart. Whatever phantoms threatened that innocent slumber, he wanted to be there to drive them away. He understood himself, and he knew these protective feelings toward her might not last for long, not when he still had so many questions and doubts. But while Megan was suffering, he couldn't turn his back and walk away from her.

He undressed in the dark. Clad in his skivvies and undershirt, he walked around the bed. He slept raw at home and had planned to do the same on this trip. If he'd foreseen that he'd be sharing a room—and a bed—with a woman he'd resolved to treat like a kid sister, he'd have brought along some pajamas.

He did have a pack of condoms in his bag, which he'd bought at the hotel gift shop in Arusha after making plans to take Megan on safari—and hopefully seduce her. But they were locally made, so he couldn't count on their reliability. Given the present arrangement, maybe that was just as well.

Doing his best not to wake her, he lifted the blanket and slid over the top sheet onto his side of the bed. The mattress wasn't king-size, or even queen-size. It was a double, like the one his grandparents had slept on all their married life. There was no boundary line down the middle, but Megan was definitely taking more than her share of space. Unless he wanted to sleep on the couch, he would have to choose between disturbing her rest to move her over or spooning around her. The latter struck him as the more appealing choice.

Easing deeper into the bed, he curved his body around hers and pulled the blankets up to his shoulders. Head on the pillow, he closed his eyes. It was late, and he was tired. With any luck he'd go right to sleep.

But something told him it wasn't going to be that easy. Megan's warmth crept around him, seeping into his senses. She smelled of the lavender soap from the shower. It was the same soap he'd used, but on her woman's skin the innocent aroma, coupled with the memory of that shower, was sensual enough to rock his libido. The notion that he mustn't touch her, mustn't have her, heated his blood like torched gasoline. He bit back a groan as his sex rose and hardened. Only the thin sheet between their bodies kept his male impulses in check.

It was going to be a long night.

Megan stirred and opened her eyes. Except for a shaft of moonlight falling through the window, the room was dark. She'd gone to bed alone. But the sound of breathing and the manly warmth radiating against her back told her she was alone no longer. Sometime in the night Cal had joined her.

As she drifted into wakefulness, she became aware of her curled position in the bed. Moving in her sleep, she'd left Cal with little more than the far edge of the mattress.

Instead of pushing her out of the way, she realized, he'd done his best to sleep around her.

Despite the awkwardness between them, she would have to give him credit for being a gentleman in this respect, at least. True to his word, he hadn't laid a hand on her. But he'd stayed close, and even in her sleep, something about his presence had made her feel safe and peaceful. Maybe that was why the dreams hadn't come tonight.

Stretching full length, she rolled toward her own side of the mattress. Looking back, she could see Cal. He lay awake with one arm propping his head. Had he been watching over her?

"Hello," she whispered. "Did I wake you?"

He shook his head. "Any bad dreams?"

"No. But I don't always have them. When did you come in?"

"A couple of hours ago. You were sleeping like a kitten."

"All over the bed! No wonder you're still awake. You should've booted me back where I belong."

His chuckle warmed her. "You looked so contented, I didn't have the heart."

"There's plenty of room for you now," she said. "Go ahead and stretch out. I won't bite you."

"I won't touch that comment." The bed creaked slightly as he eased onto his back and straightened his legs. "Ah... that's better," he breathed.

"Now get some sleep," she ordered. "And don't let me crowd you again."

Another chuckle was followed by silence, as if he'd bitten back a too-clever retort.

They lay side by side, modestly clad and separated by a thin layer of muslin sheet that might as well have been a brick wall. There was something Victorian about the arrangement, like two strangers sharing a bed in a nineteenth-century inn. Megan knew that Cal had come up with this silliness to ease her fear. But no barrier could hide the intense masculinity exuded by the man next to her.

Even when she was married to Nick, Cal's presence had given her a rush of heightened awareness. She'd willed herself to ignore the sensation, but he was so powerful, so decisive and rugged that he fluttered the pulse of every female who came within range. Next to him, even the glib and charming Nick had seemed shallow and insubstantial. Cal was like the lion they'd seen in the crater—fierce, majestic and completely sure of himself. She'd be foolish to trust him—he was every bit as dangerous as the lion. But she couldn't deny her attraction to him.

Cal had never had any shortage of women. And he was doubtless an accomplished lover. She remembered the touch of his big hands in the shower, how he'd caressed her naked breasts until she'd ached for more. He'd awakened feelings she thought she'd lost forever. She'd *wanted* him—and she'd desperately needed the release he could give her.

So why had she stopped him? What gave her fear such uncontrollable power? If only she could understand that much, she might be on her way to healing.

"Are you all right, Megan?" His throaty whisper stirred the darkness.

"Aren't you supposed to be asleep?"

"Aren't you?" He paused, then turned toward her, shifting onto his side. "Feel like talking?"

Talking? Megan could guess what that meant. He was preparing to back her into a corner and grill her again, maybe about Nick and the money, or about her time in Darfur, or even what had happened in the shower that afternoon. Why did *she* always have to be the one answering questions?

"I've done enough talking," she said. "I'd rather listen for a change. Tell me about yourself."

"Not much to tell. My story's pretty dull compared with yours. Nick must've told you most of it."

"Not really. Just that the two of you were friends in high school and decided to start J-COR after college. But I don't want to talk about Nick. Where did you grow up?"

"Fresno. White house. Picket fence. Barbecue in the backyard. Station wagon in the driveway. How does it sound so far? Are you getting sleepy?"

"Don't count on it." She shifted deeper under the covers, her hip brushing his through the sheet. The contact triggered a subtle ache—a yearning to snuggle against his side and lie cloaked in his warmth. She battled temptation, telling herself that any move on her part would only confuse the man, leading him to assume she wanted more.

Maybe she *did* want more. But a second failure on her part would be frustrating for him and scathingly humiliating for her. Better to leave well enough alone. She sighed, willing herself to remain where she lay. "Go on," she urged him. "I'm listening."

Cal's words could have painted a pretty picture of his childhood home. It would have been a true picture, as far as the description went. But that would mean leaving out the screaming, cursing fights that raged between his parents within the walls of that home. Those fights had driven him out of the house to wander the streets at all hours, afraid of what he'd see if he came back too soon.

Sharing that part of his life was painful. But Megan had been open with him about her past. He owed her as much.

"My mother left us when I was eleven," he said. "My father made sure I knew she'd run off with another man—

one who'd told her he didn't want a snot-nosed kid like me tagging along."

"You were an only child?"

"Yes, fortunately."

"And your mother never came back?"

"We got word years later that she'd died of cancer. By then I was in high school. I can't say I blamed her for leaving—my dad was pretty rough on her, and it may have been her only way out. But the fact that she didn't even tell me goodbye or write me a letter…that part was hard to take."

"Oh, Cal…"

His jaw tightened. If there was one thing he couldn't stand it was pity from a woman—especially *this* woman.

"No need to be sorry," he said, cutting her off before she could shovel on more sympathy. "I got through it fine. My dad sold cars and hung out with his drinking buddies. I took after-school jobs—mowing lawns, bagging groceries, lifeguarding at the pool. The work kept me in spending money and out of trouble. I earned my own car, bought my own clothes and still managed to do pretty well in school. Even dated a few girls and played a little football."

"And that was when you met Nick."

"Yeah. You know the rest." They'd shared a table in study hall and, for some reason he couldn't even remember, they'd hit it off. The big, scrappy kid from the wrong side of town and the handsome, smooth-talking boy who seemed to have everything—two doting parents, an imposing brick home and a black Trans Am to drive to school. They'd formed an alliance that had lasted until two years ago, when a single gunshot had ended it all.

Remembering that part still hurt like hell.

Megan stirred beside him, warm and soft and fragrant. "I know you cared about him, Cal," she said. "I cared about him, too. Nick had some wonderful qualities. But he hurt us both. I've done my best to forgive him and move on. I hope you have, too."

Cal's throat went painfully tight. He had no words—and even if he had, he wouldn't have been able to speak. All he could do was hook her with his arm and draw her close while raw emotions surged through his body. It wasn't a lustful gesture, just one of simple human need, and she seemed to know it. Her head settled into the hollow of his shoulder. Her breath eased as she fitted her body to his side. It felt good holding her like this, even with nothing else in the plan. Little by little he could feel the tension flowing out of him.

Turning his head, he brushed a kiss across her hairline. "Go to sleep, Megan," he whispered.

She didn't reply, but her nearness said enough. Lord, but she was sweet. Almost sweet enough to make him forget their shared past. But some wrongs were too grievous to put aside. For him, there could be no forgiving and no moving on until he knew the full story behind Nick's death, the stolen money and Megan's part in it all.

Megan lay still, lulled by the steady beat of Cal's heart. His skin was warm through the thin fabric of his undershirt. She closed her eyes, feeling the gentle rise and fall of his chest against her cheek.

Tonight he'd shared some surprising secrets—things that not even Nick had told her about his friend. Surely Nick had known Cal's background; but maybe he hadn't expected her to be interested. Sadly, now that she thought of it, there were a lot of things she and Nick hadn't talked about.

She tried to picture Cal as a lonely, unwanted young boy, abandoned by his mother and probably ignored by his father. No wonder he'd developed a cold manner and a cynical attitude. No wonder he'd never trusted any woman enough to develop a serious relationship.

The only person Cal seemed to have trusted was Nick. And in the end, even Nick had betrayed him. His anguish would have been as deep as her own—different, yes, but just as painful and just as lasting.

Cal's revelation gave her new understanding and an unexpected sense of peace—like a gift. She wasn't alone in her pain. In his own way, Cal was suffering, too; and he was looking for answers. Why else would he have come all this way to find her?

She was beginning to drift. Most nights she dreaded sleep and the nightmares it brought. But tonight she felt safe. Cal was here to protect her and calm her fears. For now that was enough.

Was she getting better?

But it was too soon to ask that question. The past three days had been intoxicatingly normal, with drives into the crater and along the river where the elephants came to drink. They'd seen crocodiles, great, lumbering hippos and more lions, a pride of them with cubs. They'd scouted a tree where a leopard had hung its kill and, after some searching, managed to spot the beautiful, mottled cat sprawled along a high limb.

Megan had filled her camera's memory card with photos and her head with stunning images that would stay with her the rest of her life. But did that really mean she was getting better?

She felt vital and restored; and the nightmares had yet to return. But it wasn't as if she could spend the rest of her life on safari. How would she hold up in the world she'd left behind—especially in Darfur?

As for Cal, they'd managed a cautious truce. He treated her like a friend and kept his distance both in and out of bed. If it wasn't everything she wanted—and there were times when she ached for more—at least she felt safe with him.

His touch on her arm tugged her back to the present. They were driving the crater today, on the narrow track where they'd been mired in the rain. Gideon had slowed the Land Rover to a crawl. A hundred yards ahead, a hulking dark shape moved through a screen of thornbush. Cal's lips moved, forming the words *black rhino.*

They'd cut the distance by half when the rhino burst out of the bush, coming straight toward them. The beast was immense—not tall like an elephant, but massive—long-bodied and as sleekly powerful as an old-time steam locomotive. The horn on its nose was as long as Megan's arm and looked to be spindle-sharp at the tip.

Megan forgot to breathe as the rhino paused, ears and nostrils twitching. Her hand crept into Cal's as Gideon idled the engine. They were close—too close. Rhinos were known to be short-tempered, and this one was capable of wrecking the vehicle and trampling or tossing anyone who couldn't get away. Harris had drawn and cocked the rifle—not to shoot the precious beast but more likely to try to scare it if the need arose.

The rhino snorted and tossed its enormous head. The small brown birds roosting on its back flapped upward, chattering an alarm—not a good sign.

At a touch from Harris, Gideon eased the Land Rover into Reverse and began slowly backing away. A bead of sweat trickled down the side of the driver's face. No one in the vehicle moved or spoke as the wheels inched backward.

Snorting again, the rhino lowered its head. Sunlight glinted on the deadly black horn. Megan's grip tightened around Cal's hand. His body tensed, moving slightly in front of her.

But the rhino must have calculated that the intruders weren't worth bothering with. Changing course, the huge beast turned aside and trotted into the scrub. Gideon gunned the vehicle backward, stopping only once they were safely out of range. Pulling the hand brake, he sagged over the wheel. Harris uncocked the rifle, breaking the silence with a laugh. "Well, hell, I said I wanted to show you a black rhino, didn't I?"

"That you did." Cal's arm went around Megan's shoulders, squeezing her fiercely tight. Megan managed a nervous chuckle.

"I don't suppose I can talk you into going back, can I?" she joked. "I forgot to take pictures."

Still giddy from the rush of their close call, they headed out of the crater. Sullen clouds were rumbling over the rim, and nobody wanted to be caught in the rain again. Tomorrow they'd be leaving Ngorongoro for a tent camp on the vast Serengeti grassland to the north. What remained of the afternoon would be set aside for resting, washing and packing up for a predawn start.

By dinnertime Megan had her things well organized. She'd enjoyed the lodge but she was ready for a change of scene. Over plates of coq au vin and rice pilaf, Harris described what she could expect to see.

"We'll be there for the big game migration that happens every year with the rains. Nothing like it on earth. Wildebeest, zebra and more—oceans of them—marching south to new grass. Bloody picnic for the meat-eaters that tag along. Not a pretty sight for a lady, but I shouldn't worry about you. After all, you've been in Darfur."

Cal glanced toward her. She caught the dark flicker in his eyes before he looked away. Was he thinking about the nightmares and panic attacks she'd come on safari to escape—details he'd agreed not to share with Harris? Was he worried about how she'd react to the more violent aspects of the migration?

It would be like Cal to worry. That was one thing Megan had learned about him on this outing—that he paid attention to everyone around him and seemed to feel responsible for their well-being. That included her—sometimes to her annoyance.

They finished their dessert. Then, as had become custom, Megan rose, excused herself and went back to the bungalow to shower and relax while Cal stayed to keep Harris company. Not only did the arrangement give her some needed private time, but it helped ensure that Harris would make it back to his room without drinking too much. Cal had voiced his concern for the old hunter, and Megan had agreed that Harris shouldn't be left alone at night in the bar.

After showering and dressing in her pajamas and robe, she curled up on the couch with the afghan and a paperback murder mystery she'd borrowed from the lodge's library. The book had looked promising, but the story wasn't holding her attention. She'd already guessed how it would end, and a peek at the last page proved her right.

Setting the book on the coffee table, she leaned back into the cushions and tried to imagine what the next few days would be like. She knew about the migration and had even seen video footage of it on PBS's *Nature*. But being there, actually seeing it, would be a thrill to remember.

The more she thought about it, the more she wished she'd asked Harris more questions. How soon would they get to the Serengeti? What would they see on the way?

Maybe it would help to look at a map. Cal had a map,

she remembered now. He'd mentioned that he kept it in his bag.

Crossing the room, she found the packed duffel where he'd left it on the floor of the wardrobe. Her fingers probed inside and felt the stiffness of paper in the inner pocket. Unzipping the pocket, she lifted out the folded map, which felt thicker than she'd expected.

As she unfolded the map, a sheaf of printed papers dropped out and scattered on the tiles. Bending to gather them up, Megan noticed a name at the top of one page.

Her name.

Ten

Roiling clouds blackened the night sky, hiding the moon and stars. Lightning sheeted across the horizon, followed seconds later by the subtle roar of distant thunder. Walking the brick path back to the bungalow, Cal was grateful that Harris had decided to turn in early. Otherwise he'd be running a gauntlet through the coming downpour.

As it was, he took his time. Today, under the equatorial sun, the humid air had felt like a thick flannel blanket. Tonight the breeze was cool, the air sweet in his lungs. The day had been a good one, crowned by the close brush with the rare black rhino. When Megan's hand had crept into his, he'd felt the connection of electric fear and excitement that coursed through both their bodies. In that breathless moment when the beast was threatening to charge, his foremost thought had been keeping her safe.

Was he falling for the woman? But that would be the craziest thing he could do. Megan was an emotional wreck.

And whether she did or didn't have anything to do with the stolen money, their past history didn't bode well for any kind of relationship.

But things weren't that simple. As attracted as he'd been to her beauty, he was even more drawn to her now that he'd seen her courage, her kindness and her magnificent spirit. Lying next to her in the night, separated by nothing but that damnable sheet, he'd burned with wanting her. It had been all he could do to keep from ripping away the thin muslin, seizing her in his arms and burying his swollen sex in that deep, hot wetness he craved like a drowning man craves air.

But that would be the most despicable—and damaging—thing he could do.

Reaching the porch of the bungalow, he fished for his key. The curtain was drawn, but the glow of a single lamp shone through the fabric. Would he find her awake, maybe reading that paperback she'd found in the lodge? That might not be so bad, he mused. This would be their last night in the bungalow—maybe their last chance for some relaxing, private talk.

After a polite knock to announce his presence, he turned the key and opened the door.

Megan was seated on the couch, wrapped in the afghan. Her back was ramrod straight, her fists clenched in her lap. The rigid expression on her face made it clear that something terrible had happened. Cal's heart dropped as he saw the papers laid out on the coffee table.

He stifled a groan. "Megan—"

Her look stopped him from saying more—raw eyes, filled with shock and a kind of frozen rage.

"How long have you known?" Her hoarse whisper rose from a well of pain.

Cal forced his mouth to form words. "Not long. A few

days. I can imagine what you think, but I was looking for a way to help you."

"Help me?" She flung the words at him. "By going behind my back? This was private information. You had no right!"

"That's where you're wrong. As the head of the foundation, I have the right to see volunteer records."

She glared at him in helpless fury. Cal stood his ground, hoping that a cool facade might help keep her calm. But he didn't feel cool. Heaven help him, what had he done to this woman?

"So why didn't you tell me?" Megan was beginning to crumble. "How long did you plan to keep it to yourself that I'd been...*raped?*" She choked on the last word.

Cal ached to gather her into his arms. But he knew better than to try. She was too angry to welcome comfort, especially from him. "You saw the report," he said. "The doctor didn't think you were ready to be told. Not without professional help."

"The doctor was *wrong!*" She was on her feet, eyes blazing. "He was wrong, and so were you! I'm not a child! I *needed* to know! How could I heal without understanding what happened to me?"

"I'm sorry. I deferred to the doctor's judgment. I didn't feel I had the background to make any other call." Lord, he sounded so detached. She probably thought he was the world's coldest bastard.

"You should have told me, anyway." The afghan had slipped off her shoulders. She let it fall to the floor. "It would have been a kindness to tell me, Cal. Instead, you let me make a fool of myself. That time in the shower—did you know then?"

"No. If I had, things would never have gone that far."

He took another step toward her. "Sit down, and talk to me, Megan."

"Why should I? You went behind my back. You kept a secret from me—a terrible secret—"

Her fists came up to flail impotently at his chest. He stood like a pillar, letting the harmless blows glance off him. He deserved her anger for the way he'd let her down. The last thing he'd wanted to do was to hurt her again—and yet, that was exactly what he'd done.

As her strength ebbed, she began to quiver. Her shoulders slumped. She buried her face in her palms. Sobs shook her thin frame. Cal had always prided himself on his ability to manage a crisis. But trying to reason with Megan had only made things worse. Now he had run out of things to say. There was only one thing left to do.

Without another word, he wrapped her in his arms and held her tight.

Outside, the storm had broken. Lightning crashed across the sky, flickering through the curtains as the thunder roared overhead. Rain battered the windowpanes and drummed on the roof, like an echo of the emotions that churned through Megan's body.

Pressed against Cal, she had no will to pull away. She was still furious, but she needed the solid anchor of his strength. Tonight, as she'd waited for him to come back from the lodge, she'd struggled to remember what had happened on that tragic night. The details of the brutal assault on Saida had haunted her dreams for months. But she had no recollection of the same thing happening to her.

Had she been unconscious at the time, or had her mind mercifully blocked the memory? And what of the physical signs of assault? She supposed that thanks to the swift treatment she received, and the four days she spent in a daze, the worst of the injuries had time to heal before she came back to full awareness. If only the mental and emotional damage were as easily fixed.

She had to accept that the rape had been real. Given the medical evidence and her state of mind, nothing else made sense. But the truth was still sinking in, too much truth for her ravaged psyche to process. It was as if she was tumbling through a black void with no bottom and nothing of substance to hold on to.

Except Cal.

"It's all right, Megan." His lips brushed her hair as he whispered phrases meant to comfort her. "You'll be fine, girl. You're safe."

Liar, she thought. It wasn't all right—and maybe she would never feel safe again. But she was grateful for the arms that held her, supporting and protecting her. Megan pressed her face into Cal's shirt. The fabric was wet and salty with her tears—real tears. For the first time since that awful night, she was *crying.*

"Go ahead and cry," Cal murmured. "You don't have to be strong all the time. Let it go. I'm here."

She sagged against him, drained by her furious outburst. Cal hadn't meant to hurt her, she reminded herself. He'd only wanted to help. And here, in this remote place, he was all the help she had.

Her knees were threatening to buckle. As if sensing what she needed, Cal swept her up in his arms and carried her to the bed. Throwing back the covers, he laid her on the sheet and tucked the quilt over her, tenderly as if he were tucking in a frightened child.

"Do you want me to go?" he asked.

"No. I need you to stay."

She heard the sound of his boots hitting the floor before he stretched out beside her on top of the quilts. For the first few minutes they lay still, listening to the sounds of the storm. Cal didn't speak, but his weight on the bed and the deep, even cadence of his breathing surrounded her with a sense of peace.

"I still don't remember," she said. "I've no reason to doubt what happened, but the memory isn't there."

"Maybe you're lucky," he said.

"In Darfur, in the camps, I knew so many girls and women who'd been raped by the Janjaweed. It was a form of warfare, a way to shame them and humiliate their families." She turned onto her side, spooning her hips against him. His breath eased out as he laid an arm across her shoulders.

"I used to wonder how they could bear the horror of it," she said. "But somehow they did. They survived and moved on with their lives because they had no choice. They showed so much courage. How can I expect any less of myself? I need to move on, too—and now that I know what happened to me, I will."

"I know you will," he said softly. "You're a strong woman, Megan."

"They're the strong ones. They remember everything—and they don't have a safe place to go to keep it from happening again."

Cal didn't reply, but his arm tightened around her, drawing her closer. The light pressure of her hips set off a rush of sensual warmth. The reaction was nothing she hadn't felt before with Cal. But the fact that it was still there was a surprising comfort. She snuggled closer, feeling his breath quicken in response. The tingling heat spread, flowing into the core of her body to become a subtly throbbing pulse of desire.

She wanted him—with an urgent hunger she'd feared

she would never feel again. But the risk was a fearful one. Another failure would be devastating.

"Cal?" She turned to face him. He was watching her, his silvery eyes tender and questioning. Lifting her hand, she traced a fingertip along his cheek, feeling the soft burn of whisker stubble. "Cal, would you make love to me?"

For what seemed like forever, he didn't reply, didn't even stir. Only a subtle flicker in his eyes betrayed that he'd even heard the question. What if he was about to refuse? The embarrassment would kill her.

One eyebrow quirked. "Are you sure about this?" he asked.

"Yes…" The word barely made it past her trembling lips.

"Then I have a suggestion. Why don't *you* make love to *me?*"

She stared at him, searching his face in the lamplight. Slowly his reasons dawned on her. Let her take control, set the pace, back off if she became uncomfortable. It would be the furthest possible thing from the hellish rape that was locked in her memory.

Did she have the courage to try?

Rising onto her elbows, she leaned over and kissed him—softly at first, letting her lips feather over his, then deepening the contact. As her tongue brushed along the sensitive inner surface of his lower lip, she felt the quiver of his response. She could sense the strain as he willed himself to lie still.

Her mouth nibbled a trail down his throat, tasting the sweet saltiness of his skin. Her caresses barely skimmed the edge of intimacy, but her heart was racing. She could stop anytime, Megan reminded herself. But she didn't want to. All she wanted was Cal, his arms around her and his naked body warming hers.

Tossing her robe aside, she knelt over him. Her fingers, clumsy with haste, fumbled with the buttons of his khaki shirt. So many buttons…

"Let me." He sat up, swung his feet to the floor and in a few easy moves stripped down to his tan silk briefs. With his back toward her, he opened the drawer in the nightstand and withdrew a small packet. The lamplight cast his splendid torso in bronze. The sight of him, and the awareness of what was in the packet, kicked Megan's pulse to a thundering gallop. She yanked at the buttons that held her modest pajama top in place.

When he turned around, she was kneeling on the bed, bare to the hips. The way his face lit did wonders to calm her jittery nerves. It told her that he thought she was beautiful, and that he wanted her—something she desperately needed to believe.

Hiding the packet under the pillow, he raised the covers and slipped into bed. His heavy-lidded eyes smiled up at her in the shadows. "I can't wait to have you pleasure me," he murmured huskily. "Now, where did we leave off?"

As the storm beat against the bungalow, she stretched out alongside him, aching to touch him, smell him, taste him—every part of him. She wanted to feel alive again—to feel the thrill pulsing through her body and the hot blood coursing through her veins. She wanted to feel joy—with this man.

His mouth was cool and tasted faintly of the single-malt Scotch he'd drunk with Harris. Her tongue darted to meet his in a playful pantomime of what was meant to come. Her bare nipples grazed his chest, lingering until she broke off the kiss and nipped her way down over his collarbone.

As if playing a game with rules, he kept his hands at his sides; but other parts of him were fully responsive. He moaned as her lips closed around his aureole, tongue circling the tiny nub, coaxing it to heat and swell. His flesh was salty after the day in the hot sun, his pungent sweat deliciously male. Even this…it was heaven. She couldn't get enough of him.

As his hips arched against her, she could feel his sex, jutting along her thigh. She shifted, legs parting, pelvis tilting to bring her throbbing center into contact with that rock-solid ridge. Even through layers of fabric she could feel every inch of him. She thrust harder, hungry need spiraling through her body until the gentle press of his hand on her hip stayed her.

"You naughty girl…" he growled. "Do you have any idea what you're doing to me?"

"Yes, and I'm about to do more." The sense of power was intoxicating. Giddy with her newfound courage, she shed her pajama bottoms and panties and slid her hand beneath the waistband of his straining silk briefs. Her pulse leaped as her fingers brushed, then clasped his naked erection. To her touch, he felt as big as a stallion, as hard as a hickory log and as smooth as velvet. A purr of sheer pleasure vibrated in his throat as she stroked him, intensifying her confidence and her desire.

She loved the feeling of him in her hand, but she sensed she was pushing him to his limit. And her own sweet hunger was growing more urgent. She could feel the pulsing of her own need, the slickness of moisture all but dripping from between her thighs. She'd expected to be fearful, or at least hesitant; but all she could think of was how much she wanted him inside her.

Stripping his silk briefs down his legs, she tossed them aside and reached for the condom he'd hidden under the pillow. Slipping it over his firm erection was done in seconds. Cal's lust-glazed eyes held a glint of amusement as he watched her cloak him.

"Are you all right with this, Megan?" he whispered.

She flashed him a grin. "I've never been more all right in my life."

A slow smile spread across his face. "That's good, because you're driving me crazy. I want to be inside you so much I can't stand it."

And that was enough, she thought. No pretty lies about being in love with her. No useless flattery. Nothing was settled between them except that he wanted her. And she wanted him.

Straddling his hips, she found the center of her slickness and lowered herself down the length of his shaft. He filled her, so deep that, as she settled onto him, she could feel his manly heat pulsing through her whole body.

As she began to move, he responded with a groan. Unable to keep still, his hands came into play, clasping her hips as he drove upward into her, thrusting deeper and deeper. Where their bodies joined, shimmering bursts of pleasure ignited inside her. She came, clenching around him as the climax washed over her in waves, leaving her deliciously spent.

"Don't stop," he urged, thrusting again. She matched her motion to his. This time she rode a rocket into the stars, reeling and gasping as his release mounted. He came with her, exploding with a grunt, followed by a long outward breath and a low chuckle of satisfaction.

Still feeling spasms in the depths of her body, Megan sagged over him. She was utterly spent, but she had never felt more free. Only time would tell whether the nightmares would return. But with Cal's help, she had broken the barrier of fear. He had given her hope—and so much more.

Tears of relief and gratitude welled as she leaned forward and brushed a kiss across his smiling lips. "Thank you," she whispered.

* * *

As early dawn crept through the curtains, Cal lay spooned against Megan's sweet nakedness, his hand resting on her hip. The even cadence of her breathing told him she was still fast asleep.

They'd made love again in the night, this time in the more traditional way. Cal had feared that having a man on top of her might awaken her bad memories, but his worries had been unfounded. The second time had been every bit as wonderful and revealing as the first.

She shifted against him, settling her lovely bum deeper into the curve of his body. With a sigh, he tightened an arm around her. He'd enjoyed her beauty and relished her passion. But what moved him most was her trust. That a woman who'd been through hell would give herself to him as Megan had, with nothing held back, stirred emotions Cal had never known he possessed. It was as if he'd been handed a magnificent gift he didn't deserve. He felt unworthy, humbled, overwhelmed.

With Megan he'd ventured to a place where he'd never been with a woman—and it scared the hell out of him.

After last night, the thought of letting her go was more than he could stand. He wanted to protect her from the ugliness in the world. He wanted to heal her pain and see her smile every day—maybe for a long time to come. But questions swarmed at him. What about the past? What about her determination to return to Darfur? And what if he were to find evidence that Megan had embezzled the missing money?

As long as doubt existed on any front, he'd be a fool to trust her. He'd trusted his mother. He'd trusted Nick—trust that he was now beginning to question. The last thing he needed was another betrayal from a person he cared about.

Pulling her closer, he filled his senses with the soft lavender fragrance of her hair. For now, at least, he would be here, giving her the support she needed to heal. As long as she was willing, he would enjoy every minute of their lovemaking.

But he would keep his emotions under tight rein; and he would remember why he'd come to Africa in the first place. No one, not even Megan, would ever deceive him again.

Eleven

Megan woke to the sound of the shower running. For a moment she lay still while her mind processed the realities of her new, changed world. Last night, she'd learned the shocking truth about the rape in Darfur. And later on, when she and Cal had made love, she'd responded with newfound passion. It was as if a dam had burst, forever changing the landscape of her life.

She stretched her naked body in the bed, relishing the aches and twinges she hadn't felt in so very long. She felt like a whole woman again, and she had Cal to thank for it.

Not that she believed she was healed. The brutality she'd experienced would haunt her for the rest of her days. At some point she might remember everything. Even if she didn't, she might need therapy. But she'd turned a corner. She believed and accepted what had happened; and she no longer felt paralyzed by the fears that had taken over her life.

The shower had stopped running. Facing Cal would be one more new reality. Last night they'd become lovers. But what about today? Where would they go from here?

She had no illusions about love. Not with Cal. To a man like him, sex was just sex. And if she allowed herself to want more, she'd only get her heart broken.

But on safari, she couldn't simply get dressed and leave. The two of them would be together twenty-four/seven for most of the next week. Things could become awkward between them. As for the future...but even if she wanted something with him, and even if she could somehow convince him to agree, what kind of future could she expect, given the baggage from their shared pasts?

She was sitting up, reaching for her robe, when the bathroom door opened and Cal stepped out. He was naked except for the white towel that wrapped his hips, his splendid torso gleaming with moisture. Tossing the towel aside, he strode toward the wardrobe and then glanced back at her with a friendly grin. "Rise and shine. Harris wants us out front in thirty minutes."

So it would be business as usual—and that was fine, Megan told herself. Clutching her robe to her chest, she fled toward the bathroom. After flashing in and out of the shower, she finger-combed her hair and slathered her face, neck, arms and hands with sunscreen. By the time she emerged from the bathroom, Cal had dressed and gone out, leaving his packed duffel next to the door, probably for the staff to pick up.

The message was clear. He was keeping his distance.

Had she said or done something wrong? Had last night's performance failed to meet his expectations? Or was he just making it clear that he didn't want to get entangled? Fine, she would follow his example and behave as if nothing had happened between them.

Willing herself to ignore the sting, she finished dressing, closed her duffel and made a last-minute sweep of the bungalow to make sure nothing had been left behind. That done, she parked her bag next to Cal's and opened the front door.

Cal stood on the porch, a grin on his face and a cup of coffee in each hand. "We've got a few minutes," he said. "After last night, I thought we might need this to wake up."

Megan's heart rose like a helium birthday balloon as he put the cups on the outdoor table and turned to pull her into his arms. His kiss was sweet and tender, lingering just long enough. Exactly what she needed this morning. "You're amazing," he whispered in her ear.

"You're pretty amazing yourself," she countered, playfully rubbing her head against his chin.

Letting her go, he retrieved the cups and handed her one. Together they stood on the porch, cradling the warm cups between their palms and watching the African sunrise flame across the sky. It was one of those moments made all the more perfect, Megan thought, because it couldn't last.

"Will you be all right today?" Cal asked her.

"I'll be fine." She took a sip of the hot, rich Tanzanian brew. "But I'd just as soon not share this situation with Harris. He'd have far too much fun with it."

"Agreed." He punctuated the word with a chuckle. "I'll be on my best behavior today. Just so you won't be surprised, we'll be sharing a single tent with two cots for the next few nights."

"Fine. Something tells me I don't really want to be alone in a tent on the Serengeti. I have visions of some hungry hyena wandering in to munch on my leg. You can be there to chase him away."

"I'll confess that wasn't the first advantage I thought of." The gray eyes that gazed down at Megan held a slightly naughty twinkle, and she knew he was thinking about making love to her again. It felt good, knowing he wanted her—even though she knew things might well be different later on. Cal had always been a man with an agenda. He may have put that agenda aside for now, but sooner or later it would resurface. When that happened, it would be as if this romantic interlude had never taken place.

Was she falling in love with him? Was that the reason her brain kept flashing those red warning lights? Cal Jeffords was a compelling man, but Megan knew he didn't hold her blameless for Nick's crime and subsequent suicide. Revenge might not be far from the top of his list. She'd be a fool to lower her guard—but meanwhile she was having such a wonderful time. It was like being Cinderella at the ball—but with the constant awareness that the clock was ticking toward midnight.

By the time they finished their coffee, it was time to meet Harris and Gideon for a quick predeparture breakfast. Cal helped the driver load the last of their gear into the vehicle, and they were off.

They were headed north, toward the Kenyan border where the vast Serengeti Plain spanned the two countries. In the dry season the game herds migrated north in search of water and food. At the start of the long rains, they swept southward by the hundreds of thousands, to graze on the abundant fresh grass and raise their young. It was this grand spectacle that Harris had promised to show them.

As the Land Rover sped along the narrow ribbon of paved road, Cal stole a glance at Megan. She was seated with her arm resting on the back of the seat, the breeze fluttering the green scarf at her throat. He took a moment to feast his eyes on her. True to their understanding, she gave no sign that anything had changed between them. But he couldn't forget that last night she'd been his—quivering above him, her head thrown back, while he exploded deep inside her. Right now, all he could think about was having her again, and soon.

He'd set out to seduce her, and now he'd succeeded, but with more complications than he could've imagined in his wildest dreams. Her beauty was a given. But it was her blend of courage and vulnerability that had hit him with the impact of a ten-ton truck.

She was Nick's widow. Cold reasoning told him he couldn't dismiss her link to the stolen money. But last night she'd given herself to him with all her woman's passion. She'd reached out and trusted him to lead her back from the edge of hell. How could he even think of using that trust to get the answers he wanted? But then, again, how could he not? He'd spent two years searching and had even come to Africa to learn the truth—he wasn't going home without it.

A bump in the road jarred him back to the present. The landscape had opened up into rolling hills, carpeted with pale green shoots of sprouting grass. On a flat rise, a cluster of round huts came into view, with mud walls and artfully thatched, conical roofs. Rangy-looking cattle, watched over by young boys, grazed on the slopes.

"Maasai," Harris explained for Megan's benefit. "They're all over these parts with their cattle and goats, living pretty much like they have for hundreds of years. Back in the old days, do-gooders tried to civilize them. But the rascals didn't take to civilizing. They wanted to keep their spears and their cows and their old ways. They still do."

The Land Rover had come up on a herd of goats, grazing in a hollow where the runoff from the road had nourished the grass. The young boy guarding them showed spindly legs below his crimson togalike garment. He grinned and waved as they passed.

Megan called out *"Jambo,"* laughing as she returned the wave. It was plain to see that she adored children. What a shame she'd never had any of her own. That miscarriage she'd suffered must've been devastating.

"What a beautiful boy," she said.

"Oh, they're a handsome lot, all right," Harris snorted. "And vain as all get-out, especially the so-called warriors. The women do the work, the boys herd the stock, and aside from making babies, the men haven't much to do but strut around with their spears and look pretty."

"Is it still true that a young Maasai has to kill a lion with a spear before he can be called a man?" Cal asked.

Harris guffawed. "Lions are protected these days. But knowing the Maasai, I wouldn't be surprised if it still happens. Years ago I showed up in time to save one of the young fools. His spear had snapped. The lion was about to rip him apart when I stepped in. That's how *this* happened." He nodded toward his pinned-up sleeve.

Megan shot Cal a mischievous glance, rolling her eyes skyward. A smile teased her kissable mouth. She looked luscious enough to devour on the spot. He could hardly wait to get her alone.

He was in over his head—and he knew it.

By the time they arrived at the campsite, it was late in the day. Clouds were rumbling across the vast expanse of sky, threatening a downpour.

Megan had half expected they'd be pitching camp on their own. She should have known better. Harris's competent safari staff had everything set up and waiting for them, including a savory dinner of saffron rice, vegetables and chicken cooked over an open fire.

Set on high ground, safe from flooding, there were tents for staff and guests along with sheltered cooking and eating areas. Megan was astonished to discover that the tent she shared with Cal featured an adjoining bathroom with a flush toilet and a primitive but functional shower.

"Magic!" Harris laughed at her surprise. "We can't have clients wandering out to the loo in the dark, can we? They might not make it back."

After the long, bumpy ride in the Land Rover, it was heavenly to sit in the open front of the dining tent and watch the rain drip off the canvas. The day had been spectacular. They'd seen elephants, giraffes, ostriches and a pride of lions feasting on the zebra they'd killed. White-headed vultures and marabou storks had flocked around them, waiting their turn at the leavings. In this place of raw, cruel beauty, nothing went to waste.

Megan had watched breathless as a cheetah streaked after a gazelle and brought it down in a single bound. Two cubs, hiding in the grass, had scampered out to join their mother at the feast. Death was brutal on the Serengeti, but it nourished new life.

As the darkness deepened, they sat in folding chairs, watching the rain and listening to the sounds of the awakening night—the distant roar of a lion, the titter of a hyena, the cry of a bird and the drone of insects in the grass. Harris sipped his bourbon, lantern light deepening the hollows under his eyes. He looked old and tired, Megan thought. Maybe the life of a safari guide was becoming too strenuous for him.

"Cal already knows this," he said to Megan, "but I need to make it clear for you. Once you go into your tent for the night, you zip the flap and don't open it till you hear the boys in the morning. No traipsing around in the dark, hear? You never know what's going to be out there."

Megan laughed. "Not to worry. No power on earth could drag me out of that tent in the middle of the night."

"Speaking of the tent…" Cal set down his glass, stood and stretched. "I'm ready to turn in. You should get some rest, too, Harris. It's been a long day." He glanced at Megan. Taking her cue, she rose. It had been a tiring day for her, too. But if Cal had lovemaking on his mind, she was on board. Just looking at him was enough to make her ache.

Harris remained in his chair. He really did look tired, Megan thought. Feeling a surge of affection, she bent and kissed the weathered cheek. "Do get some sleep, Harris," she murmured. "We don't want to wear you out tomorrow."

"Thanks for thinking of an old man." Patting her hand, he glanced up at Cal. "You take care of this girl, hear? She's a good one."

"She is, and I'll do that." Switching on a flashlight and opening a handy umbrella, Cal ushered her toward their tent. The storm had subsided to a steady drizzle. Exotic animal sounds, like the track from an old Tarzan movie, filled the night.

"Will it really be dangerous out here," she asked, "or was Harris just trying to scare me?"

"You can take him at his word. The staff will keep a fire going to scare off anything big. But that won't be much help if you walk outside and step on a snake."

Megan shuddered. "That's enough. You've convinced me to behave."

"Behave? You?" Cal teased. "We'll see about that."

They'd reached the sheltered entrance to their tent. Cal laid the umbrella on a chair and checked the interior with the flashlight beam. "All clear," he said. "Come on in."

Megan stepped into the tent and bent to close the long zipper that secured the flap. When she straightened and

turned around, Cal was standing in the narrow space between the cots. In the dim glow of the flashlight, his eyes
held a glint of pure, unbridled lust.

"I've been waiting all day to get my hands on you," he
growled, opening his arms and moving toward her.

Megan met him partway. He crushed her close, his kiss
flaming through her like the tail of a meteor. They tore
at each other's clothes, buttons popping, belts and shoes
thudding. Megan left her slacks wadded on the floor. Still
in her bra and panties, she hooked his hips with one leg,
bringing his erection into hard contact with her aching
sex. Wild with need, she ground against him through his
briefs, heightening the hot sweetness until her head fell
back and she came with a little shudder, ready for more.
She had never felt so free.

"What a little wanton you've turned out to be. Who
knew?" He chuckled under his breath as he unhooked her
bra and tossed it on the cot. His hand slid inside her panties, fingers stroking her, riding on her slickness. "Damn
it, but I want you. All I can think about right now is being
inside you!"

"Would you believe it's all I can think about…too?"
She shed her panties. Her hand tugged at his briefs, pulling them down to free his bulging erection. The cots were
narrow, but that was of little concern as he lowered her
onto the nearest one and slipped on protection before he
mounted her and drove in hard. Megan flung her legs
around his hips, pulling him deeper inside her. She loved
the way his length and thickness filled every inch of her.
She loved the feel of him, gliding silkily along her sensitive
inner surfaces, igniting a trail of sparks that soared through
her body. She met his thrusts, heightening the dizzy spiral
of sensations that carried her with him, mounting upward
to release in a shattering burst.

For a moment he lay still. His breath was warm against her shoulder as he exhaled, chuckled and rolled off the cot.

"Did we break anything?" he teased, grinning down at her.

"Are you asking about me or the bed?" Megan sat up and ran a hand through her damp hair. She felt gloriously spent. "For the record, I believe we're both intact."

He bent and brushed a kiss across her mouth. "You're amazing," he said.

"So you tell me," she responded with a little laugh. "Sometimes I even amaze myself."

They lay awake in the darkness, veiled by mosquito netting and separated by the narrow space between their cots. Outside the tent, the sounds of the African night blended in a symphony of primal nature.

Wrapped in contentment, Megan stretched her legs beneath the blankets. The day had been splendid, the night even more so. She didn't want this time to end. But she knew better than to talk about the future. Here, with the outside world far away, she and Cal had found something memorable. But days from now, she knew, only the memory would remain.

"I wish I could record those sounds outside and take them with me," she said. "The rain, the animals…they'd lull me to sleep anywhere, even in Darfur."

A leaden silence hung between them before he spoke. "You can't mean to say you're still planning to go back!"

"Why not?" Even as she said the words, Megan could feel her resolve crumbling. But she held fast. "I'm feeling so much better now. And those people need me. I can't just turn my back and walk away."

He sat up, a dark silhouette through the mosquito netting that draped his cot. "I'm not asking you to turn your back. I'm asking you to take more time off. Make sure you're strong enough."

"Is that all?" The words slipped out before Megan could stop them. Her heart sank. The last thing she wanted was to question Cal's motives like a whiny, insecure female fishing for a commitment.

"No, it isn't all," he said. "The past few days have been wonderful. I care about you, Megan. I want to see where you and I are headed before I let you go anywhere. Is that so hard to accept?"

Megan's throat had gone dry. Only as Cal's words sank in did she realize how she'd been yearning to hear them. She *wanted* him to care for her. She *wanted* more time with him. But believing those words could get her heart broken. Cal had come to Africa seeking one thing—justice. And he was the sort of man who'd do anything to get what he wanted. That included playing her any way he could.

She found her voice. "I didn't realize we were headed anywhere. What about the money you suspect I took? Isn't that why you came after me?"

He hesitated, as if weighing his reply. "In part—at first. But knowing you as I do now, I can't believe you're hiding anything. You're as transparent as fine crystal, Megan. That's one of the things that I…" He fumbled for the right words. "One of the things I find so compelling about you. And right now I'm here because of *you,* not the damned money."

Megan's heart leaped. She'd wanted to hear those words from him. And now she wanted to believe they were true. But were they? Or was he still manipulating her?

With a weary sigh he lay down again. The cot creaked as he adjusted his tall frame. "So what's it to be? Will you give me more time before you vanish out of my life again?"

Megan gazed up into the darkness, her emotions churning. She wanted this man in more ways than she could name. But did she want him enough to risk heartbreak or betrayal?

"I can't make that decision tonight," she said. "Give me a few days to think about it—maybe until we're headed back to Arusha. All right?"

"All right," he grumbled. "But you can expect some lobbying on my part. I'm not one to take no for an answer."

"I know." Torn, she blinked away a secret tear. "Now, let's get some sleep. Harris will be rousting us out early tomorrow."

He mumbled a reply, already drifting. Megan closed her eyes and soon fell into a dreamless sleep.

It was barely dawn when a commotion outside the tent shocked her awake. Megan sat bolt upright. She could hear the sound of shouts and running feet.

Cal was awake, too. "Stay inside," he said. "I'll see what's happening."

He was pulling on his pants when Gideon's frantic voice came through the closed tent flap. "Open up! We need you!"

"What's wrong?" Cal yanked the zipper down. Gideon's face was ashen.

"Hurry! It's Mr. Harris! I think he's had a heart attack!"

Twelve

Still in her pajamas, Megan raced outside. Harris lay gray-faced and unconscious on the canvas apron in front of his tent. Megan dropped to her knees beside him. He wasn't breathing. No time to check for a pulse. It had to be a heart attack. Willing herself not to panic, she placed her hands at the base of Harris's sternum, shifted her weight above him and fell into the rhythmic compressions of CPR. Her nurse's training had taught her to keep a cool head, but a voice inside her was screaming. This old man had grown dear to her. She couldn't lose him.

Why hadn't she paid more attention to him last night? He'd looked ill even then. If she'd checked him, she might have been able to do something sooner.

Gideon hovered over her, visibly shaken. "He came outside and fell. Is he going to die?"

"Not if I can help it." Megan kept the rhythm steady. "When did this happen?"

"Just before I called you. He has been like a father to me…" Gideon's voice broke.

Megan didn't look up. "Radio the airport in Arusha," she said. "Tell somebody to send a plane with medical equipment. Hurry!"

"No, not Arusha. I know who to call." Gideon raced for the Land Rover, which was equipped with a radio.

Cal had been standing back to give her room. Now he knelt beside her. "I can do this. Let me take over while you make sure the message gets through."

"Thanks." Megan let his hands slip under hers, keeping the rhythm unbroken. That done, she clambered to her feet and raced after Gideon. By the time she reached the vehicle, he was already on the radio, speaking in terse English to a voice that could barely be heard through the crackling static. Ending the call, he turned back to Megan.

"Flying Doctors. We have a contract with them. They can be here in half an hour and take him to Nairobi. Can you keep him alive that long?"

"We can only try." Megan raced back to where she'd left Cal with Harris and gave him the news. She'd heard of the air ambulance company that served much of East Africa, but in her haste to get help she'd forgotten. Thank heaven Gideon had thought to call them.

"That's some hope at least." Cal's strong hands kept up their pumping on Harris's chest. "Go get some clothes on. We can spell each other till the plane gets here." His gaze met Megan's, and she saw the fear that neither of them would voice. There was no way of knowing whether CPR could keep Harris alive. By the time the plane arrived, it could be too late to save him.

Rushing into the tent, she yanked on her clothes and shoved her feet into her boots. As an afterthought, she flung some essentials into her day pack and shoved her passport, with its multiple-entry Kenyan visa, into her pocket. If there was room in the plane, she wanted to be ready to go along. Harris would need someone there who knew him, and as a nurse, she was the logical choice. She would ask Gideon to find Harris's passport, as well. It would at least give the distraught man something to do.

She was closing her pack when she heard Cal's voice calling her. Stumbling over her boot laces, she raced out of the tent. Her heart dropped as she saw that he'd stopped the chest compressions. But then she noticed the relief that glazed his face.

"I'm getting a pulse," he said. "He seems to be coming around."

"Oh, thank God!" Megan dropped to Harris's near side. She saw at once that his color was improving. A touch along the side of his throat confirmed a thready heartbeat. "Water," she called out. "And bring a pillow and blanket!"

Someone handed her a plastic water bottle. Twisting off the cap, Megan wet her hand and smoothed it over Harris's face. He gasped, taking in precious oxygen. His eyelids fluttered open. His mouth worked to form words.

"What the hell...?" he muttered.

"Hush." Megan laid a finger on his parchment-dry lips. "You've had a heart attack, Harris. Lie still. The plane's on its way."

"Feel like I've been kicked by a damned elephant..." He struggled vainly to sit up.

"Stay put, *mzee*." Cal's hands on his shoulders held him gently in place. "You almost checked out on us. We want to keep you around."

Someone handed Megan the bedding she'd asked for. She tucked the blanket around Harris and slid the pillow under his head. He still looked as frail as a snowflake. The plane would be sure to carry oxygen and a defibrillator;

but until it arrived, the old hunter could go back into cardiac arrest at any time. All they could do was keep him quiet and hope for the best.

Lifting his head, she held the water bottle to his lips. "Just enough to wet your mouth," she cautioned. "And then I'm going to give you an aspirin to chew."

"Water and aspirin!" He swore in protest. "Hell, give me a swig of bourbon and let me up. I'll be as good as new!"

Megan exchanged worried looks with Cal. The old man's spunk was definitely back. But that didn't mean the danger was any less grave. In fact, he could put himself in danger if he refused to settle down. While she held his sunburned hands, her eyes gazed anxiously at the sky. Nairobi, the capital of Kenya, was only about fifty air miles away—closer than Arusha. Gideon had promised that the doctors would arrive in half an hour, but she hadn't thought to check her watch. How much longer did they have to wait?

The minutes crawled past. In a blessedly short time, they heard the drone of a small aircraft. Megan breathed a prayer of thanks as the single-engine Cessna landed on a level strip of ground below the camp. Within minutes Harris was hooked up to oxygen, strapped to a stretcher and on his way to the plane.

Megan, who'd been given the OK to come along, followed with her day pack slung on her shoulder. With one backward glance at Cal, she swung into the plane and took the last empty seat. There'd been no time to say goodbye. She would likely see him again in Nairobi, but their interlude in this African paradise was over. Whatever happened between them now would happen amid the stresses and uncertainties of the real world.

Cal watched the departing plane until it vanished into the sunrise. Harris was in capable hands, he told himself. Kenyatta Hospital in Nairobi was modern and well equipped, its doctors as competent as any in Africa. As for Megan, it had been the right decision for her to go. But there was a cold hollow inside him where her warmth had been. He hadn't planned on her being torn from him so soon—or so abruptly, without so much as a chance to say goodbye. Only now that she was gone did he realize how empty he felt without her.

He would see her at the hospital, of course, but under strained conditions. They would both be concerned about Harris and focused on his needs. There'd be little opportunity for them to be alone or to make any decisions about their budding relationship.

Budding? Was that what it was? He'd scarcely spent a week with Megan, but now that she was gone he felt damned near lost without her. What was that supposed to mean?

But that thought would have to wait. Right now he had other urgent concerns on his mind.

The plan was for Cal and Gideon to load the personal gear in the Land Rover, drive back to Arusha and make the flight from there to Nairobi in Cal's corporate jet. It was the course of action that made the most sense. With Megan gone, Cal had no more reason to stay in Arusha. And Gideon was the closest thing to family the old man had. In Nairobi, he could look after Harris's needs and see him home after his release from the hospital.

Cal would see that Gideon had plenty of money for his lodging, meals and transportation. He would also make sure there'd be no problem with Harris's medical expenses. He could afford it, and it was at least one way he could help.

Nairobi might also be his last chance to arrive at an understanding with Megan. Things had been good between them last night. But she still seemed set on returning to Darfur. He'd told her he wanted more time together, but even though she'd agreed to consider the idea, they no longer had the luxury of the rest of their safari to decide what would come next. If he was going to convince her to give him a real chance, he'd have to move very fast. Maybe he needed to open up and tell her how he really felt. Otherwise he could lose her for good—and he wasn't ready to let that happen.

"Hello, sweetheart." Harris was sitting partway up, an oxygen line hooked to his nose. Above the bed, monitors attached to his body flickered and beeped.

"Hello, you old rogue." Megan stepped to his bedside and brushed a kiss across his forehead. His color was much improved, and his eyes had recovered a bit of their twinkle, but he was far from out of the woods. A few hours ago the doctors had performed an angioplasty to clear out the clogged artery that had caused his heart attack. The attending physician had told her his chances for recovery were good, but only if he took better care of his health.

"Where's Cal?" he asked her.

"Cal and Gideon are driving to Arusha and flying from there. Unless they've been delayed, they should be here by tonight."

"Gideon's coming? Good."

"He wanted to be here. He said you were like a father to him."

"The rascal would only say that if he thought I was dying." Harris snorted dismissively, but something in his voice told Megan the old man had been touched.

"The doctor's going to come in to lecture you soon," Megan said, taking a seat next to the bed. "If you don't want to end up back in the hospital, you're going to have to make some changes. No more smoking. Cut way back on alcohol and red meat—"

"Oh, bother! Will he say I have to give up all those women who are chasing me, too?"

"You're incorrigible."

"And you're the sweetest thing to come into my life since I don't know when." His hand brushed Megan's cheek. "If I was thirty years younger and if Cal hadn't already staked his claim on you—"

"Staked his claim? Maybe he should ask me first."

"He will if you stick around. I've noticed the way he looks at you. The man's so lovesick he can barely lace his boots. Hellfire, girl, I do believe you're blushing."

"I haven't blushed since I was fifteen years old." But Megan's face did feel unsettlingly warm. Was Harris right about Cal? Surely the old man was teasing her. How could she let herself believe that? "Let's talk about something else," she said.

He looked thoughtful. "Well, I guess I could thank you for saving my life."

"I can't take credit for that. It was Cal who did most of the CPR and Gideon who called the plane."

"But you're the one who stayed with me and talked me into hanging on. So just for you, I've a confession to make." His pale blue eyes twinkled mysteriously. "I've been filling your pretty head with tall tales about how I lost my arm. If you promise to keep it a secret, I'll tell you the real story."

"You mean it wasn't a jealous husband or a rhino or a lion? This, I need to hear. Certainly I'll keep your secret." Megan leaned closer to the bed. "I promise."

"It was back in England," he said. "My family was dirt poor, with six mouths to feed. I was fifteen when I quit school to work in a coal mine. The place was a black hellhole. But it was the only job to be had for a boy like me.

One day a slab of coal fell out of the ceiling and crushed my arm. The flesh and bone were too far gone to heal, and there was no money for a doctor. When gangrene set in, the local butcher got me drunk and cut off the arm to save my life."

"Oh…" Megan gazed at him in dismay. No wonder Harris made up those fanciful stories about losing his arm. The real story was too sad to share with clients. "What did you do, Harris? How did you survive?"

"I'd always been good with a gun. It took some practice, but I learned to shoot one-armed with my father's old army rifle. To feed the family, I started poaching deer and grouse off the local estate. Got caught, of course. Barely escaped with my hide. Stowed aboard a freighter and ended up in Africa. No papers—but it was easier to get by in those days."

"That's quite a story, Harris." Cal stood in the doorway, looking rumpled and weary in the clothes he'd pulled on that morning. "I've always wondered about it myself. Trust Megan to charm the truth out of you."

The old hunter smiled, but it was plain to see that so much talking had tired him. Megan watched Cal as he crossed the room toward her. They'd been apart for only a few hours, but now that he was here she realized how much she'd missed him.

"Harris swore me to secrecy," she said. "Since you were listening, you have to swear, too. Not a word."

"Consider it done. My lips are sealed." Cal's hand brushed across her shoulder as he moved to the head of the bed. She felt his touch through her shirt and along her skin like the passing of a warm breeze. After the long, stressful day, the need to be in his arms was compelling enough to hurt.

The look he gave Harris betrayed how worried he'd been. "You gave us quite a scare, old friend," he said.

"Oh, I'll be fine." Harris winked. "Just might have to cut back on my bad habits, that's all. Where's Gideon? Didn't he come?"

"Gideon's down in the cafeteria grabbing a sandwich. He wants to sit with you tonight, so I suggested he eat first. Meanwhile, I hope you won't mind if I take Megan back to the hotel for some dinner and a good night's rest. We can stay till Gideon gets here."

Harris waved them away. "Go on. I'll be fine. There's this good-looking nurse on duty. If I'm alone when she comes in, maybe I can get somewhere with her."

Cal shook his head. "Just don't overdo it, you old rascal! We'll see you later."

Megan rose, blew Harris a farewell kiss and allowed Cal to escort her out of the room. His hand rested lightly on the small of her back as they walked through the maze of hallways and took the elevator to the hospital lobby. "I booked us a room at the Crowne Plaza." He named one of the city's premier luxury hotels. "Your things are there, and we have reservations in the dining room. I'm guessing you'll be hungry."

"Starved. But I'll settle for something quick in the coffee shop. I look a fright, and I'm too tired to get cleaned up for dinner."

The Crowne Plaza was an easy drive from Kenyatta Hospital, but the cab took time to weave its way through the tangle of evening traffic. Too tired to talk, Megan stared out the cab windows at the busy streets. She was no stranger to the big, bustling city of Nairobi. It was the jumping-off point for the refugee camps in northern Kenya and the Sudan. If she decided to go back to Darfur from here, it shouldn't be too difficult to find transportation.

But when it came to that decision, her heart was still torn. She was needed in Darfur. And going back might help her face her buried fears. But she'd found something warm and thrilling with Cal—something she realized she'd been searching for all her life. If there was a chance it might last, she'd be tempted to stay. But she'd known Cal too long not to have doubts. Was he really capable of a long-term relationship—with anyone, much less her—or was he still just a man with an agenda?

The taxi was slowing down, turning left into the hotel driveway. Other times in Nairobi, Megan had ridden local buses and stayed at one of the cheap boardinghouses frequented by volunteers like her. Now as the cab pulled up to the elegant, ultramodern complex, she felt as if she'd stumbled into a different world. The old Megan would have been right at home here. But that woman was gone forever. She was a different person now.

But when he looked at her, which woman did Cal see?

The hotel coffee shop was too noisy for serious conversation. Cal studied Megan across the table as she finished the last of her chicken and rice and sipped her mineral water. He'd planned a romantic evening in a setting where he could lay his heart on the line. But he should have known it wasn't the best idea. Megan had been rousted out of bed by Harris's heart attack, flown with him in the plane and remained at the hospital for the rest of the day. Stress showed in every line and shadow of her face. What she needed tonight was rest, not romance.

They rode the elevator up to their room, having conversed mostly about Harris, the flight, his surgery and recovery. "You look worn out," Cal said as she surveyed the room with its king-size bed. "Your duffel's on that bench by the wall. The bathroom's all yours."

"Wonderful. I could really use a shower." She rummaged in her bag, pulled out a few things and then vanished into the bathroom. Minutes later the shower came on.

Cal had retrieved his laptop from the plane. The device was functional here in the hotel, and he needed to catch up on his messages. He scrolled through his in-box, marking some for reply, deleting others. What he'd hoped to see was some word from Harlan Crandall about his search for the missing funds. Knowing where the money had gone might at least give him some closure, so he could move ahead with Megan. But there was nothing.

Impatient, he pecked out a message to Crandall asking for an update. By the time he'd finished, the shower had turned off. A moment later, Megan emerged in a cloud of steam. Wrapped in one of the hotel's oversized terry robes, she was damp, glowing and so beautiful it stopped his breath.

"Better?" he asked, finding his voice.

"Better. It's been a long day and I'm done in." She began rubbing her hair dry with a towel, fluffing and curling it with her fingers. The sight of her stirred Cal to a pleasant arousal. Although he'd planned to let her rest, the thought of Megan's fresh, naked body in his arms was giving him different ideas. But he'd had a long day, too, and he didn't exactly smell like a rose garden. He needed a shower before he shared her bed.

With a murmured excuse, he walked into the bathroom, stripped down, turned on the water and lathered his body. The shower took about ten minutes, drying off a few more. With his hips wrapped in a towel, he stepped out of the bathroom.

His anticipation sagged. Megan was curled under the covers on the far side of the bed, deep in slumber.

* * *

Megan stirred and opened her eyes. The last thing she remembered was lying awake, waiting for Cal to finish his shower and join her—for lovemaking, serious talk or whatever was meant to happen. But she'd been so sleepy, she had no memory of his even coming to bed.

Now it was full daylight, and Cal was nowhere to be seen. Only his bag on the luggage stand gave any indication that he hadn't gone for good. Sitting up, she found a note penned on hotel stationery and tucked under the clock on the nightstand.

Good morning, sleepyhead. I didn't have the heart to wake you before I left for the hospital. Since Gideon didn't call me in the night, I'm guessing Harris is fine. If he's not, you'll hear. I'll check back with you later. Meanwhile, please relax and order some breakfast. C.

Megan glanced at the clock. It was almost 9:00 a.m. How could she have slept so late? Flinging aside the covers, she sprang to her feet, then realized her mistake. Lying down for so long and getting up so fast had left her slightly dizzy. Tottering toward a chair, she banged her knee on a small side table. She managed to right the table before it fell, but as it tilted, an object crashed to the floor.

Megan bent to pick it up and recognized Cal's laptop. *Oh, no!* What if she'd broken it?

Worried, she gave the device an experimental shake. Nothing sounded loose, but she noticed that the screen had come on. Maybe Cal had left it in sleep mode—not that she had enough technical savvy to be certain. It appeared he'd been checking his email earlier. His in-box was still open on the screen.

Something popped up on the screen, drawing her eye automatically. It was a "new email" notification letting him know a message had arrived, from someone named

Harlan Crandall. Megan would have dismissed it as none of her business—but then she saw the subject line.

Re: Update on missing foundation funds

Her pulse lurched. The right thing would be to ignore the message. But this concerned *her*, and might even have some bearing on her relationship with Cal. She couldn't *not* look at it.

Racked with guilt for snooping, she highlighted the message and clicked it open.

Dear Mr. Jeffords:
You asked for an update on my investigation. I fear I have little to report. I've traced Mr. Rafferty's activities during the weeks before his suicide, but aside from some large bank withdrawals, I've found nothing that might lead us to the money.

What have you been able to learn from Mr. Rafferty's widow? If we can put our findings together, maybe some new pieces of this puzzle will emerge.
Yours truly,
Harlan Crandall

As Megan laid the laptop back on the table, a strange numbness crept over her. So Cal's motive hadn't changed. He'd pretended to care about her, but all he'd really wanted was to track down the money and prove her guilt. His tenderness, his loving patience—it had all been an act to win her trust.

At least she knew. And she knew what she had to do.

Willing herself to move, not think, she emptied her duffel on the bed and began repacking the contents for a long, rough trip.

Thirteen

Cal's gut clenched as he reread the note Megan had left in the hotel room. It was penned in a shaky script—his only clue to her anguished state of mind.

Dear Cal,
By the time you read this I'll be on my way back
to Darfur. Now that my decision is made, there's
no point in staying, or in drawn-out goodbyes. And
there's no point in explaining why I decided to leave.
I think you already know.

Yes, he did know. He'd just seen Crandall's message on his laptop and realized it had been opened and read. Lord, he could just imagine what Megan thought of him now.

Don't bother coming after me. I've told you the truth
all along—I endorsed the checks and gave them to
Nick, and that's all I know. You won't learn anything

*new by tracking me down again, and you won't find
the money. I truly believe Nick spent it all. If he
hadn't, he'd have given it back when he was caught.*

    *Please give my best to Harris and Gideon. Tell
them if I get back to Arusha I'll pay them a visit.
Whatever your motives may have been, Cal, I can't
leave without thanking you. You did some good
things for me. But now it's time for me to go back
to where I'm needed. I'm strong enough now. I'll
be fine.*

There was no closing or signature, as if Megan had
put so much emotion into the message that she'd been too
drained to finish it.

Cal's first impulse was to go after—find her, drag her
back by force if need be and convince her she was wrong
about him.

Convince her, damn it, that he was in love with her!

But he knew it wouldn't work. Even if he could track
Megan down, forcing her to come back wouldn't be an act
of love. It would be an act of control. Megan had made
her choice. If he loved her, he would respect that choice—
even though letting her go was like ripping out his heart.

He would go home to San Francisco, Cal resolved.
There, he would do whatever it took to find out what Nick
had done with the stolen funds. The answer had to be
somewhere—and when he found it, he would take the
evidence and lay it at Megan's feet. Once he could prove
her innocence, all the civil suits would go away. It would
be safe for her to come home. Maybe then she would forgive him.

Meanwhile, as she faced danger in a savage land, he could only pray that the heavenly powers would keep her safe.

Darfur, two months later

Megan filled her mug with hot black coffee and seated herself at the empty table in the volunteer kitchen. It was early dawn, the sun not yet risen behind the barren hills. But outside the infirmary, the camp was already stirring to life. Through the open window she could hear the crow of a rooster, the cry of a baby and the chatter of women going for water. The familiar scent of baking *kisra,* a Sudanese bread made from ground sorghum, drifted on the air.

Two months after her return to the camp, it was as if she'd never left. Some of the volunteers had moved on, including the doctor who'd diagnosed her rape and filled out the report. But the refugees were mostly the ones she remembered. In a way it was almost like coming home.

The long days kept her blessedly busy. It was only at night that she had time to think about Cal. The man had schemed to win her trust and get information. He had used her shamelessly, and she had let him. She knew she ought to put him out of her mind. But as she lay on her cot in the darkness, the hunger to be in his arms was a soul-deep pain that never left.

"You're up bright and early." Sam Watson, the new doctor, wandered in and filled his coffee cup. He was African-American, middle-aged, with a wife and college-age children back in New Jersey. Megan had warmed at once to his friendly manner.

"This is my favorite part of the day," Megan said. "The only time it's calm around here."

"I understand. Can I get you something before I sit

down? Some eggs? Some nice fried Spam?" He lifted the cover off the electric fry pan where the Sudanese cook had left breakfast to warm.

Megan shook her head. "Coffee's fine."

He filled his plate and sat down across from her. The smell of fried meat triggered a curdling sensation in her stomach.

"You've been off your feed lately." He stirred a packet of sugar into his coffee. "Everything all right?"

"Fine." She forced a smile, clenching her teeth against a rising wave of nausea.

"You're sure? You look a little green this morning. I'd be happy to check you out before we open for business."

"I'm fine. Just need some…air." Abandoning her coffee cup, she rose and stumbled out the back door. The morning breeze was still cool. She gulped its freshness into her lungs.

It couldn't be. It just couldn't be.

But she remembered now that she'd had her last period in Arusha—a week before Cal showed up. That had been more than two months ago.

No, it couldn't be. They'd used protection.

But now she remembered seeing the wrapper on the pack of condoms—a local brand, not known for reliability. Oh, Lord, she should have warned him. But at the time, that had been the last thing on her mind.

"Megan?"

She turned to find the doctor standing behind her.

"I'll be fine, Sam. Just give me a minute."

"I've got something else to give you," he said. "Found a stash of them in the supply closet. Something tells me you might need one of these."

He handed her a small, cellophane-wrapped box. Megan's stomach flip-flopped as she saw the label.

It was a home pregnancy test.

* * *

Megan lay on her cot, staring up into the darkness. One hand rested lovingly on her belly, where the precious new life was growing.

Her baby. Cal's baby. The wonder of it sent a thrill through her body. Two weeks after discovering her pregnancy, she was still getting used to the idea. Only one thing was certain. She wanted this child with all her heart, and she would do anything to keep her little one safe.

When, if ever, would she inform Cal? She supposed he had a right to know. But after the way he'd used her in an effort to glean information, did she want him in her life… or in their child's life?

Cal *would* be in her life, she knew, probably trying to control every aspect of his child's existence—and hers.

She'd learned that Cal could be a genuinely caring person, but his version of caring usually meant taking over. She could do without the Cal Jeffords Master-of-the-Universe brand of caring. But did she have the right to raise her child without a father—and without the advantages that such a father could provide?

So many decisions to make. However, as much as it weighed on her, the question of Cal was far removed from her present world. For now, there were more urgent matters to deal with.

Given her history of miscarriage, Sam had wisely insisted that she be evacuated on the next available plane, which would be arriving with mail and supplies the day after tomorrow. For the near future she could be posted to Arusha, where there was a small modern hospital and ready transportation out of the country. Sooner or later, Megan knew, she would have to face going back to America, where she had no home, no family, no job, few friends who'd remained loyal to her and a stack of legal charges waiting for her. When the time came, involving Cal and his lawyers might be her only choice if she wanted to spend the last stages of her pregnancy anywhere other than inside a courtroom. But for now she wanted to stay in Africa.

She'd asked Sam to keep her pregnancy out of his report, citing simply "health reasons" for her transfer. He'd agreed to her request without demanding the reason.

The hour was late and she'd worked a long day. As she closed her eyes, she could feel herself beginning to drift. Soon she was deep in dreamless sleep.

"Miss Megan! Wake up!" The whisper penetrated the fog of Megan's slumber. She could feel a small hand shaking her shoulder. "Miss Megan...it's me."

Megan opened her eyes. A delicate face, surrounded by the folds of a head scarf, peered down at her. *No! She had to be dreaming!*

"It's me, Miss Megan. It's Saida!"

Still groggy, Megan rolled onto one elbow. "You can't be alive," she muttered. "I saw the Janjaweed—"

"Yes, they took me. For many days they kept me with them. But no more. Now I need you to come."

Megan sat up and switched on the flashlight she kept next to her cot. Yes, it was Saida. But a very different Saida from the innocent girl who'd sneaked out of camp to meet a boy. There was a grim purpose to the set of her mouth, a glint of steel in the lovely doe eyes that had seen too much. Slung over her shoulder by a leather strap was an AK-47 automatic rifle.

"I need you to come," she repeated. "My friend is hurt. I need you to save her."

"You need the doctor. Let me get him."

"No. Not a man. Only you."

None of this was making sense. "Where is your friend? Can't you bring her here?"

Saida shook her head. "Too far. Our camp is in the mountains. I have horses outside. If we ride hard, we can be there by sunrise."

"Saida, I'm going to have a baby," Megan protested. "I can't ride hard."

"We will have to take more time, then." The girlish voice had taken on an edge. "But my friend has been shot. I must bring you or she will die. I made a promise."

Only then did Megan realize what was at stake. Saida had made a desperate vow, and she had a weapon. Megan's choice was to go willingly, as a friend, or be taken at gunpoint. If she tried to warn Sam he might try to stop her, and somebody could get hurt.

"All right." She rose from the bed. "Give me a few minutes to get dressed and gather some medical supplies."

Saida pulled the blanket off Megan's bed and draped it over her arm. "I'll be out back with the horses. Can I trust you?"

"You can trust me," Megan replied, meaning it. She and Saida had shared a hellish experience—the girl's far worse, even, than her own. For good or for ill, the horror of that night had bonded them for life.

As she pulled on her clothes, she glanced at the clock. It was 1:20, no more than five hours before sunrise. At least the camp must not be far away. But if they took more time, as Saida had said, the sun would be well above the horizon before they arrived.

In the supply closet, she dropped bandages, disinfectant, forceps, a scalpel, antibiotics and other needs into a pillowcase. A hastily scrawled note told Sam she'd gone to the aid of a patient in the nearby mountains, and that she'd gone willingly. She could only hope Saida would bring her back before the plane arrived tomorrow afternoon to fly her out of Darfur.

Saida had said her friend was shot. Megan had assisted with treating gunshot wounds, so she knew what needed to be done. But this time she'd be flying blind. She had no idea how badly Saida's friend was hurt, what complications the injury involved, or what would happen if she couldn't save her.

She found Saida waiting with two horses. The girl had folded the blanket and slipped it under Megan's saddle for a more cushioned ride—a gesture that reassured Megan of her good intentions. Still, she sat on the horse gingerly, ever mindful of her unborn baby.

They rode out of the camp in silent single file. Only when they were far out of hearing did Saida pull back, allowing them to ride abreast.

"I saw what they did to you that night," the girl said. "The Janjaweed made me watch before they took me away. I promised to go with them and do whatever they wanted if they left you alive."

Tears burned Megan's eyes as the words sank in. The idea that her life had been saved by the courage of this fifteen-year-old brutalized child clenched around her heart. Speechless for the moment, she reached across the distance between them and squeezed the thin shoulder.

"Thank you," she whispered, finding her voice. "I didn't know."

"When Gamal died it was as if I died, too. For a long time I didn't care what happened to me."

"How did you get away?"

The beat of silence was broken only by the sound of plodding hooves and the distant yelp of a jackal. In the east, the stars had begun to fade against the purple sky. When Saida spoke again her words were a taut whisper. "I was rescued by a band of women who had escaped the Janjaweed. Now we fight to save others."

Megan stared at her young friend, stunned by the revelation. While she had retreated into nightmares, little Saida, who'd suffered far worse, had used her pain to become a warrior. Falcon fierce, falcon proud—what a lesson in resilience. Never again, Megan vowed, would she allow herself to become the prisoner of her own fear.

Saida glanced at Megan's still-slender body. "Your baby is not Janjaweed?"

"No."

"Where is the father?"

"In America, as far as I know. We are…separated." The words triggered an unexpected ache. Megan glanced down at her hands, fighting the emotions that threatened to unleash a rush of tears. Hearing the despair in Saida's voice when she spoke of her lost love had Megan questioning the decision she'd made back in Nairobi. Should she have given Cal more of a chance? She'd been hurt and shocked by his apparent betrayal…but she hadn't shown much greater faith in him. Had her leaving been justified, or had it been triggered by hurt pride? Would she have made a different decision if she'd known she was carrying Cal's child?

"You loved him." It wasn't a question.

"Yes, I loved him." And she loved him still, Megan realized. She loved Cal, but she'd fled from him at the first flicker of distrust, giving him no chance to explain himself. Her fear had taken over yet again—the fear of being hurt the way Nick had hurt her.

What a fool she'd been—and now it was too late. Cal Jeffords was a proud man, not inclined to give second chances. Once he learned she was pregnant she could expect him to take an interest in their child, but he would never trust her again.

The way had narrowed, forcing them to ride single file

once more. With Saida in the lead, they wound through the barren hills, picking their way over loose rock slides and following windswept ridges. As sunrise slashed the sky with crimson, a sense of unease crept over her. She owed Saida her life, and she'd had no choice except to come; but she was riding into an explosive situation where anything could happen. She and her baby could already be in mortal danger.

If she could reach out to Cal now, half a world away, what would she say? Would she tell him she was sorry, or would it be enough just to tell him she loved him?

But what difference would it make? Cal was a proud man, and she'd walked out on him without even saying goodbye—just as his mother had. He would never forgive her.

Geneva, Switzerland

The three-day Conference on World Hunger had given Cal the chance to make some useful connections, but little else. During the long rhetoric-filled meetings, he'd found his mind wandering—always to Megan.

Almost three months had passed since that morning in Nairobi, when he'd come back to the hotel to find her gone; and every time he thought of it, he still felt as if he'd been kicked in the gut. He'd been ready to open up to her, to lay his heart on the line. But Megan had completely blindsided him.

The worst of it was, he couldn't say he blamed her.

He'd resolved to leave her alone until he found proof of what Nick had done. That search had proved a dead end, even for Harlan Crandall. But what did it matter? She'd never asked him to clear her name—she'd just asked him to trust her. And he hadn't. Instead, he'd let a stupid misunderstanding drive her away. He couldn't blame her if she never wanted to see him again.

Now, with the conference over, he leaned back in the cab and closed his tired eyes. He'd dared to hope that, given time, Megan would come around and contact him. The volunteer roster indicated she was still in Darfur, but he'd heard nothing from her. Maybe it was just because she'd washed her hands of him. But he couldn't ditch the feeling that something was amiss. When he'd checked with the travel coordinator, he'd learned that she was being evacuated to Arusha for health reasons. Had she caught some sickness in the camps? Had her nightmares and panic attacks returned? The more he thought about her, the more concerned he became.

The corporate jet was waiting at the airport, fueled and ready to fly him home to San Francisco. Cal thought about the long, dreary flight and lonely return. He thought about Africa and worried about Megan.

He made his decision.

By the morning of the next day, Halima, Megan's sixteen-year-old patient, was alert and wanting breakfast. Two days ago, she'd been shot in the thigh during a skirmish with the Janjaweed. The bullet had gone deep, barely missing the bone. Without medical treatment she would have suffered a lingering death from infection. Megan had removed the slug, cleaned the wound and dosed the stoic girl with antibiotics. Thank heaven she'd been able to save this one.

Megan had sat with the girl most of the night, on a worn rug in an open-sided tent. When she rose at dawn to stretch her legs, she was so sore-muscled she could barely stand. Wincing with each step, she tottered into the open.

The little band of female guerillas had set up their camp

in a brushy mountain glade, near a spring. Megan counted fifteen of them—all young, some no older than Saida. The toughened faces below their head scarves bore invisible scars of what they'd endured. All were armed with knives and AK-47 rifles.

Saida had explained to her how they lived, raiding weapons, horses and supplies from ambushed Janjaweed and accepting gifts of food from grateful refugees. Some of the rescued girls eventually went home to their families. Others like Saida, who had no families, chose to stay with the little band.

"Come with me." Saida was beside her, taking her arm. "I'll get you something to eat and a place to rest. The others can tend to Halima now."

Crouching by the coals of the fire, she uncovered two iron pots. Taking a piece of *kisra* from one, she wrapped it around a scoop of seasoned meat, most likely goat, and thrust it toward Megan. The spicy smell made Megan's stomach roil, but she forced herself to eat it. She was going to need her strength.

"Now that Halima's doing better, I'm hoping we can start back," she said. "I'm due to fly out on the supply plane this afternoon."

But Saida shook her head. "We can't leave till it gets dark. The Janjaweed have eyes everywhere. If they saw us leave here by daylight, they could follow our trail back to this camp."

Megan's heart sank. "So unless the plane is late, I'm going to miss it."

"Yes. I'm sorry." Saida reached out and took her hand. "I understand you need a safe place for your baby. And I can tell you want to be with your baby's father again. But wherever you are, this man you love, if he is worthy of you, he will find you and make you his."

Megan squeezed the thin, brown fingers. If only she could believe those words were true. But when she'd walked out on Cal, she'd closed a door that would never be open to her again.

Fourteen

Cal had hoped to take off for Africa at once, but storms delayed his flight from Geneva till the next morning. It was late that night when the Gulfstream touched down in Nairobi, once more in a heavy downpour.

After a few restless hours in a nearby hotel, he was up by dawn and back at the airport, looking for a small plane to take him to the Darfur camp, where the jet couldn't safely land. The twice-monthly flight that carried medical supplies and mail for the volunteers had gone and returned earlier that day. When found and questioned, the pilot, who knew Megan, said she'd been at the site on earlier trips, but this time he hadn't seen her.

Cal's vague sense of foreboding had burgeoned into a gnawing dread. He could try to call, he supposed, or radio, or however the hell one was supposed to communicate with that place. But he knew that nothing would satisfy him short of going to the refugee camp in person. He had to find Megan, or at least find out what had become of her.

By the time he'd arranged to commandeer the supply plane and pay for a second flight, another storm had moved in, drenching Nairobi in gray sheets of rain. With the flight put off till morning, Cal paced his hotel room, glaring out at the deluge that was keeping him from the woman he loved.

Why had he let her go? He'd told himself that she had the right to make her own choices. But if something had happened to Megan because he hadn't found her in time, he would never forgive himself.

If he found her—no, *when* he found her—and if she'd have him, he would never let her go again.

The ride through the hills was taking even longer than Megan had expected. She and Saida had mounted up after dark and wound their way down the treacherous path to the open plain below. Ever mindful of the danger to her unborn baby, she'd clung to the saddle, silently praying as the trail skimmed sharp ledges in the dark. There was no chance of catching the supply plane now. By the time they reached the refugee camp, it would be long gone. But now she was just hoping they'd reach the camp safely, without any attacks in the night.

With dawn streaking the sky, Saida reined to a halt. Her girlish body stiffened in the saddle as she listened. Megan could hear nothing except the wind, but she saw Saida's mouth tighten. "Janjaweed," the girl said. "Not far, and they're coming fast. We will have to go another way, longer but safer. Follow me and be quiet."

Megan followed Saida's horse up and over a steep ridge. Somewhere behind them she could picture the Janjaweed, arrogant as red-turbaned kings on their swift-moving camels. Saida had her AK-47, but a single girl with a rifle would be no match for the Devil Riders.

Once more Megan said a silent prayer for their safety. She wanted to live. She wanted to hold her baby in her arms. And she wanted another chance to see Cal again.

Would he forgive her for leaving? Or was it too late to mend what she'd broken?

As soon as Cal stepped out of the plane, his worst fears were confirmed. He recognized Dr. Sam Watson from his personnel photo. Tall and balding, his face a study in sleepless concern, he was waiting next to the graveled runway. Megan, who would surely have come out to meet the plane, was nowhere to be seen.

"Megan's gone missing," the doctor said after a hurried introduction. "She left a note, but I've been worried sick, about her—especially since she's pregnant."

"She's...*pregnant?*" Cal's throat clenched around the word.

"Coming up on three months. You look even more surprised than she did." The doctor gave Cal a knowing look. "Would it be presumptuous of me to ask if you're the father?"

The father. Still in shock, Cal forced himself to breathe. This was no time to weigh the implications of what he'd heard. All that mattered now was that Megan was missing in a dangerous place, and she was carrying his child.

"Tell me everything you know," he demanded. "Whatever's happened, I'm not leaving Darfur without her."

Sam was staring past him, into the distance. "You may not have to. Look."

Turning, Cal followed his gaze. Beyond the far end of the runway two mounted figures had come into sight, one small and dressed in native robes, the other taller, wearing a khaki shirt, her light brown curls blowing in the wind.

As she and Saida approached the clinic, the first thing Megan noticed was the plane, which should have departed yesterday. Then she saw the tall, broad-shouldered figure on the landing strip next to Sam Watson.

Her heart slammed. She'd ached to see Cal again, but now that he was here she was suddenly afraid. Had he found more "evidence" against her back home? Was he here to make her pay, as he'd threatened to do at the funeral?

At the end of the runway, Megan slid out of the saddle. Part of her wanted to run to him, but she was sore from riding and dreading the first words he might say to her. She kept her pace to a measured walk while she struggled to build her courage.

Cal was striding toward her, but not running. He seemed to be holding himself back. When they met in the middle of the airstrip, he faced her with his arms at his sides.

Megan forced herself to meet his gaze. He looked exhausted, she thought. The shadows under his eyes had deepened since she'd last seen him.

"Why didn't you let me know about the baby, Megan?" he demanded.

"I only just found out myself."

"Did you ever plan to tell me?"

"Of course I did." She could feel herself beginning to crumble. Her eyes were beginning to well. "This baby is your child, too. How could I not tell you?" A tear escaped to trickle down her cheek.

Something seemed to shatter in him. "Oh, damn it, Megan!" he muttered, and caught her close.

For a long moment she simply let him hold her. Only now did she realize how much she'd wanted to be in his arms.

"Are you all right?" His stubbled chin scraped her forehead as he spoke.

"I've never been more all right in my life." Her arms went around him.

"And our baby?"

"Fine," she whispered. "I should have warned you about those condoms."

"Then I suppose it's time we made an honest woman of you."

Was it a proposal or a joke? For now, Megan decided to let the remark pass. "Forgive me for leaving," she murmured. "I was so upset, I jumped to conclusions. I shouldn't have gone without giving us a chance to talk."

"And I should never have let you go." His arms tightened around her. "But maybe this was meant to happen. Maybe this was what it took, for two stubborn souls like us to work things out and find each other. I'll confess it was the money at first. But then it wasn't. It was you. All you."

"So you never found out what Nick did with the money?"

"No, and I don't give a damn. It's in the past, over and done with."

His kiss was deep and heartfelt. Megan's response sent quivers to the tips of her toes.

She nestled closer, resting her head in the hollow of his shoulder. "About what you told me a minute ago, when you said it was time to make an honest woman of me…"

He drew her closer with a raw laugh. "More than that. I love you, Megan, and I want a life with you and our child—maybe even our children. I'm prepared to marry you the minute I can get you in front of a preacher."

"You mean that?" She gave him an impish look.

"Absolutely." His arms tightened around her.

"You're sure?"

"Hell, yes, I'm sure. Why?"

"Because there's something you might not know about Sam Watson. He's not just a doctor. He's also an ordained minister."

Epilogue

They were married the next day. The ceremony had been brief and simple, performed by Sam and witnessed by Saida, a few of the volunteers and the pilot of the plane. Even with no flowers, no music, no gown and no ring as yet, it had been everything Megan could have wished for—tender, romantic and meaningful.

They'd taken the supply plane back to Nairobi. From there they'd boarded Cal's jet for America, with a side trip to Arusha.

Harris had been so delighted by their news of the baby and the wedding that Megan had almost feared another attack. Surprisingly, the old man had followed his doctor's orders. He'd cut back on his drinking and his work, handling the business end of his company while Gideon replaced him as head guide. And he'd hinted, with a sly wink, that he was dating a sexy widow.

Ironically, on the way home, Cal had received an email

from Harlan Crandall. A Las Vegas casino owner had recognized a photo of Nick as the compulsive gambler who,
under a different name, had lost millions at the gaming
tables. Nick had also bet heavily on horse races and sports
events, losing a good deal more than he won. Megan had
been dismayed by the discovery of her late husband's secret life. But the fact that he'd gambled away the money
was proof enough that Nick had been the sole embezzler,
and that the money was truly gone.

In the two years that had passed since that time, Megan
hadn't been back to Africa. With an active toddler son to
look after and another baby on the way, she was busy with
the family she'd wanted so much. But she'd left a piece of
her heart with the refugees of Darfur. Here at home, she'd
become an advocate for their cause, helping Cal set up a
branch of the foundation to educate their young people.

Tonight she stood at the darkened window of her San
Francisco home, watching the rain that streamed in a silver curtain off the overhanging roof. The sound of rain
always brought back memories of her time in Africa. Tonight, because of the precious piece of paper in her hand,
those memories were especially poignant.

"What's that you've got?" Cal had come up behind her.
His hands slid around her waist to cradle the happy round-
ness of her belly. His lips brushed the nape of her neck.

"It's a letter," she said. "From Saida."

She didn't need to tell him what the letter meant. The
last time they'd heard from the girl was a year ago, when
she'd been struggling with the decision to leave Darfur
and go to school in Nairobi. Her little band of warriors
had been shrinking. Two of the girls, sadly, had died. Others had left for a different life—marriage, babies, work, a
few for school. Passionate and loyal, Saida had been one
of the last holdouts. But finally even she had abandoned

the mountain camp to help her people another way, by getting an education.

"How's she doing?" Cal pulled his wife closer, rocking her gently against him.

"Wonderfully, it seems. She loves school, and she's getting excellent marks. She says she wants to become a doctor."

"She's a bright girl. She just might make it." Cal trailed a line of kisses down Megan's shoulder.

"I was thinking." Megan closed her eyes, savoring his closeness. "When she's ready for college, we could sponsor her and bring here, to San Francisco."

"Saida at Berkeley?" Cal chuckled. "Now there's a scary thought. I hope she's not still packing that AK-47."

"Stop it, you big tease! She'd do fine, and you know it!" Turning, Megan planted a playful kiss on his mouth.

Cal deepened the kiss with an intimate flick of his tongue. "Isn't it about our bedtime?" he murmured.

She snuggled against him. "You know, I was just thinking the same thing."

Laughing, he swept her into his arms and carried her off to bed, leaving Saida's letter alone with the rain.

* * * * *

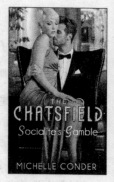

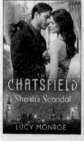

The World of Mills & Boon

There's a Mills & Boon® series that's perfect for you. There are ten different series to choose from and new titles every month, so whether you're looking for glamorous seduction, Regency rakes, homespun heroes or sizzling erotica, we'll give you plenty of inspiration for your next read.

By Request

Back by popular demand!
12 stories every month

Cherish™

Experience the ultimate rush of falling in love.
12 new stories every month

INTRIGUE...

A seductive combination of danger and desire...
7 new stories every month

Desire

Passionate and dramatic love stories
6 new stories every month

nocturne™

An exhilarating underworld of dark desires
3 new stories every month

For exclusive member offers go to
millsandboon.co.uk/subscribe

Join the Mills & Boon Book Club

Want to read more **Desire**™ books?
We're offering you **2 more** absolutely **FREE!**

We'll also treat you to these fabulous extras:

- 🌹 Exclusive offers and much more!

- 🌹 FREE home delivery

- 🌹 FREE books and gifts with our special rewards scheme

Get your free books now!

visit www.millsandboon.co.uk/bookclub
or call Customer Relations on 020 8288 2888